His Forbidden Kiss

Serpent's Kiss Series Book 3

Sherri Hayes

ABOUT THIS BOOK

She's the one woman he can't have.

Kim Langley is beautiful, sexy, and confident. She makes Justin's heart skip a beat every time he sees her. There's only one problem. She's his best friend's little sister. Off-limits. Then, she shows up on his doorstep, offering herself to him.

Justin McKay has been starring in Kim's fantasies since she was a teenager. When she finds out he's an experienced Dominant, she knows he's the one she wants to explore her sexuality with. One night with no strings.

But what if one night isn't enough for either of them? Is he willing to risk betraying his friendship to be with her?

CHAPTER 1

"Are you sure this is all right?"

Kim Langley halted right outside the door to Serpent's Kiss. There were no signs on the outside of the building. If she didn't know any better, she would have thought it was a warehouse used for storage. She knew better, however. Inside was a private club where those who were into BDSM could indulge in all their kinky fantasies.

Two weeks ago, she'd been hanging out with her best friend, Ali. They were in Ali's apartment eating rocky road ice cream and commiserating about Kim's latest bad date. It was that night, by accident when she'd been searching for a shirt in Ali's closet that Kim had stumbled on a bag full of her friend's 'toys'. It had led to a discussion about Ali being a submissive and what all that meant. Kim wasn't sure what to make of it, and she'd left with more questions than answers.

Throughout the next week, Kim couldn't forget what Ali had told her, so when they'd gotten together the following weekend Kim brought up the subject again. By the end of the night, Kim was wondering if that was what she'd been missing in the guys she'd been dating. They were all too...nice.

Not that she didn't want a nice guy—she did—but she also wanted someone who wasn't afraid to push her up against a wall and kiss her until she was breathless. She wanted a man who went after what he wanted, including her. And all the other things Ali told her about—being held down or tied up—didn't sound half bad either.

Which brought her back to tonight.

"Of course it's okay," Ali said. "I talked to Mistress Katrina. She said it was fine as long as you stayed with me the whole time and that you agreed to keep what you see, and who, confidential."

"Are they going to know I'm not…" Kim tried to get a hold on her nerves. She had no idea what was behind that door.

Ali turned toward her friend, placed both hands on her upper arms, and looked her in the eye. "We don't have to do this if you're not sure. We can go back to my place and gorge on ice cream again."

Kim grinned. "If we keep doing that neither one of us is going to be able to fit into any of our clothes."

Her friend shrugged. "It's a sacrifice I'm willing to make."

As tempting as it was to take Ali up on her offer and forget about the thoughts she'd been having, she didn't want to. If she could find the answers she'd been seeking inside the club, then she needed to face her fears and go for it. It wasn't like her to run and hide. She'd learned long ago that if she wanted something she had to make it happen. "I love you for offering, but I want to do this. I need to do this."

Ali nodded and dropped her arms. "Let's get this party started, then."

Kim took a deep breath and followed Ali through the front door. She was a little shocked, however, to find they were now in a small foyer no bigger than the bathroom in her apartment. Her friend shot her a smile before swiping a card through a reader beside another door directly opposite the one they'd entered. A light turned green and then there was the sound of the door unlocking. Ali took hold of the knob and opened it.

Again, the room they entered wasn't what she'd been expecting. They were in another foyer, but this one was much larger. It was long, and on one end there was what looked to be a coat check. There was a woman standing inside and she greeted them as they approached. "Hi, Ali. Who's your friend?"

"Bridget, I'd like you to meet my best friend, Kim. Kim, this is Bridget."

"Nice to meet you." Kim didn't miss the curious look the woman gave her. It made her wonder how often nonmembers were allowed into the club and just how many strings Ali had to pull in order to allow Kim to come with her. It was a private club, after all. She knew there were background checks and membership fees. Ali had explained it all to her the previous weekend.

"Thanks." Kim felt as if there were a big sign on her forehead that said *newbie* on it.

"Bridget, could you buzz Katrina for us?" Ali asked. "She wanted to meet Kim before we go inside."

"Sure."

The woman reached below the counter and smiled.

"Thanks." Ali grinned back at Bridget.

There seemed to be something going on that Kim didn't understand. Then again, she was sure that would happen a lot tonight. She knew very little about BDSM outside of what Ali had told her.

A minute or two later, a blond woman who looked to be in her forties strolled into the room from a door Kim hadn't even noticed only a few feet away. Kim thought she heard some noise on the other side and wondered if that was the club.

The new arrival approached them with a warm smile. "Good evening."

Ali cleared her throat. "Mistress Katrina, I'd like you to meet my best friend, Kim Langley."

Unlike before, there was no introduction of Mistress Katrina to Kim. She wondered if that was intentional.

"It's nice to meet you, Kim," Mistress Katrina said. "Ali here tells me you're curious about our lifestyle."

"Y-yes. I am." Why was she so nervous? Oh yeah. She was about to enter a club where who knew what happened and she was standing there talking to the owner of said club. Nothing at all to be anxious about.

The club mistress chuckled. "Relax. I'm not planning to use my whip on you. You're perfectly safe here."

"Sorry."

"It's fine. Everyone's first time is nerve-racking. It's to be expected."

That made her feel a little better. "Thank you."

Mistress Katrina nodded. "Ali went over the rules with you?"

"Yes. I won't say anything to anyone and I'm pretty sure I'll be plastered to Ali's side the whole night."

"Very well." Mistress Katrina seemed amused by her answer. "Relax. Have fun. If you want to try anything, let Ali know and I'm sure we can find someone willing to give you a demonstration."

Kim swallowed. "Um. Thanks."

The older woman shot Ali a look before extending her hand to Kim. "It was nice to meet you. I need to get back inside. Please take whatever time you need."

Once they were alone again, or sort of alone—Bridget was still there but she was typing away on her laptop—Kim leaned over to whisper in her friend's ear. "She was intimidating."

"She can be." Ali turned to face Kim. "You ready to go inside?"

"Now?"

Her friend laughed. "Were you wanting to stand out in the lobby all night? I thought you were curious?"

"No. I mean, yes. I am. Curious, I mean." Kim took a deep breath to calm herself. "Okay. I'm ready."

Ali looked doubtful, but began walking toward the door Mistress Katrina had disappeared behind a few moments before. Kim followed. It was now or never, right? Better to jump in with both feet and get it over with.

She wasn't really sure what she'd expected to find on the other side of the door, people chained to walls maybe? Instead it looked a lot like any other club she'd gone to. There was a bar, a dance floor, and places for people to sit and talk. The room had a small stage even though there wasn't any sign of a band.

"Doing all right?" Ali asked.

"Yeah. Fine." She was just trying to take it all in and reconcile it with her preconceived notions.

"Good. Let's get something to drink and I'll introduce you to Brandon."

As they made their way toward the bar, Kim continued to look around. While at first this looked like a regular club, she was beginning to see some differences. The main one was that there were quite a few people sitting on the floor, even some with their heads in another person's lap. That certainly wasn't something one would normally see at a nightclub.

The other thing she observed was the clothes, or lack thereof. She blinked as she saw a guy being led up the stairs by a leash attached to his penis. That wasn't something you saw every day.

"Good evening, ladies. What can I get for you tonight?" The man behind the bar grinned at them. He was cute. Maybe five to ten years older than they were, but Kim had always liked her men to be a little older. At thirty-two, she had no desire to mess around with some twenty-year-old who didn't know what he wanted or what to do with a woman. The guys her age were bad enough in that respect. She was ready for different, which was why she was here.

"Brandon, I'd like you to meet my friend Kim."

The smile Brandon shot her made her belly do a little flip-flop. Oh yeah. She could get used to that. "Nice to meet you, Kim. Is this your first time in a kink club?"

"Yes. I mean, yes, sir." That was right, wasn't it? Or was he not a Dom?

His eyes twinkled with amusement as he leaned forward, resting his forearms on the bar in front of him. "No need for formalities. At least, not yet. But I'm sure we could arrange something if you'd like."

Kim's eyes went wide.

"Maybe another time, then." He smirked, and turned his attention back to Ali.

She ordered them both sodas and while he went to fill their order, Kim took a few moments to catch her breath.

"You okay?" Ali whispered.

"I think so." Kim paused as she tried to organize her thoughts. "He's a…a…"

"Yes, Brandon's a Dom."

Kim nodded.

"Remember you don't have to do anything you don't want to. Brandon's a good guy, though, and he seems interested."

"I just think—"

They were interrupted when Brandon returned with their drinks. "Here you go. Oh. And Kim?"

"Yes?" The question didn't come out as confident as she would have liked.

"Come see me if you change your mind." He winked at her, and then moved down the bar to help someone else.

When she looked over at Ali, her friend was trying to suppress a giggle.

Kim felt off balance after her exchange with the bartender and maybe even a little annoyed, although she couldn't say if she was more annoyed with herself or Ali. Why hadn't her friend warned her? Given her a heads-up? Something. Was the entire night going to be like this?

"Come on," Ali said, bumping Kim's shoulder. "I want to introduce you to some people."

"Oh joy," Kim muttered as she followed her friend across the room.

They walked up to a group of people who smiled as Kim and Ali drew closer. An older man stood and repositioned himself farther down on the couch to make room for them.

After they'd taken their seats, Ali made the introductions. The older man's name was Daniel. There were two couples in the group, Beth and Drew, and Nicole and Jeff. Kim learned that both were female dominants and the men were the submissives in the relationships. Kim had to admit it was a foreign concept to her. Then again, so was BDSM really. But as she watched the couples interact throughout the night, the appeal began to resonate. It was in the subtle body movements and the way they touched. Watching them created an ache inside Kim she didn't understand.

"Would you ladies like something more to drink?" Daniel asked.

He was talking to Ali and Kim. She thought she saw her friend blush slightly as she said 'yes, please' and handed Daniel her glass.

Kim did the same, minus the blush, and stared at her friend. Was something going on between the two of them? Surely not. Ali was thirty-two, the same as her. Daniel had to be at least fifty.

As she was contemplating that, her attention shifted to the sound of someone behind her. The voice sounded familiar. When she turned, Kim got the shock of her life. Justin, her brother's best friend, was standing five feet away. He had his back to Kim so she was able to get a closer look. Justin was talking to a man and a woman and in his hand was a leash—a leash that was attached to a young woman wearing a barely there dress.

Kim quickly turned back around. What was he doing here? Was he into this?

Of course Kim already knew the answer. He had to be. What else would he be doing at a kink club?

"Kim?"

She glanced over at Ali. Her friend looked worried. The impact of seeing Justin must have been written all over her face. Kim couldn't help it, though. He was the last person she'd expected to see here.

During her teenage years, she'd had an ongoing fantasy that Justin would sneak into her room during one of his many sleepovers with her brother and make mad passionate love to her. That never happened, of course. He'd shown no interest in her that way. Then her brother had left for college and the next time she saw Justin was when he'd brought his girlfriend home with him when Mark had returned for spring break. At the time, she'd been crushed.

Seeing him with his girlfriend had been the kick in the pants Kim needed to wake up to reality. Justin was never going to see her as anything but Mark's little sister. She had to move on and she did. Sort of.

Two months after coming face-to-face with Justin's girlfriend,

Kim lost her virginity to Kyle Zimmerman in a cheap motel room. It had been her way of saying goodbye to Justin.

As it turned out, Kyle wasn't the best of choices. He'd shown his interest in her the entire year leading up to prom, the night she'd finally relented and gave it up. She liked him, she really did, but he wasn't Justin. Afterward he'd rolled off her, gone to the bathroom to get rid of the condom, and then began gathering his clothes. Maybe it was just her, but she'd expected there to be more…to feel something different. Instead, she felt sore and a little empty.

Ali wrapped her hand around Kim's upper arm and shook her. She blinked and refocused on her friend. Kim must have been lost in her thoughts longer than she thought.

"I'm fine," she said.

Her friend looked doubtful.

She knew she was going to have to say something. It only took her a split second to come up with a topic that would turn the tables on her best friend and put Ali in the hot seat. Leaning in so no one around could hear them, Kim asked the question that had been on her mind moments before she'd spotted Justin. "Is there something going on between you and Daniel?"

Ali flushed. "No."

Kim gave her a skeptical look.

"He's nice. He watches out for me."

"And?" Kim knew there had to be more to it than that given her friend's reaction before.

"And nothing."

"Riiiight."

Speaking of Daniel, he walked over with their drinks in hand. "Here you go, ladies."

They both thanked him, although Kim still thought there was more behind Ali's 'thank you' than simple politeness.

Daniel leaned back, resting his arm along the back of the couch. Kim didn't miss how her friend stiffened for a moment before relaxing again. Even if there wasn't anything there, she was pretty sure Ali would be open to it if he was.

"What do you think of Serpent's Kiss? Do you have any questions?" Daniel's inquiry was directed to Kim, of course.

"It's different."

He smirked. "Yes, it is. And you haven't even seen the second floor yet."

Kim froze. "The second floor?"

"That's where the fun stuff is." Nicole winked at her.

Not sure how to react, Kim swallowed nervously.

"Would you like to see?" Daniel asked. "I'd be more than happy to accompany you ladies if you'd like."

"I don't know..." Kim looked to Ali for help.

Instead, her friend shrugged. "It's up to you, but you did come here to see what it was all about."

Like it or not, Ali was right. If she was going to do this, she needed to suck it up and do it. "All right."

She stayed close to Ali while shooting discreet glances in Justin's direction. Kim had no idea who the woman was. As far as she knew, he wasn't dating anyone. But if that was the case, then who was she and why was he leading her around by a leash?

Justin was still talking to the couple as she passed within ten feet of where he was standing. Another man joined them. As she continued to spy on him, the new man took hold of the woman's leash and kissed her. Did that mean the woman didn't 'belong' to Justin? Just thinking that left her with a bad taste in her mouth, but she shook it off and looked again at the small group. Justin didn't seem upset by the other man stepping in and staking a claim.

Kim averted her gaze. So far he hadn't noticed her. That was good. She had no idea what she'd say to him if he did.

As they reached the top of the stairs, Kim could feel a change in the atmosphere. At first it didn't make sense because, while there were a few people milling about in the hallway, none of them were doing anything more than standing or talking. Then they came to the first window and Kim glanced inside.

On the other side of the glass was a woman kneeling. She was completely naked and on display for whoever chose to look. Her head was bent so Kim couldn't tell if her eyes were open or not.

A man she hadn't seen walked up behind the woman, wrapped his hand around her ponytail, and jerked her head back. He said something to her and she responded. The next thing Kim knew, the woman was being led over to some sort of padded chair-type thing. Instead of sitting, however, she placed her knees on what Kim had assumed was the seat and rested her chest on the flat upper part. When she was in position, the man placed a hand between her legs. She opened them as wide as the bench/chair would allow.

What he did next stunned Kim and had heat rushing to her core. The man ran two fingers along the woman's slit and then inserted them into her pussy. After pumping them in and out a few times, he removed his fingers. Kim had expected him to wipe them off on a towel or even lick the moisture off as she'd seen done in porn, but that didn't happen. Instead, he walked to the side and placed his fingers in front of the woman's mouth. He said something, and a second later she opened her mouth and began sucking on his fingers.

Suddenly there was a loud smacking sound as a leather paddle made contact with the woman's ass. Kim had been so focused on the woman's mouth that she hadn't noticed what the man was doing with his other hand. She felt the moisture leak out of her body. With each smack she got wetter and wetter. Did that mean she was submissive? Kim didn't know, but she was pretty sure she wanted to find out. And she knew exactly who she wanted to enlist to help her explore these new fantasies.

CHAPTER 2

Justin McKay loved owning his own business. Usually. It was days like today when he seriously questioned his decision to open his own mechanic's shop two years ago. Shaking his head, he strolled into the small utility room that contained his washer and dryer. He removed his grease-soaked clothes and tossed them into the washer with a generous amount of soap. Why couldn't he go back to the night before when he'd been hanging out with his friends at the club without the worries of employees and everything that came with them?

The morning had been a nightmare. Normally Saturdays weren't that bad. They were only open half a day and the guys spent most of their time doing simple oil changes. It all came down to Jax. He'd hired the kid about a month ago, and he was about as bright as a box of rocks. Even after hearing the explanation, Justin still wasn't sure what the kid had done exactly. All Justin knew was that one minute he was working underneath the car and the next he was being covered in dirty oil. Once he got the leak plugged, Justin had sent Jax home and spent the next two hours cleaning the oil off everything and throwing sawdust on the floor of his garage so it could soak up some of the mess. He'd have to go in early on Monday and sweep it up.

As much as Justin didn't want to fire the kid, he was only nineteen and seemed excited by the idea of being able to work on and restore vintage cars. The problem was that Justin couldn't trust Jax on his own. Every task he was given he screwed up somehow. It wasn't on purpose, but it still cost time and money. Justin had been hoping to have Mr. Smith's car back to him early next week. After today, that wasn't likely to happen.

Sighing, Justin padded naked to the bathroom. He needed a shower. While he was used to working in grease and grime, he wasn't used to wearing it.

Ten minutes later, Justin was feeling better. He'd scrubbed himself down—twice—and put on a comfortable pair of jeans. He had nowhere to be until later that night.

Thinking about Serpent's Kiss, the kink club he'd been a member of for the last year and a half, brought a smile to his face. He hadn't been sure it was a great idea with him being single and all, but it had ended up being a very good thing. There was a nice mix of singles and couples at the club and everyone was friendly. Of course, a lot of that had to do with the club mistress and owner, Katrina Mayer. She made sure things worked the way she wanted them to. If you created too much drama, then she politely asked you to leave.

He rolled his shoulders as he headed toward the kitchen for some lunch. Maybe he could find a play partner tonight. It had been a while since he'd done more than socialize at the club or keep an eye on Kate when her husband had to work late and wasn't able to accompany her to the club.

Grabbing the leftover Chinese food from the refrigerator, he dumped the contents of the container onto a plate and popped it into the microwave. Quick, easy, and ready in minutes. Considering he was starving, those were all pluses in his book.

The microwave dinged, letting him know his meal was ready. He removed the plate of beef lo mein and took it into the living room. Surely there was a game on he could watch while he scarfed down his food.

Justin had just swallowed his last bite when there was a knock on his door. He glanced up at the clock. It was half past two. Since he wasn't expecting anyone, he had no idea who it could be. A delivery, maybe? But even then, he was left scratching his head. He hadn't ordered anything recently.

Setting his empty plate on the coffee table, he walked over to the door and looked through the peephole. He jerked back and swiftly opened the door. Standing on his threshold was his best friend's little sister. Justin and Mark had been best friends since they were sixteen. In high school they'd done everything together—even went on a few double dates. Now that they were both adults, they got together at least once a month to catch up and shoot the bull while downing a few beers and yelling at whatever game happened to be on the big screen of their local sports bar.

Kim stood there staring at him with wide eyes.

"Hi," he said.

"Hi." She looked nervous.

"Did something happen?"

She shook her head. "No. Nothing…no. May I come in?"

He took a step back and motion for her to enter. Kim walked inside and he closed the door behind her. "Are you sure you're all right?"

"Yeah. I'm fine. Promise." She flashed him one of those sweet smiles of hers. It caused his chest to clench every time. He didn't see her as often anymore as he used to, but they still ran into each other on occasion. Justin had been such a fixture at their house during the last two years of high school that he was often invited to family gatherings. Whether he wanted to admit it or not, seeing Kim at those times had been a definite highlight.

He reached for the remote and turned off the television. She was obviously here to talk to him about something. "Would you like something to drink?"

"Sure."

She was acting really strange. "What would you like? I have water, soda, beer, wine…pick your poison."

His joke fell flat.

"Water. Thank you."

He nodded and ducked into the kitchen.

Justin took his time getting Kim's water. Standing in his living room fidgeting with the belt of her coat, she looked almost fragile. It threw him because he knew she wasn't any such thing. Kim had graduated at the top of her class in college and landed a job almost immediately thanks to one of her professors. She'd excelled in her position and quickly rose within the company. Last he'd heard, she was being considered for a promotion. The woman knew what she wanted and went after it. That was one of the things he admired about her—one of the things he'd always admired about her.

As he headed back into the living room where Kim was waiting, he racked his brain trying to figure out why she was here. All thoughts went out the window, however, when his gaze fell on Kim kneeling on the floor, naked. Her head was bowed, her knees parted, and her forearms rested on her thighs, palms up.

He froze. It had been seventeen years since he'd seen this much of her. And even though he'd seen dozens of women sans clothing since then, it didn't lessen the effect she had on him. Seeing her bare flesh flushed and her chest heaving with every breath had him instantly hard and his cock straining against his jeans.

The last time he'd been seventeen and he'd walked by her bedroom one night on his way to brush his teeth. She'd left the door open a crack and when he'd glanced inside, unable to resist, he'd watched her change into her pajamas. Kim was the first live woman he'd ever seen naked.

"What are you doing?" He somehow managed to choke out the question even though it felt as if he had no air left in his lungs.

She didn't look at him, which bothered Justin a great deal, but at least she answered. Sort of. "I want to submit to you."

Placing the glass he was holding down on the side table, Justin closed the distance between them. When he was in front of her, he extended his hand.

At first, she hesitated, but then she took it, and he helped her up. Once Kim was on her feet, he left her long enough to retrieve a blanket from his room, and then wrapped it around her shoulders. It didn't completely cover her, but it made things a little less distracting. He'd wanted Kim Langley from that first time he'd seen her dressing in her bedroom. The only thing that had kept him from making a move on her was her brother. Mark would kill him. Or castrate him. Maybe both.

Trying to keep a level head, Justin led her over to his couch. He sat down facing her, their knees within inches of each other. It would be so much easier if he weren't so aware of her. "Now, tell me what this is about."

Kim glanced up at him and then back down at her lap. Her cheeks were flushed and she looked embarrassed. "I saw you."

He furrowed his brow in confusion. "Saw me?"

"Yes. At Serpent's Kiss. You're into BDSM. You're a Dom, right?"

Justin's heart skipped a beat. She was at the club? Why? How?

"Anyway, I want you to be the one to show me. I want to submit to you." The words were spoken in not much more than a whisper.

It wasn't often Justin was at a loss for words, but this was one of those times. Needing some space, he stood and walked to the other side of the room.

His mind was racing and his cock was throbbing. How many times had he fantasized about her over the years? How many times had it been the memory of her face and body that had brought him to orgasm? Now here she was offering herself to him and he couldn't do it. He couldn't. If Mark ever found out he would view it as a betrayal. And as much as he wanted her, he couldn't do that to his best friend. Or to her.

The sound of sobs had him whipping his head back around in her direction. She was clutching the blanket around her and tears were streaming down her face.

Justin's heart broke. "Please, don't cry."

She shook her head and wiped at the moisture on her cheeks. "You don't want me."

"It's not that," he said as he strolled back over to her side.

"It's okay. I understand."

He lowered himself back down onto the couch and rubbed a hand over his face in frustration. "No you don't."

This time she met his gaze. He tilted his head downward toward the physical evidence that contradicted her assumption. When she looked up again, there was a clear question in her eyes.

"Kim, I can't do that to you. You deserve more than one night of kinky sex."

She straightened her shoulders and gave him a look he was far more familiar with. This wasn't the timid Kim who'd walked through his door. "What if that's all I want?"

"What about your brother?"

"Mark has nothing to do with this." Kim folded her hands in her lap. "I want to know if I'm really submissive. I think I am, but…" She took a deep breath. "Ali said that BDSM is about trust. I trust you."

He heard the tremble in her voice. "Do you?"

"Yes."

Deciding to test the waters, he ran his index finger over her collarbone and down to the valley between her breasts. Kim sucked in a deep breath.

"What did you think of Serpent's Kiss?" he asked while he continued to move his finger along her skin. His touch was innocent for the most part, but he couldn't deny how good it felt to touch her like this.

"I-I liked it."

He raised an eyebrow at her. She'd have to do better than that.

"Ali took me up to the second floor."

So she'd seen some play. "And?"

"I watched a woman get spanked."

Justin didn't miss how her breathing changed. "Did you wish it was you?"

"What?"

"Did you want to be the one who was getting spanked?" he asked.

When she didn't answer, he tried again. "Have you ever been spanked before, Kim?"

She swallowed. "No."

"Have you ever been tied up? Held down?"

"No. I…" A new rush of blood warmed Kim's cheeks. "I've only had regular sex before."

"And did you enjoy it?"

She seemed startled by his question. "The sex?"

"Yes." He skimmed the top of her breast with his fingertip. "I want to know if you enjoyed your vanilla sex."

"Yeah. I mean, of course I did. Sex is supposed to be enjoyable, right?"

Justin grinned. "It is. But I was more trying to figure out what it was that led you to your exploration of kink."

"Oh. Well, I sort of…I found Ali's toy bag. Or I guess you could say I tripped over it."

That made him chuckle. "What did you find in there? Anything intriguing?"

The blush was back. He was enjoying this. Probably too much, but how often did he have a beautiful woman sitting naked in his living room?

Kim shrugged and it brought his finger in contact with more of her breast. "She had a lot of dildos and vibrators."

He grinned and dropped his hand. His erection wasn't going away. "Where are your clothes?"

She seemed confused by the change in topic. "I didn't wear any. Just the coat."

Well, that explained her wearing a coat when it was seventy degrees outside. "You came over here in nothing but your coat?"

"Yes. I wanted you to know that I was serious. I want you to show me. I want to see if I can do this. If this is what's been missing from my relationships." She looked as if she was ready to cry again.

He took her face in his hands and brought his mouth down to hers.

It took her only a moment before she was kissing him back and, oh, it felt good. More than good. Her lips were soft and luscious and she tasted like peppermint—no doubt from a mint she'd been sucking on in the car on the way over to his house.

When he broke the kiss, Justin rested his forehead on hers and looked her in the eye. He had a decision to make. He could make her put her coat back on and send her packing, or he could take her up on her offer. They were both adults. He knew that. But could he betray his best friend by defiling his little sister?

Kim seemed to know what he was thinking. "Mark doesn't have to know. I won't tell him if you won't."

"He would never forgive me." It was the truth and they both knew it.

"Please."

Her plea did something to him. Right then he didn't care about Mark or any other member of her family. He'd wanted her for almost twenty years and here she was sitting in his living room offering herself to him.

"It can only be tonight." He had to put that out there.

"I know."

Grabbing hold of her hair at the base of her neck, he tilted her head back and kissed her hard. She gasped, but then met his aggressive tongue with an enthusiasm he knew was genuine.

When he pulled back several minutes later, he was out of breath. So was she. "The club requires we get tested for STIs every six months."

As usual, the change in subject didn't affect her in the slightest. "I got tested after I broke up with my last boyfriend."

Justin didn't need to ask her how long ago that was. He remembered Mark ranting about how the scumbag had stood his sister up one time too many and she'd finally thrown him to the curb. She'd been single for three months. How sad was it that he'd been keeping track?

He could see the hope in Kim's eyes as he sat there weighing his options. Sure, he could tell her no and send her home, but heaven help him, he didn't want to.

"Your safeword tonight will be teddy bear," he said. "If at any time I do something you don't want me to do, say it and I'll stop."

She smiled and nodded. He knew she understood the significance of the safeword he'd chosen. When she'd graduated from high school he'd gotten her one of those little graduation teddy bears.

He stood and motioned for her to follow him.

Justin led her down the hall to the room across from his bedroom. It had a bed like any other spare bedroom, but it also had several other things that he'd adapted for play.

Kim stood there eyeing everything. It wasn't anything close to the setup at Serpent's Kiss, but it fit his needs whenever he brought a sub home.

He ambled over to the spanking bench in the corner of the room and ran his hand along the leather. "Tonight you'll be my submissive."

She watched his every move.

"You will call me Sir at all times and when I give you an instruction you are to follow through without hesitation. Is that understood?"

"Yes."

He walked over to stand in front of her. "Yes, what?"

"Yes, Sir," she whispered.

"I'm sorry, I didn't get that."

Her eyes widened again at his tone, but this time she answered with more confidence. "Yes, Sir."

"Good." Justin brushed his thumb along her jaw. He would have to remember that this was her first time. "What's your safeword?"

"Teddy bear, Sir."

He smiled and trailed his fingers down her neck to where she was clutching the blanket. She loosed her grip as he began separating the fabric. The blanket slid off her shoulders, revealing her tits. Earlier he'd been in such a hurry to get her covered up that he hadn't taken the time to appreciate them, but they were truly magnificent.

Pulling the blanket completely away from her body, Justin lowered his gaze. His cock strained against his jeans as he took her in. Tonight she would be his to do with whatever he wished. Tonight he would fulfill his fantasies.

Throwing the blanket on the back of the chair, he never took his eyes off her as he extended his hand for her to take.

CHAPTER 3

KIM SHOOK as she placed her hand in his. Justin hadn't taken his eyes off her since he removed the blanket and she felt incredibly naked. Of course, that was probably because she was. But it was different. She'd slept with a handful of guys over the years and they'd all seen her without clothing. With Justin, though, it felt more intimate, like he was seeing even the parts of her that she was trying to hide from the world.

He led her over to the edge of the bed and sat down. When he released her hand, he patted his leg twice. "I want you over my lap with your ass in the air."

Was he serious?

One look at his face told her that he was.

She took a shaking breath and did what he'd instructed. It took her a minute or so to get into position with her stomach resting on his thighs and her legs and chest on the mattress on either side of him. Kim was pretty sure what was going to happen next, but she still flinched when his hand came down sharply on her backside.

"You've been a very bad girl, haven't you?" As he said the words, he landed another solid blow to her other butt cheek. "Visiting kink clubs and driving across town in nothing but a thin trench coat."

Another two hits and her behind was beginning to warm. The crazy thing was that wasn't the only thing she noticed heating up. Kim was becoming aroused. She could feel the wetness growing between her legs.

Smack.

Smack.

"A very bad girl, indeed."

Why was this turning her on? She didn't understand it at all, but the evidence didn't lie. With every swat on her ass she was getting wetter and wetter.

Then he took both her cheeks in his hands and began massaging them. It felt so good and a moan escaped from deep in her throat.

"Mmm. Something tells me you like being spanked, Miss Langley."

To her horror, he dipped his hand between her legs and ran his fingers over her pussy. She knew what he'd find. If she could feel how wet she was, Kim knew he'd be able to as well.

"Just as I thought."

Before she could form any sort of response, he moved his fingers lower and began tapping out a rhythm on her clit. Holy shit, why did that feel so good?

As he continued, she felt the energy coiling in her belly, driving her toward her climax. Her breathing picked up and soon she was rocking her hips back toward his hand, silently begging him for more. What he was doing felt good, but she needed more pressure. She needed faster. She needed…more.

Kim opened her mouth to tell him that when suddenly his hand was gone. She almost cried.

"Not yet, sweetheart, and not until I say. Tonight your orgasms belong to me. I decide when you find release."

Before she knew what was happening, he'd turned her over onto her back. The rough material of his jeans brushed against her abused backside, making it impossible to forget that she'd been spanked moments before like a misbehaving child. It should have made her furious to be treated like that. She was a grown woman and a successful one at that. None of this should be appealing to her on any level. So why was it that her entire body felt as if it were more alive than it had ever been?

All thoughts fled as Justin lowered his mouth to her breast and began sucking it into his mouth. He swirled his tongue around her nipple before scraping his teeth along the moist flesh.

When he began to pull back, she instinctively reached to hold him in place. Justin wasn't having that, however. He took hold of both her wrists, placed them on the bed above her head, and held them there.

"I want to touch you," she said though her labored breathing.

"No," Justin mumbled around the breast he was currently paying homage to.

She opened her mouth to protest and he bit down on her nipple. "Ouch!"

He chuckled and met her gaze. "Have you changed your mind? Do you want me to stop, let you get dressed and send you on your way?"

Of course she didn't want that. Was he joking?

Kim shook her head. "No, Sir. I don't want to go home."

With her answer, he took her other nipple between his teeth, worried it until it was almost painful, and then released it. She'd felt it all the way down to her pussy. It was as if all the nerve endings in her body were connected to the space between her legs. That had never happened before.

Cool air fanned over her damp breast, causing goose bumps. Then he switched sides, sucking her other nipple into his mouth, licking around her areola, and then working it between his teeth before releasing it and blowing on it. She felt cold and hot at the same time.

Kim could honestly say that foreplay had never been like this before. Most guys would have dived in as soon as they realized she was wet and ready. Not Justin. He seemed content to take his time and explore her body. Maybe it was because they were only giving themselves this one night. Maybe that was what made the difference.

He shifted his hold on her wrists, freeing one of his hands. "I'm going to make you feel good tonight, Kim. How many times would you like to come?"

"What?" She'd been lost in her thoughts and the feel of his mouth as he peppered kisses on her chest and collarbone.

She felt his lips curl up into a smile against her skin.

"I asked you how many times you wished to come tonight." Justin punctuated his statement by tracing a line up her collarbone to the curve of her neck with his tongue.

"I thought that wasn't my decision." It was difficult to concentrate with his lips so close to her neck.

"Oh, it's not, but I still want to hear your answer." He drew some of her flesh into his mouth and began sucking on it gently. Was he going to give her a hicky? Normally that would annoy the hell out of her, but she found she didn't care.

It was hard to concentrate while he was doing that, but she tried to focus. How many should she say? The most she'd ever had during a sexual encounter was two and that was only because the guy had gone down on her first. Usually one was a stretch for her. Then again, this was Justin and if he hadn't stopped earlier she would have come.

He released the skin he'd been sucking on and ran the tip of his nose up to the base of her ear. "I'm waiting."

"Two?"

Justin whispered in her ear, "Try again."

She swallowed. How many should she say? "Four."

Lifting his head, he met her gaze and shot her a mischievous grin. "I think five sounds like a nice round number, don't you?"

"Five," she said. Never had she experienced five orgasms in one night, not even when she'd helped herself.

He chuckled at her expression. "Are you doubting my abilities, Miss Langley?"

While he was talking, his free hand kneaded her breast. Kim had to keep reminding herself that she wasn't dreaming this. She was really here with Justin's hands and lips on her. And hopefully by the end of the night she'd know what it felt like to have him inside her as well.

"I've never had five before." She swallowed. "In one night, I mean."

Why did she feel shy admitting something like that to him? She was spread out naked across his lap, for crying out loud.

"There's a first time for everything."

Justin pulled her earlobe into his mouth as he lowered his hand down her abdomen to the junction of her legs. He didn't rush and the anticipation was killing her. She wanted him to touch her—to make her come.

When he reached his destination, she spread her legs for him, desperate for his touch. He cupped her pussy and used the flat of his palm to press slow circles on her clit. Her eyes rolled back in her head because it felt so good.

"Please."

"Please, what?" he asked, releasing her earlobe.

"I need to come. Please, Sir, a little harder." Kim knew she was begging but she needed this.

He shifted his hand and curled his fingers so that he had one on each side of her clit. What he did next caused her back to arch and a very unladylike sound to escape her lips. Every nerve ending in the lower half of her body went on high alert as he rolled and pinched her clit. He seemed to know how to make her body sing better than she did.

In no time at all, the energy built to the point where it had nowhere to go. With one final pinch between his fingers, Kim was flying.

* * *

Justin had to keep reminding himself this was real. Of course, the fact that his cock felt as if it were about to rip a hole in his jeans helped to drive the point home. So did seeing the look on Kim's face as her orgasm overtook her. It was absolutely beautiful how her brow furrowed and her lips pursed as if she were about to whistle. It was cute and endearing. And he wanted to see her doing it over and over again.

The heat radiating from between her legs had him wanting to dive in and taste what she had to offer. If this was their one and only night together, then he wasn't going to hold back. Everything he'd been dreaming of doing since she began starring in his fantasies was now going to become a reality. Justin was going to make sure of it.

Releasing his hold on her wrists, Justin helped her to sit up. He ran one hand up along the curve of her hip. The other hand cupped the back of her head. "That's one."

Kim was still trying to catch her breath, but she laughed anyway.

"Ready to get started on number two?"

Before she could answer, he pulled her against him and kissed her. It took her only a moment to catch up and then her hands were in his hair and she was kissing him back. She met every stroke of his tongue with one of her own. Blood was pumping through his veins and he wanted nothing more than to plunge his cock deep inside her and make her forget her own name.

If he'd been ten years younger that would have been exactly what he would have done. But he was older now. Wiser. He'd promised her five orgasms and that was exactly what he intended to give her.

Ripping his mouth away from hers, he stood and flipped her over onto the bed. The look of surprise on her face told him that he'd caught her off guard. She'd been so dazed by the kiss that she hadn't been paying attention to how he'd shifted her on his lap or moved both his hands to her hips for leverage.

He didn't let her get her bearings before falling on top of her and starting to ravish her mouth again. It felt incredible to kiss her—to have her under him. Kim wasn't a stick of a woman. She had gentle curves and a nice set of tits that demanded to be touched and played with.

With that thought, Justin shifted his weight and rolled over to reach inside the nightstand. He kept a variety of toys in there, most of which were new since it wasn't often he brought a woman home. That was one of the great things about being a member of Serpent's Kiss. Most of the women he played with were members. Given the wide variety of implements and furniture the club offered, it didn't make sense to bring them back here when playing there was more convenient for both of them.

Justin felt Kim watching him as he rifled through the drawer. It didn't take long, but by the time he returned his attention to her she was breathing normally again. He brushed the back of his hand along the side of her face, and held up the item he'd retrieved from the drawer. Her eyes widened a little when she saw the nipple clamps he had in his hand. They were a simple pair of tweezer clamps, but they had a chain linking them together. Perfect for what he had in mind.

"Have you ever worn nipple clamps before?" he asked.

She shook her head and kept eyeing them with trepidation.

A thrill rushed through him as he thought of what her reactions to the clamps might be. Every woman was different. Depending on her sensitivity and her pain tolerance, she may love them or hate them.

Not allowing her to spend too much time worrying about how the clamps might feel, he leaned down and took one of her nipples into his mouth again. It had softened, but it didn't take long to get it hard. He took his time licking and touching—bringing her level of arousal back to where it had been before.

Kim's fingers tangled in his hair as he continued to worship her tits. He took his time memorizing the texture of them, knowing he needed to store up memories of tonight to last him a lifetime.

By the time he pinched her nipple between his fingers and situated the clamp on either side, Kim was completely focused on what she was feeling. She was paying attention to what his mouth was doing, not his hands. That was until he pushed the clamp closed around her nipple. She gasped and pulled at his hair.

Justin took her other nipple between his teeth and smiled up at her. She was shaking her head. "Justin."

His only response was to dig his teeth into her nipple a little more, causing her to suck in another sharp breath. He followed that up with a soothing brush of his tongue and then he attached the clamp. If she was interested in being someone's submissive, she was going to have to learn that her Dom called the shots during a scene, not her.

He held her gaze as he moved down her torso and settled himself between her legs. She looked uncertain, but as soon as he lowered his mouth to her pussy he heard a soft moan escape her lips. Kim tilted her head back and dug her fingers into the mattress as he ran his tongue over her lips and up to circle her clit. She was still slick with evidence of her previous orgasm. He took his time devouring every ounce of it.

Needing better access, he pushed her thighs farther apart and wrapped his arms around the tops, locking them in place. It also brought the chain that was attached to the nipple clamps within easy reach. He wrapped his fingers around the center of the chain and gave it a gentle tug as he ran the tip of his tongue over her clit.

She cried out. "Justin? Sir?"

He eased up on the chain, but continued his mission between her legs. "Yes?"

"I don't…it's too much." She was breathing hard and, given how wet she was, Justin was fairly sure it wasn't going to take much to get her to that second orgasm.

His only answer was to redouble his efforts. He buried his face in her pussy and used his lips and tongue to drive her closer and closer to the edge of reason.

When he felt her legs begin to shake, he focused his efforts solely on her clit and timed each swipe of his tongue with a tug of the chain. Before long she was bucking her hips. He held her firm and steadily increased the pressure on her clit.

Less than a minute later, she opened her mouth and released a silent scream. It was one of the most beautiful things Justin had ever seen. Watching a woman orgasm never got old, but even he had to admit that with Kim it was even more special. He would give her the five orgasms he'd promised her and then he would let her go. It would kill him never to be with her like this again, but he would do it because he had to. Tonight, however, she was his and he was going to make sure she never forgot their amazing night together because he knew he never would.

CHAPTER 4

Kim couldn't remember the last time she'd had two powerful orgasms within such a short period of time. She'd known her night with Justin would be full of new experiences. What she'd witnessed at Serpent's Kiss had told her that much. She had known very little about dominance and submission before her discovery at Ali's apartment. All Kim knew was that what her friend had shared had appealed on a level she didn't understand.

She was still trying to catch her breath when Justin released her legs and began moving up her body. Without thinking, she reached for him. If she'd been thinking properly, she might have second-guessed her actions considering he was supposed to be in charge this evening but it didn't cross her mind until her hands were already massaging his shoulders.

He placed a single kiss on each of her nipples. It was only then that she realized the clamps were still attached. How had she missed that? When he'd first put them on they had hurt. The pain was still there but her body was still singing from her climax. Everything else was secondary.

"That was two."

Justin grinned up at her and she felt her belly do a somersault. She pushed the feeling aside. Tonight was about sex. That was all it was—all it could be. They both knew that.

His face grew serious. "I need to take the clamps off. When I tell you, I want you to take a deep breath and hold it. Understand?"

She nodded and braced herself, hoping the pain wouldn't be as bad as when he'd first put them on.

"Deep breath."

Kim did as he said but she still felt the pain zip through her.

Then his warm mouth was there. The soft lapping of his tongue eased the pain considerably and then took it away completely. She sighed and cupped the back of his head, holding him to her chest.

He chuckled and shifted to the other breast. "One more to go."

"No," she whined.

She felt his lips curl up into a smile against her skin. "Deep breath."

A split second later the pain hit her. Even though she'd known what to expect, it still caught her off guard. But then he was there easing her pain and making her melt all over again.

"Better?" he asked.

She combed her fingers through his hair. "Yes. Thank you."

If given the chance, Kim could have fallen asleep right there. She was completely relaxed. Her bones felt as if they were disconnected from her body. She couldn't ever remember that having happened before.

"Uh-uh. No falling asleep on me. We aren't nearly done yet."

His voice sent a pleasant tingling to the pit of her stomach even though her mind was ready to shut off. Apparently her body still wanted to fool around, not that she could blame it. Justin was by far the sexiest man she'd ever encountered.

She felt his breath on her face and opened her eyes. He was hovering above her, his lips an inch from her own. Justin had the most amazing eyes. They were a vivid green framed with the longest lashes she'd ever seen on a man. Every time she looked into his eyes she was lost.

He lowered his mouth onto hers and began kissing her as if he had all the time in the world. At first it was all gentle suction, then he traced the outline of her lips with his tongue. She opened to him, wanting nothing more than to taste him. Kim could smell herself… taste herself on his tongue. It mixed with Justin's own flavor creating something altogether new and highly intoxicating.

As he continued to kiss her, Justin lifted her right leg up over his shoulder, spreading her open. She felt exposed. With anyone else Kim would have protested, but this was Justin. This was their night. If that was how he wanted her, then she wasn't going to protest. Besides, so far she'd had two of the most powerful orgasms in her life. She would have to be crazy to not want more.

The feel of his fingers drawing circles along the inside of her thigh tickled. It caused her to tense up.

"You're thinking too much," he whispered as he brushed his lips along her neck.

Then he was tugging her hands away from where they'd been buried in his hair. Before she could protest, Kim felt something wrap around her wrists. When she looked up, Justin was using a thin red rope to secure her wrists together. He let her leg fall to the bed as he positioned himself higher to concentrate on his work.

There was a part of her that wanted to resist. This was different than when he'd been holding her down earlier and she wasn't sure she liked it.

Justin must have noticed her uncertainty because he paused and met her gaze. "Do you trust me?"

"Yes, Sir." There was no doubt about that. Kim trusted Justin more than any other man besides maybe her brother and her father. She knew he wouldn't do anything to hurt her. But that didn't mean she wasn't nervous. This was new, different…and just a little scary.

He held her gaze for a moment longer, and then went back to what he was doing. A few seconds later, he gave the rope a jerk, and ran his finger along the edge. Justin flashed her a devious smile and hopped off the bed. He knelt down beside her head, and then she felt a pull on the rope. Instinctively, Kim knew he'd tied it to the side of the bed. Even without testing the rope, she knew it was secure. Justin had been a Boy Scout the same as her brother. He knew how to tie a rope and secure it.

She breathed through her nerves and focused on the fact that this wasn't some random guy. It was Justin. And if what she'd experienced so far was anything to go by, she still had three more earth-shattering orgasms to go.

Movement had her looking up. Justin was standing over her, this time with a scarf. He held it in both his hands.

"What are you going to do with that?" She was pretty sure she already knew the answer.

The side of his mouth pulled up into an amused smirk. "I'm going to blindfold you."

In the next second, the silky fabric was being pressed against her eyes, plunging her into darkness. He lifted her head and tilted it to the side to secure the scarf behind her head. Then he placed a soft kiss on her lips. For some reason, even that simple kiss felt different. Not only could she feel his lips, but she could feel his breath against her cheek—smell the musky scent of her and him. She even caught a whiff of the soap he used.

Kim arched her back as he backed away, hoping to prolong the connection.

She heard Justin chuckle. "Not yet, sweetheart. I have plans for you first."

Maybe that statement should have made her nervous, but it didn't. If anything, she was excited for the possibilities.

There were sounds of drawers opening and closing, and then his hands were on her legs. One by one, he wound something around her ankles and attached them to the edge of the bed. She wondered if it was the same red rope that he'd used for her wrists. Either way, Kim was now lying sideways on Justin's bed, blindfolded, with her wrists secured above her head and her legs spread wide. She was completely helpless and exposed. The logical part of her brain told her that she should be upset. This wasn't normal. She shouldn't find this arousing.

But whether it made sense or not, the evidence of her excitement was right there between her legs. Her heart was racing and blood was pumping through her veins. Not because she was terrified, but because she couldn't wait to see what Justin would do to her next.

* * *

Justin had Kim exactly where he wanted her. Her wrists were tied together and attached to the bedframe. Her legs were spread as far apart as was comfortable. His mind was racing with all the things he wanted to do to her. It was taking considerable effort on his part to stay focused. If this was their only night together, he wanted to give her the full experience. But this was new to her and Justin wanted her to enjoy it. He wanted tonight to be what filled her fantasies.

It was stupid and completely irrational. Logically Justin knew that. But logic had nothing to do with this. He'd wanted her almost from the first moment he'd laid eyes on her after moving to St. Louis his junior year. The selfish part of him wanted to ruin her for any other man.

Shaking his head, he banished the thoughts from his mind. Thinking like that wouldn't change the situation. Justin knew he wasn't Kim's first lover and he knew he wouldn't be her last. She was a beautiful woman. Any man with half a brain would be thrilled to have her warming his bed every night. Justin knew he would. If things were different.

He watched the rise and fall of her chest as she lay there waiting for what would come next. To the casual observer, she looked as if she wasn't bothered by the pause in activities but he knew Kim well. Whenever she was nervous or unsure about something she would scrape her teeth along her bottom lip in the cutest way—just like she was doing now.

Grinning, Justin rested his knee on the bed between her spread legs. He placed his hands on either side of her arms, bracing himself above her. She seemed to relax some knowing that he was close. Did she really think he would leave her alone tied up like this?

"You look so beautiful tied to my bed," he whispered against her lips before moving down to the curve of her neck.

She tilted her head to the side to give him better access. "I do?"

He hummed in answer, too busy kissing her sensitive skin to break the connection long enough for words.

For the next few minutes, he nuzzled and kissed every inch of flesh from her ear down to her collarbone. There was something about a woman's neck that made him crazy. Lucky for him, most of the women he'd been with loved when he paid extra close attention to that part of their body. Going by Kim's responses, she enjoyed it as well. Her chest rose and fell more rapidly as he explored and memorized the scent of her—the feel.

Shifting his weight, he lifted one of his hands and began touching her. He started with her arms and slowly worked his way down. By the time he got to the small patch of hair that covered her pussy, she was arching her back trying to prolong the contact with his fingers as they skimmed her flesh.

"Does my bad girl want me to touch her pussy?" he asked.

"Yes."

His lips brushed her ear. "Yes, what?"

"Yes, Sir. Please touch me."

He scraped his teeth along the outline of her ear. "I am touching you. Is there somewhere specific you want me to touch? If there is, you need to tell me."

Kim swallowed. "Please touch my pussy, Sir."

Justin smiled and cupped her heat with his hand. "So hot."

Raising her hips, she tried to get him to move faster. But that wasn't how this worked. Obviously, she needed a reminder.

He retracted his hand slightly and brought it down with a firm smack against her swollen flesh.

She let out a squeak.

"We do this on my time." He hit her pussy again with the palm of his hand. "Not yours." Again he spanked her, this time landing the blow more on her clit. "Understand?"

"Yes. Yes, Sir." The words came out somewhere between a gasp and a moan. It was incredibly sexy.

He ran a finger through her slit and then spanked her again.

"Looks like my bad girl likes to have her pussy whipped as much as her ass."

As he switched between smacking and stroking, Justin noticed the telltale signs that she was getting close to another orgasm. Tugging a nipple into his mouth, he worked it between his teeth while continuing to spank her pussy.

It didn't take long for her to start tugging on her restraints and her legs to begin trembling. He picked up the pace, slapping her clit in quick succession. She threw her head back and let out a high-pitched scream as yet another orgasm ripped through her.

Justin suddenly had the need to taste her. He could feel how wet she was and he wanted it on his tongue.

Giving the top of her breast a quick kiss that was in complete contradiction to the spanking he'd just given her most sensitive area, he worked his way down her body until he was kneeling between her legs. Running his hands from her calves up the inside of her thighs and back down, he breathed in the musky scent of her sex.

His gaze narrowed on her clit poking out of its hood surrounded by her dark pubic hair. Her legs were smooth as silk and the patch on her mound neatly trimmed. He wondered if she'd shaved before she'd come to his house or if she preferred waxing.

Again, he shook off his wayward thoughts. It didn't matter. After tonight, he'd never be in a position to see or know what she did or didn't do to her lady parts.

Before he could get sidetracked again, he used his thumbs to part her lips and licked a long line from the base of her pussy all the way up to her clit. Kim's mouth fell open and she released a near-silent sigh. He didn't even want to think about how many times he'd fantasized about this.

He made sure to take his time massaging everywhere he could reach with his tongue both inside and out. Her lips had a darker hue to them after his spanking, as did the skin around them. He worshipped it all, soothing the sting of the spanking.

Before he'd even reached her clit, she was panting. He knew it wouldn't take much.

"Ready for number four?" he asked a moment before his lips engulfed her clit.

Kim sucked in a ragged breath and came on his tongue.

While she was catching her breath, Justin stood and stripped off his clothing. His erection was painful at this point. He needed to be inside her and feel her tight and wet surrounding his cock.

Rolling on a condom, he leaned over her outstretched body, his lips hovering a breath away from hers and his left hand pressed against the side of her face. The need to possess her was overwhelming. And suddenly he was filled with a longing to see her eyes staring back at him. For her to see just how much he desired her.

Pushing the fabric he'd used to blindfold her out of the way, he watched as she blinked up at him, her eyes readjusting to the light in the room. Justin waited until she was staring up at him—her eyes were still glassy and dilated. That was good since she had one more orgasm to go.

Giving her a hard kiss, he didn't hold back as he took what he wanted. When he broke their connection, he pressed his thumb into the side of her face, commanding her attention. "I'm going to fuck you now. And I'm going to make sure you'll feel it with every step you take tomorrow."

"Please," she begged.

His heart clenched. He loved hearing her all hot and needy for him. If only they had more time…more than just this one night.

But they didn't.

Reaching between them, he wrapped his hand around the base of his penis and lined it up with her entrance. He thrust his hips forward, sinking deep into her warmth. The feeling was incredible and he knew without a doubt that one night with her would never be enough.

But it was all he had, so he was going to make it an experience neither one of them would ever forget.

CHAPTER 5

Kᴵᴹ's entire body was vibrating. And that was before he pushed his way past her now sensitive labia and stretched her more than she could ever remember being stretched before.

The heat from his body burned her as he pressed her into the mattress, his hips slapping against her thighs. This wasn't making love. This was fucking. With every thrust she could feel him claiming what he wanted. He'd promised she'd feel it in the morning and Kim had no doubt that was true. But the last thing she wanted him to do was stop. She'd never been this aroused before. Never felt as if the only thing holding her to the earth was him.

She tilted her head back and closed her eyes. Every time he surged forward he brushed against her already sensitive clit. After four orgasms, Kim would have thought she would have had enough. Her body, however, disagreed. It wanted more—more of whatever Justin had to give.

"Open your eyes."

His breathless instruction had her opening her eyes and gazing up at him. Sweat glistened on his naked chest. She wished her hands were free so she could run her fingers over the muscles she saw flexing as he pounded into her pussy.

As if he could read her mind, Justin reached up over her head and released her bindings. With her arms free, she stretched, needing to feel him almost as much as she needed her next breath.

Justin fell forward, bracing himself on either side of her body with stiff arms. Even with the movement he never stopped his assault. Every time his pelvic bone made contact with her clit she felt herself climbing farther and farther up that magical peak that would give her another mind-blowing orgasm. She couldn't believe how close she was...again. How was it possible to want someone so much?

His hands were everywhere. So were hers. Now that Kim could touch him, she wanted to touch him everywhere all at once.

Justin shifted his weight, released one of her legs, and then wrapped it around his waist. He repeated the process with the other leg until both were bracketing his hips and hugging him tightly.

"You feel amazing." The words were said in between thrusts which only added fuel to the fire. He was completely focused on her. It was as if nothing outside the two of them mattered.

Her orgasm was building. She knew it wasn't going to take much more before she was falling over the edge into oblivion.

Then, out of the blue, he circled his arms around her, picked her up, and brought her back down on the bed with her head on the pillows. He never lost their connection while repositioning them.

Bringing his mouth down to meet hers, he kissed her with unrestrained passion. His tongue mimicked what his body was doing. Her heart felt as if it would beat out of her chest and as she ran her hands over his torso she could feel his own heart pounding out a quick and hard rhythm against her fingers.

The need to come became too much to take. He had her so primed and ready yet she couldn't get over that final hurdle. Kim knew what she needed, so she snaked her hand between them.

She was inches from her goal when Justin's fingers wrapped around her wrist. He broke the kiss and stared into her eyes. "What do you think you're doing?"

"Umm..."

He quirked an eyebrow at her, letting her know he expected an answer. To accentuate his point, he pushed into her hard.

"I need to come."

He brought her hand up to his lips and kissed her fingers before placing her hand back over his heart. "You don't get to come until I say, sweetheart."

"But—"

He cut off her protest by kissing her again. This was another one of those no-holds-barred kisses that had her toes tingling.

"No buts. I promised you one more orgasm tonight, but it will be on my terms, not yours. Are we clear?"

Why did that make her even hotter?

"Yes, Sir."

He thrust his hips again, rotating them in a way that had her eyes rolling into the back of her head.

When she gazed up at him again, he had fire in his eyes.

"Kiss me," he demanded.

Unable to deny him and not wanting to, Kim brought his head down and captured his lips with her own. She kissed him for all she was worth.

After that, thinking became difficult. He picked up his pace and quicker than she thought possible she was burning. She needed to come. Never in her life had she needed a release the way she needed it now. Kim felt as if she would combust right there in his arms if she didn't get some relief soon.

"Please," she mumbled as best she could around his kisses. "Please, Sir, I need…I need to come."

"Not. Quite. Yet."

Justin punctuated each word by plunging his cock deep inside her. He moved his mouth down to her neck and began attacking the skin there. Everything he was doing only added to the sensations pulsing through her body and culminating right between her legs.

Just when she thought she couldn't take any more, he took her legs and spread them wide, stretching her open as far as she could go. It drove him deeper and made her feel as if she would split in two.

Kim had no idea how long he kept pounding away at her pussy. She'd passed the point of anything but feeling.

Then he released one of her legs and brushed a single finger over her clit. She went off like a rocket. A scream tore from her throat and filled the room. Her orgasm seemed to go on and on, leaving her feeling as if she were floating.

* * *

Somewhere in the middle of Kim's orgasm Justin found his own release. He'd drawn it out for as long as he could, torturing them both in the process, but he hadn't wanted it to end. It was stupid and probably not the wisest decision he'd ever made, but the whole situation—them sleeping together—wasn't exactly smart either. Even so, Justin couldn't bring himself to regret it.

Climbing off the bed, he quickly cleaned himself up before grabbing a blanket and rejoining her. She was shaking, which, given the circumstances, was to be expected. He'd worked her hard.

Justin covered her with the blanket and pulled her into his arms. She felt soft and warm and perfect. Like she belonged there.

He closed his eyes and tried to push the image out of his mind. She wasn't his and she never would be.

"I can't seem to stop shaking," she said, huddling farther into the blanket.

"It'll pass. You need to drink some water as soon as you think you're ready."

She nodded and cuddled closer to him.

Circling his arm around her waist, he pressed his body against hers hoping to transfer his warmth.

As he lay there with her he tried to take in every detail—the texture of her hair as he tucked her head under his chin, the way every one of her curves fit perfectly against him. Even though it would be painful to remember and never be able to experience the perfection that was being able to possess Kim again, Justin never wanted to forget. He'd known when he agreed to this that once he had her he'd want more and that not being able to have it would haunt him for the rest of his life. But it was worth it. If only Mark wouldn't be so opposed...

But it was a fool's hope. Justin knew his best friend. Mark wouldn't approve of Justin pursuing his little sister no matter how honorable his intentions.

"What are you thinking?" she asked.

He noticed that she'd finally stopped shaking. "Are you ready for some water?"

It took her a second too long to answer. He knew she hadn't missed the fact that he hadn't answered her question. "Sure."

Reluctantly, Justin rolled away from her and got up to get some water from the small fridge he kept in the room. He also swiped a chocolate bar from his stash before returning to her side.

Kim stared up at him as he lowered himself back down onto the mattress. He situated himself with his back against the headboard, and then helped her into a sitting position. Before he handed her the water and chocolate, he gathered her against him once more. If this was all they got, he wasn't letting go of her until he absolutely had to.

"Thanks," she said, and took a bite of the chocolate.

"The sugar will help." He ran his fingers through her hair and down the side of her face. She was the most beautiful woman he'd ever met.

Kim was quiet for several minutes. She looked down and then back up at him. "You don't have to, you know."

"I don't have to what?" he asked.

"Take care of me like this. That wasn't part of the deal."

She'd lowered her gaze again and that just wouldn't do. Gripping her chin, he turned her to face him. "It most certainly is part of the deal. Aftercare is part of BDSM and any Dom who doesn't think so isn't worth his salt, in my opinion."

Kim swallowed and nodded.

"You're staying here tonight so I can watch you. I worked you hard and I want to make sure you're okay." The thought of her going home and experiencing subdrop alone had him feeling sick to his stomach.

"I don't—"

Justin placed his index finger over her lips, silencing her. "This isn't up for discussion. You're staying."

She turned away from him again and he hated it. There wasn't anything he could say, however. Both of them knew that when the morning came everything had to go back to the way it was before.

When she finished both her chocolate and her water, he took the empty bottle and stood. Extending his hand to her, he helped her up. Without words, he led her out of the room and across the hall to his bedroom. Normally if he let a submissive stay over he'd have them sleep in the other room. Kim was different. But then again, she always had been.

Once in his bedroom, he flipped on the light and went to his dresser to get her a T-shirt. As much as he would love to sleep naked next to her, he needed to begin the separation process or he'd never be able to let her go come daylight.

"Here," he said, handing her the dark blue shirt with his shop's logo on it and pointing to the door that led to the master bathroom. "You can wear this to sleep in. I'll wait here while you get changed. There's an extra toothbrush in the linen closet you can use."

Kim took the shirt and hugged it to her chest. It only accented her tits, which had his cock twitching.

"Go on. We both need to get some sleep." He hadn't meant the words to sound as harsh as they'd sounded, so he took a step forward and touched her cheek. Kim leaned into his touch. When he dropped his hand, he winked at her and she smiled.

"I'll be right back." She brushed past him.

"Hurry."

Running a hand through his hair, Justin grabbed a pair of underwear out of his top drawer and put them on. He knew he'd need more than just the T-shirt she'd be wearing to keep him from sinking his cock into her again. Not that clothing of any kind would completely prevent that. Kim brought temptation to a whole new level.

Justin strolled over to the bed and turned down the covers. It had been years since a woman had slept in his bed. Not since his last long-term girlfriend.

Before he could take a trip too far down memory lane, Kim walked back into the room. When he saw her he blinked several times. How was it possible she looked sexier in his shirt than she had out of it?

He crossed the short distance separating them and gathered her into his arms. Massaging his thumb along the side of her face, he looked deep into her eyes. She was too desirable for her own good.

"What's wrong?" she asked, gazing up at him.

Instead of answering her question, he refocused on the task at hand. "Climb into bed. I'll be right back."

Justin didn't wait to see if she followed his instructions. He couldn't.

Once he was inside the confines of his bathroom, he did his business and then took a moment to catch his breath. When Justin was fairly sure he could get into bed with her and not jump her again, he headed back into his bedroom. When he crossed the threshold, his gaze was immediately drawn to the woman lying in his bed. She was staring back at him with those soulful brown eyes of hers.

He tried to ignore the stirring in his groin as he got into the bed beside her. Kim pulled the covers higher as if she was shielding herself. That wouldn't do. He reached out and tucked her head into the curve of his shoulder.

"How are you feeling?" he asked as he ran a gentle hand over her head and down the smooth slope of her back.

"Fine." Her answer was quiet.

Tipping her chin up, he gave her a stern look. "I need the truth."

She tried to avert her gaze, so he tightened his hold.

"Why?" she asked. "Why do you want to know?"

"I told you. It's part of being a Dom." He cupped the side of her face. "Are you sore?"

Kim nodded. "A little."

He smiled. "Roll over. I'll massage your shoulders."

"You don't—"

"It wasn't a request." The look he gave her let her know he wasn't taking no for an answer.

Sighing, she turned away from him. Justin positioned his hands on either side of her shoulders and began to massage the tension out of her muscles. As he rubbed and kneaded her flesh, Kim began to moan. It went straight to his cock. What was wrong with him? He hadn't reacted like this to a woman in…well, ever. Even with his first girlfriend he was usually good after one hard session.

Kim moved her hips and bumped against his erection. When she felt it, she froze and turned her head to look at him. "Really?"

He'd expected exasperation or something like it but instead she seemed genuinely shocked that he'd want her again so soon. In truth, he was having a difficult time believing it as well. But it wasn't like he could deny it. The evidence was right there.

As if his hand had a mind of its own, he slipped it around her and palmed her breast. This time when she moaned it had nothing to do with the easing of sore muscles. Kim arched into his hand, seeking more. Who was he to deny her?

Releasing her long enough to sheath himself with a new condom, he returned and repositioned them so he could slide into her from behind. He'd worked her over good earlier. This time he'd take it nice and slow. Justin loved kinky sex, but as he moved in and out of Kim… as he felt her pussy pulse around him…he realized that with her slow and easy was satisfying in its own way.

Justin kept up a gentle pace until he felt her legs begin to quiver. Snaking a hand between her legs, he circled her clit with his fingers. Kim gasped and shuddered around him as she reached her climax. Feeling her come apart in his arms was almost spiritual.

Placing a kiss at the base of her neck, Justin closed his eyes and let his orgasm take him. It wasn't as explosive as their joining earlier, but it was more powerful if that was possible.

He pulled out of her and she twisted so that she was facing him. Her face was flushed. Gorgeous.

"I need to clean up," he said, kissing the tip of her nose. "I'll be right back."

When he returned, she was exactly where he'd left her. Gathering her into his arms, he held her close to his chest. They had eight hours until morning. Eight hours until he had to let her go.

CHAPTER 6

KIM AWOKE to a warm body lying beside her. It only took her a second to replay their night together. Trying not to make any sudden moves, she looked to see if he was awake. His eyes were still closed and he had the most adorable look on his face. She could have stared at him for hours and not gotten tired of looking at him. That, however, wasn't an option.

As quietly as she could, she snuck out of his bed and into the bathroom. Glancing in the mirror, her lips were a little swollen and there were a few red marks on her neck from his whiskers. That's all that was visible, but she had the most delicious ache all over her body. Never had she had sex like that. Not the kinky stuff or what had transpired later in his bed. Before she would have said that the sex she'd experienced in the past was good. What transpired with Justin last night changed her definition.

Splashing some cold water on her face, she took the toothbrush she'd used last night and brushed her teeth, then used the bathroom. As much as she wanted to get out of there before things got weird between them, Kim knew she couldn't. It wasn't as if she'd never see him again. Justin was Mark's best friend. He came to all their family functions, as well as the occasional family dinner. If things were weird, her family—and especially her brother—would notice.

Squaring her shoulders, she marched back out into Justin's bedroom with nothing on but his shirt. As promised, she was feeling the residual effects of the night before with every step she took.

He was awake when she walked into the room. "Hi."

Justin propped himself up on one arm. "Morning."

Neither said a word for several charged moments.

"I should go," she said.

He continued to look her over for what felt like forever, and then nodded. "Would you like some breakfast?"

She shook her head even though her stomach protested. They hadn't stopped to eat dinner last night, but it had been worth the sacrifice. "No. I think I should go."

Not sure what to do since her coat was still out in the living room where she'd left it, she debated whether or not to take his shirt off here or wait until she had something to cover up with. Even though he'd seen all of her there was to see last night, in the light of day things were different.

Justin must have sensed her indecision. "Keep the shirt. And grab a pair of my boxers out of the top drawer. You can wear those home under your coat."

A part of her wanted to protest, but when she thought that maybe she'd get to take home something to remember him and their night by, she couldn't say no. Doing as he'd instructed, she selected a pair of dark blue boxers to match the shirt she was wearing, and stepped into them. He never took his eyes off her the entire time.

Once she was dressed—or as dressed as she was going to be—she crossed her arms over her chest and took one last long look at him. "Thank you. For last night."

"It was entirely my pleasure."

"Well. I should go." She moved toward the door. Before she stepped through, she met his gaze once more. Everything she felt was right there reflected in his eyes. If only things were different.

But they weren't, so she took a deep breath and walked away from him. Back to her boring life. At least she'd have her memories of their night together. It was enough. It would have to be.

For now.

CHAPTER 7

Three Months Later

Kim's heels clicked on the concrete floor of the parking garage as she rushed to her car. She tugged her coat tighter around her as the cold air sent a shiver down her spine. The sun had set over St. Louis and the temperature had dropped. It was New Year's Eve and while there was no snow in sight, the wind had picked up, leaving a bite in the air.

She hurried the final steps to her vehicle and slid behind the wheel. No sooner had she started the car than the sound of her phone ringing filled the small space. Her best friend's name popped up on the screen in big letters.

"Hey, Ali."

"Hey, yourself. Are you on your way to your parents' house?"

"Yeah. I'm just leaving work. Got stuck on a call. You already there?"

Silence met her question.

Every second that passed where her friend didn't answer had Kim's heart rate kicking up a notch. "Ali?"

"Don't kill me, okay, but I won't be able to make it."

"What? Why?" Kim's voice vibrated in the small confines of the car.

"I'm sorry. You know I was planning to be there, but my mom called about an hour ago. She and her current boyfriend had a huge fight, so I told her she could stay with me for the night. She's curled up on my couch with a huge glass of wine and a box of tissues. I'm sorry."

Kim's anxiety ratcheted up another notch. She'd been counting on Ali being there...being her buffer. But it wasn't as if she could fault her friend. Ali was supporting her mom. How could she be mad about that?

"It's okay," Kim said. "I forgive you." Ali and her mom didn't have the best relationship. It was kind of messed up, actually. Ali tended to act like the parent while her mom hopped from boyfriend to boyfriend, looking for someone to fix all that was wrong in her life.

"Thanks." Ali paused. "I am sorry, though. I hate leaving you hanging like this."

"I'm a big girl. I'll be okay." Maybe if Kim said it enough times, she'd believe it.

The long pause on the other end of the line told Kim that Ali wasn't convinced. "Call me later if you need me. And give your mom and dad a hug for me."

"I will."

Kim released a loud breath as she disconnected the call and headed out of the city toward her parents' home in the suburbs. It was already after six, which meant she would most likely be the last to arrive. Not that her parents' New Year's Eve party was a major social event. It wasn't. But it was a big deal for them.

Every year, her mom and dad opened up their home to their nearest neighbors and to a few close friends. Her mom would bake dozens of cookies, make her famous punch, enough food to feed an army, and decorate her house from top to bottom. It was a big affair. As far as her family was concerned, anyway.

Normally, it was something Kim looked forward to. Her brother's best friend—the man Kim had spent the last seventeen years fantasizing about—Justin McKay, would be there. Unfortunately, he was also the reason she was dreading tonight.

Maybe dreading was too strong a word. It wasn't as if she didn't want to see him. She did. The man still starred in her fantasies. The problem was that now she didn't have to dream about what it would be like to have him touch her, kiss her. Kim knew what it was like and she got to relive their one night together in vivid detail every time she closed her eyes.

It had been three months and she'd been avoiding him since. Well, sort of. If avoiding him meant that she'd joined the private BDSM club, Serpent's Kiss, where he was a member and watched from afar as he flirted with various submissives every night.

It was torture, but she'd brought it on herself. She'd thought she could handle it. Thought she could find a connection with one of the other Doms like the one she'd felt with Justin when he'd draped her over his lap and spanked her. But so far, all being at the club had done was make her ache even more to have Justin's hands on her again.

At the club, they kept their distance. She hung out with Ali and her friends, while Justin mingled or sat at the bar talking to Brandon, one of the bartenders.

Tonight, however, avoiding him wouldn't be so easy. Her family would notice if she gave him the cold shoulder or left the room every time he entered. No, she was going to have to suck it up and face him. They were both adults. They could do this. Adults had one-night stands all the time. Right?

As she pulled up in front of her parents' house, she was still trying to convince herself. Maybe she should call and say she was stuck at work or that Ali needed her to help with her mother's latest boyfriend disaster. While Kim didn't want to put her friend in that position, she knew Ali would back her up.

The decision was made for her, however, when the door opened, and her brother peeked his head outside. He was looking straight at her. So much for ducking out before being noticed.

Turning off the engine, Kim scooped her purse from the seat and stepped out of the vehicle. As she neared the house, her brother crossed his arms to ward off the chill. "Hurry up, Sis. It's cold out here."

"No one told you to stand there with the door open. I'm an adult, you know. I can walk from my car to the door by myself."

He moved to the side to let her pass. "Gotta do my chivalrous duty to protect the womenfolk."

Kim turned and stuck her tongue out at her big brother before hanging her coat up in the hall closet. She'd barely got her coat on the hanger when she was lifted a foot off the floor. "Mark! Put me down."

Her brother laughed.

"Mark Jacob Langley, put your sister down." Belinda Langley's voice boomed from the kitchen.

"Yes, ma'am." Her brother was still chuckling when he set her feet back on the floor. "Saved by Mom."

Kim rolled her eyes and straightened her clothes. "Don't you have someone else to annoy?"

"Of course," Mark said. "But picking on you is so much fun."

"I thought you said you were looking to protect me," she said as she headed toward the kitchen, leaving him behind.

"I can do both," he called from behind her.

Ignoring him, she stepped into the kitchen to find her mother stirring a pot on the stove. Kim walked over and gave her a kiss on the cheek. "Happy New Year."

Her mom smiled and wrapped one arm around her daughter's waist, pulling Kim against her side. "How's my baby girl? Work going okay?"

"Work's good. Busy as always. Sorry, I'm late."

With a peck on the cheek, her mom released her. "I know you work hard. I'm just glad you made it." Her mom removed the sauce she'd been stirring from the stove and poured it into a bowl. "Is Ali coming?"

Kim snatched an olive from a nearby tray and popped it into her mouth. "Something came up with her mom, so she can't make it."

"That's too bad. Her mom needs to find a nice man to settle down with instead of chasing these bad boys."

Kim didn't say anything because she knew what was coming next.

Sure enough, with barely a pause, her mother continued. "Speaking of men, do you have a new fella in your life these days?"

To give herself a minute, she ate another olive, taking time to suck the pimiento out of the center before devouring the rest of the olive. She was about to answer her mother when her brother and Justin strolled into the room. They were both smiling from ear to ear, laughing at some joke, no doubt.

Justin's gaze zeroed in on her and her heart rate kicked up. The juicy olive lost all its flavor as she stared into Justin's vivid green eyes. He only held her gaze for a few seconds, but it was enough to raise her body temperature and have her clenching her thighs together. The memory of those eyes staring back at her in a much more intimate moment had her wishing for things that would never be.

Completely oblivious of the tension in the room, her brother removed two beers from the refrigerator, handing one to Justin, and before she knew it, they were gone.

"Are you okay, honey?" her mom asked, reaching up to check her forehead to see if she had a temperature. "You look flushed."

Kim gave her mom what she hoped was a reassuring smile. "Yeah, I'm fine. Did you need me to carry anything into the dining room?"

Her mom frowned but let it go. "If you could carry these two trays in, that would be wonderful."

Without giving her mom a chance to say anything else, Kim picked up the trays and headed into the formal dining room where all the food would be arranged buffet style for their guests. She breathed a sigh of relief when there was no sign of Justin or her brother. Kim knew she wouldn't be able to avoid him forever, but she was going to try and delay the inevitable.

* * *

Justin stood in the Langley's den with Mark, Mark's dad, Davis, and two of their neighbors. Music played in the background as they chatted about who they thought would make it to the Super Bowl this year. Justin liked sports, but it wasn't something he obsessed about. He'd much rather talk about cars.

Unfortunately, not even that would have been able to keep his attention tonight. His mind was still upstairs in the kitchen with Kim. She'd been sucking on an olive when he'd walked into the room and the only thing he could think of was what it would feel like to have those lips wrapped around his cock.

He stifled a groan and tried to pay more attention to the conversation happening right in front of him. Kim was thirty-two years old. Hardly a child. And sexy as hell. But that didn't change the fact that the man standing beside him, his best friend of seventeen years, was her older brother. Her very protective older brother.

The group laughed and Justin realized he'd missed something. He smiled and chuckled, trying not to draw attention to himself. He'd thought it worked until Davis excused himself to go check on his wife and their little group broke up, leaving him and Mark by themselves.

"Car or woman?" Mark asked before taking a swig of his beer.

It took a moment for it to register what his friend was asking. Justin's brain was too muddled with thoughts of Kim. Thoughts he shouldn't be thinking with her brother standing right in front of him.

"Car," Justin said, forcing his mind away from the woman he'd spent way too much time thinking about lately. "A 1970 Road Runner to be exact."

Mark released a slow whistle. "Nice."

"It needs a lot of work, but it's gonna be sweet once I get finished with it." All that was true, but he hadn't thought about the car all day. He'd known Kim would be at the party and, as much as he shouldn't, he wanted to see her.

"Man, I envy you. I wish I had your talent for cars."

"Hey, I tried to get you to take shop with me in high school, but you wanted to go the college route." Justin took a sip of his beer and waited for what he knew was coming.

"And pass up the college girls? Nah."

Justin laughed and shook his head. Mark had gone to college for a traditional four-year degree, while Justin spent that same time at a local garage doing tune-ups and oil changes. His best friend liked to think going to college somehow granted him some magic with females, especially now that he had a good job and made a decent living. In reality, Justin's sex life saw a lot more action than Mark's, but it wasn't something Justin discussed often with his friend. At least, not in recent years. Their sexual tastes had veered off in very different directions. Mark tended to stick to what people in the lifestyle liked to call vanilla sex, whereas Justin preferred a little more...variety.

Before the two could continue that line of conversation, Davis bounded down the stairs and announced that the food was ready. Everyone stopped what they were doing and made a beeline for the stairs as if none of them had eaten for days. Justin included. Belinda Langley was an amazing cook and she went all out for her annual New Year's Eve party. Justin could hold his own in the kitchen, but on his best day, he didn't hold a candle to Belinda.

There wasn't a horizontal surface in the formal dining room that didn't have some type of food or drink on it. She had everything from typical party meats and cheeses to more elaborate options like roast with the most delicious sauce known to man. His mouth watered thinking about it.

As he filled his plate, he was keenly aware of where Kim was in the room. Justin told himself it was so he could make sure he was keeping his distance, but that wasn't entirely true. He was honest enough with himself to admit that. Not that it mattered. She was off-limits and always would be. No matter how difficult it was, he was going to have to forget about their night together. It wasn't going to happen again. Hell, it shouldn't have happened in the first place.

To remove the temptation, he headed back downstairs once he'd gotten his food. Most people remained in the dining room, keeping close to the food, talking while they ate. Normally, he'd be right there with them, but he couldn't this year. He should have known he'd want more after he'd gotten a taste of her.

It was bad enough that she'd joined Serpent's Kiss. The one place where he could relax and indulge. With her there, it was becoming a place of torment.

The thing was, he couldn't even be upset about it. She was a submissive...at least in the bedroom...and she deserved the opportunity to explore her newfound sexuality. She deserved to find a Dom who could give her what she needed. It wasn't her fault that every time a Dom looked her way, Justin wanted to land a solid punch to the guy's face.

Justin was sitting near the fireplace, his plate almost empty, when Mark found him. "There you are. I was wondering where you'd disappeared to." He plopped down on the chair beside Justin. "I thought maybe you'd sweet-talked Jackie into giving you a pre-New Year's blow job and snuck off to my old bedroom."

Mark thought he was being funny. Jackie had been trying to get Justin's attention since she and her family moved into the neighborhood ten years ago. Justin was twenty-four at the time. She was seventeen. He hadn't been interested then and he wasn't now. That didn't stop her from flirting with him every chance she got. "Nope," Justin said. "She's all yours."

His friend chuckled and took another drink of his beer. Justin had no idea how many that was for Mark, but Justin could already tell his friend was getting tipsy.

To keep the subject from continuing down the path of women and sex, Justin changed the topic. "You should swing by sometime and see the Road Runner. I should have it down to barebones in a few weeks. Maybe you could get your hands dirty for once."

"I don't know," Mark said. "Women seem to like my baby soft hands. Don't want to mar their skin with any rough calluses."

Justin snorted. "I've never had any complaints."

"Well, of course you don't. The women you're with like that sort of thing."

A retort was on the tip of Justin's tongue, but he bit it back. He'd been trying to avoid talking about women and sex. How did they end up right back on the same subject again?

Oh yeah. Mark. When he was drinking, it was hard to get him to talk about anything else.

Justin stood. "I'm gonna grab a cold one from the fridge. You want another?" It wasn't like his friend was driving tonight.

Mark drained his current bottle and handed it to Justin. "Sure."

At the top of the stairs, Justin tossed his and Mark's beer bottles into the trash can. Instead of heading straight for the kitchen, Justin changed direction and walked down the hall toward the bathroom. Sounds of laughter and talking filled the house, and it was almost a relief to duck into the bathroom and shut the door.

Normally, he was a social person. He enjoyed hanging out with friends. But he was swiftly learning that anything that involved Kim became a struggle in restraint. As a Dom, he was used to drawing things out...delaying gratification...but this was more than that. There wouldn't be a reward at the end for his patience. He wouldn't be able to lose himself in the release of all that built-up tension.

Closing his eyes, Justin willed his feelings away—the ones that had him longing for more with the one woman on the planet he couldn't have.

It didn't work.

The image of Kim tucked into him as he drove into her from behind had his cock hardening despite his need to piss. A low moan left his throat as he forced his eyes open and focused on the one thing that would kill his erection faster than anything. Mark. And the betrayal his friend would feel if he ever found out that Justin fucked his sister.

It worked. At least, enough that he could relieve himself.

Zipping up his jeans, Justin flushed the toilet and washed his hands before reaching for the doorknob. He pulled the door open and took a step forward without looking where he was going...and came face-to-face with the one woman he'd been trying to avoid.

CHAPTER 8

Kim's heart felt as if it were going to pound out of her chest. She hadn't realized Justin had come upstairs. He'd disappeared downstairs as soon as he'd filled his plate with food over an hour ago and she hadn't seen him since. After her brother headed down as well, she thought she could breathe a sigh of relief. Apparently, she'd been wrong. Now she was standing in the hallway outside the bathroom with less than two feet between them.

Their gazes met for a long moment before he stepped out into the hallway. His broad shoulders seemed to take up too much space and her body reacted to the proximity. He was wearing one of those long-sleeved T-shirts that molded to every one of his muscles.

His gaze dipped down to linger on her mouth and her lips began to tingle at the memory of him kissing her. When he looked at her again, there was a heat in his eyes that told her he was remembering, too.

The air around them felt charged as they stood staring at each other. She wanted to touch him, but that was dangerous. Anyone could see them...especially her brother...and she didn't want to cause a rift between Mark and Justin. Mark wasn't exactly known for being accepting of Kim's boyfriends.

Not that Justin was her boyfriend. They'd had one night together. A night she'd begged him to give her, to show her what it would be like to submit to a Dom. He'd given her that. He'd opened her up to the world of Dominance and submission and made her realize what she'd been missing in her past relationships.

Justin cleared his throat. "Bathroom's all yours."

Kim swallowed. "Thanks."

Neither of them moved.

She had no idea how long they stood there. Eventually, their bubble burst when her brother's voice filled the hallway less than five feet from them. "There you are," he said, his words slurred. "I thought you were bringing me another beer."

Justin shoved his hands in his pockets and turned to face Mark. "Had to take a leak."

Kim watched as Justin and Mark turned and walked away, leaving her standing in the hallway alone. Justin didn't look back. Not that she'd expected him to. They weren't a couple. It was just sex. She was going to have to figure out a way to forget about it.

There were plenty of fish in the sea, right? She could find another Dom who made her feel like Justin did. One who sent her heart racing with one heated look. She just had to keep looking.

Even as she tried to convince herself, she feared it wasn't true. She'd been a member of the club for almost three months now and the closest she'd come to feeling anything like what Justin sparked inside her was when she'd watched a scene between one of the female dominants, Beth, and her submissive, Drew. It was as if Kim could feel the connection between them...feel the pull they had toward one another.

Kim finished up in the bathroom, then ducked into her old room. She needed a minute...or two.

Her old room hadn't changed much since she'd moved out. Her bed was still there and so were some of her old posters. The only addition were some boxes stacked by the closet.

Kicking off her shoes, Kim climbed onto her bed and closed her eyes, trying to focus her breathing like her yoga instructor was always telling her to. Slow breath in. Slow breath out. Slow breath in...

Five minutes later and she didn't feel any better, so she did the only other thing she could think of. She called Ali.

Her friend didn't bother with a standard greeting. "What happened?"

"Hello to you, too."

"Hi," Ali said. "And you didn't answer my question. What happened? Did you and Justin end up having crazy monkey sex on your old bed?"

Kim snorted. "No, we didn't have crazy monkey sex."

"Plain old vanilla sex, then."

Kim rolled her eyes. "No sex." At least, not tonight anyway. Ali didn't know about the night Kim and Justin had spent together. One of the few secrets Kim had ever kept from her best friend.

"Bummer." Ali sounded disappointed.

Deciding it was a good time to change the subject, Kim directed the conversation to less dangerous territory. "How's your mom doing?"

"She drank two bottles of wine and passed out on the couch." Ali sighed. "Not exactly the fun-filled New Year's celebration I'd been hoping for."

"Sorry."

"It's okay. I'm used to it."

Unfortunately, Kim knew that was true. "So does that mean she's crashing at your place until she finds the next guy?"

"Probably. It's not like she has anywhere else to go."

Ali's mom didn't have friends she could turn to because she tended to burn any friendships she developed at the whim of whatever guy she was dating. On the flip side, Ali was overly cautious when it came to relationships. Kim and Ali had been friends since their freshman year of college and Kim could count on one hand the number of guys Ali had dated in that time.

The two talked until a knock on her bedroom door brought Kim's attention away from the phone. It was her mom. "Everyone's gathering downstairs for the countdown."

Kim glanced at the clock. Sure enough, it was almost midnight. "Thanks," she said to her mom as she began scooting off the bed.

"I'll let you go," Ali said.

"I'll call you tomorrow."

"Happy New Year."

"Happy New Year."

Kim disconnected the call and tucked the phone into her pocket. The call had worked. She was feeling more like herself again.

By the time she made it downstairs, everyone was facing the television, watching the host as the clock counted down the last seconds of the year. Her dad came up beside her and handed her a glass of champagne as everyone in the room joined in with the countdown.

Ten...nine...eight...seven...six...five...four...three...two...one!

Fireworks filled the skyline on the big screen television as everyone screamed Happy New Year before taking a drink of their champagne.

"Happy New Year, sweetheart." Her dad placed a kiss on her cheek.

"Happy New Year, Dad."

The room joined in as the host led everyone in Auld Lang Syne. By this point in the night, almost everyone was tipsy. People were signing at the top of their lungs, hugging and kissing each other to celebrate the start of a new year.

Several people pulled her into their embrace and most kissed her on the cheek before moving on to the next person. The atmosphere was full of joy and hope.

She saw her mom and went to go wish her a Happy New Year, but before she could get across the room, someone bumped into her. The man turned around, brushing his arm against her breasts. With the way her body reacted, she knew who it was before their eyes met.

It was the hallway all over again. Time seemed to stop as they stared at each other before someone else bumped into Justin, seeming to break whatever trance they were in. He bent down and placed a soft kiss on her cheek, the same as at least a dozen other people in the room, but unlike those other kisses, when Justin's lips touched her skin, she felt it all the way in her belly.

"Happy New Year," he whispered before turning on his heel and walking away.

Taking a deep breath, Kim forced her feet to move. She found her mom and pulled her into a tight hug, needing the comfort of her mother's embrace. "Happy New Year, Mom."

"Happy New Year, honey."

Her mom didn't say anything about the extra-long hug, of course that could have had something to do with her brother. As soon as she'd released her mom, Mark came up behind her and lifted her off the ground again. "Happy New Year, Sis."

He was talking way too loud and she could smell the beer on his breath. "Happy New Year to you, too. Now put me down."

Mark laughed but lowered her feet to the floor again.

* * *

Justin stood in the corner, watching Kim, Mark, and Belinda. The Langleys had been good to him. He'd lost count of how many nights he'd stayed over during the last two years of high school. And when his parents had moved out of state when he was eighteen, Davis and Belinda had gone out of their way to make sure Justin was doing all right on his own.

He and Mark had met on the first day of football practice and they'd hit it off right away. Before long, Justin was spending more time at the Langleys' than he was at his own home. He ate meals with them and even tagged along on a vacation to Florida the summer before their senior year. They treated him like family.

Mark was the brother Justin never had, but the feelings Kim evoked in Justin were anything but sisterly. She was only fourteen when they first met and shy. He'd thought she was cute, but to be honest, he'd been more focused on sports at the time. Sports and cars.

But as time went on, the way he looked at her began to change, and by her sixteenth birthday, Justin was reminding himself daily why he couldn't make a move on her. That didn't mean he didn't notice everything about her down to how her glasses would slip down to the tip of her nose while she was reading and she wouldn't notice until they were on the verge of falling off. He'd wanted to be the one to push them back up or take them off altogether so he could look into her eyes, but he'd been a good boy and kept his hands to himself.

It had been easier once Kim graduated from high school and left for college. He didn't see her as much and threw himself into achieving his own goals for the future. Sure, he saw her when she came home to visit, but she'd often bring a friend with her and it was easy enough to keep his distance.

For seventeen years, he'd been a downright saint when it came to Kim Langley. A saint until she'd shown up at his home and knelt naked on his living room floor, offering herself to him on a silver platter. He should have said no, but years of attraction and longing had convinced him to give in just once.

It had been a huge mistake. Before, he'd only imagined what it would be like to sink his cock deep inside her and hear her moan and gasp as he pumped into her sweet pussy. He'd thought that was torture enough, but he'd been wrong. His body knew what being with her felt like and it wanted more. He wanted more.

An hour later, people began to head off for the night. Many lived in the neighborhood and were able to walk home. Some called for rides as they'd drunk a little too much to get behind the wheel. Except for a few sips of champagne at midnight, Justin had stopped drinking over three hours earlier. He lived too far to walk and there was no way he was crashing at Davis and Belinda's. Having Kim sleeping under the same roof was too much of a temptation.

Justin pulled into his driveway a little before two in the morning. The street was quiet other than some dogs barking. In his twenties, he'd lived in a loft downtown and he'd loved it. He could walk to bars, restaurants, and clubs. It was great.

But he wasn't twenty anymore and his life had changed quite a bit from that of a randy twenty-year-old who was out looking to get laid.

He'd learned that quality was more important and quantity when it came to sex. That's not to say he was a monk or anything, because that wasn't the case, but he was more discerning with his partners than he used to be.

Of course, thinking about his sex life brought his thoughts back to Kim. He could still feel her there. Still smell her perfume wafting in the air if he closed his eyes.

Justin needed to get over her and move on with his life, but he had no idea how. Two weeks ago, he'd taken a sub upstairs at the club to play, something he hadn't done since being with Kim. The scene went all right. He'd taken care of his sub, but there had been a disconnect for him. He couldn't get into the right headspace no matter how hard he'd tried and he knew why.

Stripping off his clothes, Justin headed into the shower. He was hoping the warm water would help to relax him and make him sleep.

The spray cascaded over his broad shoulders and down his torso. He tipped his head back into the water before reaching for the shampoo.

As he lathered his head, Justin tried to figure out what he was going to do about the one woman he couldn't have but couldn't stop thinking about. There was no easy answer he could come up with and her being at Serpent's Kiss complicated things.

The way he saw it, he had three options, and none of them were great. He could keep ignoring her as he had been, which didn't seem to be working all that well if the hard-on he'd been sporting for most of the night was any indication.

Option number two was that he could help her find a Dom. It was what she wanted. Or, at least, it was what she said she wanted.

He rolled that option around in his brain even though thinking about it made him sick to his stomach. It was a logical option. Once she belonged to another Dom, maybe his libido would get with the program and realize she was off-limits.

The third option brought back all the guilt he'd felt since that night. He could forget about his friendship with Mark—forget about all that the Langleys had done for him—and give in to what he wanted. It would be the easy solution. At least, in the short term.

Justin already knew what Mark's reaction to that option would be, but he had no idea how Davis or Belinda would feel about it. They thought of him as a son. They'd told him that many times. But that didn't mean they'd be thrilled about him dating their daughter.

Was the risk worth it?

He didn't know, and it was so hard to think around his desire to feel her in his arms again. His body knew what option it wanted.

Letting his head fall forward, he watched as the suds ran down his body into the drain before disappearing. Was he willing to flush his friendship down the drain for a woman? Not just any woman, grant you, but a woman nonetheless.

Could he break the trust of the family who'd been there for him at every turn? He was closer to Davis than he was to his own dad. Hell, it had been Davis who'd sat him down before Justin's first date with Monica Jenkins and talked to him about responsibility and being safe. All his own father had done was toss him a box of condoms and tell him not to be stupid.

And it was Belinda who'd sat with Justin for hours on the porch steps after he found out his grandmother had died.

Turning off the water, Justin reached for a towel. As much as he hated it, there was only one real option. He had to find Kim a Dom. A Dom who was worthy of her and would take care of her like she deserved. As much as the idea turned Justin's stomach, he couldn't betray Davis, Belinda, or Mark any more than he already had.

As he slipped into bed, Justin noticed a side effect of his decision. Thinking of Kim with another Dom had successfully killed his erection.

CHAPTER 9

As HER EYES fluttered open the next morning, it took Kim a few moments to remember where she was. She'd had every intention of driving home last night, but the last guest had lingered until almost two and by the time everything was cleaned and put away, it was pushing three-thirty. All she'd wanted to do was kick off her shoes and climb into her old bed.

Thankfully, she'd done a little more than that. Before crawling into bed the night before, she'd stripped off her work clothes and slipped on an old nightshirt she kept in the closet for the rare occasions when she slept over. Her mom always washed it for her, so it was ready to wear any time she needed it.

Thinking about Belinda Langley brought a smile to Kim's face. Her mom was the perfect balance of career woman and housewife. She'd stayed home with Mark and Kim until Kim was off to school, and then spent her days working as a mortgage loan officer up until two years ago when she retired. It was what Kim had always hoped to become. She wanted a husband, a family, and she wanted that balance in her life. The problem was she was now in her thirties and didn't even have a boyfriend.

She dressed in her work clothes from the night before and ran a brush through her hair before piling it on top of her head with a clip from her old nightstand. Seeing Justin last night had caused everything womanly in her to sit up and take notice. She'd read countless books where women found that connection with a man, but she'd yet to find it with anyone else but Justin. There was something about him that sparked inside her every time they were in the same room.

Closing her eyes, she tried to push thoughts of Justin McKay out of her head. Dwelling on what couldn't be wouldn't do anything but make her miserable. It wasn't going to change anything.

Grabbing her jacket from the back of the chair, she followed the smell of food to the kitchen where she found her mom and brother already sitting around the table. Belinda looked as if she'd had hours of restful sleep. Her brother, on the other hand, wore wrinkled clothes and his hair was standing up all over the place. Had he even brushed it?

"Morning." Kim went straight to the coffeemaker.

"Good morning, honey. I made cinnamon rolls for everyone, or there's bread on the counter for toast."

Kim brought her coffee over to the table, sat down, and reached for one of the cinnamon rolls. She hummed as the sugar hit her tongue. "Thanks, Mom."

"You're welcome." Belinda smiled. "How did you sleep?"

"Good." And she had. It was one of the blessings of being so tired. She'd been able to fall asleep, for perhaps the first time in three months, without dreaming about Justin.

She was halfway through her cinnamon roll when the back door opened and her dad strolled inside. He looked even more chipper than her mom. How was that possible? They hadn't gone to bed any earlier than Kim and Mark had.

"You two sleepyheads are up, I see." He gave his wife a kiss on the head before making his way to the coffeemaker. He took a loud sip of the hot liquid before joining the rest of them at the table. "Do either of you have any plans this afternoon?"

"Sleep," Mark murmured. "Lots and lots of sleep." He turned to look at his dad. "How are you not dragging this morning?"

Davis chuckled. "Well, for starters, I drank water instead of beer last night. And I always get a good night's sleep when I'm next to your mother." He winked at his wife.

Mark groaned. "TMI, Dad. TMI."

Their father grinned into his coffee as he took another sip, but otherwise ignored his son's reaction. "Think you can help me move the tables and chairs back into the garage before you catch up on that sleep?"

Her brother ran a hand through his already messy hair, then stretched his arms high above his head. "Sure."

Belinda turned her attention to Kim. "Are you going to see Ali today?"

Her mom's question wasn't unexpected. Kim polished off the cinnamon roll she'd been eating and reached for another one. "I thought I'd stop by on the way home and see how she and her mom are doing. When I talked to her last night, her mom had passed out on the couch."

Kim didn't need to fill in the blanks. Ali's mother had a pattern with men and that included showing up on her daughter's doorstep, then drowning her sorrows in alcohol until she passed out. It also meant that by noon today, she'd be taking over Ali's kitchen, cooking every sweet known to man, while going on about how men are the scum of the earth. In the thirteen years Kim and Ali had known each other, it had happened at least a dozen times and the pattern never changed.

Belinda stood. "I put some leftovers aside for her last night. To help balance out the sugar."

"Thanks, Mom. I know she'll appreciate it."

One by one, Belinda removed enough food from the refrigerator to feed ten people and placed it on the counter.

Ali rarely asked for help, but Kim knew the toll it took on her every time Ali's mom showed up on her doorstep after another breakup.

After devouring two cinnamon rolls, Kim kissed her parents goodbye and drove to Ali's apartment. She desperately needed a shower and a change of clothes, but her best friend wouldn't care what she looked like.

Kim stood outside Ali's door with two grocery bags full of leftovers. She could hear lots of movement inside and knew that Zelda, Ali's mom, must already be in the kitchen. A few moments later, the door swung open, revealing a weary-looking Ali.

Stepping inside, Kim dropped the bags on the floor and pulled her friend in for a hug. She held her there for a good minute before releasing her. "That bad, huh?"

"I should be used to it."

"Who is it?" Zelda yelled from the other room.

"Kim stopped by with some food from her mom's party last night." Even though Kim hadn't told her friend what was in the bags, Ali knew Belinda would send leftovers.

"Oh, good," Zelda said, appearing in the archway between the kitchen and the living room. "I have cupcakes in the oven and I'm almost done with the no bake cookies."

"Hello, Zelda." Kim picked the bags up off the floor and headed into the kitchen to put the food away. When she'd first met Ali's mom, she'd called her Ms. Foster out of respect, but Zelda wasn't having any of that. She insisted Kim call her by her first name.

Ali took the bags from Kim and began unloading them.

"Do you have any plans today, Kim?" Zelda asked.

"Beyond a shower and a change of clothes? Not really. I was kinda hoping to veg out on my couch and catch up on my shows."

Zelda waved her hand in the air before going back to her cookie mix. "Boring. You need to come shopping with us. We're going to have a girls' day out, right, Ali? No boys allowed."

Kim looked at Ali, but her friend was avoiding all eye contact. Ali hated shopping. Not that she didn't do it, but more that she was one of those people that if she needed something, she'd go to the store, get it, and then get out. She hated marathon shopping trips, which Kim knew was more along the lines of what Zelda had in mind.

But she also knew Ali wouldn't tell her mom no. So what was a best friend to do? "I'll need to stop by my apartment first."

"Yay! This is going to be so much fun." The look of excitement on Zelda's face was a complete contrast to the dread on Ali's. Unfortunately, there wasn't much more Kim could do until her friend stood up to her mom and Kim didn't see that happening anytime soon.

Four hours later, they were in their fifth store, Zelda combing through racks of clothes while Kim and Ali hovered around the cart that was full of clothes Ali's mom would never wear. In fact, two or three days from now, Zelda would conclude that she didn't need the new clothes and return them. This would usually come the day after Zelda had met a new man.

Something caught Zelda's eye in another aisle, leaving Ali and Kim blissfully alone for a few seconds. "Are you ready for tonight?"

Ali frowned. "No. I know *Thelma and Louise* is supposed to be a great movie about female empowerment, but just thinking about watching it again makes me want to hide."

"Maybe you could suggest another movie."

Her friend snorted. "I've tried that before. It never works. She says there's nothing that says girl power more than *Thelma and Louise*."

"Girls, you've got to see this," Zelda said from two aisles away.

Kim put an arm around her friend and squeezed. "Two more days at most."

Ali sighed. "I know. That's what I keep telling myself."

* * *

It had been two days since Kim had seen Justin. She would love to say she hadn't thought about him since, but the truth was that she couldn't stop thinking about him...about their encounter in the hallway.

She'd done her best to avoid him since their night together. It was a matter of self-preservation. He'd only promised her the one night and she'd eagerly accepted thinking it would be enough.

What a fool she'd been. It hadn't been enough. Not even close. And a part of her dreaded the possibility that their night together hadn't had the same effect on him.

But he didn't look unaffected when they'd come face-to-face on New Year's Eve. If anything, the opposite was true. He'd looked at her as though it was taking every effort he had not to push her up against the wall and kiss her.

Which was why she was currently standing outside his mechanic's shop dressed in a knee-length pencil skirt and a red blouse that dipped low enough to give a hint of the cleavage beneath. It wasn't the sexiest outfit she owned, but in order to get here before he closed, she'd had to come straight from work.

Taking a deep breath, she hiked her purse a little higher on her shoulder and strode inside.

Sandi, the receptionist slash office manager, looked up as Kim walked through the door. Her smile was instantaneous. Sandi had been working for Justin since he opened his shop five years ago and she knew all the Langleys well as they were frequent customers. "Kim. How have you been? It's been a while since I've seen you."

"I'm good, Sandi. Work's been crazy. What about you?" Sandi was two years older than Kim. She'd gone to school with Mark and Justin. In fact, at one time, Kim thought there might be something between Sandi and her brother, but nothing had ever come of it. At least, not that she knew about, anyway.

"The same." Sandi chuckled. "There's always something to do around here. Justin's reputation for fixing older cars has started to grow and business has been booming lately."

"That's great."

Sandi stood and walked around the desk to stand in front of Kim. "So, what brings you by today? Everything okay with your car?"

Kim shifted her weight from one foot to the other. Why was she so nervous? Oh yeah. Because she was there to talk to Justin. "Nothing major. It just needs an oil change. I was hoping maybe Justin could squeeze me in."

"Let me check," Sandi said. "Chuck and Zach were still working on a transmission last I checked, but I'll see if Justin's free."

Before Kim could say any more, Sandi disappeared through the door that led out to the shop area. The sound of a tool being used filtered through for the few seconds the door was open before it swung shut behind her. Kim was tempted to follow Sandi, but she kept her feet planted firmly on the floor. She wanted to talk to Justin, but not with an audience. If she'd played her cards right, Justin would agree to do the oil change and by the time he was finished, it would only be the two of them left in the shop. She didn't want to have this conversation with anyone else around on the off chance she'd read him wrong the other night.

A few minutes later, the door opened again. But instead of Sandi, it was Justin. He was dressed in overalls that had a patch with his name on it over his heart. There was a smudge of grease on his cheek and his hair was sticking up in several places.

His gaze raked over her from head to toe before coming back to her face. "Sandi says you're here for an oil change."

"Yes." Her response came out less confident than she wanted, so she tried again. "Yes. I was hoping you could fit me in before you close."

Justin glanced at the clock. "We close at six."

"Yes."

"It's five-forty."

She swallowed. "Yes."

"An oil change takes at least thirty minutes."

These were all things she already knew. "Does that mean you can't do it?"

He looked at her so long it took everything in her to stay still. Kim wished she could know what he was thinking, but he was giving nothing away.

"Give me your keys." Justin held out his hand and waited for her to drop them into his palm. "Take a seat. I'll come get you when I'm finished."

With that, he turned on his heels and strolled into the shop, leaving her alone.

Kim blew out a breath and sat down on the faux leather couch that had seen better days. She pulled out her phone and began scrolling through her emails. Eventually, Sandi returned to the desk and began closing everything down for the night. "I can go ahead and get you checked out."

Nodding, Kim tucked her phone back in her purse and dug out her credit card. Once all the paperwork was done, Kim returned to her place on the couch and reached for her phone again.

At six o'clock, Sandi turned off the lights on her desk, made sure the coffeemaker was ready to go for the morning, and strolled over to where Kim sat. "Did you need anything before I go? I hate leaving you here."

"No, I'm good. Enjoy your evening," Kim said with a smile.

Sandi gave one last glance into the shop before heading to the door. "It shouldn't be too much longer. Good night."

"Good night."

Kim watched as Sandi locked the door behind her, essentially securing Kim inside. Once Sandi pulled out of the parking lot, Kim watched as the other two mechanics who worked for Justin got into their vehicles and did the same. Kim and Justin were the only two left in the shop.

It was now or never. She stood, walked over to the door that led to the shop, and turned the knob.

Her car was at the far end of the room, its hood up. At first, she didn't see Justin, but then he appeared from behind a large toolbox that was as tall as him. He leaned over the front of her car, pulling the overalls tight over his ass. Her muscles clenched in appreciation.

Justin's head whipped around as soon as he heard her heels clicking on the concrete floor. His brow furrowed and his lips turned down in a frown before going back to whatever he was doing. "I told you to wait in the lobby."

"No, you told me to take a seat, which I did."

The scowl on his face didn't go away. "I also told you I'd come get you when I was done."

She ignored him. "Sandi ran my credit card already and locked everything up."

"I know." He stood to his full height, grabbed the top of the hood, and lowered it back into place. Without a word or a look in her direction, Justin strolled over to the sink and washed the grease from his hands. "What are you doing here?" he asked as he turned off the water.

No beating around the bush. Now or never, right? Why did this seem harder than showing up at his place and kneeling naked in his living room? Oh yeah, because a relationship was worlds different than one night of kinky fun.

She took a step forward, then stopped herself. "I wanted to talk to you."

He reached for a towel to dry his hands. "I wanted to talk to you as well."

That surprised her. "You did?"

"Yes. I know you joined Serpent's Kiss to explore your submissive nature. The best way to do that is to find a Dom, one you're comfortable with and can experiment with to find out what you like and don't like."

Justin unzipped his overalls and stripped them off, tossing them into a nearby bin and leaving him in jeans and a T-shirt that had her wanting to investigate the muscles beneath. She was so transfixed by his body that she almost missed what he said next.

"You need to find a good Dom and I've decided to help you."

Kim blinked. Surely, she hadn't heard him right. "What?"

He handed her the keys to her car before walking over to the far side of the room and turning off several lights. "Finding a good Dom can be difficult, especially given your strong-willed personality and the fact that you're new to the lifestyle. We need to find you someone who's willing to deal with your somewhat bratty nature."

"I'm not a brat," she said, somewhat offended. Over the last three months, she'd been learning more about the lifestyle and the terminology. Strong-willed? Yes. A brat? No. She didn't act out or object to be contrary or to get attention.

Justin gave her another long look. "No. You're right. You're not. But you're also not a trained submissive."

She took a few moments to digest what he was saying. "So you want to help find me a Dom."

"Yes," he said, lifting the bay door, then opening the driver's door of Kim's car for her, motioning for her to get inside. "I think that's the best solution."

Had she really misread the other night so wrong? And what about their night together? Had the sparks she felt only been on her side?

Lowering herself behind the wheel, she looked up at Justin. He seemed perfectly at ease with the conversation.

Before she could put words to her feelings at what he was suggesting, he continued. "We can start tomorrow. Meet me at the club around seven-thirty and we'll begin weeding through the prospects."

CHAPTER 10

JUSTIN SPENT the next twenty-four hours running through the available Doms at the club in his head. He'd tried to go over all the options with an open mind, attempting to keep his own feelings in check. The thought of Kim with someone else had every muscle in his body tightening and not in a good way. It was something he was going to have to get over, though. She was off-limits and always would be. Nothing was going to change that.

By the time he arrived at Serpent's Kiss on Friday night, he'd narrowed it down to three possible Doms for Kim. The first was Daniel. He was a little old for Kim, but he had a lot of experience in the lifestyle and the patience that would be needed to train a new submissive. Plus, Kim was already comfortable with him as he was friends with her friend, Ali. The second was Brandon. He acted as the lead bartender at the club, but he'd been in the lifestyle for over ten years and had an even temperament. The third option was a newer member of the club, younger than the other two. Gabe was only twenty-eight, but he carried himself well. Justin had been asked to observe Gabe's first play session two weeks ago, and despite the sub trying to push her weight around a few times, he'd handled the scene like someone who'd been playing for years.

Straightening his shoulders, Justin stepped inside the main room of the club and surveyed his surroundings. It was early. Most members didn't arrive until after seven.

Katrina caught his gaze and motioned for him to join her. Justin often helped her with new members, introducing them around, answering their questions, and making sure they understood how things worked. He was hoping that wasn't the case tonight as he was on a mission of his own.

"Good evening, Mistress Katrina." She was in her signature corset and leather pants that showed off her boobs and ass to perfection. Even though he had no interest in Katrina, that didn't mean he was blind. The woman had a body on her that would make a man drool.

Katrina smiled in greeting. "You're here early tonight."

"I managed to close up the shop a little early." While that was true, it was intentional. He'd wanted some time to get his bearings before Kim arrived.

"I see." She signaled for him to walk with her as she began making her way around the perimeter of the club's main floor. "How's Kim settling in? I haven't seen her play with anyone yet."

He hadn't expected Katrina to bring Kim up, but he shouldn't have been surprised. Kim had listed both him and Ali on her application. "We're hoping to rectify that soon. I'm going to help her find a suitable Dom."

Katrina stopped walking. She turned and gave him a hard look...one that said she wasn't liking what she was hearing.

"As a family friend, I want to make sure she finds someone who can handle her. She's new and she's quite strong-willed." The look she was giving him didn't change. "I have it narrowed down to three possibilities."

She raised one eyebrow, but still she said nothing.

He gave her the name of the three Doms he felt might be a good fit for Kim and waited to see what she'd have to say.

Instead of answering right away, Katrina began moving again. She made him wait until they were halfway up the stairs that led to the playrooms. "I don't think Daniel would be a good idea."

"You don't think he'd be willing to take on an untrained sub?" Daniel had played with inexperienced subs in the past, so Justin wasn't understanding Katrina's reasoning.

"That isn't the issue."

They were on the second floor now. He followed Katrina as she entered each of the playrooms, one by one. About an hour from now, they would be full.

"How do you think Ali would feel if Kim began playing with Daniel?" Katrina asked when they entered the fifth room. "I don't need that kind of drama at the club."

"You think Ali would have a problem with Kim being Daniel's sub?"

Katrina shook her head. "Men. You can be so clueless sometimes."

It took him a moment to understand what she was getting at. Daniel and Ali?

Justin took some time to think it over as they finished inspecting the rooms. He'd never seen them play together. Daniel did play with other subs on occasion, but that was usually because a sub would approach him, asking for a scene. The older Dom had a reputation for being a master at flogging.

Racking his brain, he tried to recall the last time Ali had gone upstairs with a Dom and he had to admit it had been a while. Granted, he wasn't keeping an eye on her all the time, but when she was at the club she was either working the front lobby or hanging out with her friends...which included Daniel.

Interesting.

"I'll mark Daniel off the list, then."

"Smart decision."

After they were finished with the rooms, they headed downstairs again and Katrina was pulled away to help with something in the women's locker room. The club was filling up fast and he knew it wouldn't be long before Kim got there. That is, if she showed up at all. It would be like her to stay home solely because he told her to meet him there.

A part of him wanted her to defy him so he could remind her she was the submissive and he was the Dominant. But then he had to remind himself that he wasn't *her* Dom. She wasn't his and he wouldn't be the one to punish her for her willful behavior. That would fall to someone else.

The thought caused his chest to tighten and the muscles in his neck to tense. He was going to have to get past these irrational feelings of possessiveness. Kim needed him as a friend. She needed his experience in the lifestyle to help her find a good Dom. One who would treat her right. One who would care for her.

Brad and his wife, Kate, saw him from across the room and began making their way over. Brad was a surgeon and often had to work late. On the nights when Kate would come alone, Justin would watch over her for Brad. Their relationship was stricter than most of the other couples that frequented the club, but it seemed to work for them.

Tonight, Kate wore a black dress that went down to her ankles, but it was anything but modest. Both sides of the skirt had slits that came all the way to her waist. And the top was almost as revealing. Cloth stretched over her ample breasts, highlighting her pierced nipples. Those two were not shy about their sexuality. Especially not while inside the club. Justin knew that because of Brad's position, they had to keep up appearances out in public.

"You're here early tonight," Justin said in way of greeting.

"No surgery today. It's rare I get a full day at the office anymore. I wanted to take advantage of it."

As they continued to talk, Brad moved his wife to stand in front of him. He slipped his hand beneath her top, plucking her nipple as the conversation moved from work to the scene Alexander and Grace, two of the club's newer members, had done a few weeks ago.

It was impossible not to be drawn to the interaction between Brad and his wife, especially as she moaned against him. But that only lasted until Kim walked through the door. Justin felt her before he saw her, drawing his attention in her direction.

The moment he saw her, he knew something was wrong. To someone who hadn't known her so well, they probably wouldn't notice, but after all these years, he knew her tells. She had her hands balled into fists at her side, a sure sign that she was upset about something.

Justin scanned the area for Ali, but he didn't see her. She was most likely working the lobby. That meant Kim was on her own tonight.

While that could be the source of Kim's tension, he didn't think so. Ali worked the front at least three times a month. This wasn't the first time Kim was on her own in the club.

His suspicions were confirmed when she noticed him staring. Her eyes narrowed and she swiftly turned on her heel and marched in the opposite direction.

Brad had noticed his distraction. "One of the new subs caught your eye?"

Justin never took his gaze off Kim. "She's my best friend's little sister."

The sound of Brad's suppressed laughter brought Justin's attention back to the other Dom. "Well, that could get interesting."

"Yeah," was all Justin said as his gaze returned to the woman in question.

An hour later, he was sitting on a barstool, watching Kim from across the room as she chatted with one of the youngest Doms at the club. The man had little to no experience and was the opposite of what she needed.

"Are you going to drink that or wear it?"

Justin McKay looked over at the bartender, Brandon, then followed Brandon's gaze to the bottle of water Justin was holding in a death grip.

Releasing the bottle, Justin turned his back on the woman he'd been watching as she leaned in to say something to the other Dom. He needed to stop. It wasn't doing anyone any good, let alone himself or his mental well-being.

"You know," Brandon said, "you could do yourself a favor and ask her to go upstairs with you. Maybe if you two released some of that sexual tension that's floating around, you wouldn't be trying to kill your water bottle."

"It's not that simple."

Brandon reached behind him and grabbed Justin a beer he hadn't asked for. He wasn't playing tonight, so having a drink wouldn't matter. Not that it would anyway as the club had strict rules on alcohol consumption whether you were playing or not.

"Thanks," Justin said when Brandon set the open beer bottle in front of him. He took a swig and let the cool liquid slide down his throat.

Someone signaled for Brandon and he walked to the other end of the bar to see what they needed. Justin was so fucked.

He tried not to watch the exchange between Kim and the other Dom, but it was impossible. It was as if she were a beacon he couldn't look away from. His gaze was drawn to her tongue as she took a drink, then licked her lips. The memory of her tongue sliding against his in a sensual dance of give and take as he'd thrust into her had his cock straining against his pants.

He couldn't take his gaze away from Kim and deep down he knew it wasn't because the Dom she was talking to was young and inexperienced. What the hell was he going to do?

Finishing his beer, Justin continued to watch the exchange and forced himself to remain firmly planted in his seat. Every time the other Dom's fingers brushed her hand, the beer Justin drank churned sour in his gut. Kim didn't pull away or send the man packing when he ran a single finger down her arm, and for a moment, Justin thought that was it. That was the night when she was going to say yes to one of the Doms at the club, maybe just to spite him, and there wasn't a damn thing he could do about it.

Squeezing his eyes shut, he tried to remember all the reasons why he couldn't...shouldn't intervene. Why, despite the other Dom being young and inexperienced, Kim finally accepting and exploring her submissive nature was a good thing.

"Looks like you dodged another bullet," Brandon said as he wiped down the bar a couple of feet away.

"What?"

Brandon nodded for Justin to look behind him.

Justin turned to see Kim rejoining her group of friends, the other Dom moving on to another unattached sub. His shoulders sagged in relief.

Brandon shook his head. "What are you going to do when she takes one of them up on their offer to play? You know Mistress Katrina isn't going to be happy if you punch one of the other Doms for laying a hand on a girl you haven't claimed."

He wasn't wrong.

Maybe Justin should stop coming to the club for a while.

But even as that thought formed in his head, he knew he couldn't...wouldn't do that. What if something happened and she needed him?

Then...what if something happened and she didn't? In theory, helping her find a Dom was the right thing to do. It was logical. But what he was feeling at that moment wasn't logical. He wasn't even sure it was sane.

Brandon rested his elbows on the bar. It was the middle of January and the club wasn't as busy as it usually was. Normally, Brandon wouldn't have time to question him, but as luck would have it, no one was currently in need of his services.

"I'm not going to punch anyone," Justin said.

The bartender raised an eyebrow. The look of doubt clear on his face.

"I haven't punched any of them yet," Justin mumbled and downed the rest of his water.

"Yet being the operative word in that sentence." Brandon stepped away for a second to hand one of the other Doms a bottle of water for their sub, then returned to stand in front of Justin. Brandon looked him over and sighed. "If you're not gonna play with Kim, then how about one of the other subs? Bridget's here tonight."

Bridget was one of the submissives Justin regularly played with. Or had been before Kim joined the club.

Justin snorted. He'd attempted to play with one sub since that night he'd spent with Kim, and it had been lacking, to say the least. It was pathetic and even he knew it. He couldn't remain celibate for the rest of his life.

As rational as Brandon's advice was, the thought of playing with Bridget or anyone else held no appeal for him. He really was screwed.

"I'll take another," Justin said, lifting the empty beer bottle in front of him. It would be his last given the club rules. Mistress Katrina didn't bend the rules for anyone.

"You know," Brandon said, "if all you're going to do is drink beer, you could do that at a regular bar. Or at home." He paused. "Of course, at home the view isn't quite as nice."

Kim was making her way to the dance floor with Lady Beth. Justin watched as Kim swayed her hips to the music, making his fingers itch to touch her. By the time they stopped dancing, he'd finished his beer and had switched back to water.

Kim headed to the bathroom, but before she went inside, she glanced toward the bar. Her gaze met his and he felt that spark all over again. The smile that had been gracing her face for the last half hour disappeared. Their gazes locked for a long moment, then her attention was pulled away when someone exited the bathroom. Justin's chest clinched as he watched her walk away. He had to do something.

Before he knew what he was doing, Justin slid off the barstool and made a beeline for the bathrooms. He took up a position right outside, waiting for Kim to come out.

Justin got several curious glances as he stood, not so patiently, against the wall. He wasn't even sure what he was doing. All he knew was that he needed to talk to her.

Her eyes went wide the moment she saw him hovering outside the bathroom entrance. Then he saw her stubbornness kick in. She straightened her shoulders and closed the distance between them.

The crazy thing was, he had no idea what he was going to say. Waiting for her to come out had been impulsive, which wasn't like him at all. He'd learned long ago that it was much better to go into things with a plan.

"Dance with me." He didn't know where that had come from, but now that it was out there, he was craving the opportunity to get his hands on her.

"I don't think that's a good idea."

"Why's that?" he asked.

She pressed her lips together like she did when she was trying not to lose her temper. For some reason, that excited him more. It was an irrational reaction, but that seemed to be the norm for him when it came to Kim.

"Aren't you worried that might give the other Doms the wrong impression?"

He took a step toward her without thinking about it. "What do you mean?"

Kim lifted her chin, not backing down despite their closeness. "I'm supposed to be finding a Dom, aren't I? If they see me dancing with you, they might think we're a couple, and we wouldn't want that, would we?"

A shot of jealously surged through him and he took another step forward, bringing her close enough to touch. He saw the muscles in her throat contract as she swallowed, and her chest rose and fell more rapidly at his proximity. She was as affected by him as he was by her, which was the problem. "Dance with me."

This time when he said it, the words were barely above a whisper. It wasn't a demand, but a plea.

Justin held his breath until she nodded, giving him the permission he was seeking. He wasted no time taking her hand and leading her onto the dance floor. Pulling her into his arms, he closed his eyes and savored the feel of her body against him. She wrapped her arms around his neck and moved with him to the slow beat pulsing out of the speakers. Mark was going to kill him.

CHAPTER 11

KIM WOULD LIKE to say it was the music that was responsible for the warmth radiating through her body as she danced with Justin, but that would be a lie. When he'd pulled her into his arms, she'd wanted to get as close to him as possible. Every womanly cell in her body was calling out to her, ready and willing to be close to him again, to feel that connection. Her fingers itched to play with the hair at the base of his neck, but she resisted. Barely.

While her body was ready, willing, and able, she was still upset. She'd gone to his shop wanting to talk to him about what had happened on New Year's Eve. To confirm that what she was feeling wasn't one-sided. But instead, he'd announced he'd be helping her to find a Dom.

She was still mad at herself for not saying anything then, but his suggestion had completely thrown her off guard. It wasn't until she was halfway home that the anger started boiling up inside her.

Kim had almost turned around and driven back to the shop to confront him, but she'd thought better of it. She had a temper. She knew that. And over the years, she'd gotten better at controlling it. Even still, as the night wore on, she'd decided that if he didn't want her, then she would take matters into her own hands. She didn't need his help. She'd find her own Dom.

While she'd spoken to several Dominants at the club since she'd joined, she hadn't taken any of their advances seriously. Not even the ones who'd asked if she'd like to go upstairs and play. She hadn't been interested.

When she'd arrived at the club tonight, she'd made a point of seeking out one of the Doms who'd been especially attentive to her recently. He was nice enough. Younger than her, but did that really matter? Age didn't necessarily dictate whether a person was a good Dominant or not.

But the entire time she'd been talking to Kurt, she could feel Justin's gaze on her. She knew he was watching, and it made it difficult to focus on what Kurt was saying. Eventually, she found an excuse to end the conversation and rejoin Ali's friends.

They didn't quite feel like her friends yet, even though they had welcomed her into their group. She was still trying to get used to all the different dynamics and how the lifestyle worked.

Outside of Ali, the one she felt most comfortable with, was Lady Beth. She wasn't sure why, but there was something about her that put Kim at ease. So when Beth had asked her if she wanted to join her on the dance floor, Kim had jumped at the chance. She needed to get out of her own head and thought maybe if she wasn't talking to another man, Justin would find someone, or something, else to focus on.

That didn't happen. She'd tried not to look in his direction as she danced next to Beth, to ignore him, but it was impossible. Kim could feel him watching her.

What she hadn't anticipated was that when she came out of the bathroom, he'd be there waiting for her. Her plan had been to avoid him, but all that went out the window when she saw him standing there.

"I'm mad at you," she said.

He opened his eyes but didn't meet her gaze. "I know."

When he didn't continue, she figured she'd have to be the one to say something. "Do you think I'm that incapable that I can't find a

Dom on my own? I know I'm new here, but Ali's been helping me, and—"

"It's not that." His hands flexed on her hips and the muscles in his jaw tightened.

"What then?"

It took him a few moments to answer. "I thought that maybe if you found a Dom, belonged to someone else, this thing between us would somehow go away."

So she wasn't imagining it. He was feeling it, too.

"That was really stupid."

Justin tugged her closer, bringing their lower halves together. She could feel the hard length of him against her stomach. "Stupid doesn't begin to cover it."

Kim didn't think he was talking about his asinine suggestion of helping her find a Dom anymore. She decided to take a leap of faith and put it out there. "I want you to be my Dom."

He pinched his eyes closed again and leaned forward to rest his forehead on hers. She could feel the tension radiating off him.

Kim knew what was going through his head. "Mark doesn't have to know."

Justin's eyes popped open.

"No one outside the club has to know."

He lifted his right hand and cupped her jaw. His touch was firm, possessive. She loved it.

"You're not going to be my dirty little secret. I won't hide you away like I'm ashamed of you."

She thought he'd be pleased with her suggestion to keep their relationship hidden, but he seemed offended by the notion. Still, she wasn't ready to let go of her suggestion. "Not forever. And I know you're not ashamed of me. But maybe this thing with us will fizzle out if we stop trying to put the brakes on. Is it really worth upsetting Mark if we're not going to last?"

Justin tilted her face up, bringing them nose to nose. "I've wanted you for seventeen years. The only thing getting a taste of you has done is make me want you more."

Her chest clenched at his declaration. She licked her lips and swallowed. Her heart felt as if it were going to pound out of her body. He'd wanted her for seventeen years? "Why didn't you say anything seventeen years ago?"

"You know why."

His gaze was on her lips now and she knew he wanted to kiss her. She wanted that, too. She wanted to lose herself in the only man who'd ever made her feel this way. "I used to lie in bed after football games and think of you in those tight pants while I touched myself."

Justin groaned. She couldn't tell if it was a good groan, or if he was upset by her confession. "When?" he choked out.

"The first time?"

He nodded.

"It was the first game of your senior year. I was wiggling in my seat the entire evening. Mom scolded me because I wouldn't sit still." Kim slid her fingers up into his hair, bringing their bodies more in line. Normally, even at a dance club, being this entwined with a guy on the dance floor would have her self-conscious. But they were at Serpent's Kiss, and what they were doing was considered tame given they both still had all their clothes on. "As soon as we got home, I shut myself in my room and...relieved the tension."

His left hand, which had been on her hip, moved lower to cup her ass. "Why does that make me horny as hell?"

Normally, she'd laugh, but the vibe pulsing through the air was thick with suppressed sexual tension. "Did you ever..."

He knew what she was asking. "Frequently."

The song they were dancing to changed, and the pulse of it beat in her veins. Justin adjusted their bodies, positioning his leg between hers. His thigh was against the heart of her need and instinctively, she pressed herself against him.

A smirk formed on his lips, and she realized he'd done it on purpose. For some reason, that only made her hotter.

The hand that was gripping her ass ground her against him with the rhythm pounding out of the speakers. It was hypnotic and sensual.

Kim felt her arousal building. She was dry humping him right there on the dance floor in front of everyone and she didn't care.

She closed her eyes, letting the sensations build. He knew what he was doing and she felt his breath on her lips as she inched closer to that elusive peak.

"Are you going to come for me?"

Her breath hitched and she nodded.

His thumb grazed the side of her neck. "Open your eyes and look at me. I want to look into your eyes as you come."

Kim did as he asked and met his heated gaze. She knew he was as turned on as she was. His erection was pressing hard against her belly, only adding to the fire burning inside her. She'd never been one for exhibitionism, but in that moment if he'd asked her to drop to her knees and suck him off, she would have done it in a heartbeat.

All thought left her as he placed both of his hands on her hips and used all his efforts to grind her against his leg. "Come for me, baby," he whispered in her ear.

His words seemed to have a direct connection to her clit. She tightened her hold on him. She was so close. All she needed was a little more...

Justin gripped her ass again, this time with both hands, and began moving her with a purpose. There was no hiding what they were doing, but that didn't matter. The only thing that mattered was what she was feeling in that moment.

Her orgasm hit her fast and hard. A squeak left her lips before she could contain it. She buried her head in Justin's chest as her body trembled with her release.

As her heart rate returned to normal, their surroundings came into focus. She glanced over at some of the people nearby and knew that what they'd done hadn't been missed. Embarrassment trumped her orgasmic high and she tried to step away.

Justin held firm. "Where do you think you're going?"

She couldn't look at him. "I can't believe I did that."

Her words were mumbled into his chest, but she knew he'd heard her.

He chuckled.

"It's not funny."

That only made his chest vibrate more. "No one cares that you dry humped me on the dance floor. Did you forget where we are?"

"No." She hadn't forgotten where they were, but that didn't change the fact that she'd never done anything like that in public before.

When she didn't say anything else, he tilted her chin up so he could see her face. "There's no need to be embarrassed."

"I know, but..."

They'd stopped dancing. "But?"

Silence fell between them as she thought about what she was feeling. In the moment, she hadn't cared. Wanted more, in fact. But now her levelheaded nature was kicking in.

Justin dropped his hand. "Have you changed your mind about me being your Dom?"

Despite her embarrassment over what they'd just done, that hadn't changed. She wanted him. The night they'd spent together had altered something in her. And not only the realization that she was submissive. She felt a connection with Justin that she'd felt with no other man.

At first, she'd thought it was because he was a Dominant. The way he'd taken control that night had set her body on fire. She'd convinced herself she could feel that with another Dom, but after months of interacting with other Doms, she learned that wasn't the case. She didn't just want a Dom. She wanted the one standing in front of her. "No. I haven't changed my mind."

Justin didn't answer right away and she hadn't missed that his left hand was still firmly on her ass. He didn't seem inclined to remove it anytime soon. "Is Ali's mom still living with her?"

She hadn't been expecting the drastic subject change. "As far as I know, but I haven't spoken to her today."

He nodded, and to her dismay, he took a step back, separating them. Before she could ask what he was doing, Justin took her hand and led her off the dance floor.

Kim followed. Not that he gave her much choice.

Stopping a few feet away, he released her. "Katrina can print out a limits sheet for you to fill out. I believe Ali is in the lobby tonight. I'm sure she can help you if you have any questions." The tone of his voice had become more serious, his demeanor more businesslike.

"Okay."

"Are you free tomorrow morning?" he asked.

Again, she was somewhat thrown by his question. "I think so."

He raised a single eyebrow.

Why did such a simple gesture from him make her want to squirm? "Yes. I'll be free."

Justin nodded. "Be at my house at ten. I'll make us brunch and we can discuss our lists."

"Can't we just play like we did before?" she asked.

"No." He ran his index finger along her jaw. His touch had the muscles in her stomach tightening again. "Before it was about you. Giving you a taste of submission."

"And now?" Her question came out in not much more than a whisper.

"We will be testing your limits. Exploring. There will also be expectations. For both of us. It's best to be on the same page before we begin."

She was happy to hear he wasn't fighting this thing between them any longer.

Justin brushed his hand down her arm as he stepped closer, invading her space once more. "I'll give it one month."

She blinked, not understanding what he was talking about. One month?

Her confusion must have been clear on her face. "If after a month we both decide we want to continue, then we'll sit down with Mark and your parents."

Kim swallowed, her nerves returning, but she nodded. This was what she wanted. Them. Together. She met his gaze. "Yes, Sir."

He lowered his head, covering her mouth with his.

The kiss was chaste. Especially after what they'd done on the dance floor. But still, her body reacted. She wanted more. She always wanted more with him.

But before she could do more than release a quiet moan, he ended it. "Get the form from Mistress Katrina. Fill it out. Talk to Ali." Justin lifted her hand to his lips, turned it over, and kissed her palm, sending a spark of heat up her arm. "I'll see you tomorrow at ten and we'll go over everything."

He didn't give her a chance to comment before he strolled over to the bar, returning to the seat he'd occupied most of the night before their dance.

Kim blew out a breath, trying to regain her bearings. Justin always made her feel off-kilter but centered at the same time. It was a strange feeling.

"Everything all right?"

The worried look on Daniel's face pulled her attention from Justin. "Yes. I'm fine."

"You're sure? You appear worried about something." The older Dom's concern touched her.

She decided to be honest. "I am. A little. I need to get a limits list from Mistress Katrina."

"Ah." The side of Daniel's mouth quirked up into a half smile. "I was wondering when you two would stop tiptoeing around each other."

"You knew?" She and Justin had barely spoken since she'd joined Serpent's Kiss.

"For those who were paying attention, it was hard to miss."

Kim wasn't sure how she felt about that.

"But if you're looking for Katrina, she's over there." He pointed to the far side of the room.

Sure enough, Mistress Katrina was talking to a couple she'd seen several times before at the club. "Thanks."

Daniel chuckled. "Don't be nervous. We were all new at one point."

He was right. And it wasn't like Justin didn't know her.

Kim shot him a grateful smile and made her way over to Mistress Katrina. She hung back, waiting for the conversation to wrap up.

When the couple walked away, Katrina turned her attention to Kim. "How can I help you this evening?"

For some reason, the woman was intimidating, but Kim stood her ground. She could do this. She dealt with intimidating people all the time at work. "I need a limits list."

Katrina nodded, not seeming to be bothered that Kim's request hadn't been filled with confidence. "Follow me to my office."

The club owner didn't wait for Kim to agree. She turned on her heel and expected Kim to follow.

They made their way down a hallway off the main room to Katrina's office. Kim had been there once before, and it still felt as imposing as it had that first time.

A large wooden desk that sat in the center of the room dominated the office. There were no windows, and on the one wall hung a variety of whips, floggers, and other implements. The first time she'd been in the room, she'd been so nervous she hadn't paid much attention, but outside the items hanging on the wall, the room could have been any office in countless buildings across the city.

"Here you are," Katrina removed several papers from the printer and handed them to Kim.

"Thank you."

Katrina grinned. "I know you have Ali, but if you need help, or have any questions, let me know."

"Thank you, again, Mistress Katrina."

With the papers in hand, Kim left Katrina's office and headed back to the main floor of the club. Almost immediately, she spotted Justin at the bar talking to Brandon. She thought about going to him but changed her mind. He'd told her to fill out her list and come to his place tomorrow morning. If she was going to be his submissive, then that meant learning to follow instructions. That wasn't going to be easy for her, but this she could do. Clutching the papers to her chest, she exited the club and found her friend sitting behind the coat check reading a book.

Ali's face lit up when she saw Kim, but then she must have seen how anxious Kim was and her excitement dimmed. "What's wrong?"

Kim shook her head. "Nothing's wrong. I-I need your help with something."

"Did something happen?"

Instead of answering her friend's question, Kim handed over the paperwork.

Ali's happy expression returned the moment she realized what Kim had given her. She knew what it meant. Her friend had been a member of the club for a few years. A limit list wasn't required if people wanted to do a scene together. That could be negotiated before the scene began. The limit list, however, was for those who wanted to enter a longer-term arrangement.

Before Ali could start asking questions, Kim decided to get it all out in the open. "And I need to tell you something else."

Her friend's delighted expression wavered. "You can tell me anything. You know that."

Kim knew that and keeping this secret from her best friend had been eating at her.

She took a deep breath and went for it. "I slept with Justin."

CHAPTER 12

ALI'S EYES looked as if they were going to pop out of her head, then she jumped off her chair and engulfed Kim in a tight embrace. Kim wasn't sure what kind of reaction she'd get from her friend, but she'd been unprepared to be squeezed to within an inch of her life.

Eventually, Ali released her. She pulled another chair from the closet and placed it a foot from the one she'd been occupying before Kim's announcement. "Okay, tell me everything. Did you two go upstairs tonight?"

Kim shook her head, and then lowered herself into the offered chair. Taking a deep breath, she prepared to spill her guts. "Do you remember the first time I came to Serpent's Kiss with you?"

"Of course. You were so nervous, I wasn't sure if I was going to be able to get you through the door."

"Well..." Kim hesitated, knowing what she would say next was going to hurt. Not because Ali would be upset she slept with Justin, obviously, but because Kim didn't tell her right after it happened. "I saw Justin here that night and figured if I wanted to explore my submissive side, he'd be the perfect one to do it with." Kim didn't look at her friend, afraid that if she did, she wouldn't get through this next part. "So, I showed up at his house the next day and..." She paused. "Offered myself to him."

Her confession was met with silence.

Kim peeked at her friend. She had a look on her face Kim didn't know how to interpret. "I'm sorry I didn't say anything earlier, but it was supposed to be a one-time thing. An experiment."

Again, nothing.

"Well?" Kim prompted. The silence was killing her.

"It explains a lot," Ali said. Then she sighed. "I can't believe you didn't tell me."

"I know. I'm sorry." Kim paused. "And what do you mean it explains a lot?"

Ali shrugged. "I don't know how to explain it. You've just seemed a little distant." She frowned. "Now I know why."

"I'm sorry."

Waving her off, Ali squared her shoulders. "It's okay. It's not like I've never kept anything from you. I mean, I was a member here for over two years before you found my toy bag in the closet."

"Still. It's not the same. I understand why you didn't tell me about this. To be honest, I'm not sure if I would have been ready to know sooner." Kim took hold of Ali's hands. "You've known about my crush for years, almost since the beginning of our friendship. This was a big deal, and I should have told you."

A tiny smile tugged at Ali's lips and the vise around Kim's chest eased. "But you've told me now, and you need my help."

Kim smiled back and nodded. "I do. He wants me to fill out this limit list. I'm supposed to bring it to his house tomorrow so we can go over it."

Grabbing a pen from the desk in front of her, Ali placed the papers on the flat surface and handed the pen to Kim. "We'd better get started then."

* * *

Justin lingered at the bar for the rest of the night, even though it meant giving Brandon the opportunity to razz him about finally getting his head out of his ass. He didn't explain to Brandon this was only a trial run. A month to see if they worked as a couple.

He still wasn't crazy about the idea, but he understood where Kim was coming from. And to be honest, he wasn't looking forward to Mark's reaction. His best friend was as vanilla as they came. Mark didn't understand Justin's need to dominate. Once he'd commented how he felt sorry for the women Justin dated, that Justin insisted they perform like trained animals.

Justin had let the comment slide. Mark had been drunk at the time and he had no filter when he was like that.

But Justin knew Mark wasn't comfortable with his lifestyle. The one and only time Justin had brought a sub around, someone he'd been dating for a few months and felt it was time to introduce them to his best friend, Mark had acted as if he were waiting for Justin to order her to her knees at any given moment.

If Justin and Kim made their relationship public, he had no idea how Mark would react. He could almost deal with any disappointment from Belinda and Davis. Ultimately, they wanted their daughter to be happy and well cared for. Over time, he could prove to them that he could do that. Mark, on the other hand, would know or suspect what was going on behind closed doors.

Mark's possible reaction plagued Justin for the rest of the night.

When Justin's alarm went off the next morning, he knew he needed to get his head in the game. He had lots to do to prepare for Kim's arrival.

Working out helped to clear his head. He pushed himself harder than he usually did, needing to feel the burn and push the concern from his mind. Today was about him and Kim. No one else. They had to be the ones to figure this out. Time had already proven whatever pull they felt toward each other wasn't going away. They needed to deal with this.

After a shower, he put on some comfortable clothes and powered up his computer. He pulled up his limits list, gave it a quick run-through to make sure everything was up to date, and then hit print. Justin knew what he liked and what he didn't. He'd been in the lifestyle for over ten years and had played with a multitude of submissives. But in all that time, he'd never been as anxious to see his partner's list of desires as he was to see Kim's. Given her inexperience, he didn't know what it would look like.

Bringing his list with him into the kitchen, he placed it on the counter and began prepping for brunch. He had one hour before Kim was set to arrive and lots to do.

At nine-fifty-eight, his doorbell rang. Justin turned off the stove and went to answer the door.

Kim stood on his front porch, clutching her purse to her chest. Unlike last time she showed up on his doorstep, she was wearing more than a trench coat.

"Come in," he said, motioning for her to come inside.

"Thanks."

He helped her remove her coat and placed it on the coat rack by the door. She wore a lovely burnt orange sweater and a snug pair of jeans that showed off her curves. His hands were itching to touch her, but first things first. "I hope you're hungry."

She gave him a shy smile. "Starving."

Justin knew she was nervous. He would normally keep things platonic between himself and a potential sub until limits were discussed, but he wanted to help put her at ease. Cupping the side of her face with his right hand, he brought their lips together for a chaste kiss. "We'll eat first, then talk. All right?"

Kim nodded and followed him into the kitchen.

He had her take a seat at the table while he brought everything over.

"Were you planning to feed an army?" she asked.

Justin laughed. "Nope. Just us."

"I know you eat a lot, but this could feed us for the entire week."

Once everything was on the table, he sat down next to her. "It probably will. Or me, at least."

She scrunched up her nose in confusion.

Handing her a plate and encouraging her to help herself, he explained, "I usually do the bulk of my weekly cooking, or at least prepping on Sundays. Since I don't always know how late I'll be at the shop during the week, it's easier to have the food ready for me no matter what time I get home."

"Oh," she said. "That makes sense."

They ate in silence for several minutes before Justin turned the conversation back to last night. "Was Ali able to help you?"

Kim swallowed her bite of food and nodded. "Yes. It was a good thing, too, because I didn't know what some of the stuff was." She lowered her voice and asked, "Do people really like to pee on each other?"

He chuckled. "Yes, there are people who like all sorts of things, including that."

"I guess I've been living under a rock, then, because I've never heard of that."

"You've never heard of golden showers?" he asked. While she might not have the variety of sexual experience he did, she wasn't exactly a virgin.

Her eyes widened for a moment before going back to normal. "That's what that means? I never knew that."

Smiling, he reached for another piece of bacon. "What else did you and Ali talk about last night?"

She glanced up at him through her lashes. "I told her we slept together."

"We did more than sleep," Justin said with a pointed look.

Kim blushed, averting her eyes. "Yes, well, I told her that, too. She tried to downplay it, but I know she was hurt that I didn't tell her. She knows I've had a crush on you for years."

He placed a finger under her chin and guided her gaze to his. "I didn't tell my best friend either."

Silence fell between them as the reason for that hung in the air.

"How bad do you think it will be?" Kim asked.

Justin frowned. "I don't know. Your brother knows about my lifestyle. Even if he doesn't know the details of our bedroom activities, he's going to at least have a clue as to what's going on." Dropping his hand, Justin picked up his plate and carried it over to the sink. "While Mark's never said anything directly to me, I've always gotten the impression that he doesn't approve. Or at least he doesn't understand my need to dominate my partner. Nor their desire to submit."

"And me being his sister..."

Her words lingered in the air as she joined him at the sink, putting her plate down next to his.

This was a strange situation they found themselves in. Normally, he wouldn't give a rat's ass what Mark thought of the women he dated, but this was different. She was Mark's sister, and he didn't want his friend thinking any less of her or their relationship.

That is, if this month-long trial went well.

Without overthinking it, Justin pulled her into his arms, resting his lips against her forehead. "If anything, he'll take his frustration out on me, not you."

"That doesn't make me feel any better," Kim said, leaning into his embrace.

Her words pulled a smile from him. Taking a step back, Justin put a little distance between them. As much as he wanted to skip to the good stuff, they needed to take care of business first. "Are you ready to go over our lists?"

"Not really."

Justin took another step back. Maybe she wasn't ready for this. One night of kinky sex was different than entering into a D/s relationship. "Have you changed your mind?"

Her eyes widened and she shook her head. "No, I haven't changed my mind. I'm just..." She leaned back against the counter, putting more space between them. "I'm worried our lists won't...mesh."

At his look of confusion, she continued. "You've been doing this for a long time."

"And you're worried I'll want something you aren't willing to do?" he asked.

"Yes." She pushed off the counter and began pacing. "I mean, I've watched stuff at the club, but my one and only experience was with you and I know now that was pretty tame."

He could see she was beginning to panic. Taking hold of her hand, he forced her to stop and face him. "Do you trust me?"

"Yes." Her answer came swift and sure.

"That's the most important thing in these types of relationships. That and communication. Everything else can be figured out and negotiated." He paused. "I think we've already figured out we're compatible in the bedroom."

The smirk on his face aimed to lighten the mood and it worked. A small grin pulled at the side of Kim's lips. "Very compatible."

Figuring it was time to get down to business, Justin led her back to the table. "Do you have your list?"

Kim retrieved her purse from the floor and removed several sheets of paper. Carefully, she unfolded them and laid them on the table in front of her. She placed her palms flat over the papers and looked up at him. "What happens now?"

Normally, they would exchange lists, read them over, and then discuss, but he wasn't sure that was the best option in this case. She was clearly nervous, and she was right. He had been doing this for a long time and he had a wide variety of interests. The last thing he wanted to do was increase her anxiety.

But he also wanted to do this right. If this thing between them didn't work out. If, and even thinking about it made him sick to his stomach...if she did this with another Dom someday, he wanted her to know what was normal. Red flags, like not going over lists and negotiating the relationship expectations first before any play began, were important to spot early.

"We exchange lists. You read over mine and I read over yours, and then we talk about it."

Kim took a deep breath in, her chest rising with the action, and he couldn't stop his gaze from drifting to that part of her body. He hadn't spent nearly enough time worshiping them. A problem he aimed to remedy soon.

She slid her papers toward him and he did the same, forcing

himself to concentrate on the task at hand. There would be time later for indulging.

For the next fifteen minutes, they read over each other's lists in silence. It didn't take him that long to get through hers. A lot of items were marked as *don't know*. She'd marked all the things they'd done during their one night together as *like*, which brought a smile to his face. The only things she had marked as *hard limit* were the more extreme items on the list, which were fine. He had no interest in hard-core S&M.

As he sat waiting for her to finish going over his list, he wondered what she'd think of his likes and dislikes when it came to play. She was correct when she said what they'd done before had been tame. He'd wanted to give her a good experience, so he'd gone easy on her. A little spanking, a blindfold, and a little bondage can go a long way with someone who's new to kink.

When she met his gaze from across the table, she looked...apprehensive. He grabbed her hand and held it between both of his. "Talk to me."

"Can I have some water?" she asked.

Not what he'd been expecting, but...

"Sure."

Returning to the table a few moments later, Justin handed her the glass of water she'd requested. She brought it to her lips and took a sip. "Thanks."

He sat back down and waited, his own anxiety creeping up the longer she remained silent. Was there something on his list that had frightened her? He wouldn't think so, but he couldn't be sure.

Finally, she met his gaze. "Does it always feel this overwhelming?"

"What do you mean?"

Kim sat her glass on the table in front of her and blew out a breath. "I mean, I knew how much there was, but seeing it all in front of me and how many things you have checked that you've tried."

She didn't continue and he felt compelled to respond. "I've been doing this for a long time."

"I know. And part of me is glad because it means you know what you're doing." She ran her hands over the papers in front of her. "Ali said if both of us were new to the lifestyle, it would be harder."

"Yes, that's usually true."

Then he noticed a tear leak from her eye and roll down her cheek. "I want to be a good sub for you but look at my list and look at yours."

Seeing her cry nearly broke him. He didn't like seeing her this distressed, and especially not over something that could be remedied with time.

Justin used the pad of his thumb to wipe the tear from her cheek. "Experience isn't everything." He didn't usually talk about past subs when negotiating a new arrangement, but this was different. Kim was different. They both knew they weren't going into this to get their rocks off. "I've played with subs who've had as much experience in the lifestyle as I do."

She groaned.

"And while they were good subs, there was no connection. Not like the one we have."

"What if you tell me to do something and I screw it up? I don't want to embarrass you at the club."

A light bulb went off in his head. "Everyone at the club knows you're new, so no one is going to expect you to be perfect out of the gate. Not even me." He paused. "But if you disobey me while we're playing, at the club or not, your ass will be feeling it."

She squirmed a little in her chair, so she knew exactly what he was talking about.

Justin grinned. "Let's get through our lists, and then we have some business to take care of before tonight."

"Tonight?"

"Yes. Tonight, you make your debut at the club as my submissive."

CHAPTER 13

KIM SWALLOWED and tried not to let her nerves get the best of her. He was right. Everyone at the club knew she was a newbie. And if she did screw up, it wouldn't be the first time. She still remembered the night Ali had brought her to visit Serpent's Kiss. She'd stumbled over herself when she'd met Brandon, calling him Sir and blushing like a schoolgirl. Kim had survived that. She could this too. And she would have Justin there guiding her. She only had to let him.

"Let's start with the easy stuff," he said. "Tell me about the blow jobs you've given?"

Her eyes went wide. "What?"

Justin smirked. "You've marked love to give on your list, but I want to know your level of experience with them."

"Um…" She had to look like a deer caught in the headlights. She felt like one. Kim had no clue what to say. No guy had ever asked her something like that before. "I don't know. Average, I guess."

When she didn't elaborate, he pressed further. "Do you prefer soft and gentle or rough and deep? Have you ever deep throated?"

Her level of embarrassment hiked up another notch. She could feel the heat radiating from her face. Did he really need to know this? She'd never talked about her prior sexual encounters with anyone besides Ali, and her best friend hadn't ever asked her if she'd sucked her boyfriend's cock down her throat. "Um…medium, I guess."

"So not too rough, but not too gentle either." He refocused on the papers in front of them, but she thought that was more for her benefit than his. "What about deep throating?"

"I tried once, but I gagged."

He nodded, then moved on to the next subject. "What about hair pulling? You marked I don't know. A guy's never pulled your hair during sex?"

"I don't think so." She blew out a loud breath. "Do we really need to go over this in such…detail?"

Justin met her gaze. "Yes. I need to know what you like, what you don't like, and what you're willing to explore. I can't do that if I don't have all the information."

While that made sense, it didn't make it any less embarrassing. "What about you?"

The smirk was back. "Which one? The hair pulling or the blow jobs?"

His eyes were dancing with amusement, but it didn't make her feel self-conscious…or at least any more self-conscious than she already was. "Both."

Reaching out, he cupped the back of her head and twisted a fistful of hair around his hand. "I love to pull my partner's hair. And as for blow jobs, I love receiving them in any form, but I would enjoy feeling my cock hit the back of your throat." He leaned in and, with a gentle tug on her hair, whispered in her ear, "We can always work on your gag reflex."

Heat surged between her legs. "Okay."

Then, to her disappointment, he released her and turned his attention back to their lists. For the next hour, he had her explain, in detail, her level of experience on everything she'd marked *love*, *like*, *dislike*, and *soft limit*.

It was strange to sit down and talk about her preferences in the bedroom and what she'd done in the past with other partners, but the more they talked, the more comfortable she felt. Kim wasn't sure what she'd expected a relationship with Justin to be like, but this much discussion about sex and preferences didn't come close to anything she'd ever done with a boyfriend.

In fact, the only conversation she'd ever really had with a guy regarding sex was with her first college boyfriend. They'd each only been with one other person before and had both been awkward and unsure of what they were doing. The whole thing had lasted no more than five minutes and consisted of whether she was on birth control and if they should wait or not since they'd only been going out for a month. It was nothing like sitting across a table with Justin and talking about what her favorite positions had been, or her level of experience when it came to blow jobs.

She'd got to ask him a few questions as well, although he didn't seem bothered by any of them. Most of them came up when they were talking about the things she marked as dislike. He had a lot of questions about those and after he asked her why she disliked anal sex, she turned the question around on him. "Why, you like it?"

Justin smirked. "Well, for one, it feels amazing. The visual isn't bad either." Then he got serious again. "Now explain to me what it is you don't like about it. Did you have a bad experience?"

Just thinking about it made her sore and not in the good morning after type of way. "You could say that."

"Tell me."

It really wasn't something she wanted to talk about or remember, for that matter, but they'd talked about every other embarrassing sexual encounter she'd had, so why not. "He was behind me and, well, you know." She blew out a breath. "It hurt. A lot. I screamed. He stopped. End of story."

Unfortunately, that wasn't enough for Justin. "Where were you when it happened? Did he prepare you? Use any type of lubrication?"

She could feel her cheeks warming again. "We were in a bathroom. It was a party and we were a little buzzed. We were both horny, so we snuck into his friend's master bathroom, locked the door, and started moving clothes out of the way."

Kim was hoping she could leave it at that, but of course, Justin wanted more. "Go on."

"There isn't much more." She shrugged. "He bent me over the counter and somewhere in the middle of it, he pulled out. When he"—she cleared her throat and looked down—"well, it tried to enter a different hole."

"So no preparation and no lube."

"I don't know what you mean by preparation, and we'd been having sex, so he was...you know...wet from..."

Justin shook his head. "That isn't enough. Anal sex requires the muscles to be stretched beforehand." He frowned. "It also takes more lubrication than the human body can naturally produce. At least not unless inducing pain is the goal."

Again, she cringed, remembering.

He took her hand in his and gave it a comforting squeeze. "We'll leave it off the table for now, but just know that when done right, anal sex can be pleasurable for both parties and I'd love it if you'd give me a chance to show you one day."

A flutter began in the pit of her stomach. The tender look in his eyes made her think that maybe with him it would be different. Their one night together had been worlds apart from her previous sexual experiences. Why wouldn't other things she'd experienced?

Once they'd gone through both their lists, Justin stood. "Do you have any other questions for me regarding the lists?"

Kim shook her head. "I don't think so. But..."

"But?"

"How? I mean, what do I do as your submissive? Even though I've watched the subs at the club, I've never done this before."

Justin helped her from the chair and led her down the hallway to the bedroom where they'd spent the first part of their night together. She was immediately flooded with memories. Heat began pooling between her thighs in preparation.

He turned to face her, cupping her cheek with his hand. "We need to talk about protocol."

"Protocol?"

"What I expect of you." His thumb rubbed along her bottom lip. "As my submissive."

"Okay." She wanted to lean into him, to forget about everything else. Hadn't they waited long enough? It had been over three months. She wanted to feel him inside her again.

"First, you will call me *Sir* whenever we are playing."

"How will I know when that is?"

He slid his hand down to grip the back of her neck. "If we're at the club, or in this room, then we're playing. Outside of that...you'll learn how to read my signals." One side of his mouth tilted up into a half smile. "If I tell you to get to your knees, that's a good indication."

Kim tried to concentrate on what he was saying. This was important. "But what if I don't want to play?"

"Did Ali talk to you about safewords?" he asked.

"Yes." Kim recalled the first time she'd heard a submissive at the club use their safeword. She and Ali had been hanging out with Daniel when another couple had stopped by to speak with him. She'd seen Alexander and Grace around Serpent's Kiss, she'd even watched them do a scene on her first night as an official member, but she'd never met them directly before that night. As Daniel and Alexander talked, the conversation turned to their time in the military. Kim had begun to space out, not overly interested in their conversation, when she'd heard Grace say *mushroom*. All conversation had stopped and Alexander had taken Grace to one of the quieter areas of the club. As soon as she'd been alone with Ali, she'd questioned her friend. Ali had explained that *mushroom* was Grace's safeword.

"Do you remember your safeword?"

"Yes. My safeword is teddybear." Then she recalled what he'd said moments before about being in this room. "Sir."

He grinned, seeming to be pleased that she'd remembered and corrected herself.

"Because you're new to this, I'd also like to use elements of the stoplight system." Her confused look must have given away her lack of understanding because he continued. "If something isn't right, say the ropes I bind you with are too tight or your leg is beginning to cramp, say the word yellow. That tells me that while you don't want to stop playing, I need to assess the situation before continuing."

She'd heard *yellow* used before when she'd ventured upstairs at the club. "What if you do something I don't like?"

"You're asking very good questions." His fingers began massaging her scalp and she let her eyes drift closed, sinking into the feel of his hands finally being on her again. "Submission is about giving up control, which means letting me guide the scene where I want it to go. If you don't like the position I've placed you in, you can say yellow, wait for me to ask you to explain, and then I will decide if I want to adjust the scene or not. Safewords, however, are to be used in situations where something isn't right and the situation needs to be assessed, not because you'd rather something different be happening. When we talk about the scene after, you can tell me what you liked and didn't like."

Kim knew that would be hard for her. Sure, she'd given up control to him once before, and she'd enjoyed every minute of it, but they weren't only talking about one night. Could she give him complete control of their sex life?

"Tell me what you're thinking?" he asked.

"I just hope I can do it. Not tell you what I want while we're...playing. Or if I don't like something."

That sly smile pulled at Justin's lips again. "I seem to remember you giving off some pretty clear signals of your enjoyment the last time."

The blush was back, but she was less bothered by it this time. Maybe it was because they were in this room and not at his kitchen table. "I just want this to work," she whispered.

Justin stepped forward, closing the gap between them, bringing their bodies flush. He tilted her head back so her mouth was a breath away from his. Her hands went to his sides. "If we talk things over with each other, the rest can be figured out."

Her heart was pounding, and she felt hot all over. "All right."

He backed her up against the wall, pressing his body into hers. She could feel his erection pressing against her belly. All she wanted to do was lose herself in Justin. Couldn't the talk of safewords and whatever else wait?

Seeming to read her mind, he brought their noses together and locked his gaze with hers. "If something isn't right and you want the scene to stop, say teadybear and I'll stop the scene."

"Are we going to play now?" Why she spoke, she had no idea. All she wanted him to do was kiss her. She didn't want to talk anymore.

His only answer was a hard kiss that pressed her body flush against the hard surface at her back.

Her eyes fluttered closed as she held on, desperate to be as close to him as she could. As his tongue played with hers, darting in and out of her mouth, she reached for the button on his jeans. She wanted to feel his cock in her hands.

Fingers wrapped around her wrist, stopping her movement. She opened her eyes and gazed up at him, not sure why he'd stopped.

"What do you think you're doing?"

* * *

Justin had lost his head for a moment, the desire to kiss her overwhelming him. That hadn't happened to him for over a decade. Normally, when he was with a submissive, he was in complete control. But his need for her was clouding his better judgment. They should have talked about safewords and protocol in the kitchen.

But it was too late now. His cock was rock-hard and he could feel the heat of her breath on his face from her labored breathing. A little voice in the back of his head screamed at him that he shouldn't be doing this with her, but it was being drowned out by a larger voice that said she was his and always had been.

He brought her hand to rest on his chest while he tried to get his own breathing under control. It was so easy to let go with her. And he wanted to let go, to lose himself in her, but they needed to finish what they'd started. Even if it killed him.

Raising an eyebrow, he waited for an answer to his question.

She blinked, her brown eyes rich with her arousal. "I want to touch you."

"When we're in this room, I'm in control. If you want to touch, you need to ask."

"I can't touch you?"

Justin moved her hand back down, this time to cup his erection. "I didn't say that. But in here, when we're playing, I call the shots. You obey." He could see her mind working. Even though Kim was the baby of her family, she was extremely independent. He knew this was going to be a challenge for her. "I'm a very agreeable Dom, though, so if you ask me nicely, I'll likely grant you permission."

"Only in here?" she asked.

"And at the club." He paused. "For now."

Her eyes opened wide. "For now?"

"Relationships evolve over time, even D/s ones. You may find you like asking my permission."

Kim looked doubtful. "I don't know about that."

Justin took her wrist and guided her hand back to the top of his jeans. He didn't say more, just waited to see what she'd do. His cock was aching, but he'd been doing this for a long time. He knew how to control himself. Usually.

Several very long moments passed before she spoke. "May I touch you?"

"Are you forgetting something?" She looked confused. "How do you address me when we're in this room?"

"May I touch you, Sir?"

He released her wrist. "You may."

Kim wasted no time slipping her hand beneath the fabric of his jeans. His cock pulsed at the first brush of her fingers. The zipper gave way when she wrapped her fingers around him.

It was still too constricting for his liking, so he pushed the jeans down his hips, freeing him the rest of the way. He rarely wore underwear when he was hanging around the house, and today he was grateful. It was one less thing between them.

She didn't miss a beat and began pumping her hand from base to tip. It felt so good to have her touching him freely like this. For so long he'd dreamed of her hands, her mouth, her tits...

He sank his fingers into her hair and captured her mouth with his, angling her head the way he wanted it. Her eager response only encouraged him. He deepened the kiss, pressing their bodies together, trapping her hand between them.

His cock pulsed in her hand, driving him mad. He wanted everything at once...her hands...her mouth...

Tilting her head back, Justin kissed down her jaw to her neck. As he neared the base of her neck near her collarbone, she released the most delicious moan. Her hand squeezed his cock and he knew in that moment what he wanted.

He released her and took a step back, waiting until she met his gaze. "Get on your knees. I want to feel your mouth around my cock."

This time, she didn't hesitate. Kim knelt before him and brought her lips a breath away from his erection. She looked up at him with a level of sweet innocence that mocked what she was about to do. "May I suck your cock, Sir?"

Instead of answering her with words, he took hold of the back of her head and guided her mouth the rest of the way home.

CHAPTER 14

Justin closed his eyes as her warm lips encircled his length. He let her set the pace, wanting to see what she would do.

She was tentative at first, gently licking and sucking his length. It was torture when all he wanted was to sink deeper into her mouth, but he forced himself to remain still. At least, for now.

After a few minutes of exploring, she picked up the pace, seeming to gain confidence. It felt amazing having her hot mouth engulf him, but it wasn't enough. He tightened his hold on her head and pressed forward with his hips, taking control.

Slowly, so she could get used to him, he increased the speed of his thrusts, going a little deeper each time until he was hitting the back of her throat. Justin both felt and heard her gag a little, so he eased up to allow her to adjust. He gazed down at her. "Relax and breathe through your nose."

He waited for her to take a couple of breaths.

"Are you all right?"

She nodded, not releasing her hold on his cock.

"Good girl. I'm not going to push you too hard today, but I am going to fuck your face and come down your throat."

She stared up at him, her eyes telling him she was as into this as he was. He wondered how wet her panties were and knew he wanted to find out, but not before he'd found release. Having her suck him off was something he'd been dreaming about for longer than he cared to think about.

"Since your mouth is otherwise engaged, if you need to use your safeword, tap on my wrist three times. Otherwise, you will take what I give you." Increasing his hold on her hair, he didn't wait for a response before surging deep into her mouth again.

She gagged again but then focused on breathing each time he pulled out. Soon, she was able to adapt to his rhythm. "That's it. Take what I give you. You look so beautiful on your knees sucking my cock, baby."

He noticed her breathing slowed even more and her eyes dilated to nearly black at his words. His girl liked it when he talked dirty. He was going to have to remember that and use it to his advantage.

With two hands fisted in her hair, he focused on watching his hard length move between her lips. Her tongue massaged the underside of his cock, coaxing his orgasm closer and closer. He could feel it building in his balls and knew it wouldn't be long.

As the surge built at the base of his cock, Justin began thrusting harder. "Swallow every drop."

It was the only warning he gave. Seconds later, he was coming—shooting streams of cum into her mouth and down her throat.

Justin felt her swallow around him and eased his grip on her hair. He took a steadying breath before stepping back. Extending his hand, he helped her to stand. Then, without warning, he crushed her to him and kissed her.

Kim didn't miss a beat. She threaded her fingers into his hair and wrapped one leg around his waist. His jeans were still around his ankles, throwing him off balance with the force of her movement.

He fell against the wall, taking her with him, but he didn't stop kissing her. Instead, Justin hiked her leg higher on his hip. The position opened her legs wider, making him wish she wasn't wearing jeans. "From now on, when you enter this room, you will either be wearing a skirt or nothing. Do you understand?"

"Yes, Sir."

Her breathing was labored, drawing attention to her breasts, but they would have to wait until later. He had other priorities.

Setting her legs back on the ground, he took a step back and pulled his own jeans back into place. "Strip."

She blinked. "Now?"

He folded his arms and waited.

After only a moment's hesitation, she began removing her clothes. Her sweater went first, revealing a brown lacey bra that clasped in the front. Next to go were her jeans. She shimmied them down her hips and kicked them over to join her sweater. Her panties matched her bra, the lace giving hints of the silky skin beneath.

She removed the bra first, tossing it onto the floor with the rest of her clothes. Her nipples were hard and begging for him to suck them as she bent to remove her panties. His mouth watered as she lowered the fabric down her legs and stepped out of them.

Before she could throw them in the pile with the others, he held out his hand. "Give them to me."

Kim froze. "You want my panties? Why?"

"Did you forget where we are?" he asked.

She glanced around the room, then back at him. He could see the wheels turning in her head as if she were trying to decide whether to hand over her underwear. After seeming to consider her options, she stepped forward and handed him her panties.

Justin took them and tucked them into his front pocket. He'd planned to get her off before they began preparing for tonight, but it seemed she needed a reminder that she was the submissive in the relationship.

He walked over to the bed and sat down. "Lie across my lap, your ass in the air."

Kim looked uncertain as she crossed the room and lay across his lap.

He waited for her to get settled. "What did I tell you would happen if you disobeyed me?"

She lowered her forehead to the mattress. "That my ass would be feeling it, Sir."

"That's correct." Justin rubbed his hand along her bottom. "And was I unclear when I told you to hand me your panties?"

"No, Sir."

Learning to give up control was going to be the hardest part for Kim and we both knew it. But if this was the type of relationship she wanted, then she was going to have to learn to obey her Dom. "You'll receive ten swats for your disobedience."

He didn't wait for a response before landing the first blow to her ass.

"Ow!" She reached back a hand to shield her ass.

"Remove your hand and keep them on the bed or I'll get rope to secure them."

Kim brought her arm to rest over her head. "I'm sorry. I didn't mean to—"

He landed two more smacks to her ass in quick succession. This wasn't a playful spanking like before. This was discipline.

"Please." Despite her pleading, she kept her hands flat on the bed.

Justin didn't want to draw this out any more than he needed to, so he ignored her protests and the tears sliding down her cheeks and finished what he was doing. After the final hit landed on her now rosy ass, he massaged the warm flesh several times before helping her to sit up.

He went to wipe the moisture from her face, but she brushed his hands away. As much as that irked him, he let it go. She was new to this and he knew that once she realized having a D/s dynamic involved more than kinky fun, she might decide this lifestyle wasn't for her.

"Are you all right?" he asked.

"I'm fine." She shifted on his lap. "May I get up now, Sir?"

"Not yet."

Her eyes flashed to his and he saw the anger boiling beneath the surface. Kim had always had a temper. He'd seen it a lot when she was a teenager, but he'd been lucky enough to steer clear of it for the most part. "Do you understand why I punished you?"

"Yes. Sir."

She was definitely angry.

Justin wondered whether he should push the issue or let her calm down first. He decided to let it go. For the time being anyway. "Get dressed, and then we have some shopping to do before we head to the club tonight."

Kim stood and marched over to retrieve her clothes. She kept her back to him while she dressed.

"I'll be in the living room. Come out when you're done."

"Is that an order, Sir?"

He sighed. "A request."

Not waiting for a reply, Justin left her to finish.

He ducked into his room and threw on a shirt, socks, and shoes before heading into the living room. Scraping a hand over his face, he fell back against the couch. That hadn't gone the way he'd hoped. Then again, he knew embarking on this with her wouldn't be easy. But he thought they'd make it past the first few hours before hitting their first hurdle. For all he knew, she would walk into the living room and tell him off.

Maybe that would be for the best. At least, they'd know they'd tried and that it didn't work. It wasn't as if they hadn't gone over everything beforehand. She'd known what she was getting into. In theory, anyway.

* * *

Kim had finished dressing and began to pace. How dare he spank her like that. Her ass was still burning.

Her gaze drifted over to the bed where he'd dulled out his punishment. This hadn't been like the spanking he'd given her the last time. Their night together had been about pleasure. There was no pleasure in what she'd just experienced.

She'd given him her stupid underwear. Granted, she hadn't given them to him right away. And she'd question him why he'd wanted them. But did that mean she deserved to be humiliated?

Kim blew out a breath. She needed to calm down. He was out there waiting for her and whether she felt like it or not, she was going to have to face him sooner or later.

Squaring her shoulders, she stepped out of the room, closing the door behind her. He was waiting for her in the living room, exactly where he'd said he'd be.

As soon as he saw her, he stood. She'd expected him to look smug, but instead he appeared worried. That took some of the wind out of her sails.

Neither said anything for the longest time. He was the first one to break the silence. "Did you want to sit down?"

"No," she snapped, unable to help herself. "My butt is a little sore at the moment."

He sighed. "We need to talk about what happened."

"There's nothing to talk about."

"Of course there is." He started to take a step toward her, then thought better of it. "Have you changed your mind?"

"Why do you keep asking me that?" That was beginning to irritate her more than her tender backside.

Justin rubbed his hand along the back of his neck, then dropped it back down to his side. "I know how strong-willed you are. Being submissive is about giving up control."

"I know that." She closed her eyes and took a deep breath before meeting his gaze again. "Look, I know I should have given you my panties when you asked. I just wasn't expecting you..."

"To spank you?"

"Yes." She crossed her arms. "I'm not sure what I expected. At the time, I just didn't understand why you wanted my underwear. I still don't."

This time, he came to stand in front of her. He must have realized the biggest part of the storm was over. "It doesn't matter why I wanted them. I'm your Dom. As my submissive, you need to do what I ask you to do or use your safeword. That's how this works."

"I'm not sure I can do that."

He chuckled. "Then you'd better get used to having a sore ass."

She narrowed her eyes at him.

Justin held his ground and waited to see what she'd do.

As much as she hated to admit it, he was right. She could either suck it up and follow the rules, not follow the rules and deal with the consequences, or throw in the towel. Walking away wasn't an option. Not after less than a day. Which meant she either needed to learn how to follow his instructions or, as he put it, get used to having a sore ass.

She decided to change the subject. "You said we had shopping to do?"

He hesitated for a moment, then answered her question. "Yes. I want to get you something to wear for tonight."

"I have clothes I wear to the club at home."

"Are you disagreeing with your Dom again?" he asked.

"We're not playing. I'm allowed to disagree as much as I want."

Justin laughed. "True." He ran the back of his hand down the side of her face and along her collarbone. "But this has to do with playing, so it falls under my domain."

She huffed, but there wasn't any heat in it. "Fine. Can I at least get my underwear back?"

"No."

Thirty minutes later, they pulled up in front of a store called Leather and Lace. She'd never been there before, but given the name, she had an inkling of what type of clothing they'd have inside.

He rounded the car and opened her door. Kim stepped out, making sure there wasn't anyone watching, then waited for him to lock up the car. Even though she was wearing jeans, she felt naked without her panties. She couldn't believe he hadn't given them back.

Justin reached for her hand and laced their fingers together like it was the most natural thing in the world. And besides her discomfort going commando in public, it kind of was. She felt...safe with him. Not that she didn't feel safe before, but it was different. "Your brother doesn't venture to this side of town often. We're safe."

He thought she was worried about her brother seeing them. Well, she was. Kind of. But in truth, it was the clothes situation that had her uncomfortable more than anything else.

Inside wasn't exactly what she'd expected. The store was bright and open with lots of clothes. As the title suggested, most of the clothing had either leather or lace.

He guided them through the racks, stopping to look closer at a few items. Kim kept her comments to herself. This was play-related and she needed to remember that he was in charge.

At one point, he held up a bodysuit that revealed more than it covered. She wasn't sure she'd be comfortable walking about the club in something like that. Some subs did. Hell, some of the subs didn't wear any clothing at all. But that wasn't her. She didn't get off on other people seeing her naked.

"Excuse me," he said to the woman behind the counter. "Do you have a fitting room?"

"Of course. Right this way."

Justin handed Kim a black leather skirt and a tiny white top. He nodded for her to follow the woman. "I want to see what it looks like on you."

Kim froze and leaned in to whisper so only he would hear. "But I'm not wearing underwear, remember?"

A grin stretched across his face. "There's nothing wrong with my memory."

When she realized he was serious, Kim debated her options. In the end, she took the clothes from him and headed toward the fitting room.

"Let me know if you need a different size," the woman said before leaving her to try on her items.

For the second time that day, Kim stripped. She took her time, folding her clothes and laying them on the bench inside the small room before reaching for the skirt and top.

To her surprise, the skirt wasn't bad. Not something she would have chosen for herself, but at least it covered everything. It hugged her curves and had the right amount of detail to be flattering. The top, however, was a different story. Not that it wasn't flattering, exactly, but it left little to the imagination. It barely covered her breasts, dipping low to show off as much cleavage as possible.

Her belly was on full display as well. Normally, she wasn't self-conscious about her body, but this outfit was definitely out of her comfort zone.

Knowing she couldn't stay in there forever, she gathered her courage and opened the door. He was right outside, waiting.

When she stopped in the doorway, he motioned her out. "I want to see the whole picture. Come closer and turn so I can see the back."

She did as she was told, turning in a slow circle.

He was smiling when she faced him again.

"It doesn't cover much," she said, even though she knew it was useless. He obviously liked the outfit and she was ninety-nine percent sure she would be wearing it tonight.

"I can always have you try on the bodysuit instead."

She should have known he'd say that. "I like this better."

"So do I." He cupped her face and gave her a hard kiss. "Get changed and we'll head back."

Without another word, she returned to the dressing room and changed back into her jeans and sweater.

She found him at the register. He already had a bag in his hand but didn't seem keen on sharing with her whatever was in it. At least not yet. Kim had a feeling she'd know exactly what was in the bag before the night was over.

"Everything fit all right?" the woman asked.

"Yes. Everything fit. Thank you."

The woman finished ringing up the items and Justin paid. Kim waited for him to finish, then followed him outside. After placing the bags in the trunk, they both climbed into the car and headed back home.

"Do you have any shoes that will go with that outfit or do we need to stop and get shoes, too?" he asked.

"I have some black boots that will work, I think."

He took her hand and brought her fingers to his lips. "Thank you for trusting me."

Trust wasn't the issue. Not the trusting him part, anyway. She trusted him with her life. Justin wouldn't hurt her. She knew that.

Her problem was she didn't know how to get her brain to shut off. But she knew if this was going to work, she was going to have to figure it out. She only hoped he didn't give up on her first.

CHAPTER 15

THE DRIVE to Kim's apartment didn't take long. Since it was the weekend, traffic wasn't too bad and her place wasn't near any major shopping areas. Justin parked in front of her townhouse and followed her inside.

The last time he was there was the day she moved in. He'd helped Mark and Davis move her furniture. It looked a lot different now that there were pictures on the walls and a nice area rug in the center of the living room.

"Is there anything else you want me to get while we're here?"

Justin had debated on the drive here whether to have her bring an overnight bag. He wanted her in his bed, but he also knew she might need some space after her first real venture into D/s. The selfish part of him, however, didn't want to give her space. He'd given her seventeen years of space. "You might want to pack an overnight bag."

"Am I staying at your place tonight?" she asked, sounding more unsure than he was used to from Kim. The last time he'd heard that tremble in her voice was the day she'd showed up on his doorstep three months ago. He didn't want her to be uncertain about their relationship. He was all in. For this one month at least.

He pulled her into him and covered her mouth with his. The kiss was long and deep, and he felt her body give against him.

When Justin broke the kiss, he waited until she was looking at him. "I want to wake up with you beside me. It's the one thing I missed out on the first time."

Thinking about that morning brought all his mixed emotions to the surface. He'd woken up to an empty bed and for a second he thought she'd left without waking him. And maybe she would have if given the chance. They'd never know.

"I wanted to stay."

He kissed her again. This time, keeping things light. "Get your things. We still need to swing by my house."

Kim nodded and disappeared into her bedroom.

Justin strolled over to the window and attempted to get himself in check. He was hoping for a good night, but after this afternoon, he wasn't sure. She had a lot to learn, and he was hoping in time she'd be able to fully trust him with her submission. Only time would tell.

After stopping by his house so he could change, they headed to the club. It was early, but he knew Ali would most likely already be there. Kim's best friend often helped to set things up before the club opened on Saturdays on top of her coat check rotation.

He swiped his membership card to allow them entrance, hung up both their coats in the coat check, and then guided Kim into the main part of the club. Katrina was making her way down the stairs. She spotted them right away and he was positive he saw a smile tug at her lips.

The sound of Katrina's heels echoed in the space with the lack of people and no music to drown out the sound. She walked toward them. "You two are here early this evening."

"We were hoping to catch Ali before everyone else got here," Justin said.

Katrina glanced at Kim, then nodded. "The last time I saw her, she was in the women's locker room."

"Thanks."

"Of course." The club mistress smiled. "Let me know if you need anything else. I'll be around." Katrina strolled off toward the bar, no doubt to continue making her rounds to ensure everything was ready for tonight.

Justin placed a hand on Kim's lower back and urged her toward the women's locker room.

"We're talking to Ali?" Kim asked.

"No. *You're* going to talk to Ali. I'm going to wait out here." He stopped in front of the entrance to the locker room.

Kim looked confused. He could see those wheels turning in her head again.

"I want you to talk to her about what happened earlier. I think you need to talk to another submissive, and since you're comfortable with Ali, she's the best choice."

He could see the urge to argue in her eyes, but she held her tongue. "Okay."

Justin closed the distance between them, tilted her chin up, and looked into her eyes. "Come find me when you're done." Then he placed a soft kiss on her lips and dropped his hand before turning on his heel and heading toward the bar.

He was hoping having Kim talk to another, more experienced, submissive would be good for her. Kim needed to get out of her own head if a D/s relationship was really what she wanted. Hopefully, Ali could help her with that.

Sliding onto one of the barstools, Justin waved to Brandon.

"You're here early."

"I wanted Kim to have a chance to talk to Ali before things got crazy."

Brandon nodded. "Beer?"

"I think I'll stick to water, for now."

The bartender fished out a bottle from under the bar and placed it in front of him. "Trouble with the new sub?"

Justin twisted the cap off the water bottle and took a long drink before answering. "She's having trouble getting into the right headspace. I'm hoping talking with Ali will help with that."

Brandon dumped a bucket of ice in the bin. "You know, I think a group of subs from the club meets once a week at Beth's café."

He recalled hearing about a new group that had formed in the past few months. Having more subs than only Ali to talk to could be good for Kim. That is, if she decided she wanted to continue this. "Thanks. I'll talk to her about it."

More people arrived. One couple went straight upstairs. He let his gaze linger on their ascent as he tried not to think about the conversation Kim and Ali were currently having.

* * *

"I screwed up, Ali." Kim plopped her butt down on the bench and immediately regretted it. Although her ass wasn't as sore as it had been earlier, it was still a little tender.

Ali stopped what she was doing and sat down next to her friend. "What happened?"

"Everything was great. We were kissing, then he told me to strip." Kim tried to pull her skirt down, to no avail. She still couldn't believe he hadn't allowed her to wear panties tonight. Okay, yes, she could. After what happened this afternoon, he probably wouldn't let her wear underwear again when they were together.

"Did you refuse?" Ali asked when her friend didn't continue.

"Not exactly." Kim met Ali's gaze. "I took my clothes off, but then he asked me to hand him my panties and instead of giving them to him, I asked him why."

"Oh."

"Yeah. He wasn't happy."

"I wouldn't think so." Ali grabbed Kim's hand. "What did he do?"

"He spanked me. And it wasn't like before." Last night when she'd told Ali about her one night with Justin, her friend had wanted details. Kim had shared with her how she'd liked it when he'd spanked her and how shocked she'd been at her body's reaction.

"It wasn't supposed to be. One was for pleasure. The other was for punishment."

"That's exactly what he said." Kim was pouting and she knew it.

125

Ali gave her a long, hard look. "Are you sure this is what you want?"

"What do you mean?"

Two women came into the locker room to change, so Ali stood and pulled Kim over to the far corner. It wasn't exactly private, but at least they wouldn't be in the way. "Submission is about giving up control and trusting your Dom."

"I trust Justin."

"Do you?"

"Yes," Kim said.

"Then why didn't you do what he asked you to do when he asked you to do it?"

That seemed to be the million-dollar question. "I just wanted to know why he wanted them. It seemed like an odd thing to want."

Ali shook her head. "The point is, it doesn't matter why he wanted them. You were playing. He's in charge. Your job is to trust him and to obey."

Kim opened her mouth to argue, but Ali cut her off.

"No buts. A good submissive obeys her Dom and trusts him to lead her. If you don't trust Justin as your Dom, then it isn't going to work."

She didn't respond right away. "What if I can't?"

Ali didn't sugarcoat it. "Then maybe this lifestyle isn't for you."

"But what about how my body reacted?"

"Maybe you just like a little kink in the bedroom." Ali stood again as more women came in. "That's not the same as a D/s relationship. You need to figure out what you want, and I would suggest you do it before you break Justin's heart."

What could she say to that? Deep down, she knew Ali was right. She'd been at the club for long enough to know how the dynamics between Dominants and submissives worked. The question was whether that was what she wanted in her own life.

"Think about it," Ali said. "Maybe try it out, see what giving up total control is like. You are at a BDSM club after all."

Kim laughed and pulled her friend in for a hug. "Thanks, Ali."

"Anytime."

She smoothed down her skirt and made sure nothing was showing that shouldn't be. "I should probably go find Justin."

"Good luck."

"Thanks."

Kim waved to a couple people as she left the locker room, but she didn't stop to talk. Justin had told her to talk to Ali and then come find him. She didn't want to disobey him again.

The club was filling up as she stepped out into the main room. Music was playing, and there was a couple already on the dance floor.

She scanned the room, looking for Justin. It took her a few moments to find him. He wasn't at the bar talking to Brandon like she thought he'd be. Instead, he was chatting with Lady Beth.

Kim debated whether to interrupt them, but Ali's words kept playing in her head. Deciding not to overthink it, she crossed the room and came to stand by Justin's side. He smiled, wrapped his arm around her waist, and pulled her against his side. She breathed a sigh of relief that she'd obviously chosen correctly this time.

"Beth was telling me about a group of subs from the club that meet at her café on Sunday afternoons."

"I'm sure they'd love to have you," Beth said. "Drew's there when he's not on shift at the firehouse. And Ali comes sometimes, too."

Ali had never mentioned going to a submissives group. Even after Kim had joined Serpent's Kiss. It made her wonder if Ali really didn't think Kim could be in a D/s relationship. "What time?"

She felt Justin's hand flex on her hip and wondered if she'd made another faux pas.

Beth smiled. "One o'clock. Since the café is closed on Sundays, there's complete privacy."

"I'll try to come. Thank you for inviting me."

"You're welcome. There are always some bumps in the road for a new submissive. Hopefully, having some other subs to talk to will help."

Kim wondered what Justin had told Lady Beth but decided to keep her thoughts to herself. "That would be good."

They spoke with Beth for a few more minutes before Justin's attention shifted and he asked Beth to excuse them.

It was on the tip of Kim's tongue to ask where they were going, but she forced herself to remain quiet. Ali told her to trust her Dom and she was going to try. What was the worst that could happen?

She found out the answer to that question a few minutes later as Justin led her upstairs to the second floor. This wasn't her first time upstairs, but it was her first time with a Dom. Her mind began swirling. Were they going to watch? Play? She could feel a mixture of panic and excitement settling in her stomach.

Justin headed for the end of the hall and opened the door on the right. It was a playroom like all the others she'd seen on this level. There were floggers, crops, whips, and several things she didn't have names for hanging up on the far wall. A spanking bench was tucked in the corner and Kim hoped that wasn't what he had in mind. She wanted to be able to sit down come Monday morning.

The sound of the door closing echoed in her ears. Was she in trouble again?

Kim watched as he moved around the room, coming to a stop in front of a long wooden table. He opened one of the drawers and removed what looked like a scarf of some kind. That didn't look too scary. Maybe he was going to tie her wrists like he'd done on that first night.

Her pulse kicked up a notch when he came behind her and brought the scarf over her head to cover her eyes. The urge to question him surged to her lips, but she managed to keep quiet. He secured a knot behind her head, and she was cast in total darkness.

"Tonight, we're going to work on trust."

She swallowed.

"Did you talk with Ali?" He was at her side now.

"Yes, Sir."

"Did you tell her about today?"

Kim closed her eyes out of habit, even though she already couldn't see anything. "I told her I screwed up."

His lips were at her ear. "And what did she say?"

Although it was a question, Kim was pretty sure he already knew what Ali had told her. It seemed to be the theme of the day. "She told me that if this was what I wanted, that I needed to trust you." That wasn't exactly what Ali had told her, but that was the gist of it.

"And is it what you want?" He'd stepped away again.

The not knowing where he was had her wanting to rip off the blindfold, but she resisted. "Yes. It's what I want. I'll try harder."

Then she felt something touch the back of her leg and she flinched.

"Tonight, we're going to work on trust. I want you to keep your hands at your side unless I say otherwise. Do you understand?"

"Yes, Sir." Kim blew out a breath and tried to prepare herself. She had to trust him.

He ran whatever it was up the back of her leg to the edge of her skirt, then moved to the other leg and did the same. It tickled a little when he reached the back of her knee, but she kept still. She could do this.

Once he'd reached her ankle, she felt him move around to her side, then a quick slap to the back of her thigh. It stung, but it didn't really hurt.

Then he came to stand in front of her and began sliding the object up the inside of her leg. Her skirt was higher in the front than in the back, and she was very aware of the fact that she wasn't wearing any underwear. She wanted to open her legs more but forced herself to remain still.

As he continued to touch her with the toy, she felt herself starting to relax. When he was finished with her legs, he moved to her arms. He brought the implement down to her hands, and she was tempted to use her fingers to explore and find out what it was he was using. But she was afraid if she did, he'd stop and she didn't want that.

Justin ran the object along her collarbone, then down her cleavage. She sucked in a breath as he skimmed over each of her nipples.

He hadn't said a word the entire time, and maybe that should have made her nervous, but it didn't. She could feel him there. Feel him watching her. Watching her reactions. It was turning her on in a way she hadn't imagined.

Kim knew the moment he stepped away and heard moving behind her. She waited to see what he would do next. The anticipation was building inside her and she wanted him to touch her.

When he returned to stand behind her, she could feel his heat radiating against her back. But instead of touching her, he ran something else along her leg. Whatever it was felt...fuller?

She wasn't sure if that was the right word, but it was all she could think of at the moment. Where the other toy had a single touching point, this seemed to have many. As she turned her mind off and allowed herself to feel, she was pretty sure it was a flogger. It felt completely different on her skin than the other toy—almost like a caress.

By the time he skimmed it along her stomach, Kim's entire body was tingling in anticipation. She didn't suspect what he would do next, but she wasn't sure she cared.

No sooner had that thought crossed her mind than she felt his finger trace a line down her chest and circle her right nipple. She hadn't been able to wear a bra with the shirt he'd chosen, so she knew he'd be able to see her body's reaction.

Still, he remained silent.

His fingers pinched and pulled her nipple through her shirt, making it hard. She bit the inside of her cheek to keep quiet. Heat rushed between her legs and she ached for more.

Then, before she'd realized what he was doing, the knot in the center of her top released, freeing her breasts. Cool air hit her warm skin, breaking some of the spell, and she gasped. Without thinking, her hands went to cover herself.

"MOVE YOUR HANDS." The command was swift and direct. She'd been doing well, but her action didn't surprise Justin. The question was, would she choose to obey her Dom or would she dig in her heels and keep covering herself.

Her head turned toward the entrance to the room, even though she couldn't see anything with the blindfold on. She didn't move as she tried to decide what to do.

He waited. What she decided would give him a good indication as to whether a D/s relationship between them would work. As her Dom, there would be times when he'd ask her to do something she may be unsure about, especially at the club. She needed to trust that he could keep her safe and honor the limits she'd set for their play. If she couldn't do that, then this wouldn't work.

Several moments passed before she slowly lowered her arms, revealing her breasts to him once more. He saw her lip begin to tremble. He knew her well enough to know that she was on the verge of tears.

Justin cupped the side of her face, rubbing his thumb along her lower lip. "Tell me what's wrong."

"I just...people are watching me." Her voice was barely above a whisper.

"Why does that bother you?" he asked.

She leaned into his hand. "I'm not used to...being on display. It feels wrong somehow."

Her breathing was steadier now. She was calming down.

He brought his other hand up to palm one of her breasts. "You are beautiful. Every part of you."

Tilting her chin up, he brushed his mouth against hers, mimicking the motion of his thumb on her nipple. She let out a breathy moan.

The tension in her body eased, and he decided to continue with what he had planned. If there was another hiccup, they'd deal with it.

Lowering his head, he took her nipple into his mouth and sucked, worrying the tip between his teeth. The hard pebble on his tongue had him wondering how wet she was.

She arched her back, begging for more, seeming to have forgotten her worries of being watched. That was good considering his plans.

Not removing his mouth from her breast, he pushed her shirt from her shoulder and let it fall to the floor. Her reaction was minimal. He noticed her clench and release her hand before relaxing back into the feeling of his mouth on her flesh.

And it was glorious flesh. Kim had the most amazing tits. They weren't huge, but they were perfect for everything he wanted to do to them.

Once he was satisfied her breast was nice and tender, he moved on to the other one, giving it the same treatment. When he was happy with his progress, he captured her mouth with his again and reached for the zipper on her skirt.

The leather began separating as he slid the zipper lower. He felt her stiffen and waited to see what she would do.

"Please."

"Please, what?" he asked.

"I don't want everyone to see me naked."

"What did I tell you before?"

She pressed her lips together for a moment before she answered, "That every part of me is beautiful."

"That's right. Every part of you from your head to your toes." He paused. "Especially your beautiful pussy."

Justin saw her swallow and then nod. He finished unzipping her skirt and pushed it down her hips. The material pooled at her feet. Kneeling, he helped her step out of it and tossed it to the side.

The sight before him was stuff wet dreams were made of. Kim stood inches away from him, in nothing but a pair of black boots that ended an inch or so below her knees. She was the sexiest thing he'd ever seen.

Unable to resist, he spread her legs and took a long lick. "Hmm. Just as I thought. You're nice and wet for me."

Not wanting to push her too far tonight, but wanting to push the point home, Justin stood and lifted her into his arms.

She let out a little squeak and grabbed hold of his shoulders for a second before releasing him. "It's okay, baby. You can hold on to me."

Wrapping her arms around his neck, she held on tight as he brought her over to a low table set up near the spanking bench. It was lower than a standard table, making it the perfect height for sex or cunnilingus.

He set her down and reached into his pocket for a condom. "Unfasten my jeans."

While she may not have use of her sight, Kim didn't have issues finding the button on his jeans. With all her issues with being naked in front of an audience, she seemed not to have the same issue with him sans clothes.

As soon as his cock was free, he ripped the condom open and rolled it down his length. Holding the base, he lined himself up and pressed his hips forward.

Her muscles clenched around him and welcomed him into her warmth. He laid her back, pressing her into the table as he picked up the pace. This wasn't a slow seduction, nor was it meant to be. And for the first time since the scene began, he felt her attention was completely on him. She wasn't thinking about the potential people watching her or seeing her naked body. She was in the moment. With him.

Justin felt his body coil tight as his orgasm approached and snaked his hand between them. He circled her clit with his thumb, increasing the pressure until he felt her body tense. "Come for me."

He punctuated his words with several hard thrusts. Kim's head fell back against the table and her nails scraped his scalp as she found her release.

Dipping his head down, he captured one of her nipples in his mouth once more while he chased his own climax. A surge of energy raced up his balls moments before his orgasm hit him.

He rested his head against her chest as he caught his breath, then propped himself up on his elbows. She was breathing as hard as he was and she was still wearing the blindfold.

Grinning, Justin stepped back so he could slide out of her, took care of the condom in a nearby trashcan, and helped her from the table. Once she was on her feet again, he reached up and untied the blindfold, letting her see again.

Kim blinked several times as her eyes adjusted to the light. She looked at him, and then as if remembering where they were, her gaze shifted toward the door and the big picture window beside it. The window that he had darkened before he'd used the first toy on her to give them privacy.

She whipped her head back to look at him. "I thought..."

Justin tucked a lock of hair behind her ear. "Tonight wasn't about showing you off. It was about you learning to trust me as your Dom."

"I'm trying."

He pulled her into his arms and gave her a hard kiss. "Get dressed and we'll go downstairs and talk."

* * *

After getting dressed, he'd taken hold of Kim's hand and escorted her to one of the many seating areas on the main floor of the club. He'd left her only long enough to retrieve two bottles of water from the bar before rejoining her on the couch. Kim took the bottle he handed to her and was about to unscrew the cap when he grasped her by the hips and lifted her onto his lap. The bottle slipped out of her hands, landing between two of the cushions.

Justin picked it up and handed it to her again. "Drink your water."

She was thirsty, so she downed almost half the bottle in one go. He brought his water to his lips and chugged the entire thing in one go. Her gaze drifted to the muscles in his neck and she had the urge to lick him. She would have thought her libido would have been satisfied, but apparently not.

"What are you thinking about?" he asked when he noticed her staring.

"I was thinking about what happened upstairs." That was true, but not exactly. Still, she really didn't want to talk about how she was becoming a sex maniac. "Am I in trouble again?"

"Do you think you should be?"

"I don't know. You did tell me to keep my arms down and I didn't."

He nodded. "This is true. Did you disobey me intentionally or was it an automatic reaction?"

She glanced down at the bottle she held in her hands. "I didn't intentionally disobey you."

Lifting her chin, he made her look at him. "I didn't think so. You covered yourself almost immediately once I opened your top."

"I wish I had known no one was watching." She wouldn't have freaked out if she'd known only he could see her.

Justin dropped his arm and sat back on the couch. He eased her weight back against him. "That would have defeated the purpose of the exercise."

He'd been testing her. She wasn't sure how she felt about that.

As if he could read her mind, or maybe it was the way her body tensed, he asked, "Does that upset you?"

"I'm not used to the guys I'm with being able to read me so well."

His chest vibrated beneath her. "A Dom needs to be able to read his sub. And it helps that we've known each other for a long time. I know your tells."

Kim took another sip of her water. She knew his tells as well. He had a muscle in his jaw that pulsated when he got angry. It didn't happen often.

He caressed the outside of her thigh as they sat there on the couch, her head resting against his shoulder. She continued to sip her water and listen to the music play in the background as people milled about around them.

Her eyes drooped, and then she noticed a woman looking at them from across the room. Kim had seen her around the club before, but she didn't know her. "Sir?"

"Yes?" He brushed some hair away from her face, sending tingles down her cheek.

"Who is that woman?"

He tilted his head to see who she was referring to. "Her name is Angela. She's a switch."

"What's a switch?" Kim had been around the club for three months and she'd never heard that term before.

"It's someone who switches from being a Dominant or a submissive depending on who they're playing with."

Kim thought about that for a few moments. She thought about Beth and Drew. "Are Lady Beth and Drew switches?"

Justin chuckled. "No. Beth is a Domme and Drew is her submissive. They don't ever switch. Not with each other and not with other people."

"But Angela does."

"Yes."

Kim pressed her lips together and debated whether to ask the question lingering in her mind. In the end, she decided she had to ask. "Has she ever played with you?"

His fingers drew circles on her bare thigh. "A couple of times."

She closed her eyes and tried not to let that bother her, but jealousy raced through her veins. Kim knew Justin had been with other women. He was thirty-four and a member of a kink club. But that didn't mean having one of the women right in front of her was an easy pill to swallow. She knew, however, that if they were to continue their relationship, she would have to get used to it.

To her surprise, he didn't try to placate her or explain away any interaction he'd had with Angela. "I'm one of three Doms she likes to play with when she's in a submissive frame of mind."

Three Doms.

Of course, Kim knew that Justin and Angela weren't in a relationship, but that didn't mean there wasn't anything there. On her side anyway.

When Kim opened her eyes again, the woman was still stealing glances in their direction, even though she was trying to be coy about it. "I think maybe it was more than just playing for her."

"It wasn't," he insisted.

Kim couldn't seem to let it go. "Then why does she keep looking over at us?"

Justin sat up, startling her. He waited until she'd gotten her bearings back and was looking at him. "I don't know why she's looking at us. Maybe she's curious about my new sub."

She opened her mouth to counter his assertion that Angela was only curious, but he cut her off.

"It doesn't matter. You are my submissive and while we're together, I won't be playing with anyone else and neither will you. Understood?"

"Yes, Sir."

"Good." Justin helped her onto her feet, then stood. "Ali's been gazing over here since we sat down. I'm sure she wants to talk to you and see how your first time upstairs went."

Kim glanced over to the far side of the room. Ali was looking at him, a mixture of curiosity and glee on her face.

They made their way over to where Ali was perched on the front of her seat, barely able to contain herself. Justin kept his fingers laced with hers as he addressed the group Ali was with. "Mind if we join you?"

"Of course not," Daniel said. He moved to another chair, freeing up the space next to Ali for them.

Justin sat down and motioned for Kim to take a seat next to him. She hadn't been sure if he'd want her to sit, but luckily, he hadn't made her guess. He leaned back, resting his arm on the back of the couch, and began playing with the hairs at the base of her neck. He'd made her put her hair up earlier, saying he wanted unfettered access to her neck. Considering she melted almost every time he touched or kissed her there, she'd have to find ways to wear her hair up when he was around more often.

"How's the shop?" Daniel asked.

"Good. We've been busy for the last few months. Our reputation seems to be growing."

The conversation turned to cars and Kim turned her attention to Ali. It wasn't that she disliked cars, but the talk of engines and fuel injectors was a foreign language to her.

As soon as she looked at her best friend, she knew the floodgates were about to open. "How did your brunch go? Did you spend all day together?"

"Okay, I guess. I mean, I've never done anything like that before with a guy. It was kind of strange talking about what you like and what you want to try." They were talking low, but she knew at least Justin could hear them if he was paying attention. He seemed too engaged in his conversation with Daniel and Jeff, though.

"It gets easier. The first time I went over my limit list with a Dom, I think I turned five shades of red," Ali confessed.

"Yeah. I don't know how many times I blushed."

"It's to be expected."

"I know. But it's still weird," Kim said.

Ali shifted a little closer. "So I know you said you got in trouble this afternoon, but you went upstairs. Did you just watch or did he take you into one of the playrooms?"

"One of the playrooms."

Her friend let out a little squeal. "How did it go?"

"I messed up again."

Ali frowned. "What happened?"

"It wasn't as bad as this afternoon, but he took my shirt off and I covered myself even though he'd told me to keep my hands down at my side." Kim sighed. "But as it turns out, no one could see me but him. He darkened the window to the room."

"You shouldn't be self-conscious. You have an amazing body. And if you haven't noticed, no one here is going to think you being naked as weird."

Kim followed Ali's gaze as she looked around the room at the other members of the club. Not five feet from them, a sub was sitting on her Dom's lap topless. From each nipple hung what looked like jewelry. "I know that. I'm just not used to being naked in front of people."

"You didn't seem to have issues being naked in front of Justin when you showed up at his house and offered yourself to him."

"That was different."

"How?" Ali asked. "You weren't in a relationship with him. You weren't even really friends. And yet, you didn't think twice about showing up on his doorstep in nothing but a trench coat and laying yourself bare for him like you were the main dish on a buffet."

Kim chuckled. "Nice visual."

Her friend shrugged. "Ultimately, it all comes back to the same thing. Trust. Did you put exhibitionism as a hard limit?"

"A soft limit."

She nodded. "Trust."

Kim knew her friend was right. Justin hadn't done anything to make her question her trust in him. Nothing he'd done had crossed any of her hard limits. Now all she had to do was get her brain to remember that every time they were playing together. Otherwise, her ass was going to be very sore.

CHAPTER 17

Justin focused on talking to Daniel and Jeff, letting Kim and Ali have as much privacy as possible given where they were. Ali had been a member of the club before he joined, and he'd seen her play a few times. She knew how to submit to a Dom and what kind of mindset was required during a scene. Hopefully, she'd be able to help Kim.

"Sir?"

At the sound of Kim's question, he shifted in his seat, giving her his full attention.

She leaned in, lowering her voice. "I need to use the bathroom."

Pleased she'd asked before just walking off, he smiled and nodded his assent.

He watched as she and Ali strolled across the room to where the restrooms were located toward the back of the club. The skirt he'd chosen hugged her hips, framing her ass. Knowing she had nothing on under said skirt had him wanting to bend her over, lift the skirt, and take her from behind. It had been almost two hours since they'd come downstairs and his cock was itching to get inside her again.

"How are things going with the new sub?" Daniel asked. The older Dom had a lot more experience than Justin. He was in his fifties and had been in the lifestyle for over twenty years.

"As well as can be expected. She has a lot to learn, but she'll get there." Justin hoped, anyway.

"Ah, confidence. That's good, but don't get too cocky about it. She strikes me as being very stubborn."

Justin snorted. "She is."

Daniel nodded. "Ali will help her. She's a good submissive."

The pride in his voice piqued Justin's interest. "I've never seen you and Ali play together."

A solemn look took hold of the older Dom's features. "No, we've never played together."

Again, his tone had Justin wondering if maybe he was missing something, but he let it go. It wasn't any of his business in any case. "Have you ever trained a new sub? One who was new to the lifestyle, I mean?"

Daniel nodded. "I have. It can require a lot of patience."

"Can't disagree with you there," Justin said, remembering what happened earlier that afternoon.

Daniel grinned. "My best advice is to take it slow and don't try and throw a lot of new things at her all at once. When you do a scene, pick one thing to test the waters on and keep consistent. It all comes down to building that trust. Once she can let go, everything else will fall into place."

Very good advice and something he would have to keep in mind going forward. As much as he feared the reaction Mark, Davis, and Belinda would have to him and Kim being together, he wanted things between them to work. Which meant he had to take it slow. "Thanks. I'll keep that in mind."

"I'm here if you have any specific questions. And there are a few other Doms who have experience with new subs as well I can recommend if you'd like another perspective."

"I appreciate it."

Kim and Ali headed toward them, and Justin stood. He was ready to go home. That little taste of her he'd gotten earlier wasn't nearly enough.

He waited until Kim was within arm's reach. "Say goodbye to Ali."

She blinked up at him but turned and gave her friend a hug. "I'll call you tomorrow."

"You'd better." Ali gave him a knowing look as she embraced Kim, but he ignored it.

Justin took hold of Kim's hand, and they made their way to the foyer to get their coats. Given how little clothing she had on, he made sure she was buttoned up tight before they left the building. The temperature had taken a nosedive while they'd been inside the club. He felt her shiver as the wind zipped through the parking lot. He wrapped his arm around her, tucking her into his side as they rushed toward his car, trying to shield her from the wind as much as possible.

Once he'd helped her into the passenger seat, he reached into the back seat and grabbed the blanket he kept there for emergencies. It was as cold as everything else, but it would warm up quick enough. He unfolded it and draped it over her legs.

"Thanks." Kim shoved her hands underneath the blanket and pulled it higher to wrap around her middle.

Happy she was as warm as he could get her for now, he jogged around the car and slid behind the wheel. He put the key in the ignition and the engine roared to life. The sound never failed to bring a smile to his face.

"What are you smiling about?" Kim asked as she huddled deeper under the blanket.

"Thinking about all the work I did on this car."

"You're smiling about work?"

Justin chuckled. "Yep."

She was quiet for several minutes. "Was the car in really bad shape when you got it?"

He hadn't thought she'd be interested. She'd never shown interest in cars before. But he had to admit it pleased him that she'd asked. "Yes and no. The body was in great shape, but under the hood was a nightmare."

The temperature gauge was finally moving away from cold, so he turned the heater on full blast, hoping it would at least get the chill out of the car before they got back to his house. Warm air steamed out of the vents and Kim held her hands directly in front of one.

"Why was it a nightmare?"

He glanced over at her, and she genuinely looked interested. "The previous owner tried to soup up the engine."

"I'm guessing he didn't do it right?"

Justin snorted. To say he'd done a shitty job would be an understatement. "Not even close."

She turned in her seat so she could face him. The car was warming up and she wasn't shivering anymore. "He wanted you to fix it?"

"He did, but he underestimated what it would take. I think he almost had a heart attack when I gave him the price." Justin recalled how the man had gone pale, then beat red. He really had thought he was going to have to call an ambulance for the guy.

"So what happened? How did you end up with it?"

Justin pulled into his driveway and turned off the car. "He didn't like my price, but after taking it to ten other repair shops that refused to touch it, he didn't have many options."

"You offered to buy it from him."

His girl was smart.

Justin blew out a breath. She wasn't his girl. Not really. Not yet, anyway. They had to see if this could work first.

"Half the car would have to be taken apart, fixed, and then reassembled. It would take weeks, if not months to complete. The guy had already put a lot of money into the car and couldn't plow that much more into it, so I made him an offer." Justin ran a hand over the dashboard before reaching for the door handle. "One of the best business deals I've ever made."

Hopping out of the vehicle, he went to help Kim, then escorted her to the door. He'd left a light on for them, but it didn't do much considering how overcast it was. There was a storm moving in. They might even have snow on the ground come morning.

Letting them into the house, he removed his coat first before helping her. Kim rubbed her bare arms, trying to warm herself up. She was shivering again.

"Come here." He wrapped his arms around her, holding her tight against his chest.

She buried her face in the crook of his shoulder. Her nose was cold against his bare skin. "It wasn't this cold when we left."

"No, it wasn't. It has to have dropped at least twenty degrees."

Another ripple went through her body as she tried to suck up more of his heat.

Seeing how cold she was, his plans for her outfit were put on the back burner. "Let's get you into bed. Then I'll make sure you're warmed up."

She gazed up at him, a twinkle in her eyes. "Promise?"

Justin chuckled and pressed his lips to hers for a brief kiss. "Promise."

They were almost to his bedroom when his phone dinged, letting him know he had a new message. He ignored it and led her into his room. It was the first time she'd been there since the morning after their night together. Memories of her in his bed had lingered for weeks.

Pulling her into his arms once more, he covered her mouth with his in a lingering kiss. "Do what you need to do in the bathroom."

She nodded, then disappeared into the adjoining room.

Digging out his phone, he checked to see who'd messaged him.

Still on for tomorrow night? - Mark

All the conflicting feelings he had about what he was doing with Kim came to the surface again. How hard was it going to be to sit across from his best friend and not mention the fact that he was involved with his sister? Mark loved to talk about women, especially when he was drinking. Even though he didn't understand Justin's lifestyle, he was always asking about the women Justin dated. The problem was, Justin couldn't tell Mark anything this time.

For a moment, he thought about canceling, but then another wave of guilt hit. If this thing with Kim worked out, he couldn't hide from his best friend forever.

Yep. See you at 5. - Justin

He heard the shower turn on and thoughts of Kim naked and wet pushed all thoughts of Mark and the potential fallout from his mind. Leaving his phone on the dresser, he removed his clothes and headed into the bathroom.

Steam was already filling up the room when he let himself inside. Kim's head was tilted back as water streamed down her body. His cock stood at attention, aching to be inside her again.

Snatching a condom from the drawer next to the sink, he made his way to the shower and slid open the glass door.

* * *

Kim startled when she heard the shower door. She hadn't heard him come into the room.

He placed something on the ledge, then backed her against the wall. The cool tiles were a sharp contrast to the water that had been spraying on her a moment before. "Hi."

His body was flush against her and she could feel him hard against her stomach. "Feeling warmer now?"

Heat that had nothing to do with the shower took over. "Yes."

She'd barely gotten her answer out when his mouth descended, cutting off anything else she was going to say. He took control of the kiss, leaving her no doubt as to who was in charge.

Fingers slid into the wet heat between her legs. "Have you ever fucked in a shower before?"

His lips moved down to her neck, licking and sucking on her skin and sending her heart racing. She held tight to his shoulders. "No. I've never—"

Justin plunged two fingers into her pussy. He wasn't gentle about it, but for some reason that turned her on more. "Hmm. You like that, don't you?"

There was no reason to deny it. He could feel how wet she was. "Yes."

He added a third finger and positioned his thumb so it was bumping her clit with every upward thrust. She found herself pushing against his hand, trying to get more friction. Her orgasm was building, but it wasn't quite enough to push her over the edge. She needed more. "More. Please."

"Please what?" He didn't even sound winded.

How could he not know what she meant?

Then she realized her error. "Please, Sir, I need more. I want to come, but I need more."

Instead of giving her more, he pulled his fingers from her pussy. She didn't have time to protest, though, before he lifted her off her feet and placed her on the opposite side of the shower. Turning her around, facing away from him, he pressed on her back. "Bend over and put your hands on the seat."

There was a small bench built into the shower on the opposite side of the showerhead. Her hands were barely on the seat when she felt his hands on her hips. He lifted her up again and used his feet to spread her legs. She felt a little like a rag doll.

His hands left her body for several moments and she heard him moving around behind her. But before she could get too worried, he was back and this time it wasn't his fingers that were pressing against her sex.

Her eyes rolled back in her head as his length entered her, sending ripples of heat radiating through her body. He lined himself up and thrust into her with enough force that she almost lost her balance. She readjusted her stance and prepared to meet every one of his thrusts.

He wrapped one arm around her waist, using that as leverage to drive deeper, harder, into her. With his free hand, he reached down and pinched her nipple, sending sparks directly to her pussy. Her climax was building...fast. It wouldn't take much more to send her flying. Without thinking, she lifted one hand to rub her clit, needing release.

"Don't you dare touch your clit. Your orgasms belong to me. I decide when you come." He landed a firm smack on her ass.

Even though it hurt, it did nothing to calm her need to come. She was too far gone. If anything, his words had made it worse. Her entire body felt as if it were on fire.

Justin didn't relent. She had no clue how long he continued to pump in and out of her before he finally snaked a hand between her legs and gave her the release she was so desperate for. Her scream echoed inside the confined space, leaving her feeling spent.

He held on to her as she caught her breath. Her body felt as if it were vibrating and she wasn't sure she could walk or not.

"Sit down while I clean up." He helped her to turn around and made sure she wasn't going to dissolve into a puddle on the floor before stepping out of the shower to dispose of the condom.

Kim rested her head against the side of the shower. She could still feel him between her legs and yet felt the emptiness of him not being inside her anymore at the same time.

When he returned, he knelt in front of her and waited for her to meet his gaze. "How are you feeling?"

"Like someone just pounded my insides."

Justin released something between a laugh and a snort. He stood, lifting her up with him. She fell into him with an *omph*.

"Think you can walk, or do I need to carry you?" he asked.

That was a good question. She eased away from him, taking a tentative step to the side, and nearly fell on her face.

The next thing Kim knew, her feet were no longer on the ground. She clung to his neck as he carried her out of the shower and placed her on top of the vanity. He left her for no more than a second to grab a towel. She went to take it, but he ignored her and began drying her off himself.

"I can dry myself, you know?"

One side of his mouth lifted in a sexy smirk, but he didn't comment.

Once he'd wiped all the water from her body, he began working on her hair. He took his time, running his fingers through the strands and gathering any excess moisture into the towel. She let her eyes drift closed as he touched her. Never in all her fantasies over the years did she think she'd be sitting on Justin's bathroom counter while he took care of her like this.

With her body and mind slowly coming down from their high, she was getting sleepy. All she wanted to do was curl up in his very comfortable bed and fall asleep.

"Put your arms around my neck."

As soon as she wrapped her arms around him, he lifted her from the counter. Kim rested her head on his shoulder. A drop of water dripped from his hair onto his neck and she stuck out her tongue to lick it up.

Justin groaned. "Behave yourself."

"Can't help it." The words were mumbled, but it was the best she could manage.

He adjusted his hold on her, then she was being laid on the bed. When she didn't release her hold on him, he chuckled. "You can let go now."

"K." She let her arms fall to the bed, rolled over onto her side, and sighed as he pulled the covers over her.

Moments later, she felt the mattress dip as Justin climbed in beside her. He gathered her into his arms, tucking her into his side. She rested her head on his shoulder again, letting her nose graze his collarbone.

"Comfortable?" His chest vibrated under her cheek.

Kim felt his lips brush her forehead. "Hmm. Very." She was warm. She was comfortable. And most of all, she felt content.

CHAPTER 18

SOMETHING warm against Justin's chest woke him the next morning. He'd been in such a deep sleep, he didn't register at first what it was, only that it felt good. But as the sleepy fog cleared, he realized someone was kissing their way down his chest, lower to his abdomen. Memories of the night before flooded his mind and his cock stood ready to continue where they'd left off.

She was heading south and he had no notion to stop her. Waking up to Kim in his bed was something he'd only dreamed about. The reality was proving better than any fantasy and he planned to take advantage of it. He laced his fingers through her hair, encouraging her to keep going to where he was aching for her.

Knowing he was awake, she scooted farther down the bed, her mouth hovering over his cock. She hesitated and glanced up to meet his gaze. "May I, Sir?"

He was pleased she'd asked permission. "Yes, you may. But don't make me come."

Her brow furrowed a little, then her eyes glazed over a bit, understanding that this was only the prelude. She was going to find out the benefits of not running from his bed first thing in the morning.

Kim's lips circled the head of his cock, licking the bead of pre-cum from the tip. He couldn't stop the groan that escaped at the feel of her tongue. If he'd thought he craved her before, it was nothing compared to now.

Justin closed his eyes as she sucked him in, using her mouth to pleasure him to the point where he wanted to explode. But coming down her throat wasn't what he had in mind. As great as her mouth felt, he wanted her hot little pussy wrapped around him, milking him dry.

Taking her by the shoulders, he hauled her up the length of his body and tossed her onto the bed beside him. She giggled as she landed on the mattress. "Did I do a good job sucking your cock, Sir?"

There was a twinkle in her eyes that he loved. And hearing her calling him Sir pulled at something deep within him. "You did a very good job sucking my cock, baby, and now I'm going to reward you by fucking you and making you come."

Her eyes darkened and a sound he could only describe as a purr emerged from her throat. "Yes, please."

Reaching over to the nightstand, he opened the drawer and grabbed a condom. She spread her legs wide, inviting him in as he rolled the protection down his length, and the sight of her sex open and wet beckoning him almost made him come all on its own.

He fell forward, bracing himself with one arm while he guided his erection to her entrance. "Wrap your legs around me."

She circled her legs around his waist and threaded her hands behind his head. He tilted his hips forward, sinking into her warmth. She was a little tight, probably because it was morning, but after a few shallow thrusts, she opened up to him and he sank into her balls deep.

Her breasts jiggled as he pumped his hips, pressing her into the bed. It was mesmerizing watching her hard nipples dance to the rhythm he set.

Unable to resist, he dipped his head down to capture one of the taut buds into his mouth. She released a contented sigh as he suckled her breast. Her head was thrown back and her eyes were closed. He could feel her nails as they dug into his scalp. The sensation sent shots of electricity to his cock and he knew he wasn't going to last much longer.

Taking hold of one of her hands, he brought it between them, guiding her to where they were joined. "Touch yourself."

She complied instantly, probably needing to come as badly as he did.

Justin sucked in a breath as her fingers brushed against his erection and he gave up on holding back. He rocked his hips faster...harder, picking up the pace.

Kim's eyes flew open and she began rubbing her clit in time with his thrusts. She lifted her hips, meeting his downward strokes with an upward one of her own. He knew she was close. So was he. The pressure building in his balls was about to explode.

"Come." He spoke the word a moment before he bit down on her nipple, sending a shot of pain through her already sensitive breasts.

It did exactly what he'd hoped. A spasm went through her body a moment before she let out a delicious scream. She rode out her orgasm as he drove into her until his own climax took hold.

He tumbled beside her on the bed, pulling her to onto her side. "You all right?"

Kim laughed. "I don't know."

"Broke you, did I?" He smiled. "How's your breast?"

Glancing down, she inspected her abused nipple. "Doesn't look like you broke the skin. I think I'll survive."

"A very good thing as I have plans for these beautiful tits of yours." He placed a gentle kiss on the red marks surrounding her nipple.

"Well, if they lead to more orgasms like that one, I won't object." She tucked her hands under her head. "I've never had so many powerful orgasms before."

"You like a little pain with your sex."

Kim frowned. "That sounds like it should be a bad thing."

Justin rested his hand on her hip, unable to keep from touching her. "Not at all. It's perfectly normal. Ask the submissives in your group today."

"That's different. They're into kinky stuff."

Justin's grin grew bigger. "Baby, I hate to break it to you, but so are you."

She was quiet for a few moments and he wondered what was going on in her mind. "I guess that's true, but I'm not sure I'm a very good submissive."

He'd been waiting for the right time to talk about last night. Ideally, they wouldn't be lying in bed naked, but he wasn't willing to let the moment pass. She wanted to talk, so they'd talk. "What makes you say that?"

"The submissives at the club seem so...submissive." He was about to point out the irony in that statement but remained quiet as she continued. "I mean, I know Ali isn't most of the time, but there she's different. And it isn't just her. All I have to do is watch someone for a few minutes and I can tell if they're a Dom or a sub in the way they interact with people." Kim sighed. "I'm just not sure I can do that."

"So you're not sure you can defer to your Dom?" He paused. "To me?" He tried not to let disappointment take over his thoughts. She was new to this and it would take time for her to figure it out. Heaven knew it had taken him a while to find his feet.

"I don't know." She met his gaze, sadness in her eyes. "I want to, but I'm afraid I'll disappoint you."

He ran a hand down the side of her face and tucked a lock of hair behind her ear. "Remember what I said last night about trust?"

She nodded.

"At the heart of it, that's what this lifestyle is. Trust. You don't have to trust every Dom you meet. You don't have to obey every Dom, either. But the connection you have with the one you choose to be your Dom should allow you to feel comfortable enough to give up control."

"What if I can't?" Her question was honest, and knowing her like he did, he could understand her concern.

"Let's just take one step at a time, okay?" She looked skeptical, but that was Kim. She liked to have a plan. "We agreed to give it a try for a month, right?"

She nodded. "I need to get out of my own head."

Justin placed a soft kiss on her lips. "Yes, you do. We're going to work on that."

A spark came into her eyes again, giving him hope. "I hope you know what you're in for."

He chuckled. "Oh, I think I have an idea." Palming her backside, he gave it a light slap. "I just hope your ass doesn't end up permanently red in the process."

She playfully pushed at his chest. "Sadist."

Justin laughed. He rolled away from her and tossed the covers off them both. "Come on, let's get some breakfast. I need to replenish my energy before I turn you over my knee again."

Kim picked up his pillow and threw it at him.

He caught it, threw it onto the floor, and reached for her. Her feet hit the floor for less than a second before he was slinging her over his shoulder, fireman style.

With her ass right in his face, he gave it another firm tap. "I thought I told you to behave."

Her response was to give his backside a slap right back.

He'd never had such a spunky submissive before, but he had to admit a part of him was looking forward to the challenge.

* * *

After picking her up, Justin carried her into the bathroom and set her on her feet. "Get dressed while I make us some food." He gave her a hard kiss, then turned on his heel and left her alone.

Kim blew out a loud breath and took a moment to center herself. So much had happened within the last twenty-four hours. She was in a D/s relationship with Justin. It may not last for more than a month, but their talk this morning had helped. Ali told her last night that Justin was really good with submissives, and that he'd help her get over her issues with giving up control.

Actually, what she said was that he'd help Kim get over her fear of giving up control.

At first, she'd balked at Ali's assertion. Kim wasn't afraid. She'd joined Serpent's Kiss, hadn't she?

But the more Kim thought about it, the more she knew Ali was right. Kim had learned early in her career to be assertive and to go after what she wanted. If she didn't, then someone else was going to get there first. She'd never be where she was at her job if she hadn't put her head down, worked her butt off, and made her intentions clear that she'd wanted the VP position.

That didn't mean she loved being in control of everything, though, did it? Especially when it came to sex, she liked when Justin took control. She liked that she didn't have to think of what would happen next. Or if she should move into a different position.

Kim did her business, washed her face, brushed her teeth, and dug out another one of Justin's shirts from the drawer. She debated throwing on a pair of his boxer briefs but decided against it. He seemed to like her without panties.

His back was to her when she strolled into the kitchen. The room smelled like bacon and her tummy rumbled in response. She'd worked up an appetite.

Walking up behind him, she circled her arms around his waist, resting her cheek on his back and taking in his scent. "Smells good."

Justin turned and circled his arms around her. "Stole another one of my shirts, I see." His hands went directly to her bottom and he groaned. "No underwear."

His response thrilled her. "I got the impression you liked it when I was missing that particular item of clothing."

"Hmm," he said, lowering his head to capture her mouth with his. "That I do."

The kiss was way too short, but she understood. He didn't want the food to burn. "Anything I can do to help?" she asked.

"You can set the table and get the milk and juice out of the fridge." He flipped the pancakes. "The food's almost done."

As she hurried to get the plates and silverware onto the table, Kim realized she was beginning to enjoy the feeling of not wearing any panties. At least, when she was in private with Justin nearby. She liked that at any time he could bend her over a chair and take her.

It was strange. She'd never had those kinds of thoughts before with a boyfriend. Of course, most of her boyfriends were rather docile compared to Justin, especially in the sexual aspect of their relationships. That is, if they got that far.

Yep, her sex life before Justin was rather boring.

"Watch yourself," Justin said as he brought the skillet of eggs over to the table and spooned a large portion onto each of their plates.

"Thanks."

He smiled, then made his way back to the stove to get the bacon and pancakes.

Everything tasted really good. She wasn't sure if that meant he was that good of a cook or if she was just that hungry. Either way, she was halfway through her plate of food before she came up for air. "Thanks for making breakfast."

His gaze raked over her from head to toe, lingering on her bare legs peeking out from the end of his long shirt. "I need to keep you fed, now, don't I?"

Heat rushed to her cheeks as a surge of feminine power flowed through her. No underwear was definitely the right decision.

They finished up their breakfast and loaded the dishwasher before heading back to his room to get dressed. In hindsight, that might not have been the best decision as they ended up back where they started...in his bed.

By the time they'd both showered and dressed, it was close to noon. "I should get back home and throw in a load of laundry before I have to pick up Ali."

"You're going to the submissive meeting today at Beth's Café?"

"Yeah." Kim grabbed her purse and placed it over her shoulder. "Ali thinks it would be good for me to talk to other submissives."

"It will be." Justin took hold of both her hands. "Remember, they've all been in your position at one time."

She blew out a breath and went to change the subject. "How is this thing with us going to work? I mean, I figure I'll see you on weekends at the club, but—"

"If you think I'm going to go a week without seeing you, you're crazy."

Warmth bloomed in her chest. She knew he'd agreed to give this thing between them a go for a month, but they hadn't really discussed what all that would entail outside of her being his submissive. "What did you have in mind?"

"Well," he said as he pulled her against his chest, "I thought maybe I could pick you up tomorrow night and we could go out to dinner."

"A date?"

"A date." He cupped her face and gave her a lingering kiss. "How does seven o'clock sound?"

Her happiness was dashed as soon as it came. "What if someone sees us?" The chances of them running into her brother while they were out to dinner were slim, but that didn't mean they wouldn't see someone they knew and it would get back to Mark.

"I told you before. I'm not going to hide you like a dirty secret, and I meant it."

She pressed her lips together and met his gaze. "I thought we were keeping things between us for a month."

He didn't answer right away, but he didn't let her go either. "I'm meeting your brother at O'Brien's tonight."

Kim took hold of his wrist and gave it a squeeze. She was asking him to keep a secret from his best friend. He'd agreed to it, but she also understood the dilemma he was facing. She'd gone through something similar when she hadn't shared with Ali that she'd slept with Justin. It had created some awkward moments and a lot of internal arguments with herself. Finally telling Ali had lifted a huge weight off her shoulders.

But things with Mark were different and both Justin and Kim knew it. The fact that Mark knew about Justin's preferences when it came to sex complicated things. How would her brother react to finding out Justin and Kim were an item?

She honestly didn't know.

"Your monthly hangout?" she asked.

"Yeah."

Kim waited for him to say something more, but he didn't. "You could cancel. Tell him something came up."

Justin shook his head. "Then I'd feel like even more of an asshole than I already do."

She furrowed her brow and scrunched up her nose. "Why do you feel like an asshole?"

"Because I'm fucking my best friend's sister."

Dropping her hands, she took a step back and he let his hands drop to his sides. "Have *you* changed your mind?"

The next thing she knew, she was pressed against a wall and being kissed to within an inch of her life. Kim clung to him, meeting the caress of his tongue with one of her own.

By the time they came up for air, her chest was heaving with each breath she took. She could feel him hard against her stomach, leaving her no doubt that he wanted her.

"Does that answer your question?" His voice was husky and deep. It sent delicious shivers down her spine.

She licked her lips and his gaze followed the movement.

"I'll pick you up tomorrow at seven. Dress in something comfortable."

"I have to work on Tuesday," she whispered against his lips.

"Mmm. So do I." His mouth descended again and she could already feel her body softening for him again. All thoughts of Mark pushed from her mind.

By the time he dropped her off at her house, her body was humming again. If not for the fact that she'd promised Ali she'd pick her up for the submissive meeting, Kim would have gladly spent the entire day in bed with Justin.

CHAPTER 19

Kim glanced over at her best friend and frowned. "I'm not." When Ali gave her a skeptical look, she clarified. "Not much, anyway."

"There's nothing to be nervous about." Ali met her on the sidewalk and they began making their way toward Beth's Café.

"Can't be worse than my first night at the club, right?" Kim squared her shoulders as the café came into view. She'd never been to Beth's Café, but she'd heard about it from a few people at work. The muffins were supposed to be phenomenal. Too bad they were closed on Sundays. She'd have to come by during the week and try it out. Especially since she now knew the owner.

Ali scoffed and knocked on the door. "I would certainly hope not."

A few moments later, the door opened and Drew greeted them, dressed in kakis and a sweater. Kim didn't think she'd seen him in anything other than jeans and a T-shirt before. "Come on in, ladies."

"Thanks," Ali said as she stepped inside and stomped her feet on the welcome mat. It had snowed the night before, leaving almost an inch on the sidewalks. Luckily, nothing much had stuck to the roads.

Kim followed Ali inside and they both removed their coats.

"I'm glad you decided to come," Drew said to Kim. "Beth told me you might."

"Ali and Justin thought it would be good for me."

He nodded and gestured for them to follow him toward the back of the café where the rest of the group waited. "I'd been with Beth for a few months when she suggested it might be good for me to talk to other submissives away from the club and all the protocols there. I thought about trying to join another submissive group that meets locally, but after attending one meeting, I knew it wasn't a good fit for me. One of the perks of being a member of Serpent's Kiss is privacy. They were meeting in a popular restaurant at lunchtime."

"Not exactly private," Ali said.

"Not at all." Drew came to a stop in front of a table full of finger sandwiches and muffins. "Help yourselves. There are some benefits to meeting here. Namely, Beth's food."

Ali picked up a plate and began loading it up. "You're a lucky man."

Drew chuckled. "Yes, I am." He glanced over his shoulder. "I'm going to get things started. Once you have your food, come join us at the table and we'll make sure you know everyone."

Kim grinned and nodded, but the butterflies were back. She recognized everyone that was there from the club and she knew Drew and Jeff and Ali fairly well, but the others she'd only seen in passing. Kate, the submissive whose leash Justin had been holding on Kim's first night at the club, was there talking to Bridget. While Kim knew who Bridget was because she also watched the coat check like Ali did, she didn't know anything else about her.

"Relax," Ali leaned over and whispered in Kim's ear.

Taking a deep breath in and then slowly releasing it, Kim tried. The problem was that she didn't know what to expect. Neither Justin nor Beth had really explained what this meeting was exactly. And when she'd asked Ali on the way there, her friend hadn't provided a whole lot of information either. Kim didn't like to go into situations blind and that was kind of how she felt. When she had meetings for work, she'd sometimes prepare for weeks. Nothing was left to chance. If someone asked her a question, she'd be ready for it.

This lifestyle, however, seemed to be all about unpredictability. At least for the submissive end of the relationship. Out of everything, the not knowing what was going to happen next was probably the hardest part for her. She could take being tied up, spanked, and a host of other things...as long as she was prepared.

Their plates full of a variety of goodies, Kim and Ali made their way over to the group. Everyone else was already seated and nibbling on the food in front of them.

Drew cleared his throat. "We have someone new with us today. Kim joined Serpent's Kiss a few months ago, so you all may have seen her around the club."

A few people around the table smiled. Others nodded. Everyone seemed friendly enough. Kim was glad the submissive she'd seen last night—the one who'd been staring her down as she sat on Justin's lap—wasn't present.

"Hi," Kim said, giving a half wave to everyone at the table.

"Why don't we all go around and say our names and how long we've been in the lifestyle," Drew said. "I'll go first. My name is Drew and I've been in the lifestyle for almost a year."

He turned to his right, prompting the next person to go. "I'm Bridget. I've been in the lifestyle for about six years."

Everyone went around introducing themselves. Jeff, Kate, Emma, Madison, Victoria, Haily, and Ali. Nine people in total. Kate had been in the lifestyle the longest...fifteen years. Kim was still trying to wrap her head around that, but given the little she'd seen of Kate's interaction with her husband at the club, she guessed that made sense.

Once the introductions were done, Drew asked if anyone had something they'd like to share. Jeff spoke up first. "Nicole has been researching the violet wand. I have to admit I'm a bit nervous about it. Have any of you had any experience with it?"

"I have," Kate said. "Master likes to play with it from time to time. It looks scarier than it is."

Jeff nodded. "Everything I've found said it feels getting shocked by touching a doorknob."

"Yes and no." Kate picked up a mini muffin from her plate.

"Getting shocked by touching a doorknob is one sharp sensation. While the violet wand feels similar, it's not one big shock and it's gone." She paused. "It also depends on how high it's turned up as well."

He shuddered. "That doesn't sound all that pleasant."

Kate laughed. "Depends on your level of pain tolerance."

The conversation went on for a while and Kim wondered why someone would want to do something like that. She understood there were people who got off on pain. Hell, when she was teetering on the edge of orgasm this morning, all it had taken was a shot of pain from Justin biting her nipple and she'd gone flying. She understood that type of pain, but lying still while someone ran something along your skin, shocking you...she didn't see the appeal. And from the sound of it, neither did Jeff. But it appeared he was still going to do it.

Kim turned to Ali. "If he doesn't want to do it, then why not tell his partner that?"

Ali grinned, then turned to the group. "Kim has a question." Her friend looked at her and tilted her head toward the group, waiting.

Nothing like throwing Kim under the bus. "If you don't want to do something, then why not just say no?"

Kate was the one who answered. "Because what we get out of pleasing our Dom is greater than having to take a little pain."

She must have made a face because Drew jumped in to add his perspective. "Beth enjoys knife play. When she first told me, I wasn't all that thrilled about trying it, but I did because I trusted her and knew she was in control of the scene and would take care of everything."

Kim hadn't heard of knife play before outside of the checklist, and since both she and Justin had marked it as a hard limit, they had skipped over it. "So she likes to cut you?"

He smiled. "No. Although, some Dominants are into cutting. Beth is more into the mind play involved."

"I don't understand," Kim said. "Mind play?"

Bridget leaned forward, resting her forearms on the table. "She likes to mess with his head."

Kim was really confused now.

"I'm always blindfolded, so I can't see what she doing, and she makes sure before we start the scene that I've gotten a good look at what she's planning to use on me." Drew paused and one side of his mouth lifted, clearly remembering. "A lot of times she uses the knives to cut clothing from my body, or sometimes she'll even put a butter knife in some ice and use it to write on my skin. The cold makes it feel sharper than it is."

She knew she had to look like a deer caught in the headlines. "Why would she do that? Mess with your head, I mean?"

"Because it heightens your senses," Emma said, chiming in for the first time since the introductions.

Bridget nodded. "You'd be amazed how stuff like that can increase pleasure in other areas."

Kim was still reeling from the conversation when it shifted to anal play and butt plugs. She was only half listening, though. Her brain was still trying to process what Drew had shared.

He wasn't a small man. In fact, he was taller than his Domme by at least six inches. And he was fit. Even through the sweater he was wearing, she could see the outline of his muscles.

Yet, by his own admission, he allowed himself to be tied up and knives ran along his skin while he was blindfolded. Kim couldn't imagine the level of trust it would take to do that.

She remained quiet for the remainder of the meeting, thinking about all she'd learned and was still learning. Could she trust Justin like Drew trusted Beth or Kate trusted her husband?

Kim didn't know.

And then the question was...what if she couldn't? What happened then?

* * *

Even though Justin had encouraged Kim to go to the submissive meeting, he spent the entire afternoon worrying. He was hoping talking to other submissives, not only Ali, would help her. She needed a support system. A place to ask questions and get opinions from others who'd been where she was.

That didn't make sitting on the sidelines any easier. He wanted their relationship to work. Waking up beside her that morning had been a dream come true and he wasn't even talking about the blow job she'd given him.

There was something about Kim that drew him in. They clicked in a way he hadn't experienced with any other woman. Having her in his arms felt right. Kissing her felt as if he were coming home and being lit on fire all at the same time. He'd suffer whatever consequences there were with Mark to have that with her for the rest of their lives. But they had to make it through their one-month trial first.

Justin spent the afternoon trying to keep himself busy. He drove to the shop to get some administrative stuff done. There was always paperwork to do for the business, especially with tax season right around the corner. But sorting through receipts and looking over payroll didn't keep his mind from wandering.

At four-thirty, he locked up the shop and headed toward O'Brien's, a sports bar downtown, a few blocks from Serpent's Kiss. He and Mark tried to meet there at least once a month for dinner and drinks. Their lives had taken very different directions. They didn't hang out with the same people anymore or go to the same functions. If they wanted to get together, they had to make an effort and so far, both of them felt it was worth it.

As Justin pulled into a parking spot and turned off the engine, he hoped his relationship with Kim didn't change things with his best friend. It would be his one regret, but he was hoping they could get Mark to understand and accept them being together. That is, if things between them went the way he wanted.

Climbing out of his car, he was reaching for the door handle when someone yelled his name. He turned to see Mark jogging toward him. "Perfect timing."

Mark smiled and ducked inside when Justin opened the door. "I wasn't sure how the roads were gonna be, so I left a little early."

It was almost completely dark, and the air temperature had plummeted. He wouldn't be surprised if tonight was even colder than last night had been. They were in a cold spell, and he was already over it. If he'd wanted cold weather, he would have moved to Minnesota.

A hostess greeted them and showed them to a table. She handed them menus and let them know their server would be by shortly.

Neither of them needed to look over the menu. They'd been there so many times, they knew exactly what they were going to order. "First time you've been out today?" Justin asked.

"Yeah. I had a shit ton of emails to go through for work."

"You do realize it's Sunday, right? Don't you get a day off?" Of course, he was one to talk. Justin had spent his Sunday afternoon working, too.

"I took yesterday off. Spent most of the day with a woman I've been seeing from the accounting department."

Their server stopped by to take their orders. Mark ordered a steak. Justin a burger. And they both ordered beers.

Once they were alone again, Justin picked up the conversation where they'd left off. "Dating someone from the office? Is that wise? You don't exactly have the best track record with women."

Mark waved away his concern. "She's an intern and only here for a few months."

That made sense. Mark wasn't exactly known for his long-term relationships. "How long have you been seeing her?"

The server returned with their beers, placing them on the table and then leaving them alone once more.

A sly grin appeared on Mark's face before he took a sip of his beer. "About a week."

More time than he'd officially been with Kim. "That new, huh?"

"Gotta keep things fresh. Getting tied down isn't my style. Too many fish in the sea and all that."

That was the difference between him and Mark. At least on the surface. Mark had no interest in a long-term relationship. Justin, on the other hand, wanted to settle down. He was all for marriage and kids. He just needed the right woman and for years the woman he wanted was off-limits.

"One of these days you're going to meet someone who'll change your mind about that," Justin said, lifting his beer bottle to his lips."

"You haven't found anyone yet, so there's little hope for me." Mark chuckled.

Justin let the comment go. He didn't want to talk about Kim. Not tonight.

To shift the subject away from women, Justin commented on the basketball game currently playing on one of the big screen televisions not far from their table. They spent the next hour commenting on the game, the players, and how St. Louis really needed to get a pro team again.

"Some guys from work are getting together next weekend to watch the game. You interested?" Mark asked as they put their coats on and got ready to leave.

"What time?"

Both Justin and Mark left a nice tip and the table, and they made their way toward the front. "Four o'clock next Sunday at my place."

The first thing that came to Justin's mind was Kim. He didn't know what her plans were, but he also didn't want to assume. They'd be together Friday and Saturday night at the club. After two days of playing, she'd probably need a break. "Sure. Want me to bring anything?"

"Bring that dip you make. It will go nicely with the wings I'm grilling."

They said goodbye at the door and Justin flipped up the collar of his coat as he walked to his vehicle. The wind had picked up again. He was already ready for spring, and it was only January.

When he arrived home, the first thing he did was check his messages to make sure he hadn't missed a call from Kim. Not that he was expecting her to call, but he'd kind of been hoping she would. His curiosity about her meeting earlier was eating at him.

Satisfied but a little disappointed that she hadn't called, he stripped out of his clothes and ambled into the bathroom to take a shower. His dinner with Mark had gone better than he'd expected. He hadn't spent the entire night dodging talk of who he was dating, but he knew that had a lot to do with the distraction the game had provided.

Mark loved sports, so if anything was going to get him off the topic of women, it was that. With playoffs right around the corner, his best friend had been invested in the outcome of the game.

If nothing else, it had given Justin some hope for the future. He and Mark could hang out without bringing Justin's relationship with Kim into it. All they had to do was get over a few rough hurdles first.

CHAPTER 20

THE MOMENT KIM walked through the door at work the next day, she was bombarded with issues. One of their clients decided they didn't like the marketing campaign they'd already signed off on and was supposed to begin running next week. She'd spent most of her morning on the phone trying to nail down what exactly the client didn't like and figuring out how to adjust it without having to scrap the whole thing.

By the time lunch rolled around, Kim needed a break. She grabbed her purse, let her assistant know she was going out, and rushed out of the building before someone could waylay her.

It was below freezing, but at least the sun had come out. All the snow from Saturday night had melted, so there weren't any issues walking to her favorite lunch spot in her heels.

Georgio's was a quaint Italian bistro three blocks from her office. She tried to make it there a couple of times a month if for no other reason than their fettuccine Alfredo. She'd once tried to make it herself at home, but it hadn't compared. Today, she was badly in need of comfort food.

The cozy atmosphere calmed her and the cappuccino she'd ordered warmed her from the inside. Kim pulled up a book she'd been

167

reading on her phone and tried to spend her lunch break relaxing. She knew the moment she got back into the office it would be full steam ahead again. They still had a lot to do before the campaign could go live and less than a week to do it.

Her lunch was over too soon, and she trudged back to the office. At five o'clock, she sent her assistant home while she continued working with the account manager. There was so much to do and so little time. She thought briefly about texting Justin and canceling their dinner plans, but she didn't want to. After the day she'd had, she needed a break. So, at six, she and the account manager called it a night and headed home.

When she breezed through the door of her apartment, she began removing her clothes as she marched toward her bedroom. There was no time for a shower, but she needed to freshen up. Bracing her right leg on the edge of the bathtub, she turned on the water and lathered up her leg. She didn't want to have prickly hair on her legs for her date.

Kim was fastening her earring in her ear when the doorbell rang. Swiping her shoes from the closet, she hurried down the hall to answer the door.

Taking a quick peek first to make sure it really was Justin, she pulled the door open. He stood on her small porch looking as delicious as ever. His hair was still damp from his shower, and he looked downright edible. Did they really have to go out?

"We aren't going to get very far if you keep looking at me like that."

Kim took a step back, inviting him in. This was the first time he'd been in her apartment. When they'd stopped by on Saturday before going to the club, he'd stayed in the car while she ran inside to pack a bag.

It felt strange having him in her space. Her apartment wasn't huge, maybe half the size of his house, but it was perfect for her. Since she didn't have a roommate and she worked all the time, there wasn't a need for a second bedroom.

He took a look around, zeroing in on the pictures she had on the wall of her mom and dad. "I don't think I've seen this one before."

She came to stand beside him. "It's from when they were dating. Mom told me that Dad proposed a week later."

Justin turned to look at her but didn't say anything.

"What? Do I have dirt on my nose or something?" She went to rub her nose, but he captured her hand in midair. He pulled her to him and she fell against his chest with a little *omph*. As she gazed up at him, there was no mistaking the look in his eyes. Or what she was feeling behind his dark jeans.

Her body responded immediately. Blood pumped through her veins and she parted her lips, ready for the kiss she knew was coming.

But instead of kissing her, he put space between them. "Are you ready to go?"

Kim blinked, trying to shift her thinking and answer his question. "Um. Sure."

He moved toward the door, reaching for the knob. When he noticed she hadn't budged, he dropped his hand. "Something wrong?"

"No." Kim shook her head. "It's just...I thought." She blew out a breath. "I thought you were going to kiss me."

"I was."

"Oh." She was confused. "Then why—"

"We are way too close to a bed and if I kiss you right now, we aren't going anywhere but into it." The heat in his gaze told her he wasn't exaggerating.

"I wouldn't complain," she whispered.

He opened the door, letting the cold air into her apartment. "I know. But I promised you a date and I intend to keep that promise."

Sensing there was no use in arguing with him, Kim put on her coat. They exited the apartment and she locked the door behind them. Justin waited to the side, hands in his pockets. She turned toward the parking lot when he grabbed her arm, halting her progress. His lips were on hers before she knew what hit her.

The kiss was swift and hard...and over before she knew it. "I thought you decided not to kiss me."

One side of Justin's mouth pulled up and his eyes danced with amusement. He was enjoying throwing her off balance. "I changed my mind."

Placing a hand on the small of her back, he led her down the sidewalk to his car. He opened the door for her and held it open while she got situated in the passenger seat. She hadn't known where they'd be going tonight, but he'd said to dress in comfortable clothes, so she'd worn a pair of jeans and one of her favorite tops. Not exactly something she'd wear at the club, but the outfit accentuated her curves and made her feel sexy.

"How was your day?" he asked as he pulled out onto the highway.

"Crazy." She chuckled and leaned her head back on the headrest.

"Want to talk about it?"

She turned to look at him. "You don't want to hear about my day."

Justin frowned. "Why not?"

"Because." Kim noticed they were headed out of town. "It's not the type of thing you talk about on a date." When he didn't comment, she added, "You don't want to hear me complain about clients."

"Isn't that what boyfriends are for?"

Something fluttered in the pit of her stomach. "Is that what this is?"

Justin's fingers flexed on the steering wheel. "I thought I made it very clear this was a relationship. Last time I checked, that would put us into boyfriend/girlfriend territory."

Biting the side of her cheek, she watched the buildings go by as they drove. She didn't say anything for a long while and he let the silence in the car linger. "I went to the submissive meeting with Ali yesterday."

"I was gonna ask you about that." He glanced over at her. "How'd it go?"

Kim looked down at her hands. "I don't know if I can do this."

A different kind of quiet settled over the vehicle. "What makes you say that?"

"Just some of the stuff they said."

"Like?" He pulled into the parking lot of what looked to be a

Mexican restaurant. Once he'd found a parking place, he removed his seat belt and shifted in his seat to face her.

She shook her head. "It wasn't anything specific. It was more...they act like it was perfectly natural to let their Dominants do whatever to them. Drew talked about Beth using knives on him and Nicole wants to use something called a violet wand on Jeff..."

Justin took hold of her hands and brought them to his lips. He placed a soft kiss on each of her palms, then made her look at him. "What is it about those things that scares you?"

The tone of his voice was soothing and helped to calm her a little. "I just don't know if I could ever trust someone that much and according to you and Ali, that's what I have to do."

"Trust isn't something that happens overnight. It's built over time." He cupped the side of her face and she leaned into his touch. "Step by step."

Moisture filled her eyes and she willed herself not to cry. "I want this to work so much."

"We have a month." His hand caressed the side of her face. "I know this is new to you. If it's what we both want, we'll figure it out. Let's not get ahead of ourselves, okay?"

She knew what he said made sense and, true to her character, she was trying to put the cart before the horse. They'd been together three days. They had a long way to go before they made any major decisions. "I'll try not to stress about it too much."

A slow smile spread across his lips before he leaned in to kiss her. "No more worrying for tonight."

Kim nodded and they made their way into the restaurant.

* * *

Justin spent the next hour trying to take Kim's mind off work and contemplating all the reasons she couldn't be a good sub. In the few times they'd been together, he knew by her body's responses that she was submissive. It was her head that was getting in the way.

Kim was the type of person who went after what she wanted. Case in point was the day she showed up on his doorstep, offering herself to him on a beautiful submissive platter. It was also what landed her the executive VP marketing position at one of St. Louis's most prestigious ad agencies. But she was going to have to let go and free herself of that need for control if she wanted to live this lifestyle with him.

Some Doms would tolerate their subs to top from the bottom. Justin did not.

In the past when a sub tried to top from the bottom, he'd put a swift and clear end to any notion they had that they were in control. With Kim, things were more complicated. She wasn't doing it to try and gain an advantage. He didn't even think she was doing it intentionally. It was a security thing for her. What he needed to do was to show her that keeping her safe was his responsibility.

"Can I get either of you some dessert? Fried ice cream, perhaps?" Their server had taken their dinner plates and was trying to tempt them with dessert.

Justin glanced at Kim to see if she wanted anything else. She held up her hand in a stop motion. "I'm good. I don't think I could eat any more if I tried."

Their server looked at Justin. "Just the check, please."

Placing the bill on the table, their server nodded. "I'll take it up when you're ready."

"I can't believe I ate all that food," Kim said, leaning back in the booth. "I'm going to have to put in some time at the gym this week."

"I don't think one meal is going to hurt." Just reached over and took her hands in his. "Besides, I happen to like all your curves."

"Is that so?"

Running a finger along the inside of her wrist, he met her gaze across the table. "Gotta have something to hold on to."

He saw color rise in her cheeks as his meaning registered. She glanced around the restaurant, confirming no one at the surrounding tables had heard him. It was going to be hard to leave her tonight.

After paying the bill, they donned their winter coats again and made their way back to his car. "Home?" she asked.

"Not quite yet." He put the key in the ignition and listened to the engine purr to life.

"Where else are we going?" she asked.

Justin grinned. She really did have a difficult time not being in control of things. "You'll see."

"Not even a hint?" She placed her hand on his thigh, a few inches below his crotch.

He removed her hand from his leg and placed it back in her lap. "Nope. You'll have to be patient and wait till we get there."

After his conversation with Daniel Saturday night at the club, he'd been thinking of different ways to build Kim's trust and get her to let go. Asking her on this date was a step in that direction. He didn't want a relationship with her that only revolved around sex, so being together and acting like a normal couple was important.

The second part of the evening, however, was about building that foundation of trust. The skating rink was five miles from the restaurant. Since it was a Monday night, it wasn't very busy. That was perfect for what he had in mind.

"We're going ice skating?" she asked as he helped her out of the car.

"Yep." He tucked her into his side as they headed inside. "Have you ever been ice skating before?"

"Not since I was six and I wasn't very good then."

Justin grinned and kissed the top of her head. He paid for their time on the ice and rented them both a pair of skates. His dad was a huge hockey fan, so Justin had spent a lot of time on the ice as a kid. He could skate almost as well as he could walk.

When they walked into the ice rink, there was only a handful of other people skating. There was a little girl and a woman he assumed was either her mother or her coach standing nearby, giving her instructions. The other three people were older and didn't look to be quite as steady on their feet.

He laced up his skates and waited for Kim to finish with hers. Then he reached for her hand and helped her up. Luckily, they only had a few feet to walk in order to reach the ice. Walking on ice skates wasn't his favorite thing in the world.

Bracing himself on the side edge of the rink, he removed the guard on his skates before stepping onto the ice. He held on to Kim's arm as she followed his lead.

As soon as she had both feet on the ice, she latched onto him, nearly landing them both on the ground. It was a good thing he was proficient on the ice. "Sorry."

He helped to steady her. "Better?"

"As long as I don't have to move."

Justin chuckled. "I think for it to be considered skating, you have to do more than stand in place."

"How about I stay right here by the wall, and you can skate to your heart's content?"

"Not a chance." He took a step back, putting a little distance between them, but not letting go of her arms.

"Don't let go!" Her voice was laced with panic. Her eyes pleaded with him, and her nails dug into his arm.

"I'm not going to let go. Relax." Before she could respond, he stalked backward, pulling her with him.

It was a small move, but like before, she overcompensated. "I'm going to fall."

"Look at me, not the ice." He waited for her to lift her gaze to meet his. "If you do what I tell you, you'll be fine."

She pressed her lips together but didn't comment.

Justin took her lack of response as agreement and continued with his lesson. "Tilt your hips forward a little." He watched as she complied. "Now slide your right foot forward."

Kim was holding on to him for dear life as he guided her step by step around the outside of the rink. She wasn't doing too bad. Every now and then, she'd wobble and grasp hold of him, but as they embarked on their second trip around the rink, she got steadier on her feet.

"Ready to move away from the edge?" Even though he asked the question, he changed their trajectory and moved them toward the interior of the ice.

She clung to him again, the fear he'd seen on her face earlier returning. "Maybe we should stick to the edge."

"Nope. You can handle this. I'm right here if you need me."

They spent another thirty minutes skating around before he led her over to the edge so they could remove their skates. Toward the end, she was skating with more confidence—he even noticed her smiling a little. She still wasn't steady enough to do it on her own, but she wasn't leaving claw marks in his arms either.

"You're really good," she said after handing in their skates. "I didn't know you could skate."

"My dad taught me. I think he was hoping I'd become a hockey player."

She slid into the passenger seat of his vehicle and waited until he was behind the wheel. "I think you're the only guy I know who's not really into sports."

He shrugged. "I like sports. I just don't eat and breathe them."

"I'm glad."

Justin glanced over at her before pulling out into traffic. "Why's that?"

"Because I'm not sure I could spend the next forty years listening to someone yell at the television every weekend."

Justin tried not to read too much into her statement. She wasn't saying she wanted to spend the rest of her life with him. But it was hard not to view it that way. "I'll keep that in mind."

CHAPTER 21

K IM DIDN'T KNOW where that came from, but she spent the remainder
of the ride back to her apartment with her mouth firmly shut. They
hadn't talked about more than one month, let alone forever. And she
wasn't stupid enough to think they were anywhere near ready to have
that type of a discussion either. There were too many obstacles they
had to overcome first.

When they arrived at her apartment, Justin walked her to her door
and waited as she took her key out and inserted it into the lock. "Did
you want to come inside?"

He hesitated for a moment, then followed her in.

"I have some cake in the fridge and I can put some coffee on," she said,
not sure what to do. Her day had ended much better than it had started,
and she wasn't ready for it to be over yet, even though it was after ten.

"I'm good."

She stood on the threshold between her living room and kitchen,
unsure what to do with herself. The urge to jump him was there, but
she wasn't sure if that was appropriate in their agreement.

"Tell me," he said.

She lifted her gaze to meet his. "What?"

"You're thinking very hard about something. What is it?"

"Oh." She bit the inside of her cheek. "I was trying to decide whether jumping you was allowed."

He raised one eyebrow. "You think I'd be upset if you threw yourself at me?"

A smile spread across her face as the tension that had been building in her body eased. "Well, when you put it that way...no." She shook her head. "I feel constantly off balance and unsure of myself. Is that normal?"

"For someone who's used to being in control of things?" He left her hanging for a few moments before providing his answer. "Yes."

Her brow furrowed. "I'm not sure I like it."

Justin closed the distance between them, pulling her into his arms. The instant relief she felt from his touch was almost frightening. "I will never object to you trying to seduce me, baby."

"I'm allowed to initiate sex, even though I'm the submissive in the relationship?" Kim asked. She'd never seen that happen at the club, but she also knew things were different there.

"Of course." He ran his hands down her back to cup her ass and gave it a squeeze. "This lifestyle isn't meant to suppress your sexuality."

She was still confused about where the line was, but Ali had told her not to get too impatient. It was one of her faults, she knew. Kim wanted to know everything, and she wanted to know it now. Another reason why letting go was so difficult.

"You're thinking really hard again." He lifted her off her feet, startling her.

Kim grabbed hold of his shoulders as he carried her over to the couch. She'd been expecting him to sit down, but instead, he dumped her onto the couch and knelt in front of her. "Tonight, when you were gripping my arms to keep yourself steady, did you ever think I'd let you go and allow you to fall on your ass?"

"No." She'd never thought that. Not once. She knew he'd catch her if she started to fall.

"Why?" He settled between her legs, his hands resting on her thighs.

From the look on his face, she knew he was trying to make a point and it wasn't hard to figure out what it was. "I trusted you."

He nodded.

"But on the ice it's different," she insisted.

"No. It isn't." He sat back on his heels and looked her in the eyes. "You were completely focused on me. If I told you to move your right leg forward, you did. If I instructed you to bend your knees, you complied...because you trusted I would take care of you."

As much as she hated to admit it, she could see his point.

Justin stood and extended his hand, helping her up. "We both have to be up early tomorrow for work. Do you want me to leave?"

A zing that started somewhere in her chest went directly to her clit. It had only been two days since they'd had sex, but already she missed having him inside her. Plus, her bed had felt very empty the night before. She'd like to wake up beside him Sunday morning. Was it possible to get used to something after only experiencing it once?

Given their previous conversation, Kim decided not to hold back. "She wrapped her arms around his neck and brought her lips close to his. "I want you to stay."

He cupped the back of her head and kissed her hard. "You have five minutes to get yourself ready for bed and be waiting for me." Justin released her and headed toward the door.

"Where are you going?" she asked, still a little unsteady on her feet after the kiss.

"I need to grab my bag." He glanced at the clock on the wall. "And you're down to four minutes and twenty seconds."

Without another word, Justin disappeared out the door.

Kim glanced up at the clock. She figured she had four minutes left and she knew he wasn't kidding about the time limit. She turned off all the lights except for the one in the living room, checked the back door to make sure it was locked, then raced into her bathroom to take care of business and brush her teeth. She was glad she'd had the forethought earlier to shave because there was no way she could accomplish that in the short time she had left.

She had just finished kicking off her jeans when she heard him come back through the front door. As swiftly as she could, she finished removing her clothing and stood, naked, at the foot of her bed, waiting for him.

The house was quiet except for his footfalls, making them sound much louder than they actually were. Her heart pounded in anticipation. He hadn't said to get into bed or kneel or give her any instructions other than to be ready for him.

His frame filled the doorway to her bedroom, his shoulders nearly spanning the frame. He paused, taking in the view. His gaze started at her face and worked its way down, lingering on her breasts and hips.

He entered the room, but he walked over to the dresser instead of to her. Kim followed him with her gaze as he placed his bag on the chair and a mug of something on the dresser. Then he began unbuttoning his shirt.

It was a slow process. He took his time, not seeming to be in any rush to undress.

Kim wasn't sure what to do. She thought about helping him—see if she could speed things up—but decided against it. Even though her fingers were itching to touch him, she'd be patient. She could do that.

Justin peeled his shirt down his arms and tossed it onto the chair beside her dresser. His gaze met hers as he popped the button on his slack and lowered the zipper. His erection bulged from behind his underwear as he pushed the jeans down his legs and kicked them to the side.

Quirking a finger at her, he beckoned her to him. She couldn't get her feet to move fast enough. Memories of what he felt like...tasted like...had her wet and aching.

The urge to remove the last barrier of clothing separating them and giving in to her urges was tempting. She'd never denied herself with anyone but Justin. Then again, she'd never had more powerful orgasms than she'd had with Justin either. The irony wasn't lost on her.

As patiently as she could, she waited for him to tell her what he wanted.

Lifting a single finger to her breast, he traced around the outside, then around the nipple itself before taking the tiny bud between his thumb and forefinger. She closed her eyes as he rolled and pulled...pinched and twisted...her already sensitive nipple.

A low moan escaped her throat and the heat between her legs grew. She loved when he played with her breasts. Almost as much as when he played with her neck. For some reason, those two areas of her body seemed to have a direct line to her clit.

"Open your eyes." His voice was soft, yet firm. There was no doubt by his tone that it was a command, however.

Kim met his gaze and was struck by the depth of color in his green eyes. She loved it when he looked at her as if she were the only woman in the world he desired.

"Tonight, we're going to do a little breast play." He gave her nipple a hard pinch before releasing it and turning to reach into his bag. A second later, he held a pair of nipple clamps. He'd used them on her that first night and while they'd hurt, the pain had dissipated quickly. "Do you remember these?"

"Yes. Sir." She'd almost forgotten. Even though they weren't in the club or his playroom, they were still playing.

He grinned, letting her know she'd pleased him. For some reason, that made her happy. She wanted to please him.

Cupping her breast in one hand, he ran his thumbnail over the tip of her nipple, flicking it several times. It didn't hurt, but it wasn't a soft caress either.

She watched as her nipple darkened at the continual attention. It was becoming more sensitive.

Justin raised one of the clamps and positioned it over her nipple. After her first encounter with them, she'd done some research and learned they were called tweezer clamps. They were good for beginners because they allowed the user to adjust the level of pressure with a simple adjustment.

He watched her as he slid the metal bar higher to tighten the clamp. Kim sucked in a breath as pain shot through her nipple. She thought he'd stop, but he kept going a little further.

"That's it. Breathe through it. The pain will be worth it. I promise." He released the chain, letting it hang, and the weight sent more pain through her.

But her body seemed to be confused. Her sex pulsed, soft and ready for him, and her clit tingled in anticipation.

Moving to her other breast, he began playing with it the same as he had the other one. She felt...distracted. There was so much feeling going on that she didn't know how to process it all. When he clamped her left nipple, the pain almost startled her.

"How does that feel?" he asked, giving the chain connecting the clamps a little jerk.

"It hurts." She paused. "But I'm okay. Sir."

Justin pressed his lips to hers in a gentle kiss. "You're doing well. I'm proud of you."

A sense of pride filled her knowing she'd pleased him.

"I want you to put your arms behind your back."

She did as he asked and the new position thrust her chest forward, making her breasts more prominent.

He walked around behind her and adjusted the grip of her hands, so she was holding a little higher on her arms. It was a strange position, but it wasn't uncomfortable. His hands went to her hips. "Spread your legs a little. Not too much, though. I don't want you to lose your balance."

Once she was in the position he wanted, Justin moved around to stand in front of her again. "I told you we were going to do some breast play tonight. I'm going to have some fun with these tits of yours and you're going to stand there and not move. Do you understand?"

She couldn't anticipate what he was going to do. Fear and uncertainty raced through her. What if he did something she didn't like?

* * *

Justin waited to see what she'd do. He could see her thinking. Her eyes had widened at his words, and he knew a hundred things were going through her head. As much as he wanted her to submit to him, he knew it had to be her choice. He couldn't...wouldn't force her. She had to trust him.

When she hadn't answered after several minutes, he lifted her chin and made her look at him. He didn't speak. Instead, he remained patient.

The muscles in her neck tensed and released as she swallowed. "Yes, Sir."

"You remember your safeword?" he asked. Not that he was expecting to push her to that point, but it was always good to check in.

"Yes, Sir." She sounded a little more confident this time.

"Very good. Let's get started, then."

Returning to his bag, Justin removed the first item he'd brought with him. The goal tonight was to build her trust in him while having some fun. He'd thought about bringing some rope but had decided against it. They'd get to rope play in due time.

Justin ran the black scarf through his fingers before holding it up so she could see it. When they'd played the first time, he'd blindfolded her, so this wasn't anything new. He moved behind her and secured the blindfold.

With a final check to make sure her eyes were covered, he went back to his bag. This time, he removed a single feather. He ran the feather along the outside of her breasts before grazing over one of her nipples. They looked perfect, all red as they were squeezed in the clamps. He was tempted to suck on them, but that would come later. First, he wanted to play.

Using only the very tip of the feather, Justin skimmed it ever so lightly over the sensitive flesh and she squirmed.

He removed the feather completely and admonished her, his tone expressing his displeasure. "Did I tell you that you could move?"

"It tickles."

Justin repeated himself. "Answer the question."

She was quiet for a long moment. "No, Sir."

"Do I need to restrain you on the bed, or can you control yourself?"

Again, it took longer than it should for her to answer. "You don't need to restrain me, Sir."

He had to give her credit. She was trying.

Removing the next item from his bag, he grazed the small flogger over the top of her breasts, letting the falls dip down over her nipples. He raised his hand and gave the flogger a gentle flick. The leather made contact an inch above the clamps.

Kim sucked in a breath but didn't move.

A smile spread across his face, and he repeated the action on the other breast.

This time, she was ready for it. Other than an intake of breath, there was no reaction.

He flipped the flogger over, using the handle to scrape against her left nipple. She tightened her hold on her arms, causing her breasts to thrust out more. "Do you like that?"

"I don't know what it is, Sir," she said in way of answering.

Justin chuckled. "You're not supposed to know. That's part of the fun." He moved to her right breast and did the same. "Answer the question. Do you like it?"

"Yes, Sir." She furrowed her brow. "It feels strange, but not in a bad way."

"These tits of yours look lovely in these clamps...so hard and red..." He leaned down and licked the nipple he'd been playing with.

"Yes." The word came out like a hiss.

He reached behind him and grabbed the little surprise he'd snatched from her freezer. After warming her nipple with his tongue, he pulled back enough to put the ice cube into his mouth. It was a decent size, so it should last for what he planned.

Returning to the same breast, he released the clamp and immediately sucked her nipple into his mouth. The pain from the clamp, combined with the hot of his mouth and the cold of the ice cube had her gasping and completely forgetting not to move.

Her fingers dug into his head. He wasn't sure whether she was trying to hold him to her or push him away. Either way, she was not obeying him and that needed to be rectified.

He stood, removed the ice cube from his mouth, and returned it to the mug. Kim dropped her arms. One clamp dangled from her left nipple.

She let out a little scream as he scooped her up without notice and laid her on the bed. "What did I tell you would happen if you did not remain still?"

This time, she answered him right away. "That you would restrain me." She pressed her lips together. "I'm sorry, Sir. It...what you did took me by surprise. I wasn't expecting—"

Justin had brought cuffs just in case. They were easier than rope and took up less space in his bag. He wrapped one wrist. "We need to work on your ability to follow instructions, but for now, these will keep you where I want you." Luckily for him, Kim's headboard had slats. It took a little maneuvering, but he was able to slip the chain around one before securing her other wrist.

Retrieving the mug and moving it to her bedside table, he removed his underwear before climbing onto the bed. He knelt between her legs, spreading them to accommodate him.

Before picking up where they left off, he gave her a thorough once-over. She was flushed and both her nipples were red and hard. Her pussy was also very wet. He could see it glistening and the musky scent had him wanting to bury his face in it.

"Are you ready to continue?"

"Yes, Sir." While she said the words, he sensed something was off.

"What's wrong?" He needed to know if there was an issue.

She shook her head. "Nothing."

Justin sighed and reached up to remove the blindfold. He needed her to look at him.

Kim blinked several times, her eyes adjusting to the light in the room. It was then he saw the moisture in her eyes. As much as he wanted to continue their sensory play, her mental well-being took priority.

"Take a deep breath in and hold it. I'm going to remove the other clamp."

"I'm okay. I—"

"I wasn't asking."

She closed her eyes but took in a breath and held it.

Bending, he held her breast with one hand, right above the nipple, and released the clamp. He soothed the pain with his tongue, sucking the abused flesh until he heard her breathing return to normal.

Next, he removed the cuffs. If she was a more experienced submissive, he might have had this conversation with her still restrained, but she wasn't.

He stood. "Get under the covers. I don't want you to get a chill. I'll be right back."

"Okay." Her voice was soft...almost childlike. He didn't like it.

As swiftly as he could, Justin went into the bathroom, dumped the ice, and refilled the mug with water. He was hard as a rock, but that couldn't be helped.

Running a hand through his hair, he headed back into the bedroom.

CHAPTER 22

KIM PULLED the covers up to her chin and waited for Justin to return. She'd screwed up again. How hard was it not to move? She knew she'd disappointed him, and she hated it, but she hadn't expected to react as she had. Tears had threatened to fall as he'd brought her over to the bed and bound her wrists.

It wasn't being cuffed that had caused the surge of emotion. He'd tied her up before. No, it was realizing she'd ruined their perfect night together.

After he'd taken her mind off her crappy day with dinner and ice skating, she'd wanted to give him her submission. She'd wanted it so badly, but in the end, she hadn't been able to do it. When she'd felt all the different sensations—pain from him removing the clamp—the heat of his mouth—and the cold from... Well, she didn't know what exactly.

Everything had hit her at once and she'd reacted before she was able to stop herself. She'd told him she could remain still on her own, but that hadn't been true.

As the seconds ticked by, her melancholy grew. She wasn't good at being submissive.

Justin strolled back into the room. She heard him approach the bed, but she was afraid to look at him. The mattress dipped with his weight as he sat down next to her. "I brought you some water."

"I'm okay," she whispered.

"Kim."

Reluctantly, she turned her head so she could see him. He was still naked.

Placing the mug on the nightstand next to her head, he took hold of her shoulders and lifted. She let out a little squeak as he moved her to a sitting position.

Kim gathered the blanket and once more attempted to cover herself. She wasn't sure why. It wasn't as if he hadn't seen every inch of her before.

She's barely gotten it over her breasts when he pulled it back down again. "No hiding."

"I'm not hiding."

"Really?" He tilted his head down and raised one of his eyebrows. "What are you doing, then?"

Not sure how to answer that, she deflected. "It's late and I'm tired."

"Is that your way of trying to kick me out?"

Was it? She wasn't sure. A part of her did want him to leave, but not because she didn't want him in her bed. She wanted him there. Always. But she also couldn't shake the feeling that she'd never be able to do the things he needed her to do. Hell, the things she wanted to do for him.

But she kept messing up. Her brain kept getting in the way. She'd watched enough submissives in the club to know how it worked.

When she didn't answer, he tilted her chin toward him and forced her to meet his gaze. "What happened tonight?"

"You know what happened."

He shook his head. "I'm not talking about you disobeying me." Justin rubbed his thumb along her cheek. "Why were you crying?"

"I wasn't crying." It was a weak denial and they both knew it. "I was just...upset."

"Why?"

"You know why."

Justin sighed. "This is going to be a very long conversation if you keep telling me I already know the answer to the question I asked. If I knew the answer, I wouldn't be asking." He paused. "Now, explain to me why you were upset."

"You told me not to move and I did. Twice. I thought I could do it. I thought I could remain still no matter what you did, but I couldn't."

Her response was met with silence. She didn't want to look at him and see the realization that she was a horrible submissive, but she couldn't help herself.

He was frowning. "Do you think the submissives at the club always obey their Doms' orders?"

Kim crossed her arms over her chest, but when his frown turned into a scowl, she dropped them again. She picked at the threads on her blanket to give her something to do besides look at him. "Yes."

Justin snorted, which caused her to glance up.

"What?" she asked.

"Even Kate, one of the best trained submissives I've ever met, disobeys her husband every now and then." He paused. "There are some harsh punishments involved for her not following his orders, but it does happen."

She didn't believe it. Granted, she didn't know Kate that well, but every time Kim had seen her at the club, she'd been a model submissive...something Kim doubted she'd ever be. "Like when?"

Justin chuckled. "Like when a repairman came by their house two days ahead of schedule and she answered the door."

"She isn't allowed to answer the door? Why?" Her voice had gone up an octave.

A knowing smile pulled at his lips. "Kate isn't allowed to wear clothes at home, so she had to put on a robe to answer the door."

"So, she has to ask permission to wear clothes inside the house?" For some reason, Kim felt angry on Kate's behalf.

He nodded.

That sounded...that was... "That's barbaric."

His eyebrows rose again. This time, in amusement. "Then I guess I shouldn't tell you what her punishment for disobeying was."

"He punished her?" Kim was sitting up. "For putting on a robe?" She wasn't sure what she was going to do, but she felt the urge to do something.

"Of course." He canted his head to the side. "Why are you angry? Kate knew what she was doing. She made a conscious choice to disobey her husband.

"But..."

The words died on her lips. But what? Justin was right. As much as she hated to admit it, he was right.

She met his gaze, pleading in her eyes. "I'll never be like that. I can't."

"Have I ever asked you to be like Kate?"

"No."

Justin took hold of her hand and brought it to rest against his thigh. He wasn't hard anymore, but that didn't mean she wasn't aware of him. How she could still be aroused after all this, she didn't know. "Kate and her husband negotiated their relationship the same way we did, but they have different kinks than we do. Kate gets off on her husband having total control over her in most aspects of their life."

That was hard to wrap her head around. She couldn't fathom someone wanting to give up that much control to their partner.

"That scares you, doesn't it?"

He was massaging the skin along her wrist, and it was distracting her. "Yes." She paused. "At the submissive group, Jeff mentioned Nicole wants to use a violet wand on him."

"I see." His tone was neutral, and Kim didn't like it. She couldn't get a read on him.

"He doesn't want to."

"You sure about that?" he asked.

Kim opened her mouth, but then closed it once more. Was she? He'd been unsure...nervous. But as she thought back to the conversation, she couldn't recall him ever saying he didn't want his Domme to use it on him.

Blowing out a tired breath, she admitted what he probably already knew. "No."

"There are safewords in this lifestyle for a reason." When she didn't say anything more, he turned the spotlight back on her. "Kim, I don't expect you to be perfect. You're new to this and you're going to mess up. Probably a lot." He shrugged. "We deal with it and move on."

"Deal with it?" She wasn't sure she liked that. Especially given their very recent conversation.

"If you break a rule, there are consequences. You know that." He paused. "And sometimes knowing you've disappointed your Dom is punishment enough."

She'd heard other submissives say that they'd disappointed their Doms at the club. Some of them had sounded as if the world were ending. Others seemed to brush it off as if it were no big thing.

Kim thought back to how she'd felt tonight after failing to hold still like Justin had asked her. Even though she hadn't been able to see his face, she'd known he was disappointed she didn't do what she'd assured him she could. The feeling of failure had overwhelmed her.

"I don't like disappointing you." The admission left her with mixed feelings.

He brought her hand to his lips and kissed her fingers. "I know."

Justin dropped her hand and stood. "Do you want me to stay tonight, or would you rather be alone?"

She pressed her lips together. He was letting her decide. Did she want him to stay or go?

Reaching over to the opposite side of the bed, she flipped the blanket down. "Stay."

He nodded, walked to the other side of the bed, and slid in next to her. She could feel his warmth and was drawn to it.

Justin reached for her, and she couldn't get into his arms fast enough. He tucked her head into his shoulder and kissed the top of her head. "Good night."

She nuzzled her nose against his collarbone. "Good night."

* * *

Justin spent the next few days thinking about how he could help Kim. He needed to build her confidence. While the advice he'd gotten from Daniel about introducing one thing at a time was sound, he was thinking he needed to break it down even further. Kim needed some wins, and it was his responsibility to help her achieve them.

He picked her up on Friday evening and headed to the club. The coat she wore covered whatever outfit she was wearing, which was both good and bad. It meant that whatever she was wearing was short and would give him easy access to her. But it also meant he couldn't see what was his.

"Hi," she said.

"Hello." His gaze raked over her from head to foot. "Unbutton your coat."

She opened her mouth to argue, then closed it again and began opening her coat.

Little by little, she revealed the red dress she was wearing. It looked to be soft...velvet maybe. The dress clung to her curves, then flared at the waist. He hadn't intended for them to start playing yet, but he couldn't resist. Besides, it was easy and would give him something to build on later. "Open your legs."

He heard her intake of breath a moment before she spread her legs.

They were still sitting in the parking lot in front of her apartment, so he needed to be discreet. As much as he'd love to finger fuck her right then, he didn't want to get caught by one of her neighbors. "Are you wearing panties?"

"No, Sir."

Pleased, he nodded. "Good girl." Then he removed the vibrator from his pocket and handed it to her. "Stick this in your pussy."

She took the vibrator from him. It was shaped like a small dildo with a flat end that had two wings. The wings were meant to go on either side of her clit.

Kim looked at him with wide eyes. "Here?"

He remained silent and waited to see what she'd do.

When she realized he was serious, she lifted her skirt, shifted in her seat, and placed the object where he'd instructed her to. When she removed her hand, he grabbed hold of it and inspected her fingers. He could smell her scent, which meant she was already wet.

Sucking two of her fingers into his mouth, he moaned at the small taste of her. It had been too long since he'd eaten her pussy. A problem he had every intention of rectifying tonight.

He released her fingers with a pop, not missing how her breathing had increased. "Put your seat belt on. We need to get going."

Once Kim was strapped in, he backed out of the parking lot and drove toward the club. They were a mile or so down the road before he slipped a hand into his pocket and turned on the device.

"Oh." Her shocked surprise brought a smile to his lips. He wanted her pussy dripping by the time they got to the club.

As they weaved their way through the city, he changed the vibrations. Every time she got too close to coming, he'd lower the setting.

By the time they reached the club, Kim was gripping the sides of her seat. Her chest was moving up and down with exaggerated breaths.

He switched off the toy and exited the vehicle. Kim didn't move when he opened the door for her. "Remove the vibrator and button your coat back up before you get out of the car."

Kim looked up at him as if only now realizing he was standing there. Her hand disappeared under her skirt as she removed the device. As she held it in her hand, he couldn't help but notice how wet it was as she tried to decide what to do with it.

"I'll take it," he said, holding out his hand.

She placed the vibrator in his palm and hurried to refasten her coat. Then, as if she was unsure her legs would hold her weight, she climbed out of the car.

A knowing grin bloomed on his face as he watched her find her feet. She narrowed her eyes at him. "This is your fault."

Justin laughed. "Come on. Let's get you inside. I have plans for you tonight."

"I'm not sure I can walk." She took a tentative step forward as he locked up the car.

"Here," he said, circling his arm around her waist. "I'll make sure you don't fall. Especially in those sexy heels you're wearing."

"I thought you might like them."

He hummed. "I'm going to enjoy fucking you in them later."

She stopped walking.

"Everything all right?" he asked.

"No."

He waited.

Blowing out a breath, she started moving again. "I'm so horny right now I feel like I'm going to explode and you talking like that isn't helping."

A deep belly laugh overtook him as they reached the club. He opened the door and ushered her inside. Swiping his membership card, he let them into the main foyer. "I'll keep that in mind for later." He winked at her before guiding her over to the coat check.

Ali was behind the desk tonight. "Hi, guys." She took their coats and hung them up in the large closet behind her.

"Are you working all night?" Justin asked.

"I'm supposed to. Did you need me for something?" Ali glanced at her friend, looking for anything amiss.

"No, but I wanted to know where you'd be if Kim needs you." He wasn't expecting Kim to need Ali tonight, but it was never a bad idea to have a backup plan.

Ali smiled. "Of course. And I'm sure Bridget will cover for me if I need her."

He tipped his head in Ali's direction, acknowledging her comment before turning his attention back to Kim. "Let's get inside."

Kim gave a little wave to Ali as Justin led her into the club. He guided her over to the bar. Chase, the other bartender, greeted them as they approached. "What can I get you tonight?"

His question was directed to Justin. Chase wasn't part of the lifestyle, but he'd been working at Serpent's Kiss long enough to know how it worked. "Two waters."

Chase grinned and ducked behind the bar to retrieve two bottles of water. He placed them on the shiny wood surface, and Justin handed over his membership card. After a quick swipe, Chase returned the card to its owner.

Justin adjusted both bottles in one hand, carrying them by their lids. Putting pressure on Kim's lower back, he turned them both toward the stairs.

"We're going upstairs?" she asked.

"Yes."

It was the only answer he gave her as they ascended the stairs to the second floor. As they neared the top, he could already hear the sounds of play. They were muted behind the doors of the playrooms, but it was hard to mask the sound of whips and floggers without soundproof rooms.

Several people were standing in front of various rooms, watching the play happening inside. Justin paused outside of the second room to his right when he noticed Daniel inside. He had Emma, an uncollared sub, secured to a St. Andrew's cross while he flogged her.

Since picking up on the interesting vibes between Daniel and Ali, he'd been paying more attention to the older Dom. As he watched the scene in front of him, he realized he'd never seen Daniel do anything with a submissive recently that involved more than tying them to a St. Andrew's cross and flogging them.

When Justin first joined the club, Daniel would play with subs often. He was very popular with the club's submissives for his expertise in flogging, even back then. But the scenes then would typically include more than flogging. Thinking back, he recalled a scene where Daniel had a sub laid out on a table, much like a gourmet meal, while he placed various food items on her body and licked them off. It had been extremely sensual to watch. But he hadn't seen Daniel do any scenes like that for at least the last year and he was now thinking that was because of Ali.

"Does that hurt?" Kim asked from beside him.

Justin looked over at her, then back at the scene. "Floggers tend to deliver more of a thud than a sting, but it depends on the type of flogger and the material it's made out of."

Not wanting to spend the entire night being a voyeur, he moved them away from the viewing window. They ended up in the same room they'd been in the week before. Justin had reserved the room because it was one of the few where the window could be blocked. Kim had marked exhibitionism as something she was unsure about. It wasn't something he wished to test this early on in their relationship.

This time, he allowed her to observe as he darkened the window, giving them privacy. Tonight was about building her confidence as a submissive, not only about building trust. He needed for her to see that she could be a good sub. It was just going to take time.

He selected a pillow from the corner and placed it in the middle of the room. "Remove your clothes and kneel. Leave the shoes on for now."

Kim pushed the narrow straps of her dress from her shoulders and shimmied it down her hips. He offered her a steadying hand as she stepped out of the dress. Kim handed the outfit to him and lowered herself to the floor onto the pillow. She bowed her head, spread her legs, and placed her hands in an upturned position on her thighs, awaiting his instructions.

CHAPTER 23

Justin took in the sight before him...took in her positioning. He removed a hair tie from one of the drawers and moved to stand behind her. Gathering her hair, he secured it up and out of the way.

"Where did you learn to kneel like that?" He'd noticed her palms up the last time she'd knelt in front of him. At the time, however, he'd been too busy trying to convince himself not to take what she was obviously offering to comment on how she was presenting herself.

"Am I doing something wrong?" The sides of her mouth pulled down into a frown. "I did some research on the internet and it showed a woman kneeling like this."

"Kneeling with your palms up is a positioning common in a very specific practice of this lifestyle. I would prefer you to have your palms facing down, resting on your thighs."

Kim made the correction.

He smiled, even though she couldn't see him.

Taking his time, he walked around her, inspecting. While he didn't normally have subs spread their legs while kneeling, he had to admit he was enjoying the view. Still, if he told her to get into a kneeling position out on the main floor of the club, he didn't want there to be any confusion. "Bring your legs together. While I love the visual, holding that position for long periods of time may get uncomfortable for you."

She did as he asked.

Once he was satisfied she was kneeling the way he wanted her to, he stood in front of her and lifted her chin. "Whenever I tell you to kneel, this is how I want you."

"Yes, Sir."

He dropped his arm and moved to the far wall that contained a variety of implements. The scene tonight would need to be simple. He didn't want to overwhelm her.

Given her curiosity regarding the flogger, he selected one that most subs loved. It was heavy and the falls were soft. When welded correctly, it felt almost like a massage.

Justin pulled her head back using her ponytail. Her neck stretched as she met his gaze. "Since you were so fascinated by the flogger earlier, we're going to explore that tonight. You've never been flogged, correct?"

"No, Sir, I haven't."

He lifted the arm holding the flogger and glided it over the front of her, letting her feel the falls as they grazed her skin. Her eyelids fluttered a little as the toy rose over her chest and up her neck.

Taking his time, he ran the falls of the flogger over her arms, her legs, her back...everywhere he could reach while she was in her current position. He paid close attention to her breathing, noting it was slow and even. She was relaxed.

"Lean forward and place your hands on the floor. I want you on all fours."

Kim shifted her body weight and adjusted herself into the new position.

"Spread your legs a little more. I don't want you losing your balance."

As she opened her legs, his gaze was drawn to her sex. Her pink lips were wet and swollen...ready for him. His cock swelled even more in his pants, demanding attention. It would have to wait, however. He wanted to play first.

Again, he let the falls of the flogger skim over her back...her butt...her thighs. He wasn't in a hurry. They had plenty of time.

The first blow landed solid on the right side of her backside. Kim liked to be spanked, so he had no doubt she'd enjoy having her ass flogged.

She sucked in a breath, but other than that, she didn't react.

Justin repeated the motion on the other side. He gave her a moment to get used to the feel, then be began alternating his blows until her ass was a nice warm pink.

Kneeling, he inspected the abused flesh, now much more sensitive, and was pleased when Kim pushed back against his hand as he rubbed her cheeks. He reached between her legs, running his fingers through her wet heat. She rocked against his fingers as he circled her clit, trying to increase the pressure he was using. "Not yet, baby."

A soft whimper escaped her lips when he moved his hand away, not giving her the release she wanted.

He stood and landed a slightly softer blow to her upper back and shoulders. Once he'd warmed that part of her body, he moved back down, this time targeting her inner thighs. With each hit, the flogger would kiss her pussy lips.

As the session continued, he noticed sweat forming on her back and neck, and her breathing had picked up. She'd been in this position for more than twenty minutes and was often easing back, almost begging for more of the flogger. Kim was completely in the moment.

That was good, but his cock was in desperate need of attention. It was pressing painfully against his fly.

Laying the flogger down, he grabbed a chair and set it a foot or so from her face. Then he unfastened his pants, pushed them and his underwear down around his ankles, and sat. "Come here."

Her eyes were glazed over when she looked up at him. He held the base of his cock in one hand, and she crawled toward him.

Justin didn't need to tell her what he wanted. Kim's mouth engulfed his erection. She began bobbing her head with an enthusiasm he hadn't seen from her before.

Closing his eyes, he relished the feel of her lips and tongue as she sucked him. He liked blow jobs as much as the next guy, but it was close to an out-of-body experience every time she got her mouth on him. Justin knew it wasn't only her skill. It was because it was Kim.

He cupped the back of her head, guiding her movements. As his orgasm drew closer, he took hold of her ponytail and removed her lips from him. He needed to be inside her and he needed to be inside her now.

The chair fell as he stood, and he didn't care. He'd worry about that later.

Justin finished kicking off his jeans. Swiping a condom from the room's supply, he ripped it open and rolled it down his very hard length.

Kneeling behind Kim, he spread her legs even more, making room for himself. It was good Katrina had chosen a padded flooring for the playrooms. They came in handy when he didn't want to be bothered to move his submissive to a higher horizontal surface.

From his new position, he could smell her arousal. The desire to taste her was nearly overwhelming, but his need to feel her tight heat surrounding him took priority. There would be time for more later. It was still early and he planned to have her in his bed that night.

He coated his cock with her juices, teasing her clit before he lined himself up and thrust his hips forward. Her head dipped as he sank into her. She pushed back against him, urging him deeper. He relished the feeling of her muscles contracting around him, welcoming him inside.

Balls deep inside her pussy, he dug his fingers into her still rosy ass and began pumping his hips. He wasn't gentle about it, but he'd learned Kim liked it that way. She met him thrust for thrust and he was soon teetering on the edge again.

Snaking one hand around her middle, he found her clit. Wanting to draw it out, he was careful not to apply too much pressure. He wanted her to beg for it.

At first, she tried tilting her pelvis to increase the pressure. When that didn't work, she spread her legs more to get lower, closer to his hand. That didn't get the desired result, either.

She let out a high-pitched whimper. "Please."

He lifted the hand still on her ass and gave her skin a hard smack. "Please, what?"

"Please, let me come, Sir. I'm...I'm so close. I just need..."

"Tell me what you need, baby."

"More. Please rub my clit harder, Sir." Her voice was full of desperation.

Justin teased her a little more, then he gave her what she wanted.

It didn't take long. Within a matter of seconds, she was grinding on his hand and chanting *Please*. And it didn't take much longer until her interior muscles were clenching and milking his cock.

She came with a scream, one that in any other place would have had anyone who'd heard it coming to see if she needed help. Given their location, it was more likely to inspire envy from the other subs within earshot.

Feeling her pussy spasm around him was the final nail in the coffin for Justin's control. His climax hit him hard and seemed to go on forever. By the time it subsided, he felt spent. Completely content, but spent.

As soon as he was able, he pulled out, disposed of the condom, and moved to check on Kim. Her head was pressed against the floor, and she was still breathing hard.

"Are you okay?" he asked, brushing a loose strand of hair behind her ear.

"I don't know. I can't feel my legs again."

He lowered himself back to the floor and gathered her into his arms. Kissing her temple, he cupped her face and met her gaze. "You did well, baby. I'm proud of you."

The smile that greeted him sent his heart racing in a completely different way. The fact that he was in love with Kim resonated in every bone in his body. He wasn't going to be able to give her up after their month was over. Seeing her look at him that way, knowing he'd put that smile on her face, did something to him. They had to figure it out. All of it. Including how they were going to tell Mark.

* * *

Kim didn't know how long they sat on the floor of the playroom before they dressed and headed downstairs. She was feeling very clingy, which wasn't like her. Justin had gone to get them some more waters and she'd been left feeling somewhat lost.

He'd returned with two bottles of water and handed her one as he sat down beside her. "Drink. I don't want you getting dehydrated."

She was thirsty. He'd made her drink an entire bottle of water before they'd left the playroom, but her mouth still felt like it was full of cotton. "I don't understand why I'm so thirsty," she said.

Justin rested his arm along the couch behind her and she moved closer, wanting to be touching him. "I worked you hard. And you're not used to it."

Her gaze darted to the people around them, but no one seemed to be paying much attention to them. Granted, it was Beth, Drew, Nicole, Jeff, and Daniel, but that didn't make her any less embarrassed about it. Having sex in the club was strange enough. She wasn't ready to announce to the world what they'd done.

As she thought about it, she realized how it sounded. She'd joined a BDSM club where people had sex, often with other people watching, all the time. What they'd done upstairs was normal.

Actually, it wasn't normal. Their scene had been in private. No one had been watching them. Of course, her very loud scream as she came couldn't have gone completely unnoticed. Heat flooded her cheeks and she recalled how the sound had reverberated in the room.

Justin turned to whisper in her ear. "Remembering what we did upstairs?"

She tucked her head into his shoulder. "Yes. Please don't say anything."

He kissed the top of her head and combed his fingers through her hair. He'd removed the band that held it away from her face before they'd left the playroom, so her hair was flowing free once more. She closed her eyes, loving the feel of his hands threading through her locks. "You have nothing to be embarrassed about. No one here will judge you."

It was true. "I know." Kim took a deep breath. He smelled of sweat, and soap, and sex. It was a dangerous combination. At least it was for her. "I can't believe I did that."

His chest vibrated beneath her. "I will very happily give you orgasms like that every day."

"It's never been like that for me," she admitted. "Not like that."

He didn't seem shocked by her admission. "I doubt you've ever given up control like that before to your partner. You are submissive, baby. You just need to embrace it."

If a man had said that to her a year ago, it would have brought her hackles up. She was no one's doormat. But the more she learned about this lifestyle, the more she realized that wasn't what submission was at all.

She tilted her head to look at Drew where he sat on the floor at Beth's feet. More often than not, that was his position when they were sitting around talking with their friends at the club. He appeared to be completely relaxed as he chatted with Jeff, who was also kneeling on the floor beside his own mistress. It wasn't typical as far as the outside world was concerned, but here it fit.

And Drew wasn't a pushover. At their submissive meeting, he'd taken charge and led the conversation like a pro. She'd known he was a firefighter, but she'd learned from Ali he was a captain. He wouldn't have gotten in that position by letting people walk all over him.

Returning her attention to Justin, she brushed her lips against his neck, and he tightened his hold on her. "I'm trying."

They ended up staying for another hour before Justin decided he was ready to leave. While she wasn't feeling as needy anymore, that didn't mean she wanted the night to end.

Kim had expected him to head back to her place, but instead he drove in the opposite direction. She wasn't concerned as to where they were going, which said a lot. Her normal need for control would have had her asking questions.

Fifteen minutes later, they pulled into his driveway. "I should have had you pack a bag," he said before exiting the vehicle and coming to open her door.

"It's okay. With this coat, you can't tell what I'm wearing." She lowered her voice, knowing what it would do to him. "I won't have to worry about doing the walk of shame tomorrow."

Justin crushed her against him and gave her a lingering kiss. The air around them was cold, but her internal temperature was heating up as his lips moved against hers. "Let's get inside."

She laced her fingers with his and they made their way to the door. His thumb grazed across the skin of her wrist as he turned the key, letting them into his house. Given the incredible orgasm she'd had earlier, she couldn't believe how much she wanted him again.

He pushed the door open and led her inside before locking the door behind them. Tossing his keys down, his gaze met hers and her heartbeat kicked up another notch. He stalked toward her, pinning her against the wall. "You're wearing too many clothes again."

Kim met his gaze, loving the heat in his eyes. "Maybe you should do something about that."

His reaction had heat rushing to her core. He cupped her face with one hand as he captured her mouth with his. With his other hand, he began undressing her.

Her coat hit the floor first. Then her dress. His hands explored with every inch of skin he exposed. He was still fully dressed...coat and all...while she stood in his living room in nothing but her shoes. For some reason, that realization made her incredibly hot.

Justin's hand grazed over her abdomen as he slid lower until he cupped her sex. He hummed as he moved his fingers through her heat. "You're so wet, baby. I've been dying to taste you all night."

"Please."

He knelt on the floor in front of her and ran his nose along the neat patch of hair between her legs. "I love it when you beg me."

She threaded her fingers through his hair, closing her eyes and letting her head fall back against the wall with a thump.

Bang. Bang. Bang.

At first, the sound of someone banging on the door didn't register.

She was too in the moment. It was only when Justin stood, leaving her, that she noticed.

Whoever it was, banged at the door again. It sounded as if they were trying to break through the door. After the third series of knocks, it was clear they weren't going away.

"Go to my bedroom. I'll get rid of whoever it is and we'll pick up where we left off."

Kim didn't bother to gather her clothes. She wouldn't need them until morning. Rushing down the hall, she ducked into his bedroom.

Mumbled conversation followed the sound of the door opening. She couldn't tell what they were saying, though. Not unless she opened the door. And given her current state of undress, she was afraid whoever it was would glance down the hall and see her.

Walking over to the bed, she sat down and waited, anxious for whoever it was to leave so she and Justin could pick up where they'd left off.

CHAPTER 24

"Thank fuck you're here. Why aren't you answering your phone?"

Justin took a step back as Mark pushed his way into Justin's house. One look at his best friend told him something was wrong. "What's going on?"

Mark ran a frazzled hand through his hair. "Dad's been taken to the hospital, and I need to get there. I told mom I'd tell Kim, but she's not answering her phone. Ali isn't either, so they're probably together. I went by her house and her car's there, but she isn't, so I tried Ali's apartment. They aren't there either. I need to find her, but I don't know where else to look."

The euphoric high Justin had been on a few minutes before turned sour in his gut. "Back up. Davis is in the hospital? What happened?"

"He went out to the car to get something and slipped on some ice, Mom said. They think he may have broken his leg."

Okay, that wasn't as bad as he'd feared. Still, Kim would want to know and be there for her parents. Hell, he wanted to be there. But first, he needed to get Mark out of his house. His best friend finding Kim in Justin's house...especially in her current state...would only make things worse.

"I tell you what," Justin said. "You go to the hospital. Be with your mom. I'll find Kim and Ali. I know a few places they might have gone."

"Are you sure?" He could see Mark was torn.

"Of course." He moved toward the door.

It was then Mark noticed the discarded dress on the floor. "Oh, man. You're on a date. I'm sorry. I'll—"

"Stop. Davis and Belinda are more important than a date. She'll understand."

He looked skeptical but nodded and went to leave. It wasn't even a question that Justin would make sure Kim got to the hospital as soon as possible to be with her family. What was more of a concern to him was how she'd take the news.

"Thanks, man." Mark embraced Justin before walking out the door.

Justin waited until his friend had gotten into his car and driven off before gathering Kim's dress from the floor and padding down to the bedroom where Kim waited. She looked up when he walked through the door.

The look on his face must have been as telling as Mark's had been. "Who was it?"

"Your brother."

She paled. "What?"

"You need to get dressed. Your dad slipped and fell. They think he may have broken his leg, so they've taken him to the hospital."

Kim snatched the clothing from him. She had the dress on in a matter of seconds. "I need to go."

"Wait," he said, grabbing hold of her arm to stop her.

She looked up at him, her eyes wide.

"Unless you want your family to know we've been together tonight, you can't go racing off to the hospital minutes after your brother left my place."

It was as if the air had been let out of her sails. She pressed her lips together. Thinking.

"Your brother thinks you're with Ali." Her brow furrowed, so he supplied the additional information. "He tried to call you both, but you had your phones off." Before she could get too bogged down in the whys, he offered a solution. "I can call the club and let Ali know what's going on. We can swing by and pick her up, then head to the hospital. I told your brother I might know where you'd be, so it wouldn't be out of the question that I'd drive you."

Kim nodded and he dug his phone out of his pocket. He'd turned it off, the same as Kim, before they'd entered the club. While it was powering up, he helped her into her coat and escorted her to his vehicle. Before backing out of his driveway, he dialed the club's main number. The phone rang in both Katrina's office and the bar.

"Hello?" Chase answered the phone. Given the private nature of the club, they never answered with anything other than a plain greeting.

"Chase, it's Justin. I need to speak with Ali. It's an emergency."

"Sure. Just a minute."

Chase put him on hold as Justin drove toward the club. A few minutes later, Ali came on the line. "Justin?"

Justin filled Ali in on what was going on. She agreed to be waiting in the front foyer for them in ten minutes.

He pulled up to the curb in front of Serpent's Kiss and moments later, Ali emerged from the old building. She was still in her club clothes, but that was okay. He and Kim had talked on the way and decided it was best to be as honest as possible. She and Ali had been out clubbing. It would have been difficult to explain their attire with any other explanation.

It took another fifteen minutes to get to the hospital and another five to figure out where they needed to go. Kim's mom saw them first. She stood, drawing Mark's attention. His best friend stood, bracing his hands on his hips. "Where have you been?"

A flash of guilt swept across Kim's face. "Ali and I were at a club."

"And you couldn't answer your phone?" Mark asked.

"Stop it," Belinda said. "No one knew your father was going to get hurt. Kim's allowed to go out and have fun."

Mark didn't seem happy with the reprimand, but he let it go.

Belinda embraced her daughter. "I'm glad you're here."

"Thanks, Mom." Kim closed her eyes and held her mother close.

Justin decided to steer the conversation in a different direction. "How's Davis?"

"They took him to have his leg X-rayed about a half hour ago and they aren't back yet," Belinda said.

It took another forty minutes before someone came out to talk to them. Unfortunately, they'd only allow family members into the door, so Justin and Ali hung back.

"You doing okay?" Ali asked.

He glanced over at her. "I'm fine." His response was clipped, but it was the best he could do. All he'd wanted to do as they sat in the waiting room was to hold Kim's hand. Sadly, he'd been forced to sit there, hands folded in his own lap, while he'd watched Kim constantly fidget with anxiety. He hated being so close to her and yet so far away at the same time.

Ali flipped the page on the magazine she'd been perusing. "It's a good thing Mark's distracted tonight. You two aren't hiding it well."

"We haven't touched each other."

Grinning, Ali nodded. "True, but that doesn't mean you haven't been sending off signals."

"What are you talking about?"

She shrugged. "All the sly glances you've been shooting each other's way. And that longing look on your face when she left the room..."

Justin wanted to deny it, but he couldn't. He'd wanted to go with them and be the support Kim needed, but instead he was left sitting on his ass feeling useless.

Not able to stand sitting any longer, he stood. "Do you want anything from the vending machine?"

"No, I'm good," Ali said, going back to her magazine.

He strolled into the hall, heading for the elevators where the vending machines were located. He heard hushed, but agitated voices.

As he drew closer, he realized who it was. "Where were you tonight?" Mark demanded.

"I told you. I was at a club with Ali." He rounded the corner and nearly lost his shit. Mark was standing way too close to Kim. Her palms were pressed against the drywall, trying to put some space between them, but her chin lifted in defiance.

"What club? And how did Justin know where to find you?"

This wasn't good.

"Since when do I need to clear my whereabouts with you, big brother?"

"Since you show up to the hospital with your back covered in strange red marks."

Oh hell. He hadn't even thought about that. By morning, the evidence of the flogging he'd given her wouldn't be noticeable, but it had only been a couple of hours and that dress of hers left a good portion of her shoulders and upper back exposed. She'd had her coat on when they'd first arrived, but she'd obviously taken it off and it was impossible not to notice the marks. Justin could see them from here. He was going to have to intervene. "Everything all right? How's your dad?"

At the sound of his voice, the two siblings turned. Kim looked relieved. Mark looked annoyed.

It was Kim who answered him, though. "Dad's going to be okay, but he's going to have to have surgery. They have to put a pin in his leg."

"Could you give us a minute?" Mark asked, although, from his tone, he wasn't really asking.

"I'm not sure that's such a good idea."

His friend's eyes narrowed. "Why not?"

"Because you're acting like a jackass to your sister when she's already upset because of what's happening with your dad. You need to back off." Justin knew he was taking a chance coming between Mark and Kim, but he wouldn't let his friend berate his lover for something Justin did to her.

Mark took a step back and looked at his sister. Then to Justin. Blowing out a loud breath, he marched down the hall without another word.

"Thanks," Kim said, sagging against the wall.

"Come here." Justin opened his arms, inviting her into them.

She hesitated. "Someone might see."

"I don't care."

Kim collapsed into his arms.

He hugged her close. "Are you okay?"

"Yeah." Her answer was mumbled against his chest. "Everything was okay until I took my coat off. It was hot in the room, and I wasn't thinking."

Justin glanced down at the skin in question. The impact marks had faded a lot, but anyone who knew her would be able to spot the redness a mile away. Closer inspection would have made it clear it wasn't from her simply pressing against something.

He kissed the top of her head and tilted her head up. "Why don't you head back to the waiting room and keep Ali company for a while. I'll see if I can find Mark and"—Justin's gaze lingered on where his friend had disappeared down the hall—"see if I can smooth things over."

She nodded and stepped away from him.

Justin stayed put until she turned the corner, then he went to find Mark.

It was after one in the morning before they'd gotten her dad a room. Kim had wanted to wait until he was settled before leaving. Her mom hadn't wanted to leave, so the nurse had a cot brought in for her to sleep on.

"Are you sure you don't want me to stay, Mom?" Mark asked.

Belinda Langley shook her head. "There's nothing you all can do tonight. Go home and get some rest."

Kim embraced her mom. "I'll be back in the morning. Call me if you need anything."

"Thank you, honey." Her mom kissed her on the cheek before turning to hug Mark.

Justin and Ali hung back near the door. Once her dad had been assigned a room, they'd been able to see him. Not that he would likely remember them being there. He'd been given some strong pain relief and was currently snoring in his hospital bed.

After saying their goodbyes, the four of them made their way down the elevator to the parking lot. Mark had been acting strange around her ever since he'd returned to the waiting room with Justin. He hadn't mentioned her back again, but she'd made sure to retrieve her coat and keep it securely on her body.

Justin hovered close, but he hadn't spoken to her either since their embrace in the hall. She'd needed that hug. And while she wasn't remotely in the mood to pick up where they'd left off earlier that evening, she wanted the comfort of his arms around her. She wanted to fall asleep knowing he was right there, strong and sure.

The cold night air hit them in the face when they stepped outside. Mark turned to Justin. "Can you give Ali a ride home since her place is closer to yours?"

"Sure," Justin said. "I was planning to take both Ali and Kim home."

"I can take my sister."

"I don't think that's a good idea," Justin said.

Kim confirmed Justin's assessment. "Neither do I."

Her brother didn't seem happy his plans were being questioned. "Why not?"

"For what it's worth, I don't think it's a good idea, either." Everyone looked at Ali. She'd been quiet most of the evening, staying by Kim's side and supporting her. Holding Kim's hand when she needed it since Justin couldn't. "I don't know what's going on between the two of you and I don't care. It's been a long night and you both need rest. Whatever it is, you can figure it out tomorrow when everyone isn't so jumpy."

Kim silently mouthed *thank you* to her friend.

Mark rolled his shoulders. "Fine. We'll talk tomorrow." Then he turned on his heel and headed off toward where he'd parked his car.

"Okay then," Ali said.

Justin began walking again. "Let's get out of the cold."

They piled into Justin's car and made their way toward Ali's apartment. Ali made herself comfortable in the back seat. "You two are going to need to come clean soon. Mark's going to figure it out before too long."

Justin flexed his fingers on the steering wheel but didn't comment. Neither did Kim.

Everyone was quiet for the rest of the drive. They parked in front of Ali's apartment, and she flipped the hood up on her coat. "Call me tomorrow morning and I'll go to the hospital with you."

"Thanks, Ali."

Her best friend placed a comforting hand on Kim's shoulder, then exited the vehicle.

They waited for her friend to go inside and turn on the lights before leaving. Ali's mom was still there and driving Ali crazy, but she wouldn't say anything about Ali getting in late. She may not even be in yet herself. Zelda had moved into her find another man stage.

Justin maneuvered out of the small parking lot and headed back to her apartment. He pulled into the parking spot nearest to her door and turned off the engine.

No words were said as they got out of the vehicle and made their way up the sidewalk. Justin waited behind her as she put the key in the lock and turned. He helped her with her coat before removing his own, then hanging them both in the closet. She'd wondered if she would need to ask him to stay, but he showed no signs of going. She fell into his arms, burying her face in his chest as she'd wanted to do for the last few hours.

The feel of his hands running along her back made her feel safe. She knew her dad would be okay, but seeing him lying in that hospital bed looking pale and not his usual energetic self had been a wake-up call. He wasn't going to be around forever. None of them were and they all had to make the most out of the time they had.

Leaning back, he cupped her face in both his hands and kissed her lips with the softest pressure. "Go get ready for bed. I'll lock up."

Kim didn't argue. She stopped in her small bathroom to take care of business and brush her teeth before heading into the bedroom.

Everything was how she left it. She'd had trouble deciding what to wear to the club. There were several outfits draped over the end of her bed. She picked them up and threw them into the corner. It was too late and she was too tired to worry about them tonight.

Water turned on in the bathroom as she removed her dress and threw it into the dirty clothes hamper before kicking off her heels. Her feet were killing her. At the club, she'd known she'd be sitting or kneeling most of the time, so wearing the heels hadn't been a big deal. The hospital floors, however, had not been kind to her feet. She'd spent way too much time walking and standing on the hard floors.

She was sitting on the edge of the bed, rubbing her poor feet, when Justin strolled into the room. He crossed the room and sat down at the end of the bed, more than a foot away from her. "Get into the bed and I'll rub your feet for you."

Kim didn't have the energy to argue. She pushed herself higher on the bed and he placed her feet in his lap.

The first few touches were almost painful as he worked the knots out of her feet. But slowly the pain began to ease and what he was doing felt so good. She rested her head on her pillow and closed her eyes, letting the feel of his fingers caressing her lift the tension in not only her feet but her entire body.

CHAPTER 25

Kim's eyes fluttered open. Light was streaming through the curtains. She stretched, then sat up, looking around her room. The other side of the bed was empty, but the crinkled sheets confirmed he'd stayed. She paused to listen and heard the faint sounds of movement in her kitchen.

Swinging her legs around, she lowered her feet to the floor and stood. Her brain felt full of fog. She glanced at the clock to see how late it was and was shocked to see it was after eleven. She'd slept for nine hours. That wasn't like her. A solid seven and she was good to go.

After another good stretch, she threw on a robe and crossed the hall to the bathroom. She splashed some water on her face, brushed her teeth, and took care of business before going in search of Justin.

The smell of coffee hit her and her stomach growled. She hadn't eaten anything since before they'd gone to Serpent's Kiss.

He heard her and glanced up from where he sat at her kitchen table. He was dressed in different clothes than he'd worn the night before. She frowned. Had he gone home last night? "You changed?"

Justin looked down at his clothes, then back at her. "I keep a change of clothes in my trunk in case I get grease on them. I never know when I need to be presentable in front of a client."

"Oh. Okay." She padded to the counter to pour herself a cup of coffee.

The sound of a chair scraping across the floor was followed by the feel of him behind her. His breath tickled her ear. "You thought I left?"

She shook her head. "I didn't think so, but then I saw your clothes."

He turned her around to face him. "I wasn't going to leave you alone last night."

Suddenly, coffee wasn't as important as feeling his arms around her. She collapsed into him, circling her arms around his waist. "Thank you. I'm so glad you were there with me last night, even though we had to keep our distance."

He rested his cheek on her head and held her close. "Ali's right. We aren't going to be able to hide our relationship for much longer."

"We said we'd give it a month." She met his gaze. "It's only three more weeks."

She saw something flash across his face, but it was gone too fast for her to get a read on what he was thinking. He kissed the tip of her nose and took a step back. "I made breakfast."

It was then she noticed the eggs and sausage on the stove. "It smells good."

Kim twisted to get a mug from the cabinet and resumed getting her coffee. The caffeine hit her tongue and she sighed. After a few sips, the fog dissipated and she could think clearly again.

As she sat down with her eggs and sausage, she couldn't shake the feeling that she'd upset Justin with her response. Was he ready to announce to her family that they were together? Did he no longer care about Mark and her parents finding out? Was she?

After her brother's reaction last night, Kim was afraid of how he was going to take the news. She was hoping since he knew Justin, trusted him, that it wouldn't be bad, but she wasn't holding her breath.

She took a few bites of her food, making her stomach happy. "Does Mark know about you being a Dom?"

Justin set down his coffee. "Yes."

Pressing her lips together, she met his gaze. The food she'd already eaten began to churn in her stomach. "How much does he know?"

"Enough to want to kick my ass when he finds out you're my submissive."

She wanted to disagree about Mark's likely reaction, but she knew Justin was right. It wouldn't be the first time her brother had laid someone out on her behalf. He'd done it once before when they were in high school. She'd been a freshman and one of the senior football players had cornered her in the hall outside the boys' locker room. She'd been there waiting on Mark to drive her home. Her brother had come out to find Toby Green snaking his slimy hand up her shirt right there in the hallway. Mark had broken Toby's nose and gotten suspended for a week. He'd viewed it as a win, though, because Toby hadn't bothered her again after that.

Kim finished the rest of her breakfast and her coffee. "I'm gonna call Mom and check in."

"I'll clean up." He stood and went to the sink and began rinsing the dishes.

Making her way out of the kitchen, she realized her phone was still in her coat. Rushing over to the closet, she fished her phone out of her coat pocket and saw she had three missed calls. One was from her mom, one from Ali, and one from her brother.

Crap.

Taking her phone into her bedroom, she dialed her mom first.

"Good morning, honey." Her mom sounded tired.

"Is Dad okay?" Kim asked, concerned something may have happened overnight.

She could hear movement through the phone before her mom answered. "Nothing much has changed since you and your brother left last night. The surgeon came in to see him early this morning. They've scheduled the surgery for this afternoon at three o'clock."

Kim glanced at the clock again. It was noon already. "I'll be there soon. Did you want me to pick up anything on the way?"

"Would you mind swinging by the house and bringing me a change of clothes?"

"Sure." Kim glanced at herself in the mirror and ran a hand

through her hair. She should have taken a brush to it earlier. "Did you want me to grab anything specific?"

"Just a pair of jeans, a long-sleeved shirt, and a sweater. It's been a little chilly in at times."

"No problem." Kim picked up her brush and began dragging it through her hair. "What about food? Have you eaten anything?"

"I had a muffin and some fruit this morning from the cafeteria."

"That had to be hours ago, Mom. I'll pick you up a sandwich on my way." She reached for a tie to pull her hair back. "I should be there before one."

"Don't rush. Your dad and I are just watching some television while we wait."

After saying goodbye to her mom, Kim removed a pair of jeans and a sweater from her closet and grabbed a bra and underwear from the dresser. She put her phone on speaker after dialing Ali's number and began getting dressed.

Her friend answered on the second ring. "Hey."

"Hey, yourself." Kim stepped into her jeans and pulled them up her legs and over her hips. She told Ali about her dad's surgery and that she would be heading to the hospital soon.

"Do you want me to go with you?" Ali asked.

Kim retrieved her most comfortable shoes and sat on the edge of her bed to put them on. "I don't know how long the surgery is going to last. Don't you have to work tonight?"

"I called Katrina this morning and let her know what was going on. She knows I might not be there."

Justin appeared in the doorway as Kim finished tying her shoes. "Was she upset?"

Her friend snorted. "No. Of course not. Why would she be upset?"

"I don't know." Kim didn't really know Mistress Katrina that well, but the woman intimidated the hell out of her.

"What time are you heading to the hospital?" Ali asked.

"Soon. I have to stop at Mom and Dad's first and get Mom a change of clothes. Then I told her I'd stop and get her a sandwich."

"I'll stop and get some lunch for all of us. You just worry about the clothes," Ali said.

Kim's gaze met Justin's. He was leaning casually against the frame of her door. "Thanks."

Disconnecting the call, she lowered the phone into her lap. He strolled into the room and sat down on the bed beside her. "How's your dad?"

"His surgery is at three. I need to pick Mom up a change of clothes, and then I'm going to head to the hospital."

He nodded. "Your brother just called me. Asked if I knew where you were because you weren't answering your phone."

"What did you say?"

"I told him you were probably either sleeping or on your way to the hospital." Justin sighed. "I don't like lying to him." He paused. "To any of them."

"It's only a little longer. We still don't know if it's gonna work between us." As soon as she said it, she regretted the words, but it was too late. They were out there, and she couldn't take them back.

His gaze lingered on her face before he averted his eyes and stood.

Kim knew she'd hurt him, and it tore her up inside. She felt as if she'd been punched in the gut. "I didn't mean—"

Justin held up his hand. "I know."

Not willing to let it go, she went to him. "No, you don't."

He looked at her and she could see that same look in his eyes again. It was a mix of sadness and hurt. She knew she had to fix it. It wasn't as if she didn't want to be with him.

Circling her arms around his neck, she pulled herself up on her tiptoes and brushed her lips against his. He placed his hands on her waist, holding her to him. "I want us to be together. For so long I've dreamed about being yours and the reality is so much better than any of my fantasies." She licked his bottom lip with the tip of her tongue. "But this thing between us isn't that simple."

She felt his cock growing against her belly and her body was warming, preparing for him. But they didn't have time for that. Not now. Still, she wasn't willing to let him think she wasn't sure about them.

"You deserve someone who can be everything you need and I'm still not sure I can."

He frowned and she knew what was coming. "You're submissive. You just need time and training."

"Maybe."

"No maybe." He crushed her against his body and kissed her hard, holding the back of her head. "If we didn't need to get to the hospital, I'd show you exactly what I mean, but that would take more time than we have. Plus, I don't want your brother getting any ideas and showing up on your doorstep." He kissed her again. This time, she could feel it all the way down to her toes. "Go to the hospital. Be there for your family."

"You're not coming?" she said when he stepped back, putting distance between them.

"I told your brother I'd be there around two."

Kim nodded. They needed to talk more, but he was right. This wasn't the time.

* * *

Justin hated to leave her, but it couldn't be helped. Unless they were going to make their relationship public, they had to arrive separately and act as if they weren't more than longtime acquaintances. It fucking sucked.

Mark wasn't exactly in the best mood when he'd called Justin that morning. A night of sleep hadn't helped to calm his friend down. When he'd caught up to him at the hospital, Mark told him about the marks on Kim's back. He was convinced they weren't from her leaning up against something as she'd told him...that instead, someone had done something to her. It was an awkward conversation where Justin felt like he was dodging arrows aimed directly at him.

After kissing Kim goodbye and promising to see her at the hospital, he drove back to his house, showered, and changed again. He didn't really need to take a shower, but it was something to pass the time and it kept him from dashing off to the hospital.

Kim wanted to stick to their original agreement and even if it killed him, he'd respect her wishes. She said it was her uncertainty about being a good submissive for him, and even though he believed her, it still hurt. He was tired of hiding. He'd been burying his feelings for her for too long already. They could never get that time back.

At one-forty-five, Justin arrived at the hospital and sent a text to Mark. **Hey, man. I'm here.**

In Dad's room. -Mark

Justin pocketed his cell phone and made his way to the elevator. The ride up to the sixth floor was slow. He stood toward the back of the elevator as people entered and exited on their way to see patients. By the time he reached Davis's room, Mark, Kim, and Belinda were all standing out in the hall.

Concern that something may have happened caused his chest to clench. "Hey."

Kim's gaze met his and Justin ached to hold her. It had been less than two hours, but the worry was etched on her face. He almost said screw it, but he held back because he knew that was what she wanted.

Belinda embraced him, and he held tight to the woman who had been a second mother to him. "Thank you for coming."

"I wouldn't be anywhere else." He released her and met Mark's gaze. "How is he?"

"They're prepping him for surgery. We're going to follow him down to pre-op, and then it's a waiting game." Mark looked calm on the surface, but he knew his friend better than most. He was worried.

Any additional conversation was cut short when the orderly rolled Davis into the hall. Justin hung back, letting Belinda, Mark, and Kim go first. They all made their way down to the second floor, where they were forced to say goodbye to Davis and were directed to a nearby waiting room.

The surgery would take one to two hours, so they had time to kill. Ali texted Kim not long after they got to the waiting room and Kim went to meet her friend and bring her to join the rest of the group.

It was a long two hours. Ali stayed by Kim's side and Justin kept an eye on Mark as he hovered over his mom.

"Mom."

Belinda looked over at her daughter, then followed Kim's gaze across the room. Davis's doctor ambled toward them, looking relaxed. Mark must have noticed it too because he felt some of the tension ease from his best friend.

The doctor approached all of them and they stood. "Everything went well. He's being moved to recovery, and once he's awake, they'll take him back to his room."

"When can he come home?" Belinda asked.

"If all goes well tonight, he should be able to go home tomorrow. He'll have to take it easy for a few weeks, but everything should heal just fine."

"Thank you, Doctor." Mark extended his hand to the surgeon.

The doctor shook Mark's hand and nodded. "You might want to take this time to get some dinner. He'll be in recovery for at least an hour." He looked directly at Belinda. "We have your number if we need to get ahold of you."

"I think that's a great idea," Mark said. The doctor walked away, and he turned his attention to his mother. "Come on, Mom. Let's get you something to eat."

Justin thought she was going to argue—it hadn't been that long since they'd eaten the sandwiches Ali had brought—but she nodded and gathered her things to leave. They didn't end up going far. One of the nurses had recommended a restaurant within walking distance from the hospital.

They were seated at a round table, so Justin made sure to take a seat next to Kim. Ali sat on her other side, next to Belinda. It wasn't as if they were close, but he felt better knowing Kim was at least within reach.

Mark sat on his other side, keeping a very close eye on his sister. Now that they knew his father was going to be okay, Mark's attention returned to Kim. Instead of addressing her, though, his gaze fell on Ali. "We haven't seen you that much lately."

"Life has been a little crazy. Work is keeping me busy. And, of course, my mom was in town for a while."

Belinda took a drink of her water. "Has she moved out already?"

Ali shook her head. "Not yet. She met the love of her life." She made quote marks with her fingers. "At a bar on Wednesday night and he's going to take her on a road trip to see The Grand Canyon. She wants to make love under the stars. They're leaving tomorrow."

"Davis and I went there before you kids were born." The look on Belinda's face said more than her words.

"Mom!"

"Way to go," Ali said with a grin.

Mark scrunched up his nose. "Ew, Mom."

Justin chuckled. "I think it's great."

"Yes, well..."

Luckily, the server arrived with their meals and everyone focused on their food. When the conversation picked up again, it changed to Davis's recovery. He was going to need help getting around for a while. A plan was made to cover showers, dressing, and keeping up with things around the house. Even though Justin and Ali weren't technically members of the Langley family, they'd both eagerly jumped in to offer to do their part.

Kim laid her fork down on her plate and pushed away from the table. "I'm gonna hit the bathroom before we head back."

"That sounds like a good idea." Justin stood and followed her to the front of the restaurant. As soon as they disappeared around the corner, he reached for her hand and squeezed. She leaned into him and rested her head on his shoulder for a few seconds.

They walked the rest of the way to the restrooms holding hands, separating at the last minute. He waited until she went into the ladies' room before ducking into the men's.

He was washing his hands when Mark strolled into the bathroom. "Something's going on with Kim and I think you know what it is."

CHAPTER 26

JUSTIN FROZE for a long moment before turning off the water and turning away from his friend to dry his hands. "Why would I know what's going on with her?"

"You knew where to find her last night."

After drying his hands, Justin moved to exit the bathroom. "That's a big leap to me knowing what's going on with her."

Mark followed him out. "I think she's seeing someone."

Keeping his gaze straight ahead, he continued to make his way back toward their table. "You do realize your sister's an adult, right? As much as you don't like to think about it, she does date. I'm sure she has sex, too."

His friend didn't respond right away, so Justin was thinking he was going to let it go. Instead, Justin felt Mark's hand wrap around his arm, his fingers digging into Justin's flesh. It wasn't painful, but it was meant to get his attention.

He turned and looked at his friend. Mark's breathing was more labored than it should have been for the pace they were walking. "Someone hit her last night."

Justin's eyes widened. "What do you mean someone hit her? She looked fine to me."

"I told you about the marks on her back. Someone did that to her." Mark took a step closer and lowered his voice. "I think they were from a rope or...what do you call it...a crop or something. I should have had you look at them."

Swallowing, Justin tried not to react to the disdain in his friend's voice. He knew Mark didn't understand his lifestyle, but he'd never heard him react this way. Then again, they'd never been talking about his sister before. "Maybe she likes that sort of thing."

Mark's brow furrowed, and he released his hold on Justin's arm. "She can't like that stuff, man. Kim's too..."

"Too what?"

His friend shook his head. "I just don't want to think about her into that kind of stuff."

He was getting irritated with Mark. Even if he didn't realize it, what he was saying was kind of insulting. "Kinky stuff, you mean."

"Yeah." Then he must have realized how what he was saying sounded. "I know that's your thing, man, and that's cool. But Kim..."

"Is a grown woman and able to make her own decisions."

Mark blew out a breath. "She's my little sister."

Justin just looked at him, not trusting himself to speak.

Running a hand through his hair, Mark averted his gaze. "What if she gets hurt?"

He wanted to say something along the lines of *I'd never hurt her*, but of course he couldn't say that. "I hate to break it to you, but you can't always protect her."

"I can break the bastard's nose."

Justin tried not to react. Luckily, Mark wasn't paying attention to him. His gaze had drifted to Belinda, Kim, and Ali as they made their way toward them. Apparently, they'd gotten tired of waiting for them to return.

"We were wondering if you two got lost," Kim said, eyeing both of them.

"Nope," Justin said. "You ready to go?"

Belinda finished doing up the buttons on her coat. "Hopefully, they have Davis back in his room. I'll feel better once I see him."

Once again, he took up the rear as they walked the short distance back to the hospital. Davis was propped up in his bed. He was a bit groggy but otherwise seemed okay. The nurse advised us not to stay long so he could get some rest.

Ali and I stood by the door and let Belinda, Mark, and Kim have a moment with the family patriarch.

"Did Mark grill you?" Ali asked, in not much more than a whisper.

Justin shrugged. He wasn't sure what he'd call his conversation with Mark. His friend was worried about his sister. He understood that. But Mark took his protective streak too far sometimes. Kim wasn't a little girl anymore and Mark needed to come to terms with that.

"Go home and get some rest, sweetheart. I'll be fine. The nurses will take care of me."

Belinda didn't want to leave his side. "I can sleep on the cot like I did last night."

"You couldn't have gotten a lot of rest on that thing, Mom," Kim said. "Go home. Get some sleep. Dad will be fine for one night and he'll get to go home tomorrow."

Mark placed a hand on his mom's shoulder. "Kim's right. You need to take care of yourself."

Realizing she was outnumbered, Belinda nodded. "Okay. But we're making sure the nurse has my number."

"Of course, Mom." Mark stood next to his mom as she kissed her husband goodbye, then walked with her to the nurse's station to make sure they had all her contact information.

Kim leaned over and kissed her dad on the cheek. "I'll see you tomorrow, Dad."

He gave her arm a squeeze and smiled up at her.

Justin and Ali both said their goodbyes to Davis, then left him to get some rest.

It was after eight o'clock by the time Justin pulled into his driveway. Kim was taking her mom home, and he was hoping after that she'd be coming to his place. These long days of having her so close but not being able to touch her were wearing on him.

His conversation with Mark was also weighing on his mind. They weren't going to make it the three weeks. He knew it in his gut. But Kim was still reluctant to take that final step. He knew she could be a good submissive for him, but he had to get her to see it as well.

He was putting a load of laundry in the wash when he heard a car door slam shut. His heart rate kicked up a notch at the thought of seeing her. It had always been that way to a certain extent, but it was different now. Before, it had been mixed with dread because he couldn't do anything about his feelings. That wasn't the case anymore.

She didn't get a chance to knock before he opened the door and gathered her into his arms. He buried his face in her hair, absorbing her warmth...her scent.

Her lips grazed his neck, and he felt a shiver travel down his spine. His love for this woman filled his chest and he wanted so badly to be able to tell her.

Taking her face in his hands, he lowered his mouth to hers. The kiss wasn't rushed. It was soft, yet firm. Loving, yet possessive. Her lips glided against his.

Justin ran his tongue along the seam of her lips, and she opened her mouth, allowing him inside. His tongue caressed hers, dancing, playing. He loved kissing her.

Kim snaked her hand between them and began unzipping her coat. Once the zipper was free, he helped her push it off her shoulders and onto the floor. "That's better," she mumbled against his lips.

He hummed and kissed his way down her jaw to her neck. "Much."

She canted her head to the side, giving him better access as she threaded her fingers through his hair. "Make love to me."

He hadn't planned on having sex tonight. Yes, he wanted to, but he always wanted to have sex with Kim. "You're sure, baby?"

"Yes." She gazed up at him. "I need to feel you inside me. I want to forget about everything but you."

Placing another kiss on her lips, he released her. "Get yourself ready for bed. I'll be there in a minute."

Kim nodded and made her way down the hall to his bedroom.

He took his time checking the doors and turning off all the lights, needing to calm down a little. The last thing she needed tonight was for him to jump her. She'd asked him to make love to her, not fuck her senseless.

The sight of her lying naked on his bed was something he wasn't likely to forget anytime soon. He'd expected to find her in his bed, under the covers, preferably naked. But she wasn't in his bed. She was on his bed. Laid out like a dish waiting to be devoured.

Kicking his shoes into the corner, he crossed his arms at the waist and lifted his shirt up his torso and over his head. He threw it onto the floor and crossed to the bed. The mattress dipped under his weight as he crawled on top of her, bracing his weight with his arms. "I thought you'd be in bed."

She gazed up at him without an ounce of shyness. "I was waiting for you. I was afraid if I got under the covers, I'd fall asleep."

Her hands grazed his chest, gliding over his nipples before she circled her arms around his neck. He gazed down at her, his erection pressing painfully against his jeans. "And you don't want to sleep."

Kim shook her head, the motion causing strands of her hair to tickle his forearms. "No. I don't want to sleep. Not yet."

His cock pulsed at her words. He eased himself on top of her and captured her mouth with his.

* * *

There were so many times today when Kim had wanted to touch Justin. Her dad rarely got sick, and seeing him in a hospital bed, hooked up to monitors, was difficult to process. It was as if all at once she was hit with the fact that he wouldn't always be there.

Sadness had gripped her and all she wanted was to fall into Justin's arms and have him tell her everything would be okay. Given how independent she usually was, it felt wrong to need someone like she felt she needed him.

But as he pressed her body into the mattress, the comfort she'd been seeking warmed her body in ways she never thought possible. She'd had boyfriends before, but never once had she felt connected to them the way she did Justin. Wanting to see him...talk to him...feel him...was a new experience for her when it came to men.

She turned her head to give him access to her neck as he licked his way down the column of her neck, and then back up to take her earlobe into his mouth. He suckled it and worried it between his teeth, sending little tingles shooting down her body. She'd never had someone play with her earlobes before and she found she liked it. At least from him.

Her hips lifted off the bed of their own accord, seeking the friction she so badly desired. She could feel his length, hard and firm against her thigh.

"Patience, baby."

"I want you. I want to feel you inside me." She paused as an overwhelming rush of emotion came over her. "I need you."

He skimmed his hand down the length of her body, resting it on her hip, and lifted his head to meet her gaze. She had no idea what he saw, but he placed a firm kiss on her lips and scurried off the bed.

She watched as he removed his jeans and socks, kicking them to the side. Then he opened the drawer in his nightstand and fished out a condom. It only took a few seconds for him to tear the package open and roll the protection down his length.

Justin stood beside the bed, looking down at her. He brushed the hair away from her face and trailed the back of his hand along her cheek. "Push yourself up onto the pillows."

Doing as he asked, she lowered her head onto the soft pillow and sighed in contentment as he positioned himself between her legs. He placed two fingers at her entrance, circling before pressing them inside.

Kim closed her eyes and arched her back as he massaged her inner walls. She was wet and ready for him.

The mattress moved under his weight, but it wasn't his cock she felt next. It was his mouth. He slid his fingers in and out of her as he licked her swollen flesh. She wanted his cock inside her, but this felt so good, too.

His tongue began to circle her clit and she felt her orgasm building. She reached down, fisting his hair, not sure if she wanted him to stop or keep going.

With his free hand, he removed her hand and placed it on the bed. "Keep your hand on the bed. I'm not stopping until you come all over my face."

Heat zinged through her and zeroed in on her clit. She arched her back, silently begging for more.

He traced her lips with the tip of his tongue before returning to her clit. It seemed to go on and on and her chest was heaving with her exaggerated breaths. She was so close, but she needed a little more. Just a little more pressure to her clit and she'd be flying.

Sweat beaded on her body and she gripped the sheets with white knuckles. Her entire body was vibrating.

Then he took her clit into his mouth and sucked as if his life depended on it.

Her body collapsed in on itself. Something between a cry and a scream left her lips as she rode out her climax. Wave after wave hit her, prolonging her release.

Then she felt him. Not his fingers. Not his mouth. He thrust his cock into her in one fluid motion, sending another shock wave through her system.

"Breathe, baby." His lips hovered over hers and she could smell herself. Her scent wafted off him, marking him as hers, and a sense of possession gripped her. He was hers.

She needed to touch him. To show him how she felt because she wasn't sure she could put it into words. No man had ever made her feel the things he did. "I want. To touch. You."

Her words were broken up between her ragged breaths, but it didn't matter. He licked across her bottom lip and whispered, "Touch me."

Kim wrapped her legs around his waist and ran her hands up his muscular back. He kissed her, plunging his tongue deep into her mouth as he pumped his hips, driving his cock into her sex. They couldn't get any closer, and yet she couldn't seem to get close enough. She wanted more. Always more of him.

His lips never left hers as his hand moved lower, bracketing her hip, holding her exactly where he wanted her. He ground his pelvis against her clit, and she felt another orgasm building.

This one didn't hit her with as much force as the first, but that didn't lessen its impact. He swallowed her screams as she rode out her climax before grunting his own release.

Justin rolled over and pulled her onto his chest. He was breathing as hard as she was and she closed her eyes, not wanting to let go of the moment.

They lay there as their breathing returned to normal. His fingers brushed through her hair, relaxing her even more. "I need to go clean up."

"Okay." She didn't move.

He chuckled. "That means I need to get up."

Reluctantly, she let him go.

Kim rolled over and watched him stroll into the bathroom. Once he was out of sight, she flopped onto her back and sighed. The man made her feel as if she had no bones left in her body every time they were together. It didn't matter if the sex was hard and fast or if it was slow and gentle. Her body would take him any way it could get him.

As that thought resonated through her post-orgasmic brain, her worries surfaced again. She wanted a future with him. Wanted it more than anything she'd ever wanted in her life. But the fear that she couldn't be everything he needed still plagued her. He deserved a submissive who could serve him without overthinking everything.

Was she able to do that?

Justin emerged from the bathroom in all his naked glory. He sat down on the edge of the bed next to her and reached for her hand. "How are you feeling?"

That was a good question. But he wasn't asking her about her mental state. Or at least not in regards to the thoughts currently swirling around in her head. "Tired."

"Your dad's going to be all right. He's strong." That grin that did things to her insides pulled at his lips. "And stubborn."

She squeezed his hand. "I know. I'm glad it wasn't worse. Sometimes he doesn't realize he's not as young as he used to be."

He smiled and brought her hand to rest on his thigh. "I know the timing might not be perfect, but I'd like to take you away for a couple of days. Just the two of us."

So many emotions hit Kim at once. Her first thought was *yes, please*. But it was quickly followed by worry about leaving her dad.

Before she could come up with a coherent response, he continued. "I don't think Mark is going to let this go. You know how he is. He's not likely to let this mystery go unsolved." Justin met her gaze. "It will be so much worse if he finds out on his own. I don't want to wait for that to happen."

"And you think the two of us disappearing for a few days is going to fix that?" She was trying to follow his train of thought, but his logic wasn't making sense.

"I don't think it's going to take him three weeks to figure out that you and I are seeing each other. He's already come close to catching us once."

She hadn't known at the time it was Mark, but the thought of her brother walking in on her, naked, in Justin's bedroom had her pulse kicking up a notch and not in a good way. "You don't want to wait the three weeks." It wasn't really a question. He'd hinted at it before.

"I don't." He lifted her hand to his lips and kissed the tips of her fingers. "The month was to figure out if you can be a good submissive for me."

He held her gaze, waiting for her to nod her agreement.

"I want to prove to you that you can."

Kim sat up, feeling strangely at a disadvantage lying down. "How?"

"We go away for the weekend. I'll pick you up from work Friday night and we can spend two days alone, just us."

"And we'd be playing the whole weekend?" she asked.

"Yes."

Kim wasn't sure what to say, so she took a moment to process what he was saying. She couldn't argue with his logic, but could she submit to him for two days straight? The whole problem was that, according to Ali, she couldn't get out of her own head. How were two days away going to change that?

On the other hand, maybe it would answer the question that was looming over their relationship. Could she be a good submissive for him?

It was the one thing holding their relationship back. He was right about that. The sex was amazing. And they had no issues out of bed either. The only sticking point—the only thing standing between them and a future together—was whether she could live a D/s lifestyle with him.

Justin stood. "Think about it and let me know by Wednesday so I can make the arrangements."

"Where would we go?"

He didn't seem bothered by her question...or surprised. "A friend of Katrina's owns a cabin about an hour from here. It will give us privacy and your brother doesn't know about it."

Two days in a cabin alone with Justin. Her sex pulsed at the thought.

Releasing her hand, he stood and walked around to the other side of the bed. He slid in beside her and gathered her into his arms as if their conversation hadn't happened.

Kim snuggled against his chest, letting what he'd said permeate her brain. The chances of keeping their relationship a secret from her brother for the next three weeks were slim. Justin was right about that. And it was only her concern about submitting to him that was holding her back. Every cell in her body wanted to be with him. It was only the fallout if things didn't work out that she feared. She knew that if push came to shove, her brother would choose her, and she didn't want him to lose his best friend.

She propped herself up on her elbow so she could look at him. "Two days?"

"Yes." He grazed his knuckles over her cheek and waited.

As much as the thought of giving over control to him for two whole days terrified her, she knew she needed to try. Their future depended on it. "Okay. I'll go away with you this weekend."

"And be my submissive?"

She swallowed. "And be your submissive. You'll be in control."

A wicked smile bloomed on his face and he brought her lips to his. "We are going to have so much fun, baby."

CHAPTER 27

KIM SAID goodbye to her assistant Friday afternoon and made her way to the elevator that would lead her to the parking garage. Originally, Justin was going to pick her up from work, but she didn't want to leave her car in the parking garage the entire weekend.

Over the course of the week, she'd talked to Ali more times than she could count. To say Kim was nervous about this weekend was putting it mildly. She was going to be giving up control of everything to Justin for two whole days. While that might not seem like a big deal to some people, for her it was huge.

As if reading her mind, Ali's ringtone filled her vehicle as she pulled out of the parking garage. "How you holding up?"

The hint of amusement in her best friend's voice had her rolling her eyes. "I'm not going to chicken out, if that's what you're asking."

"Didn't think you would."

A horn honked somewhere behind her. It was a quarter after five on a Friday afternoon in downtown St. Louis. Traffic was horrible. Normally, Kim didn't make it out of the office until after six, which meant she missed the worse of the traffic. Maybe she should have told Justin to pick her up later. "I want this to work, Ali.

"It will. Just try not to overthink it. Trust him to take care of you and let everything else go. You might surprise yourself. I mean, look at Drew. He's in charge at his job, but he submits to Beth. You've seen them together." Another horn sounded, but this time it was through the phone. "Learn to use a turn signal."

Kim chuckled.

"I hate Friday traffic," Ali mumbled.

The exit Kim was looking for finally appeared and she eased her vehicle into the lane she needed. "I'm not used to it anymore. I'm usually still at the office."

"You work too much."

"I have to or someone else will end up in my job." It was a sad reality that to be at the top of her profession, she had to put in a lot of hours. Most days, she arrived before seven and left after six. She did try to take weekends off, but sometimes she didn't even get that.

"Well, try not to worry about work while you're with Justin."

Kim breathed a sigh of relief when she turned onto her street. One of the advantages of living in the city was that she didn't have a long commute. "Something tells me I won't have a choice."

Ali giggled. "True."

When Kim pulled into her parking spot outside of her apartment, she spotted Justin already there waiting. "He's here."

"Hey." Kim looked away and turned off her engine. "Stop stressing and have fun."

Taking a deep breath in, she released it. "I'll do my best."

"Love you."

"I love you, too," Kim said. "I'll call you when I get back."

"You'd better. I want all the details. Not like I'm seeing any action lately." Before Kim could comment on that, Ali added, "Later," and ended the call.

Kim snatched her purse from the passenger seat and stepped out of the car. Justin exited his vehicle and followed her up the walkway. As she put her keys in the lock, she felt his body press against her back. She closed her eyes and turned the key, wanting to get inside so she could get her hands on him. It had been three days since they'd seen each other. Sure, they'd talked and texted since then, but it wasn't the same.

She pushed the door open and hurried inside. Within seconds, he was on her. Justin backed her against the wall and kissed her hard. By the time he came up for air, she was ready to cancel their plans and spend the entire weekend there in bed with him.

"Are you ready to go?"

It took a moment for her to register what he'd said. "Yeah. My bags are in my room."

He gave her another quick kiss, then headed toward her bedroom, leaving her leaning against the wall, still trying to catch her breath.

It felt like only seconds had gone by when he returned carrying the two suitcases she'd packed. "You do realize we're only going to be gone for two days, right?"

"I wasn't sure what to bring. You didn't tell me anything besides we're going to be staying in a cabin."

Justin grinned and opened the door once more. He gestured for her to go first, so she pushed off the wall and walked back outside.

After locking up and loading her bags into his car, he drove east toward Illinois. She sat back and tried to relax as the city gave way to open fields.

With the city lights behind them, she needed to fill the silence with something. The silence was killing her. "Have you ever seen Ali play with a Dom at the club?" Kim had been a member for almost four months now and she'd never seen her friend do anything but hang out and work.

"I have."

When he didn't elaborate, she pressed him for more information. "Who?"

Justin glanced over at her, then back at the road. "She's played with a handful of Doms. No one recently, though."

"Why?" She was pretty sure she knew why, but she wanted to get his opinion.

He shrugged.

"Come on. You've been there longer than I have. Isn't it odd that she's a member of the club and hasn't played with anyone in months?"

Again, he glanced over at her. "Have you asked Ali?"

She hadn't. Ever since Kim had joined the club, the focus had been on her. And then on her and Justin. She hadn't thought to ask her friend why she didn't play with anyone. "It hasn't come up."

They lapsed back into silence again as they continued to drive. Justin turned off the highway and they drove another twenty minutes before he turned down a two-lane road with no lines. "Are we almost there?"

He grinned. "Almost."

Five minutes later, they turned down a gravel road. There were no lights anywhere to be seen, which was something she wasn't used to. Even at her parents' house in the suburbs, there were streetlights, lights on houses, and from cars going past. Here there was nothing but trees and it was so dark she couldn't see the ones illuminated by the headlights.

The road curved, and then, as if by magic, a cabin appeared. It was surrounded by trees and about a fourth the size of her parents' house from what she could see in the dark. He stopped a few feet from a set of steps that led up to a small porch and turned off the car.

Justin opened his door, then went to the back to get their luggage. She followed his lead and exited the vehicle. It was so dark. Since he'd turned off the car, the only light that shone was from the moon overhead and the few stars that were visible in the sky.

He came up beside her and she jumped.

"Sorry." He didn't sound all that sorry.

"Don't sneak up on me like that."

Chuckling, he motioned toward the door. "Let's get inside before some creature decides to come out of the woods and eat us."

"Not funny," she said.

Kim took a tentative step on the first step, making sure it was solid before ascending the rest of the way to the small deck. She stood to the side as Justin set the bags down at his feet, then removed a key from his pocket.

She scanned the forest as he unlocked the door and hurried inside the moment it was open. His soft chuckle told her what he thought of her fears. "It's not funny. I'm a city girl. I'm not used to being out in the woods like this."

He brought the bags inside and carried them over to what she assumed was the bedroom...if you could call it that. The cabin was one big room with a small kitchen area on one end and a large bed on the other. It had a small table with four chairs and a couch directly opposite a fireplace.

It was then she noticed the door next to the kitchen. A bathroom, maybe? She could only hope. Kim wasn't sure how she'd fare if she had to go outside to use an outhouse in the middle of the night.

* * *

Justin was trying not to laugh at the look on Kim's face. His reasons for picking this location were because it was close and there was plenty of privacy. The nearest neighbor was over a mile away and the only person who knew where they were was Katrina, who had generously given him Garrett's phone number so he could make the arrangements. It hadn't crossed his mind that Kim would be terrified of the animals that might be hiding in the woods.

Garrett used the cabin for fishing trips during the summer, so he'd been more than happy to lend it to Justin. Especially after he'd explained to the other Dom the situation.

Putting some wood in the fireplace, Justin busied himself with getting a fire started. While it wasn't freezing in the cabin, it wasn't exactly toasty warm either and he had plans for Kim. Naked plans. And he didn't want her focused on how cold she was. He wanted her focused on him.

This weekend, they were going to start at the beginning and work their way up from there. He'd spent the week reviewing her limits list again and producing a loose plan on what he wanted to accomplish. Depending on her responses, it would have to be adjusted, but he was okay with that. Kim might not be sure she was a submissive, but he was. He'd seen the way she reacted to being dominated. He'd noticed the way her eyes dilated when she'd watched interactions between Doms and subs at the club. Now, he had to get her to see it and embrace that part of herself.

Once the fire was going, he stood and surveyed the room. He'd never been here before, but Garrett had given him a good description. The other Dom had also arranged to have groceries delivered earlier that day. They were stocked and ready to go for the weekend.

Justin walked over to Kim and ran his hands up and down her arms. "Warming up?"

She nodded. "I don't think I'm ready to take my coat off yet, though."

He grinned. "How about some dinner? Hopefully, by the time we're finished eating, the fire will have the room warmed up."

They moved into the kitchen, and he instructed her to sit before he began opening doors and finding what he needed. "I can help."

"That's all right. I want you to conserve your strength." He winked at her, and she blushed. He loved to make her blush. In some ways, Kim was very innocent. In others, she was a vixen. Kim was both comfortable in her body and shy at the same time. It was something he was excited to explore.

That thought brought a smile to his face. He had a million things he wanted to explore with her. Showing her off was only one of them.

"How was your day?" he asked as he moved about the kitchen. The list of grocery items he sent Garrett's property manager was simple. He didn't want to spend all weekend in the kitchen, so he'd opted for three meals they could eat throughout their two days at the cabin.

By the time he finished the pasta and salad, Kim had removed her coat. He dished out their plates of food and carried them over to the table.

"Thanks," Kim said, picking up her fork.

Justin took a bite. It wasn't anything fancy, just pasta and sauce, but it hit the spot on the cold evening. "How was your day?"

"Busy. I felt a little guilty leaving early when we have a campaign launching on Monday." She glanced up at him. "But I have confidence the account manager can finish it up and have it ready to go on time."

"I'm sure they can. You wouldn't put someone in charge of an account who couldn't handle it."

She smiled. "What about you?"

He shrugged. "I tore out an engine. Spent six hours getting the thing out, then found out we won't get the part we need for two weeks." He paused as he took another bite. "Luckily, this isn't the customer's primary vehicle, so they're in no rush for it."

"That's good."

They chatted a little more about work while they finished their dinner. He'd phoned Daniel last night and picked his brain about a few things and the other Dom stressed again to keep it simple. No hanging her from the rafters or anything.

Justin could feel her tension returning once she finished eating. "Did you want me to clean up?"

"No." He'd planned to have her too exhausted to worry about dishes this weekend.

Kim placed her hands in her lap and waited, at least sensing, if not knowing what was coming next.

Pushing his plate aside, he leaned back in his chair. "From now until we leave this cabin, you are to obey me. No talking back, or second-guessing my commands. Do you understand?"

He saw the muscles in her neck constrict and release as she swallowed. "Yes, Sir. I understand."

"Good." He pushed away from the table and stood. "While I clean up, I want you to remove all your clothes and lie on the bed. You're going to give me a show while I work."

She was halfway out of her chair when she paused and stared at him. "A show?"

Justin couldn't help but grin at the look on her face and the reaction he knew he'd get at his next words. "Yes. You're going to masturbate for me."

Her eyes went wide and her breathing picked up. He wasn't sure if that was due to excitement or nerves. He'd always been the one to get her off when they'd been together, but he had no doubt she had plenty of experience touching herself. For years, he'd jacked off to the vision of her bringing herself to release. Tonight, he was going to see it first-hand.

When she didn't immediately comply, he raised an eyebrow, letting her know he was waiting. Justin wondered if she would protest, but after a few moments, she crossed the room to the bed and began stripping. It took effort for him to pull his gaze away so he could begin cleaning up.

He gathered all the dishes and turned on the water. Getting the dishes rinsed and loaded into the dishwasher couldn't happen fast enough, but he also didn't want to rush it.

Kim climbed onto the bed and lay with her head on one of the pillows. She spread her legs wide, putting her pussy on display for him. His cock strained in his jeans at the sight. Her pretty pink lips called to him, begging to be tasted, but he resisted. The end result would be worth it.

She started off slowly, rubbing up and down her sex, gathering her moisture. He watched as she swirled her index finger around her clit, letting out the sweetest sigh as she began rubbing the sensitive flesh.

Justin forced himself to look away long enough to finish what he was doing. He'd never loaded a dishwasher so fast in his life.

After placing all the dishes inside, drying his hands, and turning it on, he made his way over to the bed. She looked up at him, her eyes telling him all he needed to know.

He glanced down at her hands between her legs, watching as her fingers moved. Her nipples were hard, sticking up like beacons begging for his attention. She was beautiful. And she was his.

Moving down the bed, he positioned himself so he could have an unobstructed view of her pussy. Her opening was calling to him, glistening with her arousal. He leaned in to get a whiff, then dipped his finger inside.

When he removed it a moment later, it was covered in her juices. He brought it to his mouth and sucked, savoring her flavor. It wasn't as good as getting it directly from the source, but it was damn good. And by her reaction, she liked watching him tasting her as well.

"Someone's being a very naughty girl, making herself all wet." He was curious as to how she would react. They hadn't gone down this road before.

But she responded how he'd hoped. "Yes, Sir. I'm a very naughty girl."

Justin couldn't hide his smile. "Well, I guess we should take advantage of that, shouldn't we? Don't stop touching yourself."

If anything, she picked up the pace as she rubbed her clit while he removed his clothes. Instead of seating himself between her legs, he cupped the back of her head with one hand and held his erection in the other. He placed his cock between her lips, and she opened for him, sucking him into the warmth of her mouth.

He began to thrust his hips, keeping pressure on the back of her head, moving it the way he desired. Each time her tongue rubbed the underside of his head, he felt his balls tighten. He alternated between watching his cock slide in and out of her mouth and her hand where it continued to pluck her clit in time with each of his thrusts.

"Does my naughty girl want to come?" he asked, feeling his own orgasm building.

She hummed against his cock, and he nearly lost it.

"Let me see you come."

In less than a minute, she was moaning and arching her back. He pumped into her mouth faster, her gag reflex kicking in, but it didn't seem to take away the moment. If anything, it seemed to trigger her climax. She came, sucking on his cock with a renewed vigor, and he couldn't hold back any longer.

CHAPTER 28

THE FIRST THING that registered in Kim's brain as she awoke the next morning was the smell of food. She ran her hand over the space beside her, recalling what had transpired last night...and this morning. Well, she thought it was morning anyway. So far, she hadn't seen any clocks in the cabin.

A smile pulled at her lips as she remembered him waking her up. He'd already been posed between her legs, his cock pressing against her opening, when her eyes fluttered open. Justin had waited for her gaze to meet his before he pushed his hips forward and entered her.

When she'd reached for him, he'd held her arms above her head and continued to move in and out of her pussy. He didn't take his eyes off her, but there was also a sense that she was being used for his pleasure. For some reason, that thought appealed to her. She knew it shouldn't, but it did. She wanted to be the one who brought him pleasure. And knowing he woke up in the middle of the night, wanting her, and then taking what he wanted, was a huge turn-on.

"You're awake." Sometime during her mental drift, Justin had walked over to her. "I was beginning to think I'd have to wake you up again."

The wicked grin on his face had her internal muscles tightening and heat rushing to her sex. She sat up, clutching the sheet to her chest.

Justin wasn't having it. He yanked the sheet down, exposing her. "There will be none of that this weekend. Ever, if I have anything to say about it." His gaze lingered on her breasts before returning to her face. Then he extended his hand, offering to help her up.

She placed her hand in his and twisted to place her feet on the ground. The floor was cold and she pulled her feet up to hover an inch from the ground.

"Did you bring some slippers or socks with you?"

"They're in my bag." Which was by the door.

He released his hold on her and went to get her bag. Justin was barefoot and didn't seem bothered by the cool floor. Then again, she rarely ran around without something on her feet.

Returning with her bag, he placed it on the bed beside her. "Put something on your feet, use the bathroom if you need to, and join me in the kitchen."

She nodded and waited until he'd gone back into the kitchen before digging through her bag to find her fuzzy, lounge around for the day, socks.

After slipping them on, she lowered her feet to the floor once more and stood. The urge to grab the quilt off the bed and wrap it around herself was hard to resist. She wasn't used to running around naked, but something told her that if she and Justin stayed together, it was going to become a regular occurrence.

She made a detour in the small bathroom before joining him. A huge stack of pancakes, a plate of sausage, and a bowl of scrambled eggs greeted her when she approached the table. "What would you like to drink?" he asked. "We've got milk, orange juice, coffee, or water?"

"Coffee, please." She needed her coffee first thing in the morning. Especially since she didn't know what the day would hold.

Justin poured two cups of coffee and in one he added milk and sugar. He carried them over to the table, placing them both side by side, and sat down. It was only then that she realized there was only one place setting, and all the food was on his side of the table.

He turned toward her, his legs spread wide. "Come eat before it gets cold."

Surely, she had to be missing his meaning. Did he really want her to sit on his lap while they ate breakfast?

But it quickly became obvious that it was exactly what he wanted. He sat there, waiting.

Still, she needed to be positive. "You want me to sit on your lap?"

"Yes." When she didn't move, he quirked an eyebrow at her in that way to let her know he expected her to act or respond.

She walked over to him and sat down on his leg, her pussy rubbing against the coarse material of the jeans he wore.

Justin lifted her, brought both his legs together, and sat her back down on his lap. Her feet dangled on the other side of the chair.

"I thought you'd be hungry," he said when she didn't move. "I know I'm starving."

It still felt odd to be sitting on his lap like this, but she began loading food on the plate.

"More."

She glanced at him, not understanding.

"That's not enough for both of us."

One plate. They were going to be sharing.

Kim placed four more pancakes onto the plate before loading it up with sausage and eggs. There was almost nothing left in the serving trays once she was done. If he knew they were going to be sharing, why didn't he just use the one plate instead of dirtying more dishes?

Kim thought she got her answer a moment later. "You will feed me a bite, then feed yourself."

"I'm feeding you?" she asked.

He ran a hand down her thigh, and it sent a warm rush of moisture to her center. She'd never fed a guy before, but if that was what he wanted from her, she could do it.

She plunged her fork into the eggs, making sure they were secure enough they wouldn't fall off, and lifted them to his mouth. His lips closed over the fork and she pulled the fork away. Then she gathered some eggs for herself and took a bite. They were fluffy and perfect.

Everything was going well until she dropped some syrup onto his chest. He glanced down at it, then at her. "You made a mess. I think you should clean it up."

Kim twisted to get up, but he held her firmly. She looked at him, unsure at first what he wanted.

Then she caught the look in his eyes. Given how their weekend had gone so far, sexy and sensual seemed to be on the top of the menu. Lowering her head, she used her tongue to lick the rogue syrup from his chest.

His response sent a thrill through her. A deep rumble sounded from his throat and his fingers dug into her hip. She was kind of liking this level of power she had over him.

Justin's hand came up to grab the back of her head and brought her lips to his. He captured her mouth and thrust his tongue inside. The taste of pancakes and syrup filled her senses as he sucked on her tongue.

All too soon, he ended the kiss and she released a quiet whine in protest. Justin chuckled. "Patience, baby. Let's get through breakfast and we can play."

"What if I want to play now?" she asked, dipping her head a little and giving him her most seductive look.

He gave her nipple a hard pinch. "Behave."

She gave a yelp. "Not fair. You can't kiss me like that, then leave me hanging."

"Yes, I can. I'm your Dom, remember?"

Kim blew out a breath and willed her body to calm down. It wasn't easy to do either with her being naked on his lap and his erection pressing into her leg. He was as worked up as she was, but she did as he wanted and turned her attention back to the food.

Everything was going okay until she placed the last bite of food into his mouth. She'd stopped eating a few minutes before, already having eaten more than she normally would. He was still hungry, of course, and ended up polishing off the rest of the pancakes, eggs, and most of the sausage.

Before he'd finished chewing, he repositioned her like she weighed nothing, placing her legs on the outside of his and her back to his chest. She was about to ask him what he was doing when she got her answer. His mouth went to her neck and his hands cupped her breasts. His teeth nibbled at the sensitive flesh between her ear and shoulder while his hands massaged her chest. She'd never thought of her nipples being overly sensitive until the first time they'd slept together. Now she knew it was because the guys she'd been with before had been too gentle...too careful. Afraid of hurting her.

Justin didn't shy away from inflicting a little pain. But she found she liked it. At least, her body did. A shot of electricity went straight to her clit every time he tortured her nipples.

"Are you wet for me yet?"

His whispered words did nothing to cool her down. She wanted to touch him, but in her current position, her access to him was limited. "Yes."

He smacked her breasts. "That's not how you address me when we're playing."

"Yes, I'm wet for you, Sir." Why did him reminding her they were playing make her even hotter?

Justin hummed against her skin, and she felt it all the way down to her toes. "I do love it when you call me Sir."

One of his hands left her breast and trailed down her stomach to her legs. She leaned back into him as his fingers skimmed over her lips and dipped into her sex.

"Such a good girl. You are getting all wet and ready for your Dom."

"Yes, Sir. I'm ready for you." She was always ready for him."

His lips brushed over her ear. "That's good, because you're going to come all over my fingers, and then you're going to ride my cock like the naughty girl you are."

* * *

Kim sucked in a breath at his words, and he felt her inner muscles react to his words, which stifled his own groan. His cock was painfully hard, confined in his jeans, but he knew if he hadn't been dressed, he'd already be buried deep inside her. As wonderful as that sounded, it wasn't what he wanted.

Bringing his other hand down between her legs, he began playing. He wanted to have a little fun, so he set out to tease her but not give her enough to find release. The benefit was seeing her reaction. Justin learned what she liked and what she loved. Like the fact that her muscles tightened and her breathing sped up when he'd played with the skin between her pussy opening and her asshole. Most guys enjoyed being stimulated there, but it wasn't an area that got a lot of attention on women.

He continued to test it and after a while, he wondered if it was the area itself or what it hinted at that contributed to her reaction. Was it the fact that she didn't know if he was going to go lower? She'd marked anal sex as a soft limit and that she'd never tried it on her list. Given her reaction, he was going to have to add that to the things for them to try and soon. The thought of plunging his cock into her ass had him nearly coming on the spot.

It meant it was a good time to end this game and bring them both some relief. "Are you ready to come, baby?"

"Yes, Sir."

She'd barely gotten the words out before he moved his fingers where he wanted them. One was poised directly on her clit, while the other thrust in and out of her hot sex. He had her so lubed up and ready for him, he couldn't wait to drive his cock into her.

Kim's orgasm built fast. She clutched at the chair, her legs, anything she could reach. "Put your arms around my neck."

Her immediate compliance meant she was rewarded as he sucked the skin of her neck into his mouth. She arched her back, thrusting her tits up and giving him a perfect view of her hard nipples. He wanted them in his mouth, but that would have to wait until later.

Her climax came the moment he bit down on her neck hard enough to leave a mark. Her arms pressed against the back of his head as a high-pitched squeal surged from her lips. She rode his fingers until the shock waves subsided, then collapsed against him.

Justin gave her a few moments to catch her breath, then he picked her up by the waist and turned her so she was straddling his lap. He took possession of her mouth and was pleased when she met him with equal enthusiasm. "Unfasten my jeans, baby. I want to fuck you."

Kim's fingers tickled the skin along his waist as she worked the button free. Once she'd pulled the zipper down, he lifted his hips enough to push the fabric out of the way. He hadn't bothered with underwear this morning, which turned out to be a great idea.

Grabbing the condom he'd left on the table within reach, he handed it to her. While he was used to using protection with his partners, he hated it with her. It was an inconvenience he didn't want. She was on birth control, so he could forgo it, but it was an extra layer of protection he'd always employed when it came to sex. And as much as he wanted to say fuck it, he would suck it up until she made her decision. Once she was really and truly his for the long term, there would be nothing between them.

With the protection in place, he lifted her and brought her entrance in line with his cock. He lowered her down in one fluid motion, not stopping until every inch of his cock was buried inside.

They both groaned as her pussy hugged his length. He gave her another hard kiss. "Put your hands on my shoulders and ride me, baby. I want to see your tits bounce as you fuck my cock."

Kim braced herself, then began to move. He held on to her hips, helping to guide her movement as she slid up and down his length. The urge to take over was strong, but he let her control the movements. Plus, it gave him the opportunity to take in the view.

He'd never seen a more beautiful sight. Kim's head was back, her eyes closed as she concentrated on what she was doing and feeling. Her breasts were calling to him as they jiggled each time she lifted and lowered onto his cock. Justin could already feel the energy growing in his balls and knew it wouldn't take much longer before he exploded. But he needed to get her there first.

Dipping his head, he captured one of her nipples into his mouth.

She gasped and her nails dug into his shoulders. He felt his orgasm building and knew he wouldn't be able to hold it at bay for much longer.

Justin increased the suction on her nipple, giving it a few playful nips as he positioned his other hand around her waist. Turning his hand, he placed his thumb directly over her clit.

She reacted exactly the way he'd wanted her to. Kim tried to pick up her pace, but her movements were erratic as she climbed higher toward her climax.

He used his other hand to guide their movements, helping her with the pace. Lifting his hips, he drove deeper, harder, aiding in the goal. Needing that release as much as she did. "Let go, baby. Let me feel you come on my cock."

"Justin." The sound of his name in that begging tone had him driving into her harder. He'd made plenty of women beg over the years, but none of them had affected him the way she did.

Then he felt it. Her interior muscles clamped down on him, released, and then clamped down again in rapid succession. He bit down on her nipple, knowing it would increase her pleasure, and was rewarded with the scream he'd been waiting for. It was his signal that he could let go.

His own orgasm hit him hard and felt as if he was giving her part of himself. If he hadn't known before that he was in love with Kim, he would be a fool to deny it now. He might be her Dom, but she owned him, and it would kill him if she chose to walk away.

"You okay?" He kissed the side of her head. After she'd come, Kim had leaned forward to rest her head on his shoulder.

"I think so. Just don't ask me to move anytime soon. I don't think I can stand anymore."

He chuckled and stood, palming her ass to hold her up.

Kim wrapped her arms around his neck. "What are you doing?"

It wasn't the easiest to walk with his jeans around his ankles, but he could manage. Besides, he wasn't going far.

The couch was only about ten steps away, but it took him twice that since he couldn't do more than shuffle given his current clothing situation. As they'd made their way to the seating area, his cock slipped out of her, driving home the fact that he needed to go clean up.

Justin placed her on the couch and draped a blanket over her. "I'll be right back."

She huddled under the cover, a look of tranquility on her face.

He bent over to pull his jeans up far enough that he could walk, then headed for the bathroom.

After disposing of the condom, going to the bathroom, and washing his hands, he went to join her. They had nothing to do today except hang out and have as much sex as they both could handle. He didn't want to overwhelm her, but he was going to push her limits a little. At some point, he wanted to play with a few of the toys he'd brought with him. But for now, he was content to sit with her, talk, and watch the fire. Besides, he needed a little recovery time of his own.

CHAPTER 29

KIM WASN'T sure she'd ever been more relaxed. And she couldn't remember the last time she was this happy.

They hadn't bothered to get dressed. When Justin had come out of the bathroom, he'd quickly cleaned up from their breakfast, then joined her on the couch. He'd gathered her in his arms, holding her as if she were the most precious thing in the world to him.

She circled her index finger around his nipple as she rested her head on his chest. His heartbeat was steady under her ear and the fireplace kept them warm.

"And what are you grinning about?" he asked. They'd been talking on and off, but it had been nice to lie there together in front of the fire, watching the flames dance around.

"I was thinking how much I like this. Being here with you."

He pressed his lips to the top of her head. "I love being here with you."

She didn't miss that he'd used the word love instead of like. Kim knew he cared about her. Hell, they never would have embarked on this experiment if there was nothing there. Physical attraction alone wasn't worth the potential fallout.

Lifting her head, she met his gaze, searching to see if she was reading too much into his words.

What she saw had her breath catching in her throat. Every logical part of her brain argued with her that it was too soon, or that it was the sex. But Justin was as naked as she was, which meant she could feel every inch of him. He wasn't aroused at the moment. What she saw in his eyes had nothing to do with sex.

And it wasn't as if they were strangers. They'd also known each other for half their lives. The only people who knew her better were her family and Ali.

She lowered her mouth to his, then hesitated, remembering where they were and why. "May I kiss you, Sir?"

He smiled and threaded his fingers in her hair. "You may."

With permission granted, Kim covered his lips with hers. She kept the kiss light, keeping her mouth closed.

His hand tightened in her hair, but he didn't deepen the kiss.

She looked up to meet his gaze. "I love being with you, too."

Justin shifted beneath her. He brought his other hand up to caress her cheek. It was his turn to search her eyes. "Are you ready to be mine? No more doubts? No more waiting?"

Kim lowered her gaze. Her fears were still there. Not about her family. She could deal with her brother, and she had a feeling her parents would be thrilled. Her mom had been wanting her to find a good man to settle down with. Justin was a good man.

No, her concerns rested on whether she could be his submissive.

So instead of answering his question, she asked one of her own. "I don't know if I can be the perfect submissive."

"Baby, there's no such thing."

She bit the inside of her cheek. "I don't want to disappoint you."

His fingers massaged the back of her head, sending delicious tingles down her neck. She felt like purring. "I think you're a better submissive than you think."

Kim met his gaze again. "What do you mean?"

"You want to please your Dom."

It was true. But was that enough? "What if I screw up?"

His other hand joined the first, and she had to struggle to keep her eyes open. "I'm sure you will."

"But—"

"So will I."

She leaned into his hands. "You've been doing this for years. Why would you mess up?"

"Because I'm not perfect either." One of his hands left her hair and trailed down her neck. Her body was beginning to soften again...prepare itself for him. "But when either of us makes a mistake, we deal with it. That's how a relationship works. Even the D/s ones."

It was hard to argue with his logic. "It's hard to concentrate with you doing that."

"Doing what?" he asked with way too much innocence. She could feel his cock growing hard once more. He wasn't unaffected by what he was doing to her.

She tilted her head back, exposing more of her neck.

Justin took advantage. He guided her flesh to his lips and drew the skin into his mouth. Heat rushed to her sex, and she squirmed against him.

He nibbled his way down to her collarbone, then back up to her ear. "Are you mine?"

Even with her body warming and her need for him to be inside her again increasing with each passing second, she knew what he was asking. "I'm yours."

His hand tightened on her hair. "Again."

"I'm yours, Sir. Only yours."

He dragged her mouth to his and kissed her hard. She gasped, and he took advantage, thrusting his tongue inside. The kiss wasn't gentle, but it wasn't meant to be. This was about possession. She belonged to him. She'd always belonged to him.

Justin spread her legs and positioned himself at her entrance. Kim felt the tip of his cock rubbing against her sensitive flesh and moaned. She needed him inside her.

As if he knew what she'd been thinking, he ripped her mouth away from his and made her look at him. "No more stalling. No more uncertainty."

She nodded.

His green eyes darkened as his pupils dilated. "Mine." He pushed her down onto his erection, not stopping until she took all of him.

One of his hands dug into her hip, helping to guide the movement. He lifted his hips up while driving her down. She moved with him, needed to feel every inch of him claim her as his.

And that was what this was. There was no mistaking that. She was his and he was making sure there was no doubt in either of their minds.

Their mouths came together again as he continued to take her. Her nipples brushed against his chest with the movement, sending sparks through her breasts directly to her clit. Before him, she'd never given much time or thought to her nipples, but now they craved to be touched...played with.

He moved his mouth to her neck once more and she arched her back, silently begging him to go lower...to suck on her breasts.

Justin nipped at her collarbone. "What do you want, baby? Tell me."

"Please suck on my nipples, Sir."

"That's my good girl." A moment later, his lips clamped around her right nipple.

"Yes!" She held his head to her breasts, not wanting him to stop.

With both his hands on her hips, he drove her down onto his cock with almost painful force. He'd bent his legs to provide more leverage and while it felt great, she needed more.

Kim wanted to touch herself, but she knew she couldn't. Not unless he told her she could. And for some reason, that sent a thrill through her. Maybe he was right. Maybe she was more submissive than she'd thought. "May I touch myself, Sir?"

He released the nipple he'd been torturing and turned his attention to the other side. He gave the nipple a bite hard enough to make her yelp. "Yes. Make yourself come, and then I'm going to come inside my pussy."

Her breath caught in her throat again, but this time for an entirely different reason. He wasn't wearing a condom. And while she was on birth control, she knew the significance. She was his.

Snaking her hand between them, she slid her fingers through her wetness to find her clit. She brushed against him as he moved in and out of her and he groaned. "Get to playing with your clit, you naughty girl, or I'll have to turn you over my knee again."

Heat rushed to her center, and she began rubbing her clit. It was swollen and sensitive. She dug her nails into his shoulder, trying to anchor herself. Between Justin fucking her, sucking on her breast as if his life depended on it, and her rolling and plucking her clit, she was ready to fly.

Her orgasm hit her, and she screamed. Ripple after ripple of pleasure coursed through her body.

"Fuck!"

A moment after the word tore from Justin's throat, she felt his cock pulse within her, shooting his cum inside her. He held her hips down against his pelvis, securing her to him until he'd emptied every last drop.

Justin licked his way up her chest to her throat before capturing her lips again. He made no move to separate them and to be honest, she wasn't in any hurry either.

He caressed the side of her face with the back of his hand. "How about a shower?"

"I thought you were in charge."

She felt a sharp pinch to her ass. "I was trying to be nice, but if you insist..."

The next thing Kim knew, he was on his feet, striding toward the bathroom.

* * *

They spent the rest of the weekend in various stages of undress. Well, he did. She wasn't allowed more than socks and the occasional blanket to cover up with when she was cold. Kim had never spent so much time naked before. But considering how often they were having sex, or he was playing with her in some way, clothes would have just gotten in the way.

Sunday afternoon came way too soon. Kim wasn't ready to go back. She wanted to stay in their cocoon for a while longer.

"Got everything?" He came up behind her and placed a kiss on her neck. She was going to need to dig into her makeup drawer to find some concealer. Her neck was not only red, but there were a few hickeys as well. She loved it when he sucked on her neck, though.

"Yeah. I think I've got everything."

He picked up their bags, and she took one last look around. It had been less than two days, but so much had happened. She didn't want to leave.

"Kim?"

She shook herself out of it and joined him at the door. "Sorry. I just..."

"We can always come back. Maybe for a long weekend next time. I'm sure Garrett wouldn't mind." He opened the door, letting the cool air in. Justin had doused the fire an hour ago, wanting to make sure it was out before they left, so there wasn't anything to ward off the cold outside air.

Justin had told her more about the cabin's owner. He was from Chicago but came down to the cabin to get away from the city. "I'd like that."

After loading the bags into the trunk of his car, Justin slid behind the wheel. The car was nice and warm already, which she was grateful for. Since they were in the middle of nowhere, he'd started the car and let it warm up before they'd left—something he wouldn't be able to do in St. Louis.

They hadn't been outside the cabin since they arrived, so this was the first time she was getting to see their surroundings in the daylight. While the trees had looked ominous in the dark, they were tall and majestic with the sun shining down on them. As they drove down the drive to the main road, she almost felt sheltered by them. Safe. Of course, that might have something to do with the person sitting beside her as well.

Kim rested her head on the headrest and smiled. She'd been so worried about their weekend, but it had turned out better than she'd hoped. Not only was she feeling better about her submissive role, she was beginning to embrace it. She loved seeing his reaction when she called him Sir. Or the way his breath hitched when she ran her tongue along the underside of his erection.

She was so lost in her sexy memories that she almost missed the fact that he'd said something. "I'm sorry, what did you say?"

He chuckled. "I won't ask what you were thinking about over there, you naughty girl, but I asked when you wanted to tell your family. Did you want to see if we can get together for dinner sometime this week?"

The thought of telling her family was a sure way to throw a cold bucket of water on her libido. "I'll call my mom when we get home and see what her schedule is."

"Let me know and I'll be there." He paused. "I want to get this over with."

It should be funny, but it wasn't. Them announcing they were a couple was a big deal and one that would change a lot of things. Justin had been part of their family for almost two decades as her brother's best friend. She was hoping he'd still be that but going forward he would also be hers.

"I think Mom will be pleased. She likes you."

He glanced over at her, then back at the road. They were on the highway now and already halfway home. "It's not your mom I'm worried about." Then he corrected himself. "I am, but your dad and brother are the wild cards here. I think we can win your dad over, but I don't know how bad your brother is going to react. He's going to feel betrayed, and I can't do anything to fix that." Justin reached for her hand and laced their fingers together. "I'm not letting you go."

That warm feeling bloomed in her chest. "I'm not letting you go, either."

Justin brought their fingers to his lips and gave the back of her hand a kiss before lowering them to rest on his thigh. They drove the rest of the way in silence as they made their way back into the city.

* * *

Justin parked in front of her apartment and turned off his car. He wanted to go inside with her. Hell, he never wanted to spend a night without her again. That right there told him how head over heels he was for her.

"Move in with me." The words were out before he could stop them.

"What?"

He turned to face her, taking both her hands in his. "I want you in my bed. Always."

The muscles in her neck contracted as she swallowed, and she pressed her lips together. "Don't you think it's too soon?"

"No. We've waited seventeen years. I'd say it can't happen soon enough. Besides, if you're in my bed, I can have my wicked way with you any time I want."

He was hoping to make her laugh, and it worked. Sort of. She let out the cutest little snort. "My lease isn't up for another two months."

"That's too long."

Kim held his gaze for a long moment. "You're serious."

"I am." He squeezed her hands. "I'm done waiting. I want a life with you, and I want it now. Not in two months. Not in two weeks."

She released a loud breath. "That's a big step."

"Not as big as me asking you to marry me."

Her eyes went wide.

"I'm not asking. Yet." He ran his thumb along the inside of her wrist. "Move in with me. Share my bed. My home."

He wasn't sure what she was going to say. Kim didn't make rash decisions. She was a planner. He knew he'd thrown her a curveball, but he was hoping she'd take the chance.

Kim looked toward her apartment, and he felt his hopes sink. She wasn't ready.

"I'll need boxes."

It took him a moment to register what she'd said. When he did, he could barely contain his joy. "Is that a yes?"

She bit her lower lip and nodded.

Justin nearly leaped into her lap and kissed her. "I love you."

When she froze, he pulled back, concerned something was wrong. He searched her face. "What is it?"

"That's the first time you've told me you love me."

He hadn't thought about it, but it was true. Holding her face between his hands, he brushed his lips against hers. "I love you."

Kim looked as if she were blinking back tears. She rested her forehead against his and held his gaze. "I love you, too. I have for a long time."

"I know," he said, tucking a lock of hair behind her ear. "We've wasted so much time. No more waiting."

She smiled. "No more waiting."

CHAPTER 30

JUSTIN ENDED up spending the night at Kim's apartment and she had to admit she could get used to sharing a bed with him. She liked waking up beside him. Of course, that also meant morning sex, which she wasn't complaining about.

"I'll meet you here at seven and we'll start packing." He crushed her against his body, his hands going directly to her ass. "I'll bring pizza."

Kim couldn't believe they were really doing this. She'd lived by herself since graduating from college. It would be a huge change to share her space with someone else again. She was equal parts excited and nervous. He was right, though. They'd waited long enough. "I'll throw together a salad."

He scrunched up his nose. "If you must."

She laughed. "Vegetables won't kill you."

"Guess I'll have to get used to eating more of those, huh?" He gave her butt a squeeze as he lowered his mouth to hers.

"Definitely."

She circled her arms around his neck as their tongues tangled together. He tasted like coffee mixed with her mint toothpaste.

He released her and sighed. "I need to get going. I'll see you tonight."

Kim nodded.

After one more quick kiss goodbye, he jogged out to his car and drove away.

Heading back to her bedroom, Kim laid her clothes out on the bed and crossed the hall into her small bathroom. It was hard to believe she was leaving this place.

She turned on the water and began going through her morning routine. They'd gotten up a half hour early so he could run home before he went to the shop. As it turned out, he was barely going to make it to work before they opened because he'd convinced her they should shower together.

A huge smile grew on her face as she remembered the details of that shower. He'd made her come twice, and that was on top of the orgasm she'd had before they'd made it out of bed. She'd never come so much in her life. Before him, she'd thought multiple orgasms with a guy were a myth.

Reaching for her makeup bag, she began applying concealer to her neck. He really did love to mark her. She'd even noticed a couple of spots on her breast.

By the time she finished applying her makeup, did her hair, and dressed, it was almost seven-thirty. It was a good thing she only lived fifteen minutes from the office. Otherwise, she'd be late. And she hated to be late.

Kim strolled into the office with five minutes to spare. Her assistant was already at her desk. "Good morning, Brenda. How was your weekend?"

"Good." Her assistant tilted her head, looking at her.

"Everything all right?" Kim asked. She was tempted to touch her neck, fearing she'd missed a spot, but willed her hands to remain at her sides. It wasn't as if she could feel a hickey.

"Yeah. Fine." Brenda averted her gaze. "Um, you just missed a call from your brother. He wants you to call him."

The last time Mark had called her at work was when he'd gotten a promotion. Given it was only eight on a Monday morning, she highly doubted that was the case this time. "Thanks."

Kim flipped the light on in her office and took a seat at her desk. After placing her purse in the bottom drawer of her desk, she picked up her phone and dialed.

Her mom answered on the second ring. "Hi, honey. How was your trip?"

She'd told her mom she was going out of town, but given her job, it wasn't uncommon for her to have to travel to New York or Chicago, her mom hadn't asked for details. "It was good. How's Dad doing?"

"Going stir-crazy." Her mom chuckled. "He wants to get up and do things. The doctor told him not to overdo it, but you know your dad. He's not used to sitting around the house doing nothing. It's driving him crazy."

Her dad wasn't a big television or movie watcher. He preferred to be doing things. He liked to garden and tinker in his garage. "Maybe he can find something to do in the garage that doesn't take a lot of movement."

"We are talking about the same man, right?"

Kim laughed. Her mom was right. Her dad would never sit still. He'd find something he had to get or do that would require him to defy the doctor's orders. "Sorry, Mom. When does he go back to the doctor?"

"Tomorrow." Her mom blew out a breath.

"Sorry, Mom." Kim bit the inside of her cheek. Maybe dinner with her family this week wasn't such a good idea. "Is there anything I can do?"

"No, honey. It is what it is. We're okay." Her mom paused. "I'm sure your dad would love to see you if you have time this week."

Well, that was an opening if she ever saw it. "Why don't we all get together on Wednesday? Justin can join us. I have some news I want to share with everyone."

Her mom didn't answer right away, and Kim was wondering if her mom radar was going off. Should she not have mentioned Justin? But then it would have seemed odd if he'd shown up.

"That sounds like a great idea," Belinda said. "I'll throw together a roast. Justin has always loved my roast."

It was true. Justin always raved about her mom's cooking. Then again, his mom didn't cook all that much. A home-cooked meal to her was usually a frozen dinner she threw in the oven. "Do you want me to bring anything? Dessert?"

"No worries. I'll make some cupcakes or something. It will keep me busy."

"Okay. Well, call me if you need anything."

She hung up with her mom and debated whether to call her brother right away. Mark was not on her list of favorite people right now. He'd been a jackass at the hospital and he'd yet to apologize for it. She got why he was so protective, but his response was over-the-top. He needed to realize she wasn't a little girl anymore and she could take care of herself.

Deciding not to put it off, she dialed her brother's office. "Mr. Langley's office."

"Hi, Meg. It's Kim. Is my brother in?"

"Hi, Kim. Yep, your brother's in. Let me make sure he's not on the phone." There was a long pause. "Nope. Okay, hold on and I'll put you through."

It took almost a minute for her brother to pick up the line. "I wasn't sure if you were going to call me back or not."

Kim leaned back in her chair. "Does that mean you're calling to apologize?"

She heard a chair squeaking in the background, and then her brother sighed. "I'm sorry if I overreacted. I just...I worry about you. And when I saw those marks, I freaked. I don't like the idea of someone hurting you."

"No one hurt me." She needed him to know that. And he was going to have to get used to seeing marks like that on her from time to time. She'd really liked it when Justin had flogged her.

"Are you..."

When he didn't finish his sentence, she wondered what was going through that head of his. Probably the worst-case scenario. She only hoped his worst-case scenario wasn't her dating Justin. That might make Wednesday's dinner more eventful than she wanted it to be.

She decided to change the subject. "Can you come to dinner at Mom and Dad's on Wednesday night? Justin's invited, too." Again, she decided to add that, so it wouldn't be weird right off the bat for him to be there. She wanted to tell her family when everyone was calm and happy.

The other end of the line was quiet, and she wondered what he was thinking. "Are we going to find out about this new guy?" Mark asked.

"How do you know if there's a new guy?"

He snorted. "Please. You haven't been at your apartment the last two times I've stopped by, you had red marks all over your back at the hospital after you said you were out clubbing with Ali, and you disappeared this weekend."

She rolled her eyes. "Guess you're just going to have to come to dinner on Wednesday and find out what my news is."

"So, there is news."

"There is. And if you want to know what it is, then you'll be there."

"I'll be there."

Kim reached for the stack of papers in her inbox that needed her attention. "Good. Now, be a good brother and apologize for being a big jerk."

"I'm not a jerk." When she didn't respond in any way, he chuckled. "Fine. I'm sorry for being a jerk. Are you happy now?"

"Yes. Very." She scanned over the page in front of her. "Now, I have work to do. I'll see you Wednesday night."

"Later, Sis."

Kim rolled her eyes again. "Later."

* * *

Justin was having the day from hell. The moment he walked in the door, Sandi had pounced. A customer had come in on Saturday for an oil change and tire rotation, but when he was told he also needed some major front-end work, he'd gone off on the tech. And Sandi. The customer had only left when she had threatened to call the police.

If that wasn't bad enough, he found out the parts he'd been waiting on for two months weren't coming. His supplier couldn't source them, and so he'd had to spend three hours on the phone looking for new parts.

By the time he arranged for the parts with a new vendor and called to update the client, he knew it was going to be a late night. There was no way he was going to make it to Kim's apartment to help her pack. That only soured his mood more.

Then there was the text he'd gotten from Mark inviting him to dinner with the family on Wednesday night.

Family dinner Wednesday night. Can you come? - Mark

Justin kept his response short, not wanting to give his friend anything to read into.

Sure. What time? - Justin

The answer came back right away.

6 - Mark

Justin was relieved they weren't drawing this out, but that didn't mean he wasn't nervous about it. Kim didn't think her parents would have an issue with them being together and maybe she was right. Davis and Belinda liked him. But he still didn't want them to feel as if he were betraying their trust by defiling their daughter. He could only hope they'd realize how he felt about Kim and at least be okay with it. Especially once they found out Kim was moving in with him.

No, it wasn't Davis and Belinda that most worried him. It was Mark and there was no amount of stressing or planning or prepping that was going to alter his best friend's reaction. He was only hoping they could work through it and remain friends.

Wiping the grease off his hands, Justin noticed the time. It was almost five and not only was he not even close to being finished for the day, but he hadn't eaten anything outside of the candy bar he'd gotten from the vending machine in the lobby two hours ago.

He dug his phone out of his pocket and dialed Kim. She answered on the first ring. "Hi, sexy."

Justin laughed and it felt good. "Shouldn't that be my line?"

A door closed in the background, and he wondered if it was a car door or if she was still in her office. "I think it fits you more than me."

He leaned back on the toolbox behind him and took what felt like his first full breath since he'd arrived that morning. "I beg to differ."

She giggled.

The sound sent all kinds of warm tingles through his body. He opened his mouth to say something dirty but caught sight of one of his techs striding toward him. His heart sank and he held up a finger, letting the tech know to give him a minute.

"Hey, baby, I'm not going to make it over tonight. Today's been a nightmare and I have no idea when I'm gonna get out of here."

"That's okay. I can pack some things up on my own."

"I'm sorry." He was the one who'd suggested they move in together and he should be there to help her pack up her things. Plus, he was supposed to be bringing the boxes. "I'll do my best to get out of here early tomorrow."

"It's okay. Really. I'll be fine. I should probably sort through my closet first anyway. No need to move stuff I never use."

He could see his tech shifting on the balls of his feet twenty feet away and sighed. "I need to go. I'll call you later tonight." He paused. "I love you."

"I love you, too."

Justin hadn't wanted to hang up. Talking to her was the bright spot in his shitty day and from the look on his tech's face, there was another issue that needed his attention.

The last customer left at six and his techs not long after that. It had been a bad day all around and he couldn't blame his guys for wanting to hightail it out of there as fast as they could.

"Did you need anything before I go?" Sandi asked, peeking her head into the shop.

"No, I'm good. Just glad for the quiet. Hopefully, I can get this engine finished up."

Sandi nodded. "Don't stay too late. You need your rest, too."

He smiled. "I won't. Have a good night."

She waved and closed the shop door behind her. He listened as she walked out the front door and locked it behind her. Then there was nothing. Utter silence. It was bliss.

Justin turned back to the engine he'd been working on for what felt like forever and got to work. It was only at night when he was able to really settle into what he was doing. He loved working on cars. That was why he'd become a mechanic. But it was only at night when he was there by himself that he could let go and enjoy the process. During the day there were too many people needing his opinion, or customers to deal with.

Time fell away and he got lost in the work, which was why it took him a while to hear the tapping sound coming from outside.

He grabbed a clean towel, wiped his hands, and walked around the car to the bay door. There on the other side was Kim...holding a pizza box.

Justin hit the button to raise the door and as soon as it was waist high, Kim ducked underneath. He quickly hit the reverse button. It wasn't as cold as it had been outside, but it was still January in St. Louis.

"What are you doing here? I thought you were home packing?"

"I thought you might be hungry," she said, holding up the pizza.

He was starving, but now that she was inside in the light, he got a good look at what she was wearing. "That's not what you were wearing this morning."

She grinned and he saw mischief in her eyes. His groin tightened. "I stopped home and changed into something more comfortable."

More comfortable. Not exactly the words he'd choose to describe the skirt and sweater she was wearing. The skirt ended four inches above her knees. It wasn't tight-fitting, but that meant it wouldn't take much to flip it up and out of the way. The sweater, in comparison, clung to her chest, hugging her tits. His mouth was watering, and he wasn't sure which was causing more of the moisture: the pizza or her outfit.

He took the pizza from her and carried it to the bench he used.

Clearing off a space, he set it down, then went to wash his hands in the sink.

Kim pulled up a stool and sat down. His gaze drifted to her legs, and he had to will his libido to calm down. As much as he wanted her, he also needed food. He didn't want to get lightheaded or faint while he was taking her.

And take her he would. One of his long-time fantasies had involved her on the hood of a car. She was here. They were alone. And he was going to make that fantasy come to life tonight.

CHAPTER 31

"You look tired," Kim said as they dug into the pizza.

"Long day." He took a bite of pizza and met her gaze. "It's much better now."

"Because of me or the pizza?" She was teasing him, and it felt great.

"Both." His gaze trailed over her body before returning to her face. "Definitely both."

He scarfed down the first slice of pizza and took another, biting into it as if he hadn't eaten in days. "Did you eat lunch today?" she asked.

"I had a candy bar around one."

She frowned. "That's not lunch."

Justin shrugged. "It was all I had time for, and I barely got that down before I had to put out the next fire."

"I'm sorry you had a bad day." It was a complete contrast to hers. After her phone call with Mark, she'd had two client meetings and an executive lunch. The rest of her day had been spent catching up on emails and returning calls.

"It happens." He polished off his second slice of pizza, then smiled at her. "Part of owning my own business. Besides, if I remember correctly, you had a not so stellar day last week that I helped you forget." His wicked grin returned, and he was no longer paying attention to the pizza.

Kim slid off the stool and onto the floor. Luckily, there was a mat where they were sitting, and she didn't have to be on the concrete floor. She knelt in front of him and ran her hands along the legs of his jeans. "Would you like me to help you forget, Sir?"

He nodded and her hand went to the button on his jeans. She released it, then lowered the zipper. He was wearing underwear today, but she could work with it.

Lifting his hips, he helped her move his jeans out of the way. Without the constricting fabric of his pants, his erection stretched the fabric of his underwear. She pressed her lips against the bulge, and he groaned. "You're gonna pay for teasing me, baby."

"You don't like it when I tease you, Sir?"

Justin chuckled. "I didn't say that."

Deciding to push her luck, Kim skimmed her nose along his length before pulling the fabric out of the way. His erection sprang free, standing proud and begging for her attention. She met his gaze as she closed her mouth on the head of his cock.

The rumble that sounded deep in his chest went straight to her clit.

For some reason, she wanted to tease him. She wanted to drive him crazy. So instead of taking more of him in her mouth, she concentrated on the tip. She ran her tongue around the ridge and massaged his hole, all the time providing gentle suction with her mouth.

His hands went to her head. He fisted her hair, sending a shot of pain through her skull. She noticed he didn't tell her to stop, though.

Taking a little more of him into her mouth, she flattened her tongue along the underside of his shaft, dragging it up, and then returning her attention to his head. She did this over and over and his hold on her hair tightened. Giving a blow job had never been so much fun. Or had made her this hot.

She'd been about to take him to the back of her throat when he ripped her mouth away. His cock was glistening from her mouth, but she didn't get to look at it for long. Justin lifted her by the arms and set her on her feet. Then he flipped her around and bent her over his lap.

Kim knew what was coming before his hand connected with her ass. The sting was an electric shot to her system that sent liquid heat to her sex.

He massaged her butt before he spanked her again. "No panties?" Smack. "You deserve this spanking even more than I thought." He landed three more blows in quick succession. "You like teasing your Dom, don't you?"

"Yes, Sir."

More smacks and Kim began squirming against him, needing friction. She wanted him to touch her clit. She wanted him inside her. She wanted...more.

"My needy girl wants to come, does she?"

"Please, Sir."

But he didn't let her come. Instead, he continued to smack her ass until it was burning. Then he put her back on her feet and dragged her across the room to stand in front of a car that looked older than she was.

He left her long enough to flip the light switch on the wall behind them, cloaking them in darkness. The only light came from over his work bench twenty feet away. She could still see him, but anyone who happened to be outside wouldn't be able to see more than shadows.

Justin returned to stand in front of her. He slipped his hands under her skirt and cupped her bare cheeks. The next thing she knew, her feet were off the ground again.

Kim grabbed his shoulders as she was lifted. But before she could wrap her legs around his waist, he deposited her onto the hood of the car—the cool metal soothing the abused skin of her ass.

She didn't have a lot of time to think about that, however, before he lowered himself on top of her and captured her mouth with his. He hitched her leg up until it was braced on his shoulder. She was open and exposed and completely and totally ready for him. Her sex pulsed in anticipation of him filling her.

He probed her opening before pushing two fingers inside. His tongue mimicked the movement of his fingers, plunging in and out, twisting and massaging. She was so close to coming. All she needed was a little pressure to her clit and she'd be flying.

But he didn't give her what she wanted. Instead, he moved lower, rimming her asshole with his finger. "Once you're in my bed permanently, I'm going to start plugging your ass. I want you nice and ready for me when I take you here."

She sucked in a breath. They'd talked a little about anal sex when they'd gone over their lists, but she hadn't thought too much about it. Anal sex was one of many things she'd never tried, but she'd seen it at the club. It was something that both intrigued her and made her nervous to try. "Will I like it, Sir?"

"Based on your reaction to me just doing this..." He ran his finger once more around the outside of her hole, then pushed the tip inside.

She sucked in a breath. It wasn't painful, but it felt weird and so...forbidden.

"But not tonight." His hand moved to her hip. He reached between them, and then she felt the tip of his cock.

When he didn't move, she arched her back, trying to encourage him.

He slapped her hip in response. The sting heated her skin even more. "Stop being so impatient. You'll get my cock when I say and not a moment before, understand?"

"I'm sorry, Sir. It's just that I've been dreaming about this all day, and I want to feel you inside me."

Justin groaned and he shifted. He pushed them higher onto the car until they were both on top of the hood.

The movement had pushed her clothing up even more. Her sweater was bunched up around her armpits. She debated whether to wear a bra or not when visiting him. Going without panties was one thing, but no bra was another thing entirely. She wasn't a big girl in that respect, but she wasn't tiny either.

In the end, she'd left her bra at home. A decision she was now very happy about. Justin's gaze lowered to her breasts and without a word, he sucked her nipple into his mouth.

Kim moaned and threaded her fingers into his hair. She'd never been a big fan of men playing with her nipples before, but now she was realizing that was because they were too gentle. There was no light suction or licking. Justin went all in when it came to sex and that included playing with her breasts.

He grabbed her wrists and brought them above her head—pinning her hands against the windshield. Heat rushed to her pussy. She loved it when he held her down like this. There was something about it that sent her pulse racing in the best possible way.

Then he flexed his hips and thrust into her. His cock filled her, pushing inside until he couldn't get any farther. She felt full and hot and needy. "Please, fuck me, Sir. I need your cock."

Justin groaned, pulled out, and plunged deep into her. He released her nipple and devoured her mouth instead. The hard surface of the car was a sharp contrast to his body as he took her. Her ass was still burning, but it was all sensation and she welcomed it.

He began rolling his hips each time he thrust, giving her clit the friction it so desperately needed. She was so close. All she needed was a little...

Her orgasm hit her, and she couldn't stop the scream that tore through her. He attempted to swallow her cries, but they echoed in the spacious room.

As she was coming down from her high, she felt him shudder as he found his own release. His groan sent another shock wave of pleasure through her system, and she treasured it. He was hers.

"What the fuck?"

* * *

It took Justin a moment to register the words. He'd been so caught up in Kim that nothing else had mattered. When he turned his head, though, all the pleasure he'd felt was replaced with dread. There, standing on the other side of the bay, was Mark.

Justin released Kim's wrists, but that was about as far as he got before Mark was on him. His best friend grabbed him by the back of the neck and pulled him off Kim. He stumbled, the jeans constricting his ability to find his balance, and he hit the floor with a solid thud.

Scrambling to his feet, his gaze went to Kim. She was staring wide-eyed at her brother, who was advancing on Justin. Her clothes were still in disarray, and she seemed more concerned with the situation than with her current state of undress.

It was because he was focused on Kim that he hadn't seen Mark's fist coming. A jolt of pain surged through his jaw.

He shuffled back a few steps, then stood to his full height, rubbing his jaw. Nothing felt broken, but it was going to leave a bruise.

Mark took a step forward, but Justin was ready for him this time. "You caught me off guard before. Try it again and I'll put your ass on the ground."

It wasn't an idle threat. Justin had at least forty pounds on Mark and was in better shape. In a real fight, there was no doubt which one of them would win. Justin didn't want to fight his best friend, but he wasn't going to be his punching bag either.

Conflict in his eyes, Mark seemed to be considering his options. "What the hell are you doing to my sister?"

"Mark—"

Mark whirled around, facing Kim for the first time. "Fuck! Kim, are you all right? He didn't hurt you, did he?"

She adjusted her clothes, covering herself. "I'm fine." She slid off the hood of the car. "At least I was before you showed up and decked my boyfriend." Her hands went to her hips, and she stared her brother down.

Pride filled him. His woman was a spitfire. It only made her willing submission to him more meaningful.

Justin took the opportunity to put his jeans back in place while Mark's attention wasn't on him. He wasn't worried about Mark hurting Kim. Yell at her? Get in her face? Yeah, maybe. But Mark was usually more bluster than action. He had to be really worked up for it to come to blows and he would never hit a woman.

"Your boyfriend?" Mark's voice went up an octave.

Kim stood up straight and met her brother's gaze. "Yes. My boyfriend."

When Mark turned back to Justin, he didn't look anywhere close to pacified. "What are you doing with my sister?"

"Mark—"

"I'm asking him, Kim." Mark narrowed his eyes at Justin. "You have no idea the twisted games he likes to play with women. What he likes to do to them. What he gets off on. You probably don't know that he's—"

This time, she cut him off. "He's a Dominant."

Mark's head whipped back around, and his eyes widened. Justin could see the wheels turning in his friend's head as he put the scene he'd walked in on into perspective. "You can't..."

Kim stalked toward her brother and pointed a finger at his chest. "You don't get to tell me what I can and can't do, big brother. I'm thirty-two years old. I can have sex with whoever I want, any way I want. Got it?"

Silence hung in the air for what felt like forever. Justin wanted to go to Kim, pull her into his arms, and make the last few minutes go away. Her showing up at the shop had been a bright light to the otherwise miserable day. And loving her was the icing on the cake. It made everything that had gone wrong seem unimportant. When she was with him, the rest of the world didn't matter.

But had he known the evening would end like this, he would have left his work and followed her home. They could have warmed up the pizza, and she wouldn't be standing in the middle of his shop having a stare down with her brother.

Mark finally got his voice back. "You're not submissive."

"How would you know what I like in the bedroom?" She wasn't backing down and Justin felt a smile tug at his lips.

Again, his friend was tongue-tied.

Justin wanted to go to Kim, but that would mean he'd have to get within arm's reach of Mark, and he was trying to prevent a fight. Kim didn't need to see that.

Then Mark walked over to the wall and leaned against it. Justin wasted no time going to Kim's side. He wanted to hold her, but he kept his hands to himself for now.

Mark ran a hand over the top of his head. "How long?" He swallowed. "How long have you been fucking my sister?"

Justin blew out a breath. Before he answered, he circled his arm around Kim's waist, staking his claim. "Officially, a little over two weeks ago."

His friend snorted. "What about unofficially?"

Kim answered this time. "About four months."

Mark's eyes narrowed and he stared at Justin. Then his gaze moved to Kim. They weren't as hostile, but they weren't overly friendly either. "This is what you wanted to tell the family Wednesday."

It wasn't a question, but Kim answered anyway. "Yes." She looked up at Justin, her eyes softening. "We want to be together, and we're tired of hiding."

"You shouldn't have hidden it in the first place," her brother snapped.

Justin pulled his gaze away from Kim's and looked at Mark. "You would have been okay with it if we'd announced our intentions first?"

"Hell no!" Mark pushed himself away from the wall. "I can't believe you would betray me...our friendship like this."

"My relationship with Justin has nothing to do with your friendship," Kim said.

"Of course it does." Mark shook his head as if trying to clear it. "He's told me about some of the things he's done to the women he's been with. I can't...I can't think about him doing that kind of stuff to you."

Kim started to respond, but Mark held up his hand to stop her. "I can't do this right now. I need to think."

Mark started to the door and Kim made to go after him.

Justin held her back. "Let him go."

"But—"

"He's right. He needs time to process everything. Let's give him that."

Justin thought she might argue, but she nodded and turned to rest her head on his chest. After a moment, she lifted her hands to his face. "How's your jaw?"

"Sore. It'll be bruised by morning."

She rose on her tiptoes and placed a soft kiss on his skin. "He shouldn't have hit you."

Justin shrugged. "I'm sleeping with his sister. It could have been worse."

Kim didn't look any happier. "We should put some ice on it."

"I've got some at home." He cupped her face and rubbed his thumb over her bottom lip. It was still swollen from his kisses.

She leaned into his touch. "I didn't want Mark to find out this way."

"Neither did I, but what's done is done. We can't change it." He let his arm fall to his side. "Give me a minute to lock things up, and then we'll get out of here."

It took a little longer than that to make sure everything was secure and make their way out to their vehicles. He gave her a soft kiss before she climbed behind the wheel of her car. "I'll see you at home," she said before closing the door.

Home. Their home. He really liked the sound of that.

CHAPTER 32

I_T HAD BEEN_ two days since Mark had walked in on them at Justin's shop. Kim had thought that maybe he'd call or text her, but there'd been nothing. She wasn't sure if that was good or bad.

Justin hadn't heard from Mark either. He'd sent him a text Tuesday morning saying they needed to talk, but Mark hadn't replied.

There'd also been no spontaneous calls from either of her parents, so she was assuming Mark hadn't gone to them and spilled the beans. Her mom had texted her and Justin individually to confirm they were both coming to dinner, but there was no indication that she knew what was going on. Kim only hoped her parents took the news of her relationship with Justin better than her brother had.

The door opened and Justin rushed inside. "Hi, honey, I'm home."

Kim laughed. "You're late."

"One of my guys wanted to adjust his schedule for next week. Took way longer than I expected." He picked her up, gave her a kiss that was full of promise, and set her feet back on the ground. "Give me five minutes to clean up, and I'll be ready to go."

She nodded and watched as he raced down the hall to his bedroom.

Kim grabbed her coat and purse from his closet and sat down on the couch to wait. For all intents and purposes, she'd already moved in. He'd cleared out space in his closet and two drawers for her and she was slowly moving her things out of her apartment. Barring any unforeseen obstacles, she was hoping to have everything done by the end of the month.

As promised, Justin reappeared five minutes later, hair damp from his shower and wearing a green button-down shirt and a pair of black jeans. He looked good enough to eat, and she had to remind herself of where they were going tonight. No matter how delectable he looked, she needed to keep her hands to herself.

She stood, slipped her coat on, and headed for the door. Justin stopped her and pulled her against him. "No matter what happens tonight, remember I love you."

"I know." Kim brushed her fingers over his bruised jaw. He looked as if he'd been in a barroom brawl. They'd put ice on it as soon as they got back to his house, but it had still turned black and blue. Her brother hadn't been playing when he'd landed that punch.

He took her hand in his and kissed the inside of her palm. "We need to go."

Kim nodded and let him lead her out to the car. They'd decided to ride together. In less than an hour, her entire family would know about their relationship.

Justin held her hand on the drive to her parents. He was quiet and she let the silence fill the small space. They were both worried. Not only about her parents' reactions to their news, but neither of them had any idea if Mark would be there. And if he was, what he would say or do.

They got part of their answer when they pulled up in front of Kim's parents' house. Mark's car was parked in the driveway.

Looking over at her, Justin squeezed her hand. "Ready?"

She wasn't, but there was no point in delaying it. "Yeah."

He got out of the vehicle and came around to open her door. She let him help her out and leaned into him when he reached for her hand again as they walked to the front door. They separated before Kim opened the door and let them inside.

The house smelled of food. They weren't greeted by screaming or fists flying, so she counted that as a good sign.

Then they rounded the corner. Mark was sitting in her dad's recliner with a beer in his hand. He stared at them for several long moments before getting to his feet.

Justin moved her behind him, bracing himself for whatever it was Mark was going to dish out. The tension in the room was thick. "I think we need to talk," Justin said.

Her brother downed the rest of his beer, then set it down on the coffee table with a little more force than necessary. "Yes, let's talk." But instead of talking to Justin, he turned his attention to Kim. "He's the one who put those marks on your back, isn't he?"

She wasn't going to lie and maybe this was a good thing. They needed to clear the air. Although, she would rather not be doing it in her parents' living room. "Yes."

"How could you let him hurt you?" His voice was a mixture of disbelief and hurt.

She moved toward her brother. Justin didn't stop her, but she felt his gaze on her. "He didn't hurt me."

"I saw the marks. He hurt you."

Kim shook her head. "That's not the way it is. You must know that. You know Justin. He wouldn't hurt me."

Mark shook his head, but the conversation was cut short when her dad hobbled into the room on a pair of crutches. "I thought I heard voices in here. You two must have snuck in."

"I need another beer," Mark mumbled before fleeing the room.

Her dad raised an eyebrow, but she ignored it.

"Hi, Dad." Kim gave her dad a hug. "How are you doing?"

He returned the embrace as best as he could. "Hi, honey." Davis Langley looked over Kim's head and nodded his greeting to Justin. "Doctor says the leg's healing up fine. Another two or three weeks and I should be able to lose the crutches."

"That's great news, Dad."

They made their way into the kitchen to find her mom. Belinda was setting the food on the table. "Oh good. I thought I heard voices." She looked at her husband. "I told you I wasn't hearing things."

Kim placed a kiss on her mom's cheek. "Need help with anything?"

"Nope. Everything's pretty much done. All we're waiting on is for the rolls to come out of the oven."

They all took a seat. It was then her mom noticed her brother was missing. "Where's Mark?"

"He said he was going to get another beer," Davis said. "Maybe he went down to the basement."

Justin stood. "I'll go find him."

His gaze met Kim's and held for a long moment before he headed down the stairs to the basement to find Mark.

When Kim turned her attention back to her parents, her mom tilted her head to one side and gave her a little smirk. "Something you want to tell us?"

Kim swallowed. This wasn't exactly how she'd envisioned telling them, but she supposed now was as good a time as any. And besides, maybe it was better if it was only her and her parents. Especially with the way Mark was acting. "Justin and I are...dating."

Her dad had been about to take a drink of his water but stopped mid sip. He didn't say anything right away, though. His gaze went to the stairs Justin had disappeared down, then back to her. "How long has this been going on?"

His voice was even and monotone. That wasn't always a good sign. "It started about four months ago." No need to go into detail that it all started with what was supposed to be a one-night stand.

Her mom's eyebrows rose almost to her hairline. "Four months?"

Kim nodded. "We wanted to make sure before we told anyone." She paused. "Especially Mark."

Belinda Langley frowned. "I guess that explains your brother's sour mood."

"He sort of...walked in on us together." She chanced a glance at her dad. His face was unreadable, and it was making her nervous. "He punched Justin."

Her mom's eyes held a mixture of shock and concern. She seemed to be taking it all in.

"You were together at New Year's?" her dad asked.

This was where it got complicated. "Not exactly. We were trying to figure things out. But a few weeks ago we decided to really give a relationship a try."

"A few weeks? I thought you said you've been together for four months?" Her dad's tone had darkened.

She needed to turn the conversation around before both males in her family lost their heads over her relationship. "Things between us first started four months ago, but we both struggled with whether to get serious."

"And now it's serious?" her father asked.

"Yes." Kim met her dad's gaze. "We're moving in together."

Her dad began to stand, then faltered.

Both women shot out of their chairs and reached out to prevent him from falling. He pushed them away. "I'm fine."

Then their attention was pulled away by the sound of a crash coming from the basement.

* * *

Justin wasn't sure what he'd find when he went downstairs. He and Mark had been friends for a long time, so it wasn't the first fight they'd had. But this was different.

It was dark when he got to the bottom of the stairs. Mark hadn't bothered to turn on the lights. Justin flipped the switch on the wall and scanned the room, looking for his friend.

It took him a few seconds, but he spotted him sitting on the couch along the far wall. His hands rested on his knees and his head was leaning back.

"Hey," Justin said from the bottom of the stairs.

Mark opened his eyes and sent a death stare in Justin's direction. Not exactly encouraging.

Justin took a couple of steps into the room. "Can we talk?"

"Nothing to talk about."

"Of course there is."

His friend stood and walked over to the bookcase to his right. It was full of family photos. "I shouldn't have stopped with one punch. You deserved much more for hurting Kim."

"I didn't hurt her. I love her."

"Bullshit!" Mark whirled to face him. "I saw the marks."

Justin blew out a breath. "They were from a flogger."

Mark nodded. "You hit her. I knew it wasn't from her pressing against something. You fuckin' hit her." His voice rose in volume and Justin hoped it didn't carry up the stairs.

"It's not like that and you know it."

"Isn't it?" Mark narrowed his eyes once more and took an aggressive step forward. "Isn't that what you do as a Dominant? Cause your submissives pain?" He let out something close to a growl. "You hurt Kim and then got off on it."

If this wasn't Mark and they weren't talking about Kim, Justin would have decked his friend. "I don't do anything to the women I play with that they don't want me to do."

"So you're saying Kim was asking for it?"

This was so not going the way he'd hoped. "Stop making it sound like I'm abusing her. I'm not knocking her around."

"You're just using toys"—he put the word toys in air quotes—"to get your rocks off."

"You are such an ass sometimes, Mark, do you know that?" Justin blew out a breath. "Kim has found she likes certain things when it comes to sex. Things I enjoy as well. She has her safewords if she ever needs or wants me to stop our play."

If looks could kill, Justin would be a dead man. Then, without any warning, Mark lunged.

Justin fell backward, right into the large square coffee table in the center of the room. The corner jammed into his back, sending a jolt of pain down his side. He couldn't focus on it for long because Mark was on top of him. The next thing he knew, Mark's fist was on a collision course with his face. He managed to block it, but not well enough.

Mark's elbow hit Justin's lip and an instant later, he felt the coppery taste of blood.

Using his body weight, Justin flipped them over and pinned Mark beneath him. His friend struggled and it took all Justin's strength to keep him down.

"What's going on down here?" Belinda's voice came from the stairs.

He glanced up to see Kim, followed closely by her mom, descending the stairs. Both women looked frantic, no doubt coming to investigate the noise.

"Mark Jacob, what are you doing?" It was his mother's voice that finally got Mark's attention.

Fairly confident fists weren't going to start flying again, at least not with Belinda and Kim standing there, Justin released Mark's wrists and rolled off him. He got to his feet, not wanting to be caught in a vulnerable position should Mark decide to resume.

"I'm waiting on answers." Belinda was looking at both Justin and Mark.

Mark blew out a breath. "We're just having a...disagreement."

"Does this have something to do with your sister and Justin dating?"

His friend snorted. "Yeah. It has to do with them *dating*." He put extra emphasis on the word dating.

Belinda didn't respond right away. She seemed to be considering her answer. "I have to say that I'm a bit shocked with the news, but I don't think that justifies you two breaking my furniture. You will clean this up." She looked at Justin as well. "Both of you. And then you will come upstairs and have dinner with the family like civilized adults. Do you understand?"

"Yes, ma'am," Justin said, tentatively touching his now bloody lip. He was going to need more ice.

Mark sent Justin another scathing look. "Yes, ma'am."

Belinda straightened her shoulders, took hold of Kim's hand, and turned toward the stairs. "Come on. Let's leave these two *men* to clean up."

Kim sent a concerned glance Justin's way. He nodded, and she disappeared up the steps with her mom, leaving Mark and Justin alone again.

Justin shoved his hands into his pockets and faced Mark. "Look, I know you don't like the idea of me dating your sister."

He snorted.

"Okay, you don't like the idea of me having sex with your sister, especially in the way I like to have sex." Justin paused. "But like it or not, she's an adult, and she can have sex with whoever she wants however she wants. You don't have to like it."

"You're supposed to be my friend."

"I am your friend. That doesn't have to change." Justin waited.

"I don't know if I can stand the idea of you doing that kind of stuff with her. It was one thing when you were telling me about it when it was women I didn't know, but Kim..."

Justin thought about how to approach this. It really wasn't any of Mark's business, but he also felt compelled to plead his case. "Kim came to me."

Mark's head snapped up and Justin knew he had his full attention.

"I'm not going to go into details, but she came to me and asked if I'd introduce her to the lifestyle." He paused. "I won't hurt her, man. I love her, and...we're moving in together."

His friend took a step forward, then stopped himself. "You're serious."

"I'm serious." Justin removed his hands from his pockets and moved closer. "We've had feelings for each other for a while, but both of us were holding back. We didn't want to upset things. You or Belinda or Davis. I get that it's sudden for you, but it's not for us. This has been a long time coming."

Mark's shoulders relaxed, and Justin figured the storm was over. At least for now. "I'm just not sure. It feels wrong."

"Maybe you should talk to your sister." Justin paused. "And by talk I mean listen to what she has to say. She wants this as much as I do. Also, do you really think your sister would let me do something to her she didn't want me to? She's not exactly the passive type. She knows what she wants and she goes after it."

After a long moment, Mark nodded, then looked at the mess on the floor. The coffee table was on its side and everything that had been on it was now scattered across the floor. "We should probably clean things up before Mom comes back down."

Justin grabbed one end of the table, while Mark gripped the other. They picked it up and set it back in its place. Luckily, nothing appeared to be broken.

Once everything was where it was supposed to be, they made their way upstairs. But they weren't greeted by the serene family scene they'd expected. Davis was balancing on his crutches and Belinda and Kim were standing on the other side of the table. From the looks of it, there was another storm brewing, and they hadn't even had dinner yet.

CHAPTER 33

KIM HAD ABOUT HAD it with all the testosterone. It was bad enough her brother was acting like an idiot. Now her dad was grilling her as well. He'd paused long enough to confirm no one downstairs was missing any limbs, then started in. "Now, finish explaining to me how you and Justin are moving in together."

"It does seem rather fast, honey." Her mom didn't look upset, just concerned.

She understood that to them it might seem that way. "It's been seventeen years."

"You haven't been dating for seventeen years," her father said.

"No, Dad. But we've known each other. It's not like he's a stranger."

Her father stared at her for a long moment. "I still think you should wait."

She opened her mouth to respond, but her attention was drawn to Justin and Mark coming into the room. Justin's lip was busted, the area around it already swelling.

Kim narrowed her eyes at her brother and crossed the room to Justin. She skimmed her fingers over his face before turning toward her brother. "Can't you manage to talk without using your fists?"

Mark didn't seem overly concerned with her chastisement. "He's lucky I didn't do more than that."

She blew out a frustrated breath. "Unbelievable."

Justin cupped the side of her face, then rested his hand on her shoulder before addressing her parents. "I know our news caught you all off guard, but it's not going to change how we feel."

Her mom walked over to place a hand on Justin's arm. "It's not the fact that you're dating." Her mom paused. "I mean, we're a little surprised, but it's the moving in together. That's a big step."

"Yes, it is."

No one said anything as that hung in the air for several long moments. It was her dad who broke the silence. He looked Kim in the eyes. "I don't like it. I wish you'd wait. For another year at least. But you're an adult, and I can't stop you."

"Dad, we've waited too long already," Kim said.

Justin gave her shoulders a squeeze, then looked at Davis. "I'll take care of her. I promise you."

Her dad lowered himself into his chair, propping his crutches against the wall behind him. "You'd better. I won't be using these damn things forever."

"Understood, sir."

Davis Langley nodded once, then turned to his wife. "Do you have an ice pack or something for Justin's lip? Looks like a nasty cut he's got there." Then he scooped up a heaping spoonful of mashed potatoes and deposited them onto his plate as if they'd been discussing the weather.

Her mom retrieved an ice pack from the freezer and wrapped it in a towel before handing it to Justin. He winced as he pressed it against his face. Kim didn't miss her brother's smirk.

Everyone took a seat around the table and for a while, the only sound was the scraping of dishes as food was piled on plates. Justin sat between her and her mom, which was the safest place at the table for him. Kim still didn't trust the men in her family to behave themselves.

Eventually, her mom approached the elephant in the room again.

"I don't want any more fighting." She glared at her son and husband. "But when are you two planning to move in together?"

Kim met Justin's gaze before answering her mother's question. "I've already begun moving some of my things, but there's not a huge rush. I have the apartment until the end of next month."

"That's where you were the night of Dad's accident," Mark said. "You two were together." He paused, seeming to process the information he now knew, then narrowed his eyes at Justin. "She was the woman."

She knew exactly what was going through her brother's mind. The discarded dress she'd left on Justin's living room floor painted a pretty good picture of the situation. Justin answered her brother, but not in the way she'd thought. "Of course she was. I don't cheat. Kim's the only woman I've dated since we started seeing each other four months ago."

Kim looked over at him and hoped she didn't look as surprised as she felt at the news. She hadn't been with anyone since that first night, but she hadn't known if he had. Their first night had been a no strings type deal. They'd made no commitments. No promises. But she couldn't deny she liked this new information.

Mark stabbed a piece of meat on his plate and shoved it into his mouth. She guessed that was better than him leaping over the table to take yet another shot at Justin.

"I'm not going to lie," her father said. "This is going to take some getting used to." He looked at Justin. "It's not that I don't like you. Hell, you've been like a second son to us, but I've never gotten a hint from either of you before tonight that you saw each other this way."

Justin placed a hand on her knee under the table. "We were really good at hiding it."

Her mom speared a carrot. "What I don't understand is why." She waved her fork in the air. "I mean, obviously these two aren't thrilled about it, but if you both felt this way for so long..."

She let that trail off, obviously expecting an answer. Kim met her mother's gaze. "I didn't know he saw me as anything more than

Mark's sister. I thought my feelings were one-sided." Kim glanced over at Justin. "We both did."

Belinda shook her head. "You're not exactly like any of Kim's previous boyfriends."

Justin snorted, then winced. He was trying to eat, but she could tell it hurt to chew. He was eating more of the mashed potatoes than anything else.

"No, he's not, but that's a good thing. There's a reason why my other relationships didn't work out." She wasn't going to mention that the main reason they didn't work out was because she'd realized she was a submissive and she needed a man who could take control in the bedroom. That was the type of information her mother didn't need.

Conversation was stark for the rest of the meal. Her brother kept sending glares across the table at Justin, while her dad appeared extremely interested in the food on his plate. It was one of the strangest family dinners they'd ever had.

Kim breathed a sigh of relief when her dad asked Mark to help him with something in the garage. Normally, Justin would have gone with them, but he stayed back. She couldn't blame him. He'd had a rough few days with the men of her family.

"Do you need some help cleaning up?" Justin asked her mother.

"No, but thank you for asking. I've got it. There isn't much to clean up in any case." She inspected his face. "You should keep putting ice on that throughout the night to keep the swelling down." She smiled. "Maybe Kim can help you with that."

"You're okay with this? Us being together?" Justin asked.

"As long as you make my girl happy, I'm happy." Belinda took hold of his free hand. "Be good to her."

"Yes, ma'am." He tried to smile and winced again.

Kim gave her mom a hug. "Thanks, Mom. For everything."

"You're very welcome, honey." Belinda released her daughter and took a step back. "Now go home and take care of your man. He needs your attention more than I do tonight."

"Do you think it's safe to say goodbye to Dad?" Kim asked, eyeing the door that led to the garage.

"I think maybe you should give your dad a day or two to adjust."

After giving her mom another hug, Kim and Justin retrieved their coats and made their way to the car. "Do you want me to drive?" Kim asked.

He opened the passenger door and motioned for her to get inside. "I'm not hurt that bad."

Kim shook her head and waited until he got behind the wheel. "You don't have to be all macho with me. I know it hurts. I saw you wincing at dinner."

The engine purred to life, and he pulled away from the curb. "I've had worse."

"Still. He shouldn't have hit you." She paused. "Again."

"He's your brother." Justin shrugged. "It could have been worse."

"You keep saying that."

He glanced over at her, then pulled away from the curb. "Because it's true."

She thought about that for a moment. While she hated to admit it, Justin was probably right. "He needs to get over it."

Justin reached for her hand and tucked it against his thigh. "It doesn't matter."

Kim wasn't sure she agreed with him. If her brother tried to deck Justin every time they saw each other, it would make family gatherings impossible. She didn't want that. She wanted her family— all her family—to accept her decision. Was that so much to ask?

At least her mom seemed to be in their corner.

* * *

The next couple days passed with no word from Mark or Davis. Kim had spoken to her mom, but the two Langley men were staying silent. Justin supposed that was better than the alternative.

The bruising on his face was going down. He still had a busted lip, which meant he'd been unable to really kiss Kim...or suck on her nipples the way he wanted. It was making him cranky.

It was Friday evening, and he was more than ready to head to the club. He needed to put everything else out of his head for a while and be Kim's Dom.

They were halfway to the vehicle when they noticed Mark's car parked behind them. Justin blew out a loud breath. "We don't need this tonight."

Kim placed her hand on his chest. "Maybe it's a good thing."

Mark got out of the car and strode toward them. Justin wrapped his arm around Kim's waist. Luckily, it wasn't too cold out. He hadn't planned for them to be outside for long and the outfit he'd chosen for Kim to wear wasn't exactly made for warmth.

Stopping a few feet from them, Mark shoved his hands in his pockets. "You're heading out."

It wasn't said as a question, but Justin answered anyway. "We are."

Mark nodded.

When he didn't say anything more, Justin grew impatient. "Was there a reason you stopped by?"

"Mom says I need to apologize." Mark ran a hand over the top of his head, then looked at Kim. "She thinks I was out of line thinking I have a say in who you can date. But she doesn't understand everything and it's not the kind of thing I want her to know."

Justin felt Kim stiffen in his arms. "My relationships are none of your business."

"You're not submissive, Kim." His voice was pleading. "You don't know some of the things he'd done to women he's..." Mark paused. "Played with."

"I don't need to know what he's done with other women. All I care about is what's happening now and what we do together."

Mark shook his head. "That's not how it works."

"What do you mean that's not how it works?" she asked.

Her brother pulled at his hair, something he only did when he was really frustrated. "He's the one in control. He gets to decide."

Justin wanted to step in, but he knew this had to come from Kim. He could talk until he was blue in the face—tell Mark that all play was negotiated ahead of time—but he doubted his friend would believe him.

"No," she said. "I get to decide."

Mark shook his head and opened his mouth to argue, but Kim didn't let him get a word in.

"Justin gets to decide *when* we do things, but he doesn't do anything I haven't said is okay. I've talked more about sex with Justin than I have with any other man I've dated. He knows what I like, what I don't like, and what I'd like to try."

Her brother scrunched up his nose when she mentioned sex, but that was his only reaction to what she'd said.

Kim lowered her voice and looked her brother in the eye. "Justin's who I want to be with, and you need to respect my decision."

"And if I can't?" Mark asked.

"Then you need to at least keep your opinions to yourself." Kim glanced up at Justin, then back at her brother. "And stop hitting people."

Mark sighed. "As much as I hate to admit it, you're right. It's not my decision. But that doesn't mean I don't worry about you. You're my little sister."

Kim walked over to her brother, and Justin flexed his fist before dropping it to his side. "While I appreciate that you want to protect me, you don't have to protect me from Justin."

He glanced between them. "I'll try to"—he paused—"keep that in mind."

Going up on her tiptoes, she circled her arms around her brother's neck and kissed his cheek. "Thank you."

He returned the embrace. "I still don't like it, though."

Kim chuckled. "You don't have to like it. Just keep your mouth shut about it."

Mark snorted, then he ran his hands along her back. "Are you wearing anything under that coat?"

She took a step back and raised a sassy eyebrow at him. "You sure you want to know the answer to that question?"

Her brother paled and Justin couldn't help but grin when Mark threw his hands up in surrender. "No. Definitely not."

"Good answer," she said.

Mark looked up at Justin. Their gazes held for a long moment, then Mark nodded. "I'm gonna head out."

"Good night." Kim smiled and waved.

Walking up behind her, Justin placed a hand on her hip. "Come on. Let's get you in the car. I think we've tortured your brother enough for one night."

She giggled but let him lead her to the car. "I couldn't help it. His holier than thou attitude is getting old."

"I can't disagree, but taunting him probably isn't going to give us the end result we want."

"True."

They arrived at the club twenty minutes later, having been waylaid in some lingering downtown traffic. It was a nice night for January, and people were taking advantage. That also meant the club was likely to be busy.

Justin parked the car in the small parking lot next to the club and walked around to the passenger side to help Kim. When she placed her boots on the ground and stood, it was like a wet dream come to life. The black boots came up over her knee, and all he could think about when he saw those four-inch heels were how they tilted her ass into the perfect position for him to pound into her.

Kim took his hand, allowing him to help her to her feet, giving him a knowing smile. She knew exactly what he was thinking. That probably had something to do with the fact that he'd pulled her against his crotch before they left and mentioned how much he liked her new boots.

As he removed his keycard from his pocket, his fingers brushed against the other item he had tucked inside. Kim's collar. He'd thought about presenting it to her at home, but the club had been where everything started for them. It was where she'd first seen him as a Dom and decided to approach him. And it was where they'd both decided to give a relationship between them a go. It seemed fitting to being the next stage of their D/s relationship there as well.

After leaving their coats with Bridget, they headed into the club.

Justin took a quick look around and found Ali exactly where he expected her to be.

He placed his hand on Kim's lower back and steered her in Ali's direction. Her friend saw her and smiled. "I wasn't sure if you two would be here tonight with the moving and all."

Justin motioned for Kim to take a seat next to her friend. "I'll leave Kim to fill you in. I'm going to get us some drinks."

"So?" Ali asked as he turned away and weaved his way to the bar. He figured he'd give them a few minutes alone. Since he and Kim had gotten together, she and Ali hadn't had much girl time. He was going to have to rectify that.

Brandon greeted him with a smile. "I heard you checked out Garrett's cabin last weekend."

"Word travels fast." Justin chuckled.

"I may have been around when you called Katrina for Garrett's number."

Justin raised an eyebrow.

Brandon waved a dismissive hand. "Nothing like that. We were going over ordering. As great as Katrina is, she's not my type."

The bartender was a Dominant. Justin had never seen him bottom for anyone. And in the two years he'd been coming to the club, he'd never known Mistress Katrina to bottom for anyone either. The image of the two of them trying to play together was almost comical. All he could picture was each of them trying to top the other.

Justin shook his head and chuckled. "No, she isn't."

Brandon grinned. "So what can I get you"—he glanced behind Justin toward the couch where Kim and Ali had their heads together —"and your lady this evening?"

"Two waters for now."

Within seconds, Brandon placed two bottles of water onto the polished wood.

Justin handed over his membership card, and after a quick swipe, he thanked Brandon and made his way back to Kim. He placed the waters on the table beside the couch, sat down next to Kim, promptly picked her up, and settled her on his lap. "How are you doing tonight, Ali?"

She smiled. "Not as good as you two."

Reaching for their waters, he handed one to Kim. "No argument there."

He made himself comfortable and listened while Kim and Ali continued to talk, content to hold her for a while. As the night wore on, however, he couldn't keep himself from touching her. He ran his hand up her thigh and under the hem of her skirt. It was blue tonight. Midnight blue to match the corset he'd picked out. He wanted to finger her, but he knew she wasn't ready for that.

Leaning in, he brought his lips to her ear. At the same time, he skimmed his fingers along the inside of her thigh. "Tell Ali you'll talk to her later."

Kim's breath hitched, and then she licked her lips. "I'll talk to you later, Ali."

Not waiting, Justin stood, bringing Kim with him. He steadied her on her feet, making sure she was stable, then took hold of her hand as he led her up the stairs to the second floor.

CHAPTER 34

KIM HAD TOLD Ali what had happened with her dad and brother. Her best friend had been sympathetic. "They'll come around. It's just going to take some time."

She really hoped that was true.

Thoughts of Ali and her family were pushed to the back of her brain as she and Justin reached the second floor of the club. It was almost nine and the club was in full swing. That meant the second floor was busy. Individuals and couples lingered in the wide hallway, peering into the rooms, watching the play taking place inside.

The sound of a paddle smacking against skin drew her attention to a room on the left as they passed by. Justin hadn't used anything but his hand on her, but she figured he would eventually. And the woman on the other side of the glass didn't seem to be complaining. In fact, Kim thought she heard the woman moan.

One of the first things Kim had learned when she joined the club and ventured up to the second floor was that the walls were thin. Or at least there'd been no effort to deaden the sound. While those in the hall typically couldn't hear the words that were being spoken between the people playing, the sound of paddles, whips, and floggers carried.

Justin paused and pulled her over to the window. She gazed inside and sure enough, a woman was tied to a spanking bench with her bare ass showing for all the world to see. Her Dom stood with a long wooden paddle in his right hand, getting ready to land another blow to the submissive's already rosy backside.

When the Dom's arm came down and the paddle landed solid on the submissive's flesh, Kim felt Justin move to stand behind her. His lips pressed against her ear. "She seems to be enjoying her Dom's paddle."

A second later, the Dom reached between the submissive's legs, moving his fingers through her folds several times. Then he brought his fingers to his mouth and sucked.

Kim's interior muscles clenched. Justin had done that, dipping his fingers into her center and tasting her after he's spanked her. She didn't understand why being turned over his knee and disciplined like a child turned her on so much, but it did. And she was learning that her reactions weren't so strange, after all. Other women liked to be spanked, too. "Yes, Sir."

Justin's hand grazed the outside of her hip and moved lower until he reached the hem of her skirt. Her breath caught again when he began moving his hand upward. This time, there was no clothing between her and his fingers.

She glanced around, nervous about someone seeing, but no one was paying attention to them. The hallway was dim, and people were either watching what was going on inside the rooms or they were on their way to a room themselves.

Then his fingers brushed over her lips. Heat and moisture rushed to her sex.

"Relax and watch the naughty girl get spanked." His whispered words were punctuated by a gentle tug of her clit.

Kim couldn't stop the soft moan that escaped. His fingers felt so good and she found she was less worried about who might see them than the need for him to keep touching her. As the Dom behind the glass turned the submissive's ass a nice shade of red, Justin continued to play. His fingers massaged and tugged at her skin and she could already feel the wetness dripping down the inside of her thighs.

When the Dom finally laid the paddle down, he swiped a condom from a large bowl next to the door. He dropped his pants around his ankles, rolled the protection on, then spread the submissive's cheeks. But instead of driving into her pussy, he reached for a bottle on a nearby table. He squeezed and drizzled what she realized had to be lube down her crack.

It was then Kim realized what he was going to do. She watched in fascination and a little trepidation as he swirled the lube around her hole, then pushed his fingers inside. He pumped them several times before lining up his cock and thrusting his hips forward.

His hips slapped against her red ass and Kim heard her moan. Her body clenched as heat coiled in her belly watching the scene. Had Justin planned this? They'd been talking about anal since they came back from their weekend away. She was nervous about it but seeing this was changing her mind. The submissive didn't seem to be in pain. If anything, she looked as if she were about to burst with pleasure.

Then the Dom reached for a small vibrator that looked no bigger than a finger. He turned it on and held it between the sub's legs, directly on her clit. The sub cried out and Kim's sex pulsed in response.

Justin moved his fingers onto her clit and began circling. "Alexander and Grace love anal sex. It's one of her favorite things and he gives it to her often."

Kim blinked and focused on the couple before her. She knew who Alexander and Grace were. They'd given an anal sex demonstration before the entire club on her first night as a member. She hated to admit it, but she hadn't watched much of it, afraid of what she might see. But this was...hot. Sexy. And with Justin playing with her clit, she was close to coming.

"She's going to come," Justin whispered in her ear.

Grace's entire body was flushed all the way down to her toes. She was moaning and her fingers gripped the soft pads of the bench. Then, less than thirty seconds later, she screamed out her release.

Justin dropped his fingers, leaving Kim aching. He turned her around to face him, cupped the side of her face, and kissed her hard.

Her head was spinning when he released her and she almost tripped over her own feet when they started walking again. He kept his arm around her waist, though, apparently aware of her precarious balance situation.

They entered the room they'd played in twice before and she looked around. There was already a pillow on the floor in the center of the room. He shut the door behind them and lowered the blinds on the window.

She stood, waiting. They'd never played with clothes on before, but he hadn't instructed her to remove them. While she might not be the best submissive yet, she knew it was best not to do anything until he told her what he wanted her to do.

Justin turned and smiled. He extended his hand, and she took it.

They walked to the middle of the room, the pillow next to her feet, but he didn't tell her to kneel. Instead, he dropped her hand and stood in front of her. He looked serious and she wondered if she'd done something wrong again.

"I wanted to do this at the club because this is where everything began. It's where you first saw me and decided you wanted me to be the one to show you what it was like to submit. It's also where we decided to give a relationship between us a go."

Warmth grew in Kim's chest as she listened to his words. Justin could talk dirty to her and send her body flying, but there was something about hearing him talk about how their relationship started that pulled at her heart.

He removed something from his pocket and held it out so she could see it. In his palm lay a silver chain. It was simple and plain. "I wanted something you could wear, even at work." His gaze held hers. "Once I put this on you, I never want you to take it off."

Kim swallowed. Even though he hadn't said it, she knew exactly what it was. He wanted to collar her. To make her his.

The thing was, she was already his. She always had been. Even before their one night together. It was why no other man had measured up. She'd always been Justin's.

He held it up in front of her. "Will you wear my collar, Kim?"

She couldn't stop herself from smiling. "Yes, Sir."

Justin grinned back at her and came around behind her. "Lift your hair."

Kim gathered her hair and held it off her neck.

His fingers skimmed her neck and collarbone as he placed the collar around her neck and secured it. He placed a kiss on her shoulder, his lips lingering on her skin. "You look beautiful wearing my collar."

She released her hair and brought her hand up to touch it as it lay flat at the base of her neck. "Thank you, Sir."

"Thank you, baby." He brushed her hair aside and continued to place kisses along the back of her neck, following the line of her new collar. "I plan on making you a very, very naughty girl. Are you ready for that?"

The seriousness of the moment turned in an instant to anticipation. "Yes, Sir. I'm ready."

And she was. Very ready. Whatever they had to face, it would be okay if they did it together. Everything felt right when she was with Justin.

He turned her in his arms and crashed his lips over hers. "I love you, Kim. I always have and I always will."

Kim gazed up at him, seeing the love in his eyes. "I love you, too, Sir. I wish we hadn't waited so long."

Tucking her hair behind her ears, he kissed the tip of her nose. "It doesn't matter. We're together now and I plan on keeping you."

"What if I want to keep you?" She knew she was playing with fire, but she didn't care.

A wicked look came into Justin's eyes and before she knew it, she was being hoisted over his shoulder and carried over to the spanking bench. She guessed it was time for him to discipline his naughty girl.

EPILOGUE

MARK STROLLED into the kitchen carrying two more boxes. He placed them on the table and turned to his sister. "I think this is all of it."

"Did you get the boxes that were in the front seat?" Kim asked.

"Yep. Dad and I put them in the living room. Did you want me to bring them in here?"

Kim shook her head. "I'll go through them later. They're mainly knickknacks."

Mark glanced around the room, then behind him. Ali frowned. She knew what he was doing—looking for Justin. As far as she knew, the two hadn't spoken since the family dinner. They also hadn't fought either, so there was that. And Mark and Kim's dad had shown up to help today, bearing cookies from Belinda. Ali had needed the sugar. She hadn't been sleeping well for the last week.

"Justin's in the back bedroom with Drew and Daniel setting up my old bed if you guys want to help," Kim said to her brother as her dad came into the room. It had been about six weeks since Davis's fall and he was getting around a lot better. He'd ditched the crutches for a cane as soon as his doctor had given him the okay, but still seemed irritated at his limited mobility. She couldn't exactly blame him.

Shoving his hands in his pockets, Mark rocked back on his heels. "Did you need help with anything else, Sis?"

It was Kim's turn to frown, disappointment clear on her face. Her friend had hoped her family would have come around by now. At least they'd shown up to help today. Ali hadn't been sure about that. Neither had Kim. "No. We're about finished in here and all the furniture's either here or in storage."

Mark nodded and glanced over at Davis. "I think Dad and I are going to take off then, if you don't need us anymore."

Kim sighed. "Okay."

Davis limped over to give his daughter a hug and kiss her cheek.

"Thanks for coming, Dad," Kim said.

"Of course."

The two men exited the room and Kim's shoulders slumped at the sound of the door closing behind them. Ali's heart went out to her. Kim was close with her family and to have them react like this to such a major decision in her life was hard. Davis seemed to be slowly coming around. He'd even said hi to Justin when they'd all met at Kim's apartment that morning.

It took them another half hour to empty the new boxes Mark had brought. Ali removed the last mug from the box and placed it in the cabinet to the right of the refrigerator. "Is that everything?"

Kim glanced around the kitchen. "Yeah, I think so. In here at least." She gathered the empty boxes from the table. "We should probably go see if the guys need any help."

Justin, Drew, and Daniel were tackling the bigger stuff while Davis and Mark had carried in the smaller boxes. Kim and Ali had worked to put things away. It was the best division of labor considering the tension and Davis's injury.

Ali and Kim made their way down the hallway to the spare bedroom. "Not sure we're going to be much help carrying furniture." Ali yawned.

"That's the third time you've yawned in the last hour. What's up with you?" Kim bumped Ali's shoulder.

"Nothing. I just haven't been getting a lot of sleep lately."

"Oh?" Kim asked. "Someone been keeping you up at night?"

Ali snorted. "I wish."

They made their way to the spare bedroom. "What then?"

As they walked into the room at the far end of the hall, the sight of Drew's backside as he bent over to connect the footboard to the rest of the frame greeted them. Daniel was facing him, holding the metal part, and Justin was on the other side of the bed, trying not to laugh.

"Need some help?" Kim asked.

Justin looked up and smiled when he saw her. "I think we've almost got it."

Drew grunted as the frame finally slipped into the slot and stood. "That was more challenging than I thought it would be."

"It was sticking when we took it apart the other day," Justin said.

Daniel shook his head. "Hopefully, you won't be needing to take it apart again for a very long time."

Kim ran her hand over the dark wood. "I don't plan on going anywhere anytime soon."

"Damn straight." Justin grabbed her hips and pulled her back against him.

She chuckled and wiggled her ass into him.

Ali grinned. It was nice seeing Kim and Justin happy together. "Is there anything else that needs brought in or put away?"

"Are you ladies finished in the kitchen?" Justin asked.

Kim tilted her head to the side so she could look up at him. "Yep. All done."

"Then I think that's everything." Justin kissed the tip of her nose. "You're officially all moved in."

Daniel cleared his throat. "And with that, I think it's time we said goodbye."

"You don't have to run off."

Justin cut Kim off. "Yes, they do."

Drew and Daniel both chuckled and Ali shook her head.

They all made their way to the living room. Daniel helped Ali with her coat, and she had to suppress her reaction to his fingers as they brushed the back of her neck. He didn't feel that way about her. They were friends.

Her body, however, had trouble remembering that. Every time he touched her, it sent tingles down her arm or her leg or wherever they connected. She'd been attracted to him from the start. Everything about him turned her on, from his lips to his hands to the way he took care of her. She wanted to be his.

But that wasn't going to happen. He wouldn't even play with her at the club. The few times she'd mentioned wanting to play, he'd found another Dom for her to play with.

"Everything all right?" Daniel asked as they headed to their vehicles.

"I'm fine. Just a little tired."

He stopped them both and frowned. "Why?"

This was what was so frustrating. Sometimes he acted as if he were her Dom, but then it never went anywhere.

Daniel waited for an answer.

"I've got new neighbors."

He furrowed his brow in concentration. "They're keeping you up?"

She nodded as she stifled yet another yawn.

"Did you report them to your complex management?" he asked.

"I can't."

Daniel crossed his arms. "If they're making noise at all hours of the night, you should report them."

"It's not..."

"What?"

Ali glanced around, but they were alone. Justin and Kim had stayed in the house and Drew had already left. She sighed. "They have very loud sex."

He raised an eyebrow.

"She's very vocal and he's...well, he's not quiet either." She felt her face flush. "I can't exactly call management and report my neighbors for having sex."

Daniel thought about it for a long moment. "When's your lease up?"

"Not for another six months." Ali rubbed her hand on her forehead. "It'll get better." She hoped.

It took him a while to respond. When he did, it wasn't how she'd expected.

He took hold of her elbow and walked her to her car. "I'll follow you home."

"Why?" Was he going to talk to her neighbors? She wasn't sure how she'd feel about that.

"Because you're going to pack a bag and come home with me."

Her eyes went wide and she opened her mouth to argue.

He cut her off. "Just for a night. I'm sure I can find you something tomorrow."

"But what about my lease? I can't afford to pay rent on two places."

"Don't worry about it." He opened her car door and gestured for her to get in. "I'll figure something out."

"Daniel, you don't need to. I'll be fine."

He braced himself on the car and leaned in. Her gaze was drawn to the silver at his temples. It made him look distinguished. "You are not fine. Your eyes are bloodshot and you're slouching. You never slouch."

Out of habit, Ali straightened. He was right. She'd been slouching.

"That's not to even mention how many times you've yawned since we've been here."

Had she really yawned that much? She didn't think so. At least not when he'd been around.

When she didn't answer, he stood and met her gaze once more. "Do you feel awake enough to drive?"

She nodded. "Yes."

He gave a curt nod. "If that changes, pull over. Understand?"

Again, he was acting like he was her Dom. It was all so confusing, but she was too tired to argue. "Yes."

True to his word, Daniel stayed behind her while she drove to her apartment. She got out of her vehicle and within seconds, he was beside her. "Do you want some help?"

Ali shook her head. "No. I'll only be a few minutes." She wasn't sure she could handle him being in her space. Eventually, she'd have to come back here. She didn't need images of him leaning against her bedroom door filling her head.

In less than ten minutes, she had a suitcase packed with all her essentials and enough clothes for a week. Maybe after she got some rest, she'd be able to think clearer about her situation.

With her bag in hand, she stepped outside and turned to lock her door. Ali felt Daniel come behind her, and she bit her lip when she heard his voice so close. "I'll take your bag for you."

She handed him her bag without protest. But instead of going to her car, he continued walking to his. "Um?"

Daniel turned. "I'll bring you back to your car later. Right now, you're not alert enough to be driving."

"I made it home, didn't I?" Even that sounded lame to her own ears.

"Do you really want to stand here and argue about your driving?"

No, she didn't.

Resigned, she made her way to his car. He opened the door for her and she got in. The plush leather seats were soft against her skin, cradling her. They were warm, as if someone else had been sitting there.

She sighed and closed her eyes. Seat warmers were a wonderful thing. He must have had it on during the drive to her apartment, so it would be warm for her.

The driver's side door opened, then closed. A faint hint of his cologne or soap tickled her nose. It had her entire body relaxing.

"Are you comfortable?" he asked as he started the car.

"Hmm."

He turned on some soft instrumental music. The melody soothed her, making her entire body feel heavy.

She was in Daniel's car. She was going home with him.

Snuggling down in the seat, she let herself enjoy the moment. Even though she may never have him as her Dom, he was her friend, and she knew he'd take care of her.

A soft smile tugged at her lips as she drifted off to sleep.

***

Read Daniel and Ali's story in CLAIMING HIS KISS.

CAN'T WAIT FOR SHERRI HAYES' NEXT BOOK?

Let her know by leaving a review and telling her what you liked about
HIS FORBIDDEN KISS (SERPENT'S KISS #3)

ALSO BY SHERRI HAYES

Finding Anna

Slave (Finding Anna, Book 1)

Need (Finding Anna, Book 2)

Truth (Finding Anna, Book 3)

Trust (Finding Anna, Book 4)

Finding Anna Boxed Set (Books 1-4)

Indulge: A Finding Anna Novelette

Change (Finding Anna, Book 5)

The Daniels Brothers

Behind Closed Doors

Red Zone

Crossing the Line

What Might Have Been

Daniels Brothers Box Set (Books 1-4)

Serpent's Kiss

Welcome to Serpent's Kiss

Burning for Her Kiss

Longing for His Kiss

His Forbidden Kiss

Tangled In His Embrace

Liberty Crossroads

Seducing Janey

Strictly Professional

Strictly Professional

A Christmas Proposal

<u>Box Sets</u>

Finding Anna Boxed Set (Books 1-4)

Daniels Brothers Box Set (Books 1-4)

Boys In Blue: Everyday Heroes

ACKNOWLEDGMENTS

Thank you to Mack and Rae who make sure all the BDSM elements are accurate. They are the first ones to see the story, including all my typos.

Editors and proofreaders are the unsung heroes of the book world. Without them, our books wouldn't be nearly as good. They painstakingly go through each and every word to help us clean up and polish our work. Thank you to Emily Lawrence and DeAnne Taylor for all the work they did to help get this story reading to be published.

Covers are often the first thing a reader notices about a book, so a great cover design is important. A huge thank you to Amy with Qdesigns for the beautiful cover.

ABOUT THE AUTHOR

Sherri picked up her first romance novel when she was twelve and immediately she was hooked. She would stay up reading long after everyone else in her house had gone to bed, needing to see the hero and heroine get their happily ever after. But Sherri never imagined becoming an author.

At the age of thirty, all that changed. After getting frustrated with the direction a television show was taking two of its characters, Sherri decided to try her hand at writing an alternative ending to give the characters the happy ending they deserved.

Since then, writing has become a creative outlet that allows her to explore a wide range of emotions, while having fun taking her characters through all the twists and turns she can create.

facebook.com/SherriHayesAuthor

amazon.com/Sherri-Hayes/e/B004MIO9O4?ref=sr_ntt_s-rch_lnk_1&sr=8-1

bookbub.com/authors/sherri-hayes

Chapter 1

Prince Isaac straightened his jacket, which hung awkwardly over the medical board on his hindwing. Ran a finger under the upper edge of his stiff, starched, painfully white cravat. Soon it would be warm enough to venture out from their home in the stately old maple tree, armed and ready to defend themselves against all varieties of arthropods—wasps, spiders, termites, and so on.

There were a thousand things he should be doing to prepare for the dangerously early spring that was coming. And instead he was here, standing awkwardly to one side while his best friend, Sir Stuart, dressed for the wedding. He was in good company—including that of his own father, Wood Fairy King Walter.

It had been a difficult decision for Stuart and his bride, Princess Gallica, choosing to marry during the winter while travel was impossible. Stuart's family lived far away and would be unable to attend; but beginning almost the moment the weather was negotiable, both Stuart and his bride would be too busy to do more than wave in passing. They all would.

Isaac swallowed a painful lump in his throat while mixed emotions swirled through him. His initial reaction to their engagement was complete shock. When had his two best friends fallen in love? Happiness for them was soon tainted with envy, which only intensified with each passing moment that he spent in the company of the reserved and yet oh-so-kissable Lady Cassidy.

"Isaac." King Walter's hand settled lightly on his son's shoulder. Like Isaac and Stuart, Walter wore a snow white, double-breasted suit of the finest barkcloth. "Why so serious? This is supposed to be a celebration."

"Yes, of course." Forcing a smile, Isaac resisted the urge to tug at his cravat again. "I just have a lot on my mind and precious little time to do it in."

Spring would bring a wonderful new age to Fairydom with the re-uniting of the five tribes. It would also open travel, making it all too easy for Cassidy to slip away from him. Though he knew they could use a powerful advocate in the seven regions of the Water Fairies while their councils discussed the future, he wanted her to stay with him. But for all the times he'd professed his love for her, she had yet to reciprocate. Their kisses were another matter, yet how he longed to hear her say the words.

"I understand." King Walter smiled sympathetically, then turned Isaac to face the room full of cheerful fellows. "Just remember. This time. These few hours. They come but once. You should be fully present." Smiling fondly, perhaps at memories of his own wedding day, King Walter patted Isaac's shoulder and flitted over to where Stuart stood.

Some of the tension eased from Isaac's shoulders as he watched his father help Stuart straighten his sash, a task any valet could have done.

Determined to act on his father's advice, Isaac picked up the box containing Stuart's Wrangler decorations. "Let's see." Holding one up, Isaac cleared his throat. "It's probably too much to have you and Gallica wearing identical medals, so that leaves…" He pretended to rifle through the box.

Stuart punched him in the arm before he could get any further and the others erupted in laughter.

Isaac made a show of rubbing his arm while allowing someone to nab the box from him, then joined in the good-natured ribbing as Stuart finished dressing. He must've overdone it a bit, because…

"Oh, sure, very funny." Stuart interrupted Isaac's greatly overstated retelling of their first post on skunk duty with a glare. "Isn't there someplace you should be? Something you need to do?"

"Who, me?" Isaac tapped his chin and looked about as though he had no idea what Stuart was talking about. "Hmm. Can't think of a thing." Giving the others a sidelong wink, he shrugged. "However, if I'm no longer welcome here, perhaps my sister will take pity on me."

"Now there's a thought." Walter set his glass of kiwi nectar aside. "And I suppose I could go check on the wedding preparations." He frowned severely. "I'd like to talk with the fellow who's performing this ceremony."

"Mm, good idea." Isaac nodded. "Make sure his license is in order, that sort of thing."

Stuart made an incoherent noise, but somehow refrained from reminding them that Isaac was escorting Gallica to the ceremony— which King Walter had agreed to perform. Clamping his mouth shut, he bowed politely and turned his back on them.

Chuckling, Isaac held the door for his father, then followed him into the hallway.

"I recommend against teasing your sister." Walter offered the advice with a twinkle in his eye as they walked down the corridor. "Brides have more important things to be gracious about than bad jokes."

"I have no desire to die an early and painful death." Isaac raised his hands in an exaggerated gesture of surrender and they both laughed.

He nodded at his father when they parted ways at diverging tunnels, but suddenly each footstep seemed to resonate through his body, traveling up his legs to his *healthy* spine. It raised bumps on his arms to think of how quickly he had recovered from paralysis once he began taking Doc—*Lady* Cassidy's treatments.

Thanks to her expert care, combined with Wood Fairy medicinal potions, he would be flying again soon. Just in time for spring. And…

With an effort, Isaac kept his thoughts from being carried away like a dust mote in a stiff breeze. He would spend enough of the days ahead overseeing the massive immigrations and resettling that were coming. Today belonged to Gallica.

Taking the hallway to his right, Isaac stopped and gaped at the transformation. Imitation tree leaves, fashioned from cloths and metals and woods and a dozen other materials, lined the walls and ceiling in a recreation of the bower the couple would've walked through in any other season. Luminescent button fungi, carefully cultivated by the Plant Fairy gardeners, were cunningly concealed in every white apple blossom, making them glow.

Isaac softly touched the dogwood and plum blooms as he passed them, and nearly stopped to smell the exquisitely carved cherry blossoms. Chuckling at himself, he strode along until he reached the door of his sister's chambers.

An all-female Wrangler ceremonial guard, resplendent in their full-dress uniforms, waited for their princess just outside her doors. Typical Gallica, that. She could've had a parade of bridesmaids and blossom girls pass in review before the entire town of Weetu, making a royal spectacle of her wedding. Instead she chose to recognize twelve women as her sisters-at-arms.

"All in order, sir," advised the ranking officer, offering a salute as he drew nearer.

As the current commanding officer of the Wranglers, he returned her salute crisply. Narrowly inspected the first row of women and what he could see of the second. Every uniform had been pressed to knife-like creases. Every medal and button and boot shone from polishing.

"Exactly as I would expect," he approved. Then, as their prince, he offered twelve amazing women the courtesy of a deep bow. "Our princess could have chosen no finer peers to accompany her this day."

Straightening, he smiled and turned to face the door to his sister's rooms. The arm he raised to knock felt like it was made of lead, and he was quite glad to find that the sitting room was empty. He hadn't hesitated to agree to act as his sister's escort, but the thought of walking the wedding path with his younger sister on his arm made him feel thousands of years old.

Perhaps it was the memories that crowded this room? In his mind's eye he could see Gallica's slippered feet poised on the arm of the couch before she launched herself for a joyful bout of bouncing on the cushions. Or the patch in the far wall—which, though artfully done, couldn't quite conceal from him the hole he and Gallica made when they decided to play Wranglers and Spiders one particularly rainy day.

He ran a hand longingly over the back of the couch. Oh, for a nap!

"Tired?" Lady Cassidy peeked at him out of the overflowing dressing rooms. Easing through the gap in the door, she shut it behind her and leaned against it, needing a break from the noise and the stress…and the noise. The only child of a studious man, she'd never experienced anything quite like the sheer giddiness of so many women preparing to participate in a wedding.

Startled, Isaac nearly jumped out of his boots as he whipped around to face her. "Cass." The woman before him was a vision of loveliness in a pink spider silk gown that gathered at the waist and her mother's pearl choker shimmering at her neck. Her curls, brown, bounced loosely about her face.

Her dress wasn't quite as pink as her natural hair color, yet it served to remind him that although she had learned to blend into his world, she was in truth a guest from the previously hidden Water Fairy Tribe.

"You are so beautiful." He spoke without meaning to, yet he meant every word. Again.

She blushed, pleased with his obvious approval, but hurried to reprove him. "Please don't." This wasn't one of the many informal suppers they'd shared during her recovery from her wound. Primly she reminded him, "Your Highness, we're entering a very delicate phase in our negotiations." She'd agreed to work with him on the grafting committee without considering that her growing feelings for him might compromise her ability to negotiate in the best interests of her own tribe, the Water Fairies. Thank goodness her father and tri-Baron Duncan Edgins were handling the trade contracts!

"Yes, of course." He sighed, hating that what he'd hoped would bring them together had become yet another obstacle, but knew she was right. He couldn't give the job away, either. He had to show her that he loved her despite everything that had happened between their tribes, and this was the best way he knew how to do that. Nevertheless he resisted her logic, adding hopefully, "And when the negotiations are over?"

"What do you want me to say?" She gestured as if to wave the question away. It wasn't the right one, anyway. She already knew he wanted her for his wife. The desire to accept his offer swept over her like a rogue wave, threatening to drown her good sense.

Could she, though? Could she promise to stay on the surface? She'd been giving it a lot of thought lately. There would be plenty for her to do if she did. There were hundreds of doctors in the other tribes to be trained in Water Fairy medicine. Not to mention the decades she might devote to researching surface herbs and treatments. Or the possibility of children.

"Isaac, we have to…" The imploration died on her lips at the *click* of an opening door.

Women began pouring out of the dressing rooms like ripe figs out of a storage bin. Extremely pretty, well-dressed figs.

Isaac hastily bowed to his mother, Queen Fiona. His eyes sent both a plea and a mischievous warning to Cassidy, assuring her that his campaign wasn't over.

"Isaac!" Fiona assessed her son approvingly, even as she smoothed his wide lapels and surreptitiously checked his white suit for smudges. "You look magnificent." In fact, he looked so much like his father that her heart squeezed unbearably. It really wasn't fair to have such grown-up children at her age.

"Thank you, Mother." Capturing her hands, he kissed them both, then held her out for his examination. "Will we ever have a more exquisite queen?"

"That's up to you, me lad," quipped one of the bridesmaids, setting the room to laughing.

Cassidy nearly choked when his eyes flashed to hers. How could she have forgotten she was being courted by the Wood Fairy *crown prince*?!

Gallica, observing their exchange, hastily inserted, "Leave it to a brother to overlook the bride on her own day." She twirled prettily, intent on distracting everyone from Isaac's marriage prospects.

Isaac flushed, ashamed of his selfishness, and weakly joined the laughter at his expense. Facing Gallica directly, he bowed.

"Perhaps it is only a brother who can fully appreciate the metamorphosis of his wonderful, daring childhood playmate," he took Gallica's hand gently and tucked it into the crook of his elbow, "into a woman of strength, beauty, and grace." He looked her in the eyes as he spoke, trying to convey the full depths of his sincerity.

Gallica stared at him, too surprised to have a word of response.

"Now, Isaac." Fiona intervened just in time to prevent Gallica from giving him a bear hug that would've crushed her gown and mussed his suit. "It isn't nice to make the bride cry *before* the ceremony."

A handful of subdued chuckles followed her words, for the entire party had been struck solemn by Isaac's heartfelt pronouncement.

"Then we'd best be off." Isaac winked at Gallica. "I know Stuart is more than ready to stand."

Gallica blushed a brilliant pink and suddenly the room was once again brimming with giddy energy.

The doors opened and the procession began making its way down the corridor. The honor guard cleared the way of celebrating citizens, and were followed by two bridesmaids, then Gallica and Isaac. Queen Fiona trailed behind, arm in arm with Cassidy.

Properly speaking, they should've flown to the ceremony, but in deference to Cassidy's stern warnings about reinjuring Isaac's hindwing, they walked.

Summoning his best smile, Isaac escorted his sister through the increasingly dense throngs of fairies and into Weetu's great hall, the largest chamber in all of Weetu. Special platforms rigged for the occasion lined the walls in tiers, creating extra standing room for spectators at this, the highlight of winter's activities.

Gallica shivered as they crossed the threshold. "Isaac," she whispered, not quite stopping, "I wish Stuart's parents were here."

"His entire family loves you, you know that." He squeezed her fingers reassuringly. They *were* in for a shock, though. At winterfall, Stuart and Gallica were only friends. What would his family say when they learned of the marriage? King Walter himself might've insisted on a longer engagement if they hadn't been friends for four or five hundred years prior to their sudden mutual romantic inclinations. "They'll be happy for you, I'm sure."

Gallica nodded and allowed him to ease her along a bit more quickly, but her eyes stayed glued to Stuart's beaming face, making Isaac wonder if she'd heard him at all.

Cassidy smiled shyly at Queen Fiona and slipped away to join her father on the edges of the crowd, where she tried to take up as little room as possible. Had she ever felt more like an outsider than she did at this moment? A Water Fairy at a Wood Fairy wedding. Unthinkable a mere decade ago. Possible now only because she'd permitted her cousin, Kuntza, to persuade her to visit Weetu. She didn't regret her choice—much—though she wished she could've done some things differently.

Her father, Councilor Volt Clark, looked down at her in surprise when she pressed closer to his side. He knew of Isaac's intentions toward her and couldn't help wondering how much that had to do with her present discomfort. Unfortunately, each time he tried to bring the subject up, she refused to discuss it.

He slipped an arm around her shoulders and tried to remember the last time they'd talked about something besides trade negotiations, the treaties, or other such business.

At the center of the room, Gallica went from leaning on Isaac's arm to fairly dragging him along as they climbed the stairs to where their father and Stuart waited.

The honor guard split at the top of the stairs, encircling the group and standing ready to defend against an attack.

Isaac knew without question that he pitied the spider or termite that challenged their blades. In a recently discarded tradition, there would also have been a short duel between himself and Stuart to prove the groom's courage. Or, since Gallica was a princess, a feat might've been demanded of Stuart, such as taming a wild ant for the king's colony.

Somehow, in an exceedingly odd quirk of fate, those traditions were replaced by, of all things, a speech of acceptance by the bride's family. Yes, instead of simply trading a few blows and being done with it, Isaac was expected to explain to everyone in attendance why he thought Stuart was a good choice for Gallica's husband.

Handing Gallica off to Stuart, Isaac turned to face the assembly. His own life was so wound up in Stuart's that he'd struggled to separate himself from the stories he'd chosen to demonstrate the suitability of his soon-to-be brother-by-law. Despite his best efforts at not overpraising him, Stuart was an unbecoming shade of red by the time he concluded.

"I have watched him grow into his title of Sir Stuart of Ouray until I fear he has surpassed it. It will be my privilege from henceforth to call

call him brother."

The crowd cheered enthusiastically, then settled itself so King Walter could perform the ceremony.

Isaac didn't listen as well as he should've, but it wasn't really his fault. From his position by his mother, he could see Cassidy clearly, and couldn't help wishing she would agree to marry him.

The crowd erupted suddenly, snapping him back to the present in time to see the real wedding couple exchanging a kiss.

Hundreds of children raced through the crowd to swarm the wedding party, singing as they escorted the newlyweds down a short corridor to a room filled with heavily laden tables. Isaac, caught up in their midst, joined in the singing, wishing the bride and groom a lifetime of happiness and children to enrich their years.

Though he kept both eyes open, hunting for Cassidy, he didn't see her anywhere in the crowd of well-wishers.

Chapter 2

Cassidy locked the door to the queen's private sitting room behind her and took a seat at a desk on the far wall. With a little Water Fairy ingenuity, they'd constructed a crude signal station using the small sink hidden behind a wall panel. Some heavily modified instruments, provided by the city's highly skilled metalsmith, increased the range of Agnes' traveling transmitter-receiver greatly. Enough that they were now able to communicate with their tribe without taking over Weetu's pump maintenance room, which was a huge relief to them all.

Of course, they couldn't leave it unattended. As much as they wished to trust the Wood Fairy Royal Family, there were Water Fairy laws to consider.

From the bag she'd settled at her feet, Cassidy withdrew three critical parts and reassembled the machine. At home they would've had a team of operators ready to spell each other for a message this size, or perhaps even one of the new automated recorders that were under development. Here, however, there were only the five of them and they were all dreadfully busy of late.

Cassidy flexed her fingers, shuffled a stack of blank paper, and checked to make sure she had at least three quills cut and ready to go. Then it was time to flip the switch, opening the connection.

Ready, she tapped out on the key at her end. *Surface, ready.*

Urpean, ready. The vessel responded. *Transmitting.*

Cassidy wrote name after name until her fingers cramped, but she got them all. About halfway through, she detected a change in the signal rhythm, telling her that a different operator had taken over.

Urpean, waiting.

Capping the inkwell, Cassidy wriggled her fingers and then tapped out her reply with her left hand.

Surface, complete. Thank you.

The vessel sent a final message to close and she sank back with a soft groan.

"I may never operate again," she sighed as she massaged her weary hand.

"That doesn't sound good," Isaac remarked from where he was leaning against the door. He'd checked her quarters, the hospital, and even the room where she and her nurses liked to train before thinking to come here. And arrived just in the nick of time, by the looks of it.

"Isaac!" She shot to her feet, turning to face him—and block his view of the machine. *Blasted Water Fairy law.* It was a little harder to conceal what she was doing in the comfortable slacks and blouse that she'd changed into before coming over than it would've been in the spider silk gown, but that was her only regret in having changed.

"I didn't come here to see that hunk of scrap metal," he teased. He dropped a slow wink, enjoying her answering blush, then obediently looked away while she did something to that precious machine of hers.

"You shouldn't be here at all," she protested. Even as she said it, she groaned at herself. If anyone had a right to be here, it was the Wood Fairy Royal Family. In the end, trying to keep one eye on him while removing pieces at the same time resulted in a minor disaster. "Ouch! Oh, bother." Hastily she wrapped the pieces and stuffed them into her bag. "Alright."

Instantly, he was at her side, her injured hand cupped in both of his. "Cass, you're bleeding."

"It's just a scratch." She could forget almost anything while looking up into his gorgeous brown eyes. Even that horrid nickname. The one she was slowly coming to like despite herself.

"Here." Leading her over to a couch that was a hundred times more comfortable than the stiff-backed chair she'd been using, he seated her carefully. "Let me get the aid kit."

"I'm fine." She caught his fingers as he started to leave. "I just need a little something for the pain."

Smiling, he stooped to kiss her tempting lips. "How's that?"

"Better." She pretended to pout until he kissed her again. "Mmm, much better."

Chuckling, he retrieved the kit, then eased himself onto the couch beside her. In a matter of moments he'd treated the scratch and pasted a small dressing on there for protection.

"And how's this?" Tenderly, he began kneading the muscles in her sore hand.

"Oooh." She sucked in a breath when he hit a sore spot, but nodded. "Wonderful. Don't stop."

"Must've been a long list this time." He leaned over and kissed her forehead.

"Nearly two hundred survivors." She nestled closer. "The *Minaka* must've been an uncommonly large windship."

"I guess so." His tribe built the best windships in Fairydom, but without looking it up, he'd never be able to remember a single craft by name.

"Isaac?" Straightening, she drew her hand away. "We can start telling them now." Now that the time had come, she couldn't help feeling a little terrified.

"Yes. I was able to set up a meeting for tomorrow, as you requested." He shifted uneasily. "I wish I knew how they were all going to respond."

"Expect the worst, darling." Her stomach flipped and she was suddenly glad she hadn't stayed for the celebration after the wedding. Better to be a little hungry than a lot nauseous.

"I suppose you're right." Picking up her other hand, he began working it over as well, careful to avoid the bandage. "I think we've done all we can to prepare from our side. Now it's just a matter of letting folks know that…" He cleared his throat but still couldn't bring himself to say it.

"That their relatives are alive and well?" she finished for him, eyes searching his face as she spoke. She'd almost lost him when he first found out about this. "That they've been detained by a forgotten fairy tribe?" She wouldn't hide from what her tribe had done. She could even defend it.

"They're coming home," he reminded her softly. "Let's be glad of that."

She managed a smile despite her natural misgivings. "Are you still determined to be in the first scouting group?"

The ice outside the city's greenhouse was getting thinner every day and it would soon be time for the Wranglers to get to work. Especially those assigned to scout out the new village sites. King Walter had agreed to accept twelve thousand of the *galdu toka*, as the descendants of the surface fairies called themselves, and there simply wasn't enough room for all of them in the current Wood Fairy villages.

Not that they were sure all of them would have Wood Fairy ways. Aptitude tests were being given in every city in the seven regions, but there was still the chance that some would choose the Wood Fairy Tribe even though their talents lay elsewhere. To stay with family, or simply because they could.

"Yes. I think I should be." He looked down at their joined hands. Even after six months away from the sun, his skin was so much browner than hers that the difference was striking. "I'd like you to come with us."

"Me?" Startled, she stared at him. "But…why? I don't know anything about the surface. Or what makes a good village site. Or…anything. I can't imagine how I'd be of any use."

"No, I suppose not," he admitted. "I suppose I just want you with me." Oh, how he wanted to kiss her right then. "You've never seen a sunset over a snowbank. Tasted wild nuthatch cooked over a campfire. Listened to a Wrangler chorus." He almost snickered at that last. When the chorus was particularly bad, things could get rowdy quickly.

"That sounds amazing." Needing some space to think in, she got to her feet with a smile and made her way over to the desk, where she began collecting the rest of her things. "As you know, I've also never seen a spider. Or an aphid."

"It's too early for aphids." Rising, he followed her.

"I've never even been truly cold." She slid the list of names into a special folder. Picked up the bag of parts. "Unless I was running a temperature sensitive experiment." How long ago that was.

"All the more reason for you to come." He tried to slip an arm around her waist, but allowed her to push him away instead. What else could he say? "New experiences for you."

"What about the meetings?" Hand on the door knob, she stopped to give him a troubled look. "I realize the grafting committee is responsible for finding homes for your returning tribesfairies. Up to a point. But I also have duties as both a surgeon and a Water Fairy to consider."

"I understand." He sighed and rubbed the back of his neck, which still itched from the cravat he'd been wearing earlier. How could he persuade her to change her mind? Tell her the bald truth? That her presence on one of the scouting crews would help convince his tribe to approve their marriage? The marriage she still hadn't agreed to?

No, not tonight. He'd save that as long as he

could, because if she said no to that, there was no hope for them at all.

"Isaac?"

Her puzzled tone roused him from his thoughts and he forced a smile.

"Come on." Striding over, he opened the door for her. "I'll walk you to your quarters."

Neither of them slept well that night, despite their best efforts. Arriving early, and a little bleary-eyed, at the meeting room, they nodded to each other but kept their distance.

One by one the rest of the chairs filled until everyone had arrived. As the last fairy wandered in, a servant closed the door, temporarily sealing them off from the rest of Weetu.

Isaac got to his feet, his features carefully arranged in a smile. "Ladies and gentlefairies," he greeted them. "Thank you for joining us this morning."

"Awful early for formalities, ain't it?" called a Wrangler from the back.

"Middle o' the night fer me," snickered another. Weetu never truly slept during the winter.

"All of you had family on the windship *Minaka*." Isaac sensed the second his words registered with his audience, for several of them sat up straighter. Others scowled.

"That was thousands of years ago," growled one man through a particularly thick beard.

"And we have just learned that there were survivors." Shocked gasps and muttered exclamations filled the air, and he briefly let them go unchecked. Then, as more of the crowd began directing questions to him, Isaac held up one of the lists Cassidy and her tribesfairies had so meticulously compiled. "Here are the names of your surviving family members. I'd like to read them."

He read the names aloud, the recitation attended by occasional soft weeping and cries of joy as names were recognized. That was when he realized they'd neglected to bring any sort of tissues.

"Your Highness." A tall, lanky Plant Fairy got to his feet. "This is grand news and we're all grateful for it." He wiped damp eyes on his sleeve cuff. "But I think we'd all like to know where they've been."

"We'll answer as many of your questions as we can," Isaac assured them. "However, I must ask you to refrain from discussing what we're about to share with you until the king makes an official announcement in a week's time." This time he cut off the answering mutters sharply. "If you cannot abide by that one, simple rule, you need to leave. Now."

Startled glances were exchanged throughout the room, but no one moved to leave.

"You all know Doctor Cassidy Clark." Isaac gestured to her as she stepped up beside him. Then, as hard as it was, he let her take over.

"Good morning." She refused to lick her dry lips in an effort to hide her nerves. "As Prince Isaac said, we're here to answer your questions. I ask for your patience while I provide some necessary background information."

Though there were a few grumbles, most of the faces looking back at her seemed resigned to the delay.

"Anciently, the four surface tribes were locked in a battle so fierce that it threatened our very destruction. Instead, a treaty was signed, bringing peace to Fairydom." She paused to breathe and calm her voice, which had begun to shake. This was all vaguely reminiscent of the times she'd presented to her regional scientific council. Except, she'd never been afraid they might physically harm her. "But that is only part of the story. The treaty was not signed by four tribes. It was signed by five."

A flurry of responses were hurled at her like a storm of razor ring weapons and she physically stepped back as if to avoid them.

"Five?" called a voice.

"What do you mean?" shouted someone else.

"Impossible!" scoffed a third.

"It's not only possible, it's true." Isaac's voice rang out over the clamor. "Please, retake your seats, everyone. We will not shout over you." Folding his arms across his chest, he waited until they complied. "Doctor?"

"The fifth tribe," she continued as calmly as she could, "is the Water Fairy Tribe. We maintain the waters, keeping them clean and directing the streams, rivers, and so forth."

"We?" A single voice called from the back of the room.

"Yes." Cassidy pulled a dry cloth from her pocket and wiped the brown dusting powder out of her pink eyebrows. "I am Lady Cassidy Clark, of the Botere tribe in the Mugan region."

"Why are you here?"

"Mugan region? Where is that?"

"How come we've never heard of your tribe?"

Again the voices cried out for answers, filling the room.

Isaac caught her gently by the elbow and drew her away from the front row. Shook his head when she tried to speak. He longed to put his arm around her to still her trembling, but didn't dare. Even his own tribesfairies would be suspicious of his loyalties if they thought he was putting protecting Cassidy ahead of their interests.

As the hubbub slowly died down, Isaac and Cassidy took turns explaining the role the mysterious Water Fairy Tribe had played in the disappearance of their relatives.

"I know it's difficult to imagine your peaceful world awash with violence. Before the treaty, however, my tribe truly feared that the ongoing war would result in our complete annihilation. Our only safety seemed to lie in fading from the memories of the four surface tribes." Cassidy indicated the list of names Isaac still held. "And in order to remain forgotten, the decision was made to detain any who might betray us to the other tribes."

"Young woman." An older Sky Fairy woman rose and fixed Cassidy with a steady gaze. "The war has been over for nearly ten generations. And yet you continued to take and hold our family members prisoner."

"That is correct." With an effort, Cassidy didn't shrink from the glares aimed at her. "It is only recently that we began to consider that the surface might truly have found peace. We had our first official contact with the surface tribes mere months ago and were lied to by the pirates."

"Bane's own daughter tried to persuade the Water Fairies that we were still locked in conflict." Isaac hastily spoke before the others overcame their shock and emotions erupted. The very injuries Cassidy was treating him and various other Wranglers for were primarily sustained in the last pirate conflict; many here had lost loved ones there, as well. "The pirate treachery helped to convince the Water Fairies to seek the truth." He saw with relief that his words were being well-received. "At this very moment, Prince Cambrian of the Sky Fairy Tribe and Historian Wagner of the Silver Fairy Tribe are guests of the Water Fairies. It is with their help that our family members are being restored to us."

They did their best to answer the rest of the questions, though it was hard when they didn't have all of the answers yet. The names of those committed to returning to the surface were still being gathered; while some few had chosen to remain. To complicate matters further, thousands that might choose to come to the surface were of mixed tribal heritage and faced the difficult decision of which tribe to claim.

At length, Isaac called a halt to their questions and dismissed them with a stern reminder not to discuss what they'd learned until after the king's official announcement.

It was all Cassidy could do not to slump into the nearest chair, but somehow she remained standing at Isaac's side even after the doors closed behind the last of their audience members.

"How are you doing?" He wanted to pull her into his arms. To kiss some color into her wan cheeks. To tell her everything would be fine.

"As well as can be expected." She took a step toward the door. Stopped and reached back for his hand. "Come. We should tend to your wing."

"Ah, wait." He pulled out a tiny mirror and held it up for her to see her brilliant pink eyebrows. "I hope you remembered the dusting powder."

Half-laughing, half-groaning, she retrieved the box of brown powder from her own pocket and deftly dabbed it on.

"I will be so glad when this charade is finally over," she sighed, snapping the box shut.

"As will I." Retaking her hand, he kissed her fingers. She looked too tired to resist even the smallest advance on his part, so he gallantly began leading her toward the door. "Now, about my wings. I know you're worried about reinjuring my hindwing, but I was hoping you might approve…"

He teased and wheedled all the way to the examination room, where she examined his progress and documented it in his file.

"I suppose." She shook her quill fiercely at him. "If you give me your word that you will only exercise your forewings…I suppose I can approve light use."

He lost the battle then and swept her into his arms for a long-overdue kiss.

"Oh." Rosie, Weetu's Chief Nurse, stopped abruptly, hand still on the door knob. She coughed and looked over her shoulder as if expecting someone to appear beside her in the hallway. "Is this a, um, bad time?"

Cassidy gave Isaac's cheek a quick kiss, then drew away. "Not at all."

Rosie cleared her throat, then finished letting herself in. Even as Rosie accepted his file from Cassidy, she noted that Isaac didn't seem the least bit ruffled at getting caught, the rogue.

Chapter 3

"Cassidy?" Volt Clark dropped the papers onto his table and hurried to the door, alarmed at the uncharacteristic slump in his daughter's shoulders. "Come in, come in." He practically pulled her into his arms for a hug. "What's wrong, teyn?"

"Just a long day, Papa." Cassidy sighed at the sound of his pet name for her and hugged him back fiercely. Since childhood, his hugs had made her world right again.

"Another meeting about the, um, galdu?" He gave her a final squeeze, then eased her into a chair. After a lifetime of referring to the pris…*former* prisoners as the 'advena,' he didn't always remember to call them by their chosen name of the 'galdu toka,' but he was trying.

"*Two* meetings today, Papa. Isaac says he'll have to leave soon and these meetings must be finished first." She pushed an errant *brown* curl out of her face and tried not to grimace. It would be such a relief to no longer need to disguise her identity! To be able to rinse the brown dye out of her hair and just be herself once more.

"Hmm." Volt wasn't exactly surprised that Isaac had come up so quickly. And while they definitely needed to talk about Isaac's relationship with Cassidy, it didn't seem fair to

Volt to start the conversation now, when Cassidy was one yawn short of asleep-whilst-sitting-up. "Here." Lifting her hair aside, he began gently massaging her neck.

"Oh, Papa." Sighing, she brought her arms up on the table and rested her head on them. "That feels so good. How did you know?"

"Because you're just like your mama." He felt a subtle change as his fingers worked her muscles. "She carried her tension in her neck and shoulders, too."

"I don't remember much about her." Her eyes strayed to an oval frame on her father's dresser. In the painting, a much, much younger Volt had an arm around his new bride, a lovely young stranger with curly pink hair and a smile that looked like it could eclipse the brightest lightning globe in all of Margua. Had he chosen this particular portrait because it was the smallest, most compact option? Or because he cherished his memories of their wedding day?

"No, I suppose not." He moved his focus to her trapezii, kneading them with his thumbs. Frowned at the knots he gingerly worked to loosen. "I used to tell you stories about us at bedtime, as I recall." Her answering chuckle was accompanied by a general relaxing of muscles.

"It's been a long time since you've told me a story." She had a sudden mental image of herself, holding a curly-haired little boy on her lap. He was dressed in his nightclothes, his damp hair pressed against her cheek while they both listened to Isaac spin a tale of his Wrangler days.

The image faded almost at once, but the feeling remained, pulling her in two different directions. If she closed her eyes right then, would she be able to re-enter the dream? Live it out, or at least explore it a bit?

Her logical side laughed at the thought, coolly pointing out that she'd reach her future faster—whatever it was—by staying awake and making something happen.

Her eyelids drooped despite herself.

"Perhaps I should tell you a bedtime story now," Volt teased when she yawned.

"I'm sorry, Papa." Sitting up, she smiled at him as she turned her head from side to side. She'd been thinking about something. Something terribly important. But what? "That feels so much better, thank you." Whatever she'd thought of was gone, like steam coming off the sea on a cold morning.

"Yes, of course." He kissed her forehead and seated himself beside her. "Teyn, we need to talk."

"We are talking, Papa." Her lips smiled, but her eyes were sad. "We talk every day."

"Every day I, Councilor Clark, discuss business with Lady Clark." He took her hands in his. "I need to talk to my daughter. I miss her."

Cassidy's heart melted and she leaned forward to rest her cheek against his. "I miss you, too, Papa. When did we get so busy?"

"We were always busy," he admitted ruefully. "If we weren't in our research labs, I was off at a council meeting. Or attending a lecture." How dreadfully unimportant all of that seemed right then.

"And yet you were ever in my thoughts."

"I have an idea." Straightening, he tapped her lightly on the nose. "Let's shelve the paperwork and business for tonight. At least until after supper."

After a brief hesitation, she smiled and nodded. "I'll go to the kitchen now," she offered. Her father had chosen to keep his hair pink due to his official role as a Water Fairy Councilor and quietly loathed the hooded cloak he had to wear whenever he went out in public. "I can be back in a few minutes and then we can talk."

"Wonderful."

Cassidy hurried through the corridors, feeling as light as a feather for the first time in weeks. She kept an eye out for a page, intending to send a note to Isaac explaining why she wouldn't be joining him, and somehow missed seeing the fairy straight ahead of her.

"Oh!" She gasped when two strong hands settled on her upper arms, stopping her in her tracks. "Sugar! I...oh!!"

He picked her up without warning and swung her out of traffic, setting her down by the wall. His broad shoulders shielded her from the jostling of passersby as he leaned down. "Tell me about the windship crashes, Doc."

She tried to swallow but it felt like she had a mouthful of sand from the play areas of her childhood. Intense brown eyes searched her face while she desperately tried to think past the fact that their warnings not to discuss the meetings had clearly gone unheeded.

"Not here." Nobody had stopped to stare, but more than one passing fairy had looked a fraction of a glance too long.

"Where, then?" His eyes narrowed. "And when?"

"Sugar, please." She put her hands on his and tugged them away from her waist. Held them between hers as she tried to speak reason to him. All of the invitations to the last few meetings had already been sent. Was Sugar to attend one of them? Blast it, she couldn't remember. And yet, why would anyone tell Sugar if he didn't have a surviving relative on one of the windships?

"You already know where and when," she tried, deciding to assume he actually was invited. "Surely you can understand the why, too."

He hesitated, hands clenched under hers. "I

can't wait on procedure, Doc, not when it's this important. I have to know now. She…"

"There you are!" Isaac breezed up to them, slipped an arm around her waist and slapped Sugar lightly on the shoulder. "Sugar, how are you?" He already knew the answer, given Sugar's elevated color and the intensity of the tone Isaac heard as he approached, but he asked to give his friend an opening to explain himself.

Cassidy couldn't take her eyes off Sugar. He looked like he was going to strangle on the words he hadn't spoken. Her common sense fought her heart to a standstill in the painful *thud* of a heartbeat.

"Isaac. Enough." Lacing her fingers through his at her waist, she whispered, "We can't keep them waiting any longer."

He expelled a slow breath, but notably didn't try to move away from Sugar before responding. "Are you sure? We decided to do smaller groups…" He might've said 'for safety reasons' if she hadn't interrupted.

"I know." She nodded and tried to shake her head at the same time, nearly pinching a nerve in the process. In a moment of clarity, she'd remembered. Sugar was definitely *not* on one of the lists. "Isaac, word is getting out. Those reasons don't apply anymore."

He frowned as he considered, yet in the end he had to agree. Letting whispers and rumors precede the official announcements would only allow misinformation and half-truths to grow into anger. They had to speed things up now, for everyone's safety. Not just Cassidy's.

"Alright." He looked up at Sugar even as his arm tightened protectively around her waist. "We'll gather them all in. Tell them tomorrow."

"I can't wait that long!" Sugar all but exploded, drawing questioning stares from up and down the corridor. "You know why," he added much more softly.

"Yes, I know. But you'll have to." Isaac's words came out clipped. "I can't just pull together a meeting like this with a snap of my fingers. I don't even know where we'll meet yet."

"I do." Cassidy couldn't seem to help interjecting. It was as if the pain in Sugar's eyes pulled the words from her. "The great hall, where the wedding was held. Isaac." She hurried on when he started to object. "There will be plenty of room. And, if we start sending pages at once, we can set the meeting for, well, immediately."

"You're not going to be dissuaded, are you?" Isaac raked his fingers through his hair, then glared at them both when they started to speak. "Don't thank me. It's not as simple as either of you think, but we can't discuss it further here. Come on."

Cassidy started to follow only to jerk to a halt.

"My father!" Pressing her hand to her mouth, she gave them each an apologetic look. "I have to go tell my father…something. I'll meet you in the great hall as soon as I can!" The truth. She would tell him the truth, of course. And make supper plans with him for another night.

"Marvelous." Isaac muttered the word under his breath as he watched her zip away, wings pumping.

Acutely aware of Sugar's rising irritation, Isaac first found and gave instructions to the senior page, then interpreted Cassidy's 'light use' of his wings to his own advantage.

"Hey!" Sugar caught up with him quickly. "You shouldn't be flying!"

"I'm cleared for this." Isaac ducked away, taking a short-cut and arriving first.

As soon as Sugar landed, Isaac braced him. "There's a reason I didn't tell you sooner."

Sugar's face lit up. "She's alive! I knew it!"

"Sugar!" Isaac would've dearly loved to shake the man, but he could no more shake an oak tree than the giant before him. "Listen to me."

"Why didn't you tell me sooner?!"

Groaning, Isaac checked the door. They were still alone. Good. He'd seen Sugar mourn his sweetheart three hundred years ago and if he could, he'd spare the man an audience.

"Lieutenant Qaletaqa Campbell, attention!" To Isaac's grim satisfaction, Sugar pulled himself together enough to at least focus. "We know Suna's alive. That's all. They sent us lists hundreds of names long, but no details." Sugar's smile started to slip and Isaac rushed on. "She could be married, Sugar. They told her she would never see the surface again. For her, that meant never seeing *you* again."

Cassidy arrived just in time to see a mountain crumble.

"Sugar!" She rushed toward the staggering man only to have Isaac grab her by the arms and set her aside. "Is he hurt? What's wrong?" Her near-wail sounded nothing like her usual calm, confident self.

"Sugar." Isaac steadied his friend. "I don't *know* either way. But that's just it. We *won't* know until after the spring thaw, when they start to arrive. I didn't tell you sooner because I thought I could save you a few days of the curse of wondering, that's all."

"I see." Sugar swiped at his eyes. "And there's no way to…"

Isaac started shaking his head as soon as he heard the hint of a question in his friend's voice.

"Everyone has questions," Cassidy explained in a low voice. "We have only a very limited communication, so." Her shoulders rose and fell. "I'm so sorry."

Sugar didn't like it, but understood that it couldn't be helped. "Here's a question I think you can answer, Doc."

Her lips trembled as she tried to force them into a smile. "You want to know why."

"Isaac!" A long-legged Wrangler ambled into the hall. "What's so all-fired important I had to be dragged away from my game of Stratagem?"

Isaac gripped Sugar by the arm and spoke quietly, quickly. "Everyone else who comes tonight will also want to know why. Do you think you can manage to wait for that answer?"

Sugar wiped his hands on his trousers and nodded. Took himself off to find a seat.

"Noland will arrive in a minute with the lists," Isaac whispered to Cassidy. "Hold onto them until we're ready to start."

Turning to the door, where a small group had begun to collect, Isaac grinned. "Important? This is so important it couldn't wait a minute longer than it has to." Raising his hands, he beckoned to them. "Come in, come in and find a seat, my friends. This is a night you will long remember."

He certainly would never forget it. The questions flew like hatchets, some veering wildly off-center and others burying themselves in the heart of the matter.

An excruciating hour and a half later, Cassidy leaned against Isaac's shoulder unabashedly in the otherwise empty great hall. "It was worth it, I think."

"Oh?" He rested his cheek against the top of her head. "And why is that?"

"Because now we only have the citywide announcement to endure." Closing her eyes, she stifled a yawn. "Our fathers are in charge of that."

"I hadn't thought of it like that," he admitted. He'd been too busy counting them lucky that nothing got broken and not a single punch had flown throughout all of their meetings. Wood Fairies could be an unruly lot, though rarely given to malice, and he'd privately feared for Cassidy's well-being should a temper be lost—or thrown away—before she could explain.

"Hey." He jostled her slightly. "Why don't we skip that meeting?"

"And go where? Silly," she chuckled, "it's a citywide meeting. The shops will all close for the first time since winterfall and even the few hospitalized patients will be brought by their nurses."

"We could go scouting."

Something about the way he was holding his breath made her stop to consider before answering.

"I'll come with you, Isaac." She straightened away and looked him in the eyes. "If you'll explain why you want me to. Why you *really* want me to."

An odd sort of peace settled over him as hazel

eyes searched his. Carefully, he reached up and removed her glasses, which she wore only as part of her disguise. Traced one of her vividly pink eyebrows with a fingertip.

"I started falling in love with you the moment I saw you." Folding her glasses, he set them on the chair beside him. "You weren't just beautiful, you had a certain poise that caught my attention. Every time I look at you, I see a future queen."

Cassidy felt herself blushing and looked down at where her hands were clasped in her lap.

"Darling, I've half-proposed to you a dozen times or more since winterfall. Rash, impetuous declarations of love and the hope that you felt the same." Tentatively, he tilted his head forward, trying to catch her eye again. "In a way, your persistent refusals have helped me grow into the prince I needed to be. Which is why I have to face the fact that our tribes have a long, long way to go before they are fully reconciled."

She rose abruptly and took three swift steps away from him. Consternation rippled through her as she unraveled his full meaning. Baldly stated, she would be about as much use to him on this scouting trip as, oh, a dancing slipper. Worse, her inexperience could put someone else in danger. She'd attended a few lessons with the Wrangler apprentices, it was true; and what little she had learned only served to underscore all she had yet to learn.

All of which Isaac was perfectly aware of. Yet he proposed to take her along—why? Her eyes narrowed.

Pivoting, she marched back over to him and sat down. "You believe I will be more acceptable as the future queen of your tribe if," she inhaled shakily, "I come on this scouting trip with you." She wasn't sure whether she was upset with him or impressed at his ingenuity.

"I do. Awful, isn't it?" He wiped a tear from her cheek with his thumb. "You've put in hours of work making arrangements for the galdu to come home to us. You've talked yourself hoarse translating for various ministers. All of that and more on top of your daily hospital rounds and treatments." He held out his hands, palms up. "But all of that was done in secret. Even when the Wranglers and others learn of it, they won't understand your sacrifices because they've never had to…to oversee a trade council."

She groaned in mock frustration. "Wouldn't it be simpler to arrange for them to sit in on a council than to cart me along on a dangerous scouting trip? You won't have room for someone who can contribute absolutely nothing to your quest."

"We'll make room," he promised swiftly. "It

won't be easy, on any of us, but it's for a very, very important cause."

In the following silence, emotions flew between them that no one before or since will ever find a way to put into words.

At length, he kissed her hands and murmured, "A few months ago I would have thrown caution to the wind and fled with you to anyone who would've performed the ceremony for us."

"Anyone," she murmured, "on the surface."

He stilled. "A few months ago," he repeated. "Yes. Since then I've done a lot of thinking and…"

She touched a finger to his lips, stopping him from making a pledge she worried he couldn't keep. "I've done a lot of thinking, too. There's nothing for you in the seven regions." She bit her lip, pained at having to admit it, then plunged ahead. "On the other hand, the surface holds boundless opportunity for me. If I stay." She dropped her hands to his chest and fiddled with a button on his shirtfront. "Only promise me that we will visit sometimes. Please?"

Isaac lunged to his feet, pulling her with him. "Cassidy, do you mean that?"

"Shhh!" She pressed her hands over his mouth, his words seeming like a shout in the silent room. "Yes, my darling. Our tribes willing, I mean that I will live on the surface."

"As my wife." He hastily clarified and was rewarded with the most beautiful blush he'd ever seen.

"Yes." She leaned into his hand as it cupped her cheek, then relaxed into his kiss.

"Oh!" He slapped his forehead. "Your ring!"

"My what?" She laughed and shook her head at him.

"Your ring!" Backing away, he started patting various pockets. "I've carried your ring with me everywhere for the last month." Frustrated with himself, he threw up his hands. "And tonight I didn't bring it."

Chapter 4

The next morning, Isaac smoothed a hand nervously down the front of his barkcloth suit, then allowed himself to pace in front of his sitting room fireplace. He'd dismissed Noland without accepting breakfast and now his empty stomach was doing backflips that a trained gymnast would envy.

At least he'd found the ring; right where he'd left it on his dressing table. Opening the box, he took it out. Just holding it evoked memories of the hours he'd spent harvesting and working the yew wood. Shaping it. Smoothing it. Ornamenting it. Slivers of precious gems—deep blue sapphires, fiery red rubies, and the extremely rare milkstone, each large enough to buy a bottle of the best perfume—were embedded at random in the gold layer around the outside of the band.

Delicately, he traced one of the lines of dark summerwood still visible through the coating of gold. Similar lines ran all around the ring, imitating the look of tree bark and creating the illusion of texture on the perfectly smooth surface.

Any Wood Fairy woman would be pleased by it, he felt sure. Unhappily, he didn't have the traditional Water Fairy bridal gift of carved lavender taaffeite. More was the pity, that. He would've loved to have given her what she'd probably dreamed of since childhood.

Closing the box with a tiny sigh, he returned it to his pocket. Now he just had to transfer it to Cassidy's hand. With their parents looking on.

While reluctantly parting last night, he and Cassidy had agreed to invite their parents to be present for the occasion. Isaac volunteered his rooms because, in the first place, they agreed that they wanted to take some time to celebrate their engagement as a family before it became a matter of public—or official—knowledge. And in the second place, Cassidy's office and examination rooms didn't quite suit the occasion.

He touched his forehead and frowned when his fingers came away dry. Was it his imagination or was the room as hot as a metalsmith's forge? Odd. He hadn't felt the least bit nervous when proposing. Of course, this was the first time she'd said yes.

He paused in his pacing to adjust a log in the fireplace.

Yes, that was it. Requiring someone else's permission to marry would make anyone anxious. After their parents congratulated them—he hoped—then the Wood Fairy King, the Wood Fairy Queen, and Councilor Clark would have to consider all the ways their proposed union could impact the tribes. Or, as some might argue, all of Fairydom.

A sudden, urgent pounding jerked him out of his reverie. He spun to face it in time to see both doors burst wide open.

"Isaac!" Skite clapped his hands in obvious glee. "Found you!" Gesturing to someone behind him, Skite barged right in.

"There you are!" Roared a beefy Plant Fairy, who entered the room brandishing an old-fashioned ruler. A slightly damp ruler. "Your Highness, you missed it. I got up this morning and went to the main greenhouse to measure…"

"We're free!" Skite howled like a restless wolf. "The ice broke this morning! Less than an hour ago!"

Isaac's chest reverberated with Skite's celebratory slap, sending his heart bouncing around wildly. His thoughts, too. Was this a good thing? Or a bad thing? Or, maybe, the best thing that could've happened?

"Hey!" Skite shook him. "C'mon. We've got to get things rolling, me lad!"

"Aye!" Another Wrangler cheerfully rattled Isaac with a 'friendly' punch to the shoulder. "There's supplies to pack, windships to inspect, maps to hand out…"

Without really meaning to, Isaac looked at the doorway. And there they all were. His parents, Cassidy, and Volt. Volt looked unnervingly severe in the brown wig he wore to disguise his identity in public.

"Get out." Isaac grabbed Skite and another Wrangler by the shoulders, hauling them toward the door while those standing there hastily cleared the way. "Call assembly. Apprentices, too. Start loading the windships. I'll be along as soon as I can."

"But, Isaac!" A dozen voices clamored for him to go with them, like strings pulling at a kite.

"Shall we call Sir Stuart?" suggested Skite a tad desperately.

"What? Are you daft?" Isaac glared at them all. "Just get on with what I said. You won't have time enough to get into any serious trouble before I join you."

He all but slammed the doors in their faces. Stood there a moment, trying to catch his breath. How did his father do it? One wife, two children, three—no, four—other tribes, and millions of Wood Fairies. *How* did his father stay sane?

"Son?" Walter frowned uneasily. He'd rearranged his entire morning schedule so he could be here for…whatever was about to happen, and now Isaac looked like he was about to hyperventilate just because it was spring again.

Fiona slipped her arm through Cassidy's for support. Spring was a joyous time in Weetu. Usually. It was also incredibly busy, and Fiona suspected it would be difficult for them not to be able to see as much of each other as they were used to. Especially with Isaac leaving to lead an expedition soon.

"Cassidy." Isaac flew across the room and dropped to one knee in front of her. Pulling the jewelry box from his vest pocket, he lifted the lid and displayed the contents. Heard his mother catch her breath as the light hit the gemstones. "May I?"

Cassidy freed her arm from Fiona's and held out her left hand. Smiled tremulously as he slipped the cool metal band on her index finger, then kissed her hand and pressed it to his forehead.

Rising, he slipped an arm about her waist and they faced their parents together.

"I expected to have time to help answer your questions." He half-smiled, half-grimaced. "Unfortunately, duty is shouting for me. I'm sorry, darling." He addressed that last to Cassidy, who nudged him lightly with her shoulder.

"Go." She offered her cheek for a kiss, watched him bow to the others, and tried not to worry as he left the room. When she'd agreed to go with him, she hadn't expected the ice to thaw quite so quickly.

"Well." Volt cleared his throat of disappointment at how quickly and casually things had just happened. "I suppose you will have to get used to that." Then, fearing he'd sounded too stern, he switched to their native tongue as he came forward to kiss her forehead. "Egun ontsua, teyn." *Happy day, my little darling.*

"Thank you, Papa." Cassidy was more than a little relieved to see the sincerity in his eyes.

"Congratulations, dear." Fiona hugged her warmly, then held her out at arm's length. "I hope you know what you're getting into. Just between the four of us," her smile included Volt even as she lowered her voice in mock confidentiality, "Wood Fairies can be an acquired taste."

"Yes." Cassidy laughed a tad sheepishly as she thought back over the time she'd spent getting to know Isaac. "I know."

"For myself," Walter came to stand shoulder-to-shoulder with his wife, "I can't think of anyone I'd like better for a daughter-in-law. I've seen how happy you two are together." He'd also watched as they overcame obstacles together, growing closer with each experience.

She nodded and stepped away from Fiona at the same time. "But there is more to consider than our happiness."

"It might make things easier," Volt smiled at Cassidy, then at Walter and Fiona, "for you to know that it was never forbidden for a Water Fairy to marry an adv…um, a surface fairy."

He compromised abruptly, realizing as he spoke that Isaac had never been advena or galdu.

"Yes, um. Excellent." Walter did his best not to frown. He'd worried about how his own tribe would react to the marriage even while he'd hoped Isaac would succeed in persuading Cassidy of his love. Now, Volt's near misstep raised the disturbing question of how this marriage would be perceived by the other tribes.

Would the Water Fairies consider it a sign of weakness? As though Isaac, a mere surface fairy, was being offered in tribute to a more powerful tribe?

Or, worse, would the other surface tribes consider this a dangerous alliance—dangerous to *them*?

Accustomed to the weight of leadership, and having had some small experience with the king and queen, Cassidy thought she knew what was troubling them.

"Isaac and I have agreed that we will remain here, in the Deep Woods, for the most part." She slipped her arm through her father's as she promised, "We also plan to visit the seven regions from time to time." She'd barely had time to explain it to her father over breakfast, and felt badly that he hadn't had more time to come to terms with it.

"I see." Volt's stomach sank, again, but what could he say? That she must return to the seven regions for his sake? After a moment, he was able to ask, "And your research?"

"I left my research to come here." She leaned on his arm, feeling as it were, the pain of the more permanent separation already. "I am confident that the assistants I gave charge over it are perfectly capable of finishing it."

"Of course." It was such a logical answer that Volt was left quite speechless for the moment.

Turning back to Fiona, Cassidy bit her lip. "I must confess to needing your advice."

"Oh?" Fiona lit up, delighted at the thought of helping arrange another wedding. Even one fraught with the difficulties of combining the traditions of two very different tribes.

"Yes. I've never been on a scouting trip, but Isaac thinks it will be good for," Cassidy hesitated, "all concerned to see me taking action in this matter."

Startled, Fiona held a brief, wordless conversation with her husband, then turned back to Cassidy. "I think I understand what Isaac has in mind and 'tis a bold plan. However, my dear," she directed this at Cassidy, "a scouting trip in this weather is far too dangerous."

King Walter held up a hand to stay Cassidy's protest. "She's right. If the weather turns foul, a scouting party is trapped in whatever shelter they can find or make, trying not to freeze and eating what they've managed to pack along." He scowled. "If the weather stays true, that can be even more hazardous. On the surface, warm weather brings forth predators of all sizes, shapes, and locomotion. And you have no experience with any of them."

"There must be some way I can go," she pleaded. "Something that can be done."

"Scouting parties are made up of Wranglers and as few civilians as possible." Walter shook his head. "And even those civilians must pass the defensive test."

"The what test?" She leapt at the chance he'd unwittingly offered her. Hadn't Isaac said something about a test last night? She'd been too tired at the time, and yes, too distracted, to listen as she should've, but now she gave it her full attention.

"The defensive test." Queen Fiona hesitated, remembering suddenly that when Cassidy defended Weetu against another Water Fairy, it was Cassidy who had survived. With that in mind, it seemed highly unlikely this paltry test of her reflexes would prove any sort of a challenge. "All civilians must pass it before they can be approved for assignment to a Wrangler team."

"Then I can at least try," Cassidy asserted firmly. "And when I succeed, then…"

"No, Cassidy." Volt shook his head. This was the first he'd heard of the idea and if the Wood Fairy king and queen were worried, it had to be a terrible idea. "You'll be needed here. There is far too much work for just the five of us."

"But Father, spring is upon us. Water Fairies will soon be able to travel anywhere on the surface—including seasoned councilors, expert interpreters, and yes, even better surgeons than I." She took a deep, steadying breath. "Also, we will benefit greatly from having someone in an advanced position during the spring thaw."

"You're thinking of our promise to manage the water levels." Volt scowled as he hadn't in a thousand years. Blast. He couldn't help that his heartstrings were tangled up in his daughter's happiness, any more than he could claim a surety that he would survive her untimely death should she succeed in obtaining permission to join a scouting party.

"Yes, Papa." More for the benefit of the Wood Fairy king and queen than for Volt's, she continued solemnly, "If the snowcaps melt and flood the lowlands, even our outposts will only be able to do so much without endangering the chemical balance of our sea."

"I know." His scowl deepened and he clasped his hands behind his back. "I wish I could say you are wrong, but." He shook his head. "Of the five of us, you are best suited to that task."

Fiona and Walter exchanged worried looks.

"Come with me, my dear." Fiona gestured toward the door. "I will do what I can to help you prepare for the test."

Cassidy allowed herself to be led from the room despite noticing the grave expression on King Walter's face. She'd known there would be difficult conversations ahead.

"Councilor Clark, forgive me." King Walter could see no way around what he was about to ask. "While this is neither my first nor my only concern in this matter, as Wood Fairy King I am under a grave obligation to inquire as to what would happen between our tribes should your daughter, Lady Cassidy Clark, go on this trip and not return."

The blunt question hit Volt in the heart like a jolt from a lightning wire. Unable to breathe, he could only shake his head.

"I will be devastated, the same as you would be should something," remembering how his daughter came to be there, Volt delicately added, "happen to Prince Isaac again."

Walter nodded. Indicating one of the comfortable chairs, he suggested, "Shall we sit down?"

Halfway across Weetu, Isaac flew into what could only be described as a madhouse. Young Wrangler apprentices scurried here and there, bumping into each other as they fetched and carried.

"Isaac!" Skite hurried over. "Assembly's been called for an hour from now. And here's a tentative list of civilians going with the scouting parties."

"Good." Isaac accepted the paper without looking at it. "How about the windships? We'll need a minimum of six and I don't want so much as a blanket taken onboard until after they've been thoroughly inspected."

"I'll tell the shipwright." Skite vanished into the forest of scrambling fairies.

Isaac moved from station to station, directing and redirecting energies until an older apprentice came to let him know the assembly was ready.

"Right, I'm coming." Beckoning for the cartographer to walk with him to the door, he handed her a list of twelve destinations. "Get started on copies of these maps, please. One of each."

Hours later, Isaac was reviewing the inventory of dried food supplies when a hand touched his arm.

"What is it?" He blinked away some of the bleariness and double-checked his figures. "Oh, rot." As he moved to cross out the last line on the scrap of paper he was using for calculations, the nubby quill broke in his hand. "Wonderful!" Irritated, he threw it aside.

Shoved his fingers into his hair and took a deep breath.

"Let me." Cassidy broke the string that bound a sheath of fresh quills and expertly used a short-bladed knife to shape one for writing.

"Thanks." Isaac leaned back and smiled wearily up at her. "How are you?"

Setting quill and knife aside, she glanced around, then pulled up a chair beside him. "I'm well enough, but what about you? Have you eaten anything?"

"Eaten?" He frowned, trying to remember. "I ate…um…"

"That's what I thought." Catching hold of his ink-stained hand, she tugged on it. "Surely you can spare time to eat."

He looked around the room, only just realizing that he was the last one there.

"You know? I think I can." He had to stomp his foot to wake it up when he rose, but Cassidy was quick to offer her shoulder for him to lean on, so he didn't mind the pins and needles of each step too badly.

As Cassidy led him along, she waited for him to ask where they were going. He didn't even seem to notice when they passed by the turnoff to the restaurant section without stopping.

The rumbles of his stomach roused him at last and he looked away from her beautiful face long enough to recognize that they'd arrived at his quarters.

"I'm…not sure it's proper for us to eat alone together." He frowned and turned her hand. Her bare-fingered hand? "Now, don't tell me I dreamed everything?" The thought nearly drove the hunger from his belly.

"We won't be alone," she promised. "And no, it wasn't a dream." She leaned against him and ran a finger under the gold chain Fiona gave her earlier, raising his ring from its hiding place under her collar. "Your mother suggested we wait until after my tribe has been announced to the rest of Weetu before making our engagement public."

Opening the door to his sitting room, he ushered her in. Making sure they were alone, he asked, "And you agreed?"

"Yes, of course." Releasing his arm, she went to his desk and took a bottle from the top drawer. "Let's see if we can't get some of that ink off your fingers before Noland arrives with a cart."

He came over obediently and leaned on the desk, where he watched her intently while she worked.

"Now, don't be cross." She kissed his cheek and dampened a fresh swatch of well-used cotton, perhaps a strip off an old shirt, with the solution from the bottle. "If we shock everyone too many times, too close together, they'll never accept me." The cloth in her hands quickly turned a dirty gray. "Even if I do manage to pass the defensive tests."

Chapter 5

A little over a week had passed since the citywide announcement about the fifth tribe and the clamor in Weetu was slowly dying down. News was hard to come by in the winter, so the uproar had been general: everyone telling and retelling the same stories; asking the same questions; and making the same speculations all over the city.

The return to near-normalcy was largely due, no doubt, to the sheer amount of physical effort that went into fitting and loading six windships for the spring expeditions. Just keeping track of everything required the efforts of Isaac, Gallica, Stuart, and others.

It was that process which had drawn Isaac to the Weetu shipyard, located in the outer bark ring of the tree. Before they first came to inhabit the majestic old maple tree, lightning had struck her, splitting off a branch and exposing the softer wood to the ravages of time. It had been the work of two generations to clean out the decay and enlarge the hole a bit to make a proper shipyard.

Now Isaac stood in the mouth of the enormous cavern, surveying the fruit of their industry. In addition to the windships intended for the scouting trips, a dozen more hung half-finished in their berths, ribs sticking out and masts waiting impatiently to be mounted. Once the temperature in the shipyard reached a constant, moderate temperature, work would resume on those windships. They had a schedule to keep, after all. Commitments to provide the best windships in Fairydom to the other tribes.

"Loading is complete, sir." A Wrangler appeared beside him and offered him a stack of papers. "We could leave in an hour, if necessary."

"Thank you, Lieutenant." Isaac accepted the completed bills of lading and dismissed the officer with a nod. He appreciated the man's enthusiasm, but there was a lot left that needed doing outside of the windships. Including one very, *very* important thing. Which, if he was being honest, he'd been putting off.

"Have you made the assignments yet?" Sugar asked from where he stood by, having just delivered a load of nails, metal fasteners, and sundries. His father, the best metalsmith in Weetu, knew it was early yet to expect the shipyard to be up and flying, but had an urgent need for the space in his storage room.

"I'll post the notices after lunch. Still a few, um, civilian slots to nail down." Isaac eyed his friend warily. "You're sure you want to be assigned to one? The first news of…anything," he delicately avoided mentioning Suna by name, "will come here with the official pouches and delegates.”

“I’m sure.” Sugar’s mouth twisted in a hard smile. “I’d go mad sitting here, waiting, while the weather swings from cold to colder and back again. Wondering when things would start happening.”

“Right.” Isaac cleared his throat and secured the stack of papers under his arm. “Lucky for all of us that Prince Cambrian is with them.”

“Aye.” Sugar squinted at the massive doors that blocked out the sun. And the cold. “A Sky Fairy will know better’n anyone what the weather’s got up its sleeve.” They ought to, as it was their tribe that tended the sun and skies.

“Not to mention knowing when it’s truly safe to travel.” Isaac agreed. They had their own ways of judging the weather, but travel plans this early were always accompanied by meticulous emergency plans.

“About those civilian slots.” Sugar scratched his chin and grinned knowingly. “You got any particular civilians in mind for your crew?”

“As a matter of fact, yes. As you know well enough.” Isaac started to walk away and Sugar fell in beside him.

“Now, don’t go fretting. I’m sure she’ll pass the test.” Sugar offered a smile with the pleasantry.

“Do you mind if we talk about something

else?" Isaac felt a little ridiculous talking about it when, if he didn't hurry, he was going to miss it altogether.

"Sure, sure." Sugar waved the subject away amiably. "Let's talk about you. Where're you stationed?"

As commander-in-chief of the Wranglers, Isaac could've sat back while others flew into danger, but that wasn't the Wrangler way. If they'd had an unofficial motto, it would've been something like, 'It's impossible to lead from the rear.'

"I'm assigned to the *Itxar*, heading out to the Lauta site."

Sugar missed a step and hurried to catch up. "That's too far north! There's a bad flood risk in that area," he protested.

"Correct." Isaac hesitated. This wasn't exactly confidential, but... "You know it's an early spring."

"Everyone with a calendar knows it," Sugar scoffed. "And that means high water all spring. You can't be serious about putting a village in Lauta."

"Not on the ground, no." Isaac took the tunnel that led toward the Wrangler academy. "However, our last report indicates a healthy stand of hackberry trees." Trees were naturally the Wood Fairy residence of choice, but it took a special kind of tree to flourish where drought and flood took turns.

"Hackberries?" Sugar followed along silently for a few steps before grudgingly admitting, "Might work."

Any explanation Isaac might've given about how the Water Fairies planned to control the flooding *was* confidential, so he let the conversation lapse.

"Hey, slow down, will you?" Sugar grumbled.

"What? Oh." Isaac started to comply, then threw Sugar a look of disbelief. Usually he was the one loping along, trying to keep up while Sugar meandered. "You're kidding, right?"

"Sort of." Sugar grinned down at him. "You're letting your nerves show, my friend. Don't want her to see them, do you?"

Abashed, Isaac eased back. "Do you really think she'll pass?"

"Word is she's a," Sugar's forehead knit together as he hunted for the word, "zal-something?"

"Zaldun." Isaac slightly emphasized the 'oo' sound in the second syllable.

"Right!" Sugar brightened. "Some kind of warrior?"

"Right." The memory of his first encounter with a suge, a Water Fairy weapon, hit Isaac like a kick from a juvenile ant. And he hadn't even been in danger from it. No, by the time he got there, the pointed end of Sir Derrick's suge was embedded in Cassidy's side.

"Well, here we are." Sugar jerked back in time to keep from running over a gaggle of kids. "What in…" Staring about, he saw civilians stacked from one end of the chamber to the other. Inside the arena itself was the only truly clear area in view. "Good turnout today."

Isaac forced a smile when he would've rather ground his teeth. "They're all here to see her try." Everyone in Weetu now knew her as Lady Cassidy of the Water Fairies, but even before that she'd attained a certain level of notoriety with her advanced medical techniques; including the one that restored Isaac's ability to walk.

Sugar caught himself mid-grimace and instead muttered something uncomplimentary under his breath about idlers and gawpers.

"You're not wrong." Isaac touched his friend's arm, then gestured toward where Cassidy stood in a short line of handpicked candidates. "If you'll excuse me?"

The crowd groaned, a sure indication that one of the other candidates had failed the test, and Cassidy moved forward with the rest of the dwindling line. Peeking around the tall fellow just ahead of her, she watched as the test began anew for the next candidate. Fist-sized balls were lobbed at him. They came slowly at first, and he had no trouble swatting them away with his quarterstaff. The pace increased incrementally until a ball slipped past his defenses and caught him in the chest.

Frowning, Cassidy drew back. Thankfully, the test permitted the candidates to use the weapon of their choice, and while she didn't feel this was the appropriate time or place to introduce Weetu to suges, the next best option was a whip. She was a little out of practice, but hoped attaching the weight to the end would help it mimic the more familiar suge.

Thoughtfully, she rolled the small, finger-shaped weight that around in her palm, second-guessing herself. It was silly, of course. Hadn't she used the hospital scales to measure it against her own weapon? The end of her suge and this piece both weighed precisely seven specks.

The line moved again, sooner than she'd expected. The tests were unpredictable that way. Any given candidate might be disqualified in the first level and another might last through all three. Not many had made it to the end so far. They seemed to be mostly engineers, from what she could tell from their chatter. A couple of cooks.

The weapon rack came into view just in time for her to see someone selecting a short-handled axe. Hanging on the weapon rack not far to the left of the axes were six whips, three with wooden handles and three with woven handles.

She bit her lip, wondering how whips made

of mammalian leather would behave. Every time she'd tried to carve out time to practice with one, something had come up. Now she could only hope they wouldn't be too different from the whips she'd trained with, which were made of pyrsis, a leather-like substance common to her Water Fairy Tribe.

A hand settled on her arm, making her jump.

"I'm glad you're so convinced this scrum is the wisest way to spend our time." Volt did his best to smile at her. While he was happy his daughter had found someone, he hated that they felt it necessary for her to risk her life on a scouting expedition.

She chuckled, grateful for his presence. "I know there's other work waiting for us, Father. But Isaac is right. This is my chance to do something beyond planning where to relocate the fairies we've been detaining. To set a good example."

"Beyond?" Volt barely disciplined a snort. "Exhibition fighting to please the baser instincts…"

"Father." She put her hand on his arm. "This isn't a fight. It's not even an exhibition. There are no amusement seekers present." A roar of displeasure from the spectators made her stop with a wince.

"Remember. You wanted to be seen." Volt quirked an eyebrow, faintly amused at how badly she'd just lost their little argument.

"I remember." Cassidy choked back a groan, but his friendly jibe did help her relax a little.

"Which one will you use?" Volt asked, gesturing to the weapons' rack.

"They're probably all alike." She shrugged, eyeing the whips again. Except they weren't. Half of them had wooden handles while the others had handles made of the same braided leather as the body. She was accustomed to fishbone handles, so either of those would feel strange. "Would you hold this, please?" She gave him the padded weight. "And, keep my place in line?"

Acutely aware of her audience, she tried to focus on why she was doing this. It helped a little that in her Water Fairy training program the tests to progress from level to level always included a group of officiators. A handful of spectators, as it were.

Isaac, who had finally been back-slapped and elbow-jabbed and jollied over to her general vicinity, nodded at Volt and stopped to watch Cassidy testing the two options. His eyebrows rose as she skillfully maneuvered both whips at the same time, one in each hand. He grunted when Sugar reappeared at his side and leaned an elbow on his shoulder.

"Sure you want her to do this?" Sugar grinned down at him. "Might be a little embarrassing if she loses." Truth be told, he was backing the Doc.

Isaac snorted to cover his own misgivings. He never would've guessed that there would be an audience of over a hundred to witness her test. "It's foolishness to try to classify *Lady Cassidy*," he stressed her Water Fairy title even though Sugar had no real concept of what it meant yet, "by any one aspect of her life." She looked so graceful right now as she moved through what looked to be a set series of motions, a…um… He fumbled for the word she'd used—a taithí? Yes, that sounded right.

"Fair point." Sugar straightened up before Isaac folded in half under his weight. "Doctor. Scholar. Looks like maybe she's a dancer, too."

Just then, Cassidy finished. Agitated, she brushed her pink curls back over her shoulder. She'd tie her hair back for the match, but hadn't thought to bother with it before. With a grimace, she coiled the whips and replaced the one with a woven handle. The wooden handle, worn smooth from years of use, wasn't quite as rigid as the fishbone handles she was used to, but it would do.

She kept her eyes on the whip as she maneuvered back to her father, who had moved forward a few places already. To her pleasant surprise, Isaac stood beside him.

"Lady Cassidy." Isaac bowed and ignored the mutters from the nearby fairies. "I'm so pleased that you've joined us today." Her tight smile did nothing to reassure him that she would pass. "I do hope you qualify. We would certainly benefit from having someone with your skills at the Lauta site."

Sensing that was a remark designed to help further their cause, Cassidy summoned a smile she usually saved for tedious social gatherings.

"I still say Lauta is a bad site." Sugar verbally stomped on Isaac's carefully-planned moment with all the finesse of a worker ant. Catching Cassidy's eye, he exaggerated, "Who ever heard of building a village in a swamp tree?" Those around them started to nod their agreement.

Cassidy couldn't help laughing aloud at his—to her—dreadfully obvious ploy. His booming voice had drawn far more attention than Isaac's discreet comment. What a dear friend Sugar was!

"I won't be sure until after I can survey the area…" She cast a side-long glance ahead as the last fairy between herself and the test flew forward. Hastily, she gathered her hair back out of her face and tied it firmly as she spoke. "But Prince Isaac makes a good point. Having a Water Fairy present can be very useful in a soggy situation."

While only a handful of their listeners tittered at her weak joke, the majority of them gave her a good looking over, as if thinking that

Water Fairies might not be so bad after all. Maybe.

"Cassidy?" Volt finished attaching her weight to the end of the whip she'd chosen and handed it back. "Are you ready?"

She looked around to see the last candidate cradling his arm against his chest, a longbow on the floor beside him. Which made it…her turn. Her heart banged its head on the top of her rib cage, then sank, shivering, to the bottom, where it seemed in serious danger of staying.

"Remember." Volt lifted his chin subtly. "Dignum fiducia nostrae."

How could she argue with their tribal motto? 'Worthy of our trust.'

Her heart lunged back into position and began beating normally. The weight of centuries of responsibility settled on her shoulders, grounding her as she stepped through the narrow entrance to the arena. Let them watch, for she was no longer one Water Fairy. She was Cassidy Clark, a descendant of the first settlers of the seven regions; heir to all the rights, privileges, and yes, obligations, inherent in their position as the first defenders against outside attack.

Netting now separated her from the spectators, who quieted themselves when they saw who was in the ring.

"Take a moment to warm up," advised a lanky Wrangler apprentice, whose assistants were scurrying about, retrieving the balls from the edges of the netted area.

Cassidy flicked the coiled whip out to one side. The weight stayed on, a very good sign. Deftly, she walked the end of the whip back to her, flicking it from side to side in short, sharp motions that would ordinarily have produced the *snapping* sounds commonly associated with whips.

As a final experiment, she spread her wings and lifted off. The ceiling and floor were the only truly empty 'sides' of the cavern, so she oriented herself to face the floor. Once she was about halfway between the floor and ceiling, she gave the whip a mighty snap forward. Dropped to the floor and examined the weight once more.

Satisfied that the weight was still firmly attached, she signaled for the apprentices to start.

"There are two colors of balls." The tallest apprentice held up one of each. "If you don't hit the gray balls or if they hit you, you're done. If you do hit a yellow ball, you're done."

"I understand." Could it really be that simple?

She knocked the first few gray balls aside with the middle of the weighted whip, not for dramatic effect but for practice with how the whip handled. A second apprentice joined in throwing and she had to pick up the pace, though she still strove for precision in her strikes.

Front snap at one ball and side bounce another off the middle. Step right, snap left. An easy crisscross blocked the next two balls.

Suddenly a yellow ball was in the air! It came from the direction of the third apprentice, catching her completely off-guard. Already mid-strike, Cassidy jerked the whip back and twisted nimbly to one side, narrowly avoiding being hit by a gray ball or striking a yellow.

Her left hand dropped to her belt, grasped the second whip she'd hung there, and launched it with a *crack* that made the apprentices freeze in surprise. The gray ball she'd had to avoid abruptly changed direction and she ducked under another yellow ball before settling back to the ground.

The apprentices began throwing again and she was hard-pressed to keep up, even with two whips snaking through the air. The *cracks* of the unmodified whip seemed odd in comparison to its silent, weighted companion, as if one was brashness in action and the other stealth incarnate.

All at once, the lanky apprentice raised one hand and Cassidy was startled to see that he held two balls! He let them fly—one gray, one yellow, travelling so closely together that they would never separate in time for an easy score.

Twisting aside to avoid tosses from the other

apprentices, Cassidy brought her right arm back behind her waist. Bending her torso forward, she let the weighted end of the whip rise, rise, rise and curl…

She executed a full spin with the whip in motion and knew the instant its tip struck. The yellow ball sailed harmlessly past her cheek on its original course while the gray ball popped up toward the ceiling!

Planting her feet, she prepared for the next challenge, but it never came.

The apprentices looked as dazed as she felt as they showed each other their empty buckets. Someone, somewhere, started clapping and soon a thunderous applause, broken only by shrill whistles, beat upon her eardrums.

Cassidy hovered in place, trying to build up her wing strength while she waited. And waited. Sven, Sugar's father, was the best metalsmith in all of Weetu. If anyone outside of the seven regions could make the armor she needed, it was him. Which she would be needing sometime in the next week, if the weather didn't change.

Things were happening so fast! With Isaac and Agnes' help, she was trying to think of everything she might need—and reasonably bring—on the expedition. She would be one of forty fairies on a small scouting windship; what little storage space they had would be given over to food stuffs and tools.

Hence, her emergency visit to Sven's forge after passing the defensive test three days ago. She didn't exactly regret leaving her suit of armor in Noddfa; it would've been ludicrous to pack it at the time. But now she rather wished she had it. Made of plate metal and fitted to her by Water Fairy armorers trained specifically for such things, it would be next to impossible to replace it.

"Lady Cassidy." Sven gave a stiff half bow as he came out of the depths of his workshop. A row of apprentices trailed after him like miniature shadows. "Sorry to have kept you waiting."

"No, please." She shook her head as she landed. "I hardly noticed." How could she? What were a few minutes compared with over three hundred years of separation for his son, Sugar, and Sven's-almost-daughter-by-law, Suna? How she wished she had more information for them!

Sven gave a noncommittal grunt and waved the nearest apprentice forward. "Took us a few tries to get it right." He lifted a metal shirt from the lad's arms as if it weighed no more than a sheet of paper. Hundreds of small pieces of metal, all roughly the same size and shape as Sven's broad thumbnail, glittered in the light of the foxfire hanging from the ceiling above.

"Oh, Sven!" Running her hand over it, she was able to instantly confirm that each row of metal scales overlapped the row below it, exactly as she'd requested. It was as if he'd reached through time and space and plucked a piece of fish scale-inspired armor off a Water Fairy forge! "It's perfect!"

He grunted again, but with perhaps the faintest bit of professional pride this time. "Best try it on afore you go scattering compliments like leaves in a windstorm," he grumbled.

She settled for a smile this time and half-raised her arms as he raised the shirt to lower it over her head. The metal, still warm from being kept near his forge, felt strange to her sensitive fingertips as she separated the front from the back and ducked inside, wings tightly folded against her back out of habit.

Sven coughed. "You'll be wanting to turn around," he suggested, not unkindly.

Surprised, she nevertheless obeyed at once, only then noticing the wing slits cunningly placed in what must be the shirt's back. They were padded with something thick on the edges to protect her wings! Brilliant!

"It doesn't weigh very much," she remarked in surprise. Uneasily, she rolled her shoulders and bent her knees. It weighed nothing like she'd expected, in fact. Granted, she expected nature and misfortune to be her worst enemies on this expedition, but would this armor be sturdy enough even to handle those?

"You may recall as how I had my doubts about this, this *scale* armor." Sven scratched his cheek as if he didn't know what to do with his hands. He'd made a few shields in his time, but most Wranglers preferred a thick leather cuirass, limb braces, and a helmet to the much more restrictive metal. Of course, this shirt would wear almost like cloth—if he did say so himself. "Glad I took the job now. Gave me the chance to finally use a new alloy I developed a few years back."

"A new alloy?" Sugar echoed as he came

into the workshop. Spotting Cassidy, he offered her a tired smile, then spoke again to his father. "You mean the one you thought would replace silver and gold in jewelry?"

Sven slipped his thumbs inside the bib of his leather apron and grinned proudly at his son. "That's the one. Lightweight, malleable, and incredibly strong."

"I remember." Sugar took something from another apprentice and tossed it into the air. A piece of her armor, a coif of the same scale armor shaped to be worn on her, jingled merrily when it landed in his palm. A glimmer of white spoke of a spider silk lining. "You won't mind a little test, then."

"Not a bit." Sven folded his arms across his chest, straining the cloth that made up his sleeves.

Sugar turned the coif in his hands so that it was upside down. Gripping opposite sides of the hole Cassidy's head was supposed to go through, he set himself and began to pull.

Cassidy watched in fascination, not sure whether she should protest or cheer. Granted, she'd rather have the armor fail here, in Sugar's hands, than in the field when a mischance sent her suge doubling back on her. On the other hand, how would they ever replace the armor in time if they had to start over using traditional metals?

Sugar exhaled explosively and gasped another

breath without ceasing to try to rip the coif in half. His arms were shaking when he finally exhaled again and relaxed. Sucking in a couple of deep breaths, he tossed the armor to his father.

"Congratulations." Sugar shook out his hands, trying to get the blood running again. "I'd say you have a winner."

It wasn't until Sven held the coif aloft that Cassidy realized a crowd had begun to gather around the entrance to the forge.

"You all saw what happened," Sven bellowed at the spectators. "The military orders have been filled for now, so I'm available for private orders. Temporarily." He gestured at his senior apprentices, who mingled with the crowd, discussing possibilities. With the advent of spring, Weetu would resume the practice of exchanging money for services and Sven was probably glad for the business.

Cassidy chuckled to herself as she tentatively extended her wings, then reached back to touch the slits. A thick line of something soft ran all the way down the edges to protect her wings. "Is this…spider silk?"

"It is." Sven confirmed at once. "Spider silk can be cut, but it'll stand up to that finished metal edge just fine."

"Incredible!" She stopped trying to examine the wing slits from her current position and instead lifted her arm so she could look down the sleeve. Pressed experimentally on the inside with her finger. "Is this padded?"

"Well, sure. Some. You said it needed a backing that was tough but flexible and I got to thinking…" Sven waved his hands in exasperation. "I know you'll be wearing it with your insulated clothes, but this shouldn't affect the fit too much. And, it'll help absorb…"

"The blows, yes, of course." She finished the thought. Curious now, she stretched her arms high over her head and bent to touch her toes. Once upright again, she spread her wings and rose into the air. A quick flip to one side and a dip to the other and she resumed her feet. "Sven, you are," she ran her hands down to the shirt's hem, about six fingers below her waistline, "an artist!"

"Some have said so." His cheeks were a tad ruddier than they usually were when he was away from his forge, but he managed to keep a straight face. Beckoning to the next apprentice, he lifted out a single metal tube and held it out to her. "What did you call these again?"

"Call them?" Cassidy studied them a moment, then smiled as she recognized the shapes. "Greaves." Taking the tube from him, she separated it into two half-tubes and bent to buckle them around her lower legs. "Did you make these from the same metal as the scale armor?" She tapped one greave with a fingernail and listened to the sound it produced.

"Aye, and that's what took so long." Sven scratched his stubbly chin. The fancy metal shin guards wouldn't have been so much trouble except that he hadn't really worked with his new alloy ever since the jewelers gave their dismal reports of trying to sell it. But the sheer tediousness of crafting the scale armor, as she called it, coupled with the intricacies of the other items! "Well. And these. I've never tried making metal gloves before."

Cassidy accepted the items eagerly. Slid one gauntlet on and wiggled her fingers. The plates slid over each other in a smooth articulating motion. She rotated her wrist as if flicking a whip forward, then to the side. The palm and insides of her fingers featured only the thick leather lining and the plates on the back of her hand extended over her wrist to cover her forearm.

"May I have the coif, please?" Cassidy slipped it over her head and spread out the mantle so it lay properly. The spider silk lining protected her hair from snagging on any wayward scale edge.

Forgetting the onlookers, she shrugged her shoulders. Did a few torso twists. Bounced up and down a few times. Threw a combination punch that transitioned into a side snap kick.

"Will it serve?" Sven arched an eyebrow at her, impressed despite his feelings about her tribe.

She relaxed and lowered her arms to her sides. "Admirably."

She was still glowing a few hours later when she demonstrated the armor for her nurses, Daphne and Agnes.

"I must say," Agnes hefted the coif, "it *looks* exactly like something one of our armorers might've made."

Cassidy's enthusiasm dampened a little at Agnes' cautiously optimistic tone. "You seem concerned."

Agnes sighed. "I fear it doesn't have the weight to protect you, not even from an accidental suge strike."

"Yes." Cassidy deflated a little more. "That had crossed my mind."

"Easy enough to test, though." Daphne mimed holding a suge handle in her gauntleted hand and swung a blow at nothing. Smiled as if pleased with the way the gauntlet handled. "We can hang the shirt on a dummy torso and try to cut it on purpose. If it holds up to that," she removed the gauntlet and placed it on the table, "you won't have to worry."

"Where would we get a dummy torso?" Agnes shot Cassidy a glance, wondering what their incorrigible younger friend had gotten into now.

"There must be a hundred of them, abandoned, in a room deeper in the maze." Daphne shrugged as if to say she had no idea what the Wood Fairies were thinking, either. "The dust on them is so thick I expect them to start sneezing any moment."

Agnes couldn't help chuckling at the mental image that invoked.

Cassidy managed a smile. She couldn't dispute the simple wisdom of her younger nurse, but she did grumble a little. "There goes the 'new armor' shine."

Together, they carried the scale armor to the room of abandoned dummies and Agnes, she being the most skeptical of the alloy, did the honors.

"Enough." Cassidy stopped her after the fifth solid blow. The fact that the shirt wasn't hanging off the dummy in tattered strips of metal gave her hope. "That should be quite enough evidence."

"Indeed." Agnes, in the process of coiling her suge, pointed at a nick in the blade. "I do believe I am convinced."

Shocked, Cassidy flew up to the shirt and ran a hand over it. "It's completely intact!" There should've been at least one dented scale from where the weighted end of Agnes' suge struck it.

"How is that possible?" Daphne joined her and bent so close to the shirt that her nose was almost touching it. "There's not so much as a scratch!"

"A deliberate suge attack like that should've

done some damage," marveled Agnes, shaking her head at finding yet another notch in her blade. It would take her hours of work to grind the blade down to a smooth edge again.

"Agnes." Cassidy mused aloud. "Do you suppose Sven could be persuaded to part with the precise composition of his new alloy?"

"Not if he's as smart as I believe him to be." Agnes shook her head.

"Then the Wood Fairies have one more thing to offer Fairydom!" Cassidy grinned triumphantly.

"Oh dear." Daphne straightened up and bit her lip. "Should we tell them?"

"Yes, of course." Agnes chuckled. "We'll gain nothing by hiding what they'll soon find out on their own."

So, Cassidy brought it up that evening at supper with Gallica, Stuart, and Isaac.

"You're sure?" Stuart crumpled some of his hard roll into his bowl to soak up the last of the stew and eyed the empty serving bowl longingly. He understood that food stores were low, but he missed butter and thips and roast robin and... Gritting his teeth, he redirected his thoughts back to the conversation. "I mean, it sounds like quite an opportunity for Sven."

"Yes, very sure." Cassidy valiantly stirred her stew in preparation for another spoonful. It was ingenious the way they boiled dried meat with vegetables and spices to make a nourishing stew, it really was. The dried meat never really recovered, unfortunately. It stayed as flat and tough as leather.

She set her spoon down and reached for a piece of bread instead. Hard bread. Why was it hard? Did they dry it, too? No, that was silly. Then it would be a cracker. Or something.

"The alloy has great potential for use in armory." She finally answered Stuart. "Agnes is even discussing the idea of buying a quantity from Sven to take back with her so that she might have a suge made from it. If it will hold an edge, of course." Cassidy smiled as she discreetly squeezed the bread between her fingers. Did they eat like this every winter? How different from life in the seven regions, where food was always plentiful. Why, it might be the dead of winter and she could still sit down to a meal of succulent crab cakes and a fresh dabberlock salad. Just thinking about it made her mouth water.

Taking a small bite of the hard roll, Cassidy screwed up her courage and stuffed a spoonful of stew into her mouth.

"Pity we're only just finding out about it." Isaac took a long drink of water to try to wash the pepper out of his mouth and pushed his empty bowl aside. "Can you imagine a scout ship made with only this lighter-weight metal?"

"Except the shot," teased Gallica. "Our weapons have little enough effect on the birds and such as it is.”

The question made Cassidy lose what little appetite she had left.

“Done already?” Isaac murmured under cover of Stuart’s reply to Gallica.

“Yes.” She hesitated, then wrinkled her nose apologetically and whispered back. “It’s not very good.”

“No, it isn’t.” Smiling, he took her hand and brought it to his lips. How could he take offense at the truth, so gently offered? “I’ve had worse, though.”

Cassidy’s mind seized. Was she supposed to voice a similar sentiment? Or in some other fashion agree with him? How could she? Not since her grandmother, Damaris hired a new cook… Oh!

“I suppose I have as well.” She made a face at the memory. “Our head cook took ill and her apprentices filled in for a few days.” From the corner of her eye, for she was looking at Isaac, she saw Stuart and Gallica exchange a glance. A worried glance?

“That must have been awful.” Gallica observed, a tad too brightly.

Cassidy stilled. “The food was undercooked or overdone and sometimes both in the same meal. All the meats tasted of brine due to poor washing and preparation. Only the bread and butter were dependably edible, and my father maintained that was so because those were bought at market."

Isaac, sensing that his sister was bracing herself to deliver a dire warning about the possible fate of expeditions, decided to shoulder the burden himself.

"Cass." He squeezed her hand. "Do you remember what I told you about the expeditionary windships? That once we land, we'll have to wait for warmer temperatures before we can return to Weetu?"

"Yes, I remember." The air in the room seemed to have gone heavy all at once. Cassidy struggled to breathe and wondered fleetingly if there was something wrong in the pump rooms.

Doing his best to ignore Gallica's intense stare, Isaac stated the facts as simply as he could. "Food supplies may run low. We'll have hunters out every day, and we *will* eat." He stopped, torn between wanting to be honest and not wanting to frighten her.

"Sometimes," Stuart leaned toward Cassidy, "it's best not to ask *what* you're eating."

"Ah." Cassidy sucked in a deep breath, relieved at last of the impression that the air in the room was running out of oxygen. "Is that all?" Three pairs of wide brown eyes blinked at her. "If it's survival food you wish to speak of," she caught one of her curls and slowly pulled it away from her head before letting it spring back, "I can tell you tales that will twist your hair to rival my own."

For the next hour she kept up a brave chatter about the months of survival training she'd endured as part of earning the rank of zaldun. She even made them cringe once with her description of a meal of cave slime.

"That's absolutely disgusting." Gallica took a huge drink of water as if she could rinse away the thought of the slime coating her mouth.

Isaac and Stuart said considerably less, but they went a bit pale around their noses and mouths, which spoke volumes.

"But easily accessible. It grows on the walls of lava tubes in some places, when the conditions are right," she explained, trying to get their minds off her clearly too-vivid description. "And it's very nourishing."

Isaac, Stuart, and Gallica reached for their water glasses simultaneously.

Chapter 7

Cassidy sat on the floor beside her bed, knees bent and feet together. Her arms moved slowly through the air in a seated taithí, a weight clutched in each fist. The purposes of this form were threefold: the weights would strengthen her arms for the times she wielded her suge; it allowed her to practice the exact same motions as the standing form but in a relatively tiny space; and, hopefully, it would drive Daphne's exaggerated youthful energy from Cassidy's mind.

Daphne spent all that morning bustling about their suite, packing and rearranging and repacking the small suitcase Cassidy had finally given her in a desperate attempt to escape the younger woman's advice on what to take.

To make things worse, Daphne seemed to find it necessary to utter some form of, "You're leaving tomorrow, you know!" with every other breath.

Yes! I know! Cassidy wanted to scream, or at the very least pull her hair out, but she didn't. It would be undignified. Besides, she knew that Daphne's fidgets were fueled in part by concern for her.

So, instead, she sat in her room behind a closed door, and tried to puzzle through a way to make time move faster. After the mad rush to prepare the expedition, it felt like most of Weetu had taken a very long, very deep breath and was now holding it.

Unfortunately, Isaac was not among those at leisure. She would've much rather spent her morning with him.

She drew in a deep breath of her own and slowly exhaled it. Started the taithí over. Her arms wound up, over her head. One moved left and the other right for balance while moving.

Once again, the Wood Fairies had taken her by surprise. King Walter accompanied Isaac nearly everywhere now, like a shadow. A grim, imposing shadow in a dashing Wrangler uniform…a visual reminder that while his son was gone, he was in command of the corp. The line of authority would not waver.

Several of the Wood Fairies perked up every time they saw him, but Cassidy got the shivers every time she almost mistook the king for her fiancé. It was as if they were all trying so hard to be prepared in case something bad happened to the expedition that they were *willing* it to happen.

"Couldn't he have waited until we were aboard the windships," she sighed to no one in particular as she rose gracefully, "to be quite so prepared to take Isaac's place in the day-to-day Wrangler operations?" She stretched up toward the ceiling, then bent to press her palms flat to the floor.   Straightened and smoothed her blouse into its customary position.

It was altogether too quiet on the other side of the door, which made it time to check on her junior assistant. Bracing herself for the flood of Daphne's fifty new questions and suggestions and concerns, Cassidy opened the door and stepped through into the little room they sometimes used as a dining area.

"Daphne?"   How odd.   The vivacious young woman didn't appear or even answer Cassidy's call.

Stranger still was the tan tablecloth on the round table before her. A quick count of the place settings showed that someone was expecting five fairies for lunch.

But who was expecting whom?

Spotting her suitcase lying open on a counter across the room, she made her way over to it. A small jumble of discarded items rested beside it and she couldn't help chuckling over some of them. A bottle of scented dusting powder, which would've attracted every mosquito for leagues. A set of ornate hair pins, which would be a nightmare to wear under her coif. The slippers, light enough to dance in, gave her pause.

Slowly, she traced the slipper's bow while she thought. At Rosie's insistence, she'd gone to a cobbler and gotten sturdy boots. She'd also worn them for a few hours every day, trying to soften the stiff leather by using it.

The scale armor. The boots. Her suge. Her medical knowledge. Even her Water Fairy skills. Would it be enough? Or would she still be a dancing slipper in a world of snow and ice?

"Topa?" The greeting, spoken in Margua, the language of the Water Fairies, was accompanied by a knock as someone entered the outer office. "Is anyone here?"

"Papa?" Cassidy closed and latched the suitcase before turning to greet him. "Papa, it's so good to see you!" It was something of a surprise to see him in his shirtsleeves outside of his room, though she thought he looked quite handsome in his simple, black spider silk waistcoat and white, long-sleeved shirt. The gold embroidery on his waistcoat lent a bit of dash to him, as well, making her pause and wonder how it was that he'd managed to remain unmarried all the years since her mama had died.

"And you, my darling." Volt smiled broadly and met her halfway for a hug. "But, where are the others?" They both continued as they had begun, speaking in Margua.

"Others?" She shot a puzzled glance at the table settings—there were five of them. When it finally dawned on her what must be happening, she shook her head with a laugh. "We're all having lunch together? Even Duncan and Agnes?"

"Yes." Volt winked at her. "It's an old Wood Fairy tradition, I'm told."

So much so that he'd accidentally shocked a few of the Wood Fairy officials when he'd tried to make appointments with them for today. They'd refused him point-blank despite the rapidly shrinking calendar and insisted he spend time with his daughter before she left. Naturally, he'd assured them that he'd like nothing better, but was only now realizing how true that was.

"Yes, of course. Family and friends gather to spend time together before an extended mission." Cold despite his arm around her shoulders, she drew away to fuss over the silverware. "The Wranglers will be at the Eagle later." As would Isaac. She would probably go as well, for any member of the expedition was welcome. She hoped.

"Yes." Volt watched with troubled eyes as some of the light seemed to go out of her. "I understand their wish to take warm memories with them."

She hesitated, then dropped her arms to her sides and looked at him directly. "I have a bad feeling, Papa. As if…as if all of this good cheer and comfortable speaking of how they will miss us is building toward our failure. Our," she swallowed, hard, "permanent failure."

Volt frowned to himself as he watched his only child study the design on a fork handle.

Or, at least pretend to study it. Of all the things he'd been applauded for or congratulated on in his life, it was of her that he was the most proud. Like her mother before her, she'd crested a peak in the mountains of science and guided others on the same trail, benefitting the entire tribe.

And here she was, another mountain chosen. A mountain he wouldn't always be there to help her navigate. Well, then. He'd best point her in the right direction now, hadn't he?

"I begin to see why these Wood Fairies of yours are so boisterous." He did his best to smile warmly. If pressed, he would admit that he found their rowdy behavior shocking at first. The more time he spent among them, however, the easier it was for him to see past their relatively rough exteriors and into their hearts. "I was thinking about this just the other day."

Approaching Cassidy, he gently removed the fork from her unresisting fingers and replaced it on the table. "Winter is arguably the safest time of year for them. The few predators that don't sleep the winter away are safely on the far side of an impenetrable tree trunk. Yet somehow all this," he waved one hand at the thick walls surrounding them, "security seems to stifle them. They remind me of you, in a way."

Startled, she lifted her head to stare at him.

"You could've stayed in your laboratory, content with the current wisdom that surface fairies were forever doomed to war. But you knew you were needed here." His lips twitched in an admittedly sad smile as he remembered reading the note she'd left for him. "You might've performed a single surgery and stayed locked up in your rooms, never venturing out or learning anything of use. But that would've served no one. Knowing that, you seized the opportunities to expand your knowledge, even to expand their knowledge, and laid your brick alongside Kuntza's in building the foundation of a new Fairydom."

Cassidy shook her head, blushing crimson. "You make it sound so noble. As if I looked into the future the way I might a microscope and said to myself, aha! You must go or nothing good will ever happen again in Fairydom!"

He couldn't help laughing at her dramatic outburst and after a moment, she joined him.

"Yes, indeed." Wrapping an arm around her shoulders, he kissed her forehead, still warm from the blush. "You have a great deal in common with these Wood Fairies of yours."

"They aren't *my* Wood Fairies," she protested, twitching the tails of his cravat as she had when she was a child.

"Don't you think they should be?" Drawing back, he tapped the chain she wore around her neck these days. Prince Isaac's ring was on the end of that cord, hidden from prying eyes. "In fact, my dear, I rather think you can do better than simply accepting that you will soon be forever part of this tribe. You must learn to love them, *all* of them, as your own family." He ended his brief lecture with a kind reminder. "After all, my darling daughter. You have agreed to one day be their queen."

"Yes, Papa, I know." Reaching up, she touched the small bump nestled in the hollow at the base of her throat. "It will be nothing like serving on a city council." She hadn't served in Noddfa very long, accepting her release as soon as it was offered so that she might pursue her experiments. Even then, she'd shared the responsibility of grave decisions with six other councilors, making it the barest hint of what lay ahead for her.

"I'm afraid not," he agreed. Then, to let her try her future role on for size in a controlled setting he observed, "You'll carry a far heavier load, with only two pairs of hands to do the work and two heads to make the decisions." He tsked and shook his head glumly.

"Oh, Papa. You speak as if you knew nothing of their ministers and ambassadors," she teased lightly. "And the Wranglers, why, they're practically an extension of the royal family."

The startled expression on her face as her own words, so casually spoken, sounded in her ears, prompted him to chuckle. She smiled wryly back and soon they were both laughing.

"What's all this?" Agnes entered on the arm of her husband, Duncan. They, like Volt and Cassidy, were dressed simply, as though they'd stopped by on their way to the office or one of the markets at home. "Have you started the party without us?"

"Not exactly." Cassidy dabbed at her eyes with her sleeve kerchief. "We were just, well…"

"Contemplating the future." Volt rose to pull out a chair for Agnes, who accepted with a smile.

"Oh, good! You're all here." Daphne grinned as she rattled into the room, a serving cart in tow. Parking the cart by the table, she bowed with a flourish and somehow had a towel draped over her arm in waiter fashion when she straightened up. "Today we have something extra special for lunch, ladies and gentlefairies."

They all watched with interest as Daphne ladled out a thick, white soup into bowls for them. A platter of rolls was placed in the center of the table by Duncan, who then seated Daphne.

"This," Daphne picked up her spoon and stirred the soup lightly, "is called vegetable chowder. Made with fresh vegetables from the greenhouses, a bit of flour, and butter."

"It smells wonderful." Cassidy was the first to take a bite. The buttery flavor exploded on her tongue while carrot and potato pieces gave her the satisfaction of chewing a bit. "And tastes delicious!"

"Indeed!" Agnes had also taken a cautious sip. She still preferred Water Fairy food, but was learning to enjoy some Wood Fairy offerings. "Hmm." She closed her eyes. "I think this might taste rather good with clam in it, too."

A chorus of approval came from around the table and they all dug in. Soon a cheerful conversation began that lasted through the meal and for over an hour after.

"Just make sure you stay with the group," advised Duncan. "I never went on a training camp yet that didn't have problems a little common sense wouldn't prevent."

Cassidy smiled and agreed with them as they each offered a piece of advice, then accepted hugs, even from Duncan, who by now was more like an uncle than anything else.

Daphne packed up the dishes and trundled them off to the kitchen, leaving Cassidy alone again with her father.

Feeling sentimental, he slipped an arm around her shoulders and kissed her hair.

Likewise reluctant to let him go, though he

surely had appointments elsewhere, Cassidy put her arm around his waist and hugged him.

"Papa?"

"Hmm?" Resting his cheek against her hair, he waited for her to respond. And waited. At last he felt her shoulders rise as if with a deep breath.

"Did you ever want to marry again?" She felt his body shift as if she'd knocked the wind out of him.

"Ma-marry?" He stumbled over the word. "Again? Me?"

"Oh, Papa." Catching his hands in hers, she stepped back and looked him over briskly. "You're a young man still. Certainly you are handsome enough to have attracted someone." She squeezed his hands and moved closer when it seemed he was about to speak. Met his hazel-blue eyes directly. "I won't ask again, I promise. But I wanted you to know it would be alright with me."

Volt stood where he was, gaping at her, as if someone had tied ballast to his feet and knocked him senseless to boot.

"Wh…" He tried again. "Whatever possessed you to say such a thing, child?"

Cassidy was much too old to be reprimanded thus and she proved it by not laughing at him for it.

"I don't quite know, Papa," she answered truthfully. Looking down at their joined hands, she shook her head helplessly. "It just seemed like something that needed to be said."

"Well." Overcoming his shock somewhat, he sternly informed her, "I'm happy as I am, young lady. I'll never know what I did to deserve a woman as wonderful as your mother, or how you turned out so wonderfully without her to guide you."

"I had you, Papa." Dropping his hands, she hugged him with both arms, suddenly feeling as young as he seemed to think she was.

He sighed softly and hugged her back. "That's very kind of you, my dear, but we mustn't completely forget the role your grandmother played in your upbringing."

"Mmm." She nodded, her cheek moving easily on the shoulder of his spider silk waistcoat. "And Doctor Tzatu."

"Doctor Tzatu?" he echoed. "Why, what do you mean?"

"Didn't you know?" She stepped back and smoothed his waistcoat for him. "She was mama's best friend when they were little girls and sometimes she'd come take me for walks to the observation domes. We would watch the fish for hours while she taught me their names." Cassidy smiled fondly at the memories.

"That does sound familiar." He squinted at nothing for a moment. "Ah, yes. Doctor Tzatu. I met her at the wedding. Didn't realize you two had become such good friends, though."

"She's head of ichthyology studies at the university now."

"A prestigious position." Volt was genuinely impressed. To head the study of fish in a tribe that lived under the ocean was no small feat.

The water clock on the counter chimed twice and Cassidy sighed. "Bother. It's getting late."

Volt forced a smile. "You do leave quite early tomorrow, I'm told."

"We leave an hour after sunrise." Which meant arriving at the shipyard for loading and final preparation an hour before that. She suppressed the shiver that came with just thinking about it. Her visits to the greenhouse, though few, had been memorable. One had to wear a coat if they intended to get anywhere near the ice disk that sealed the enormous hole in the tree's bark.

"I see." His heart twisted with fear for her, for all of them. While he'd never experienced the extreme cold of a winter on the surface, he was all too familiar with the limits of fairy bodies.

"Did I tell you?" Desperate to distract him from the telltale emotion in his eyes—before they *both* cried—she hurriedly explained, "I'm to be the doctor for our party. Rosie has spent every spare moment stuffing my head with knowledge since it was decided. And, Isaac gave me this."

Flitting away from her father, she reached into the small bag on top of a much larger bag and pulled out a pocket-sized book.

"This," she proudly showed it to her father, "is the apprentice Wrangler's guide to all things medicinal."

"Wonderful." Volt produced another smile and feigned a deep interest in the book as he flipped through it. Most of the plants were foreign to him, but he took a moment to appreciate the care taken with each drawing and the detailed descriptions found beneath them. "Excellent."

"Yes, I think I'll be using this a lot." She chuckled and accepted it back, a little relieved that he'd completely missed the directory section with its lengthy list of maladies and injuries and so on. "That is, I hope to not need it."

"I understand, my dear." He cleared his throat and made a show of checking the water clock. They were clumsy things compared with the lightning-powered time pieces he was accustomed to, but since everyone here used them, they all managed to be early and late at more or less the same times. "I'd better be going. Mustn't keep the Plant Fairy Minister waiting." The words were ordinary enough, but his voice was suddenly thick with emotion.

They shared another hug, and then she was alone with her plans for the future.

Chapter 8

Early the next morning, Cassidy put her fork down with a sigh and picked up her napkin instead. If she didn't start getting some of the food in her mouth instead of on her chin or cheeks, she would faint from hunger before they stopped for lunch. Not that a windship could actually *stop* once it got going. They would land eventually, but that wasn't the same…

She forced herself to stop. Lifted one hand to massage her forehead. She'd slept badly, waking twice from nightmares. She *never* had nightmares. And, as vivid as these were, it was their silence that woke her. They were so unnaturally silent.

Her fingers curled around her napkin as she tried to objectively review one of the dreams. It should've been easy to hold it up for examination now that she was more or less awake, but the blasted thing squirmed and twisted, once again becoming real.

Some*thing* lurked just beyond her vision. One of the dozens of different kinds of surface monsters. Did it really matter which one? They were all enormous and most were fiendishly fast.

She couldn't hear it or smell it any more than she could see it…but she knew it was there.

A hand on her shoulder made her jump. Heart racing, she gripped the solid edge of the table, re-centering herself in the blessedly small room, with its comforting walls, ceiling, and floor. Nowhere for monsters to hide in here.

"It's just me," said Daphne softly. She left her hand on Cassidy's shoulder, wishing she knew a better way to soothe her. "Someone's here for your baggage."

Cassidy nodded and fought down the food she'd managed to swallow before it could finish climbing back up her throat.

"I'll take care of it." Daphne swept into the outer room, where she briskly instructed the fifth-year Wrangler apprentices which bags to take.

Cassidy focused on Daphne's voice, using it like a shield against the fear trying to swamp her. Grasping her fork, she resumed shoveling food from the plate, taking care to get each bite into her mouth.

There really wasn't that much to eat. A bowl of hot, boiled grains with a dollop of butter and bits of rehydrated apples mixed in. A draught of milk, not chilled. A small wedge of white cheese.

Finished, she rose and stacked the dishes for Daphne, then joined her in the outer office.

Per Isaac's advice, she'd sent her armor ahead to the windship, to be stored with other such gear where it could be accessed easily.

Presently, her traveling outfit consisted of leather calf boots, leather britches, and a loose leather tunic over thin woolen slacks, woolen socks, and a woolen shirt. While not ideal for casual meandering about in, the inner layer of 'woolens,' as they were called, would serve as a liner that could be relatively easily changed to keep the 'leathers' fresher longer.

Rosie had taken time out of Cassidy's medical training to explain how the pieces of the outfit worked together to keep her warm enough. The double-layer leather britches and jacket were soft and supple, but the secret to their warmth lay in the carefully preserved fur, which created a protective air pocket that insulated against the extreme cold.

"I'll carry that." Cassidy took the coorelum leather tunic from Daphne and draped it over one arm. The fur on the outside tickled her bare wrists and she tugged the sleeve of her woolen shirt down to cover them. "Take care of yourself while I'm gone, won't you?"

Daphne held her head up high, but the slight wobble of her chin gave her away.

Cassidy dropped the tunic back on the desk and wrapped the younger woman in a hug. "I'll miss you."

Daphne hugged her back fiercely. "Dreadful of you to go off and have an adventure without me." She sniffled, but only just. "Promise you'll tell me all about it when you get back?" Daphne's hold tightened painfully with her request, signaling that she truly feared Cassidy might never return.

"I promise." Cassidy's words were nearly a gasp and she wondered if Daphne had always been this strong. "I'll go over your records and treatments, too. Odds are, you'll be a full-fledged doctor before much longer."

Now Daphne sniffled in earnest, but she had the grace to withdraw and produce a handkerchief to mop her face with.

"I'll look after everyone for you," the young nurse pledged gravely.

"I know you will." Cassidy picked up the tunic again and dropped a rare wink. "Don't forget to let Agnes help, alright?"

"Agnes wouldn't mind a bit of a vacation," announced the older woman as she peeked in the hallway door. Chuckling, she pulled Cassidy into a hug, tunic and all. "You're sure about this?" she whispered near Cassidy's ear.

"Positive." Cassidy whispered back.

"Well, then." Agnes lifted the tunic from Cassidy's arms and motioned toward the door. "I've come to walk you to the shipyard, Lady Cassidy."

Daphne went with them as far as the turnoff to the infirmary, where she took her leave.

"She'll make a fine doctor," Cassidy mused aloud.

"Absolutely." Agnes chuckled. "Though I thought for a while after we arrived that she might abandon science in favor of spinning tales like the ones she discovered in the library here."

Cassidy laughed, too, grateful for a light-hearted topic. "She still may." She nodded at Agnes' incredulous stare. "Don't tell her I know, but I found a sheaf of paper in the bottom drawer of the desk the other day. She's writing the tale of Anders the Wise, with a great deal of emphasis on his successes in sea harvesting."

Agnes scrunched up her eyes in mock horror and they laughed together. "Do you think we should encourage her?"

"An interesting idea." Cassidy slowed, suddenly realizing that the groups of fairies they were encountering were mostly families. Strong men and women of varied ages, dressed in comfortable Wrangler uniforms, were on their knees, hugging children goodbye; or wrapped in the arms of their parents; or kissing their loved ones goodbye. Some groups were a mix of all three.

There was an odd hush in the corridor, as if nobody wanted to interrupt anyone else's goodbyes.

"I, um." She cleared her throat. The entrance to the shipyard was around the next corner and she suddenly couldn't bear to take

Agnes that far. Parting there would be too much like being abandoned, even though they both knew Agnes had never intended to come along on the scouting expedition. "I want you to keep this for me, please."

Startled, Agnes looked down at the rectangular box of mother-of-pearl Cassidy had all but shoved into her hands. "Cassidy, no!" Sensing others scowling at them, she lowered her voice. Her agitation showed just as clearly, though, in her choice of words. "I can't keep your mother's pearls, child. These belong to your family!"

"And I trust you with them." Cassidy folded Agnes' fingers around the box firmly. "What would you have me do? Leave them with my father just in case?"

Agnes stilled abruptly. "No." She shook her head. Cassidy was all that Volt Clark had left of his precious wife. "No, I suppose not. He needn't have this weighing on him."

"We're in agreement, then." Cassidy squared her shoulders. "Should anything happen to me, please deliver them to my grandmother, Lady Damaris. She'll know who should wear them next."

Agnes bit back a sob. "I know what this is about. You explained it all well enough." She shook a finger at Cassidy, something she hadn't done since…well, ever. "But you had better come back in one piece, my lass."

"Isaac will see to that." Cassidy promised as soberly as she could while torn between the desires to laugh and cry. "This is just a precaution." She tapped the box almost tenderly—she had little enough to remember her mother by—then hugged Agnes as hard as she could.

"Oh, my." Agnes cleared her throat softly. "Will you look at that?"

Stepping back, Cassidy followed Agnes' line of sight to... "Daphne?"

"Who's that she's with?" Agnes half-whispered the words, the mood of the corridor having overtaken her.

"I think it's..." Cassidy squinted, trying to imagine the handsome young Wrangler in a different sort of uniform and smiled. "Her friend the librarian."

"Her friend?" Agnes echoed, her lips twitching, though not unkindly. She'd double back to the infirmary and make sure things were taken care of. Daphne had probably made arrangements for the morning so she could slip off and say goodbye to her friend, but it wouldn't hurt to check. "I blame myself. I should've kept a better eye on the both of you!"

Cassidy chuckled with her, then suggested, "Perhaps we'd do well to encourage her storytelling after all."

"Mm, yes." Agnes didn't hesitate to agree. "It will give her something to do. And, the

Wood Fairies do seem exceptionally fond of adventure stories. This might be an excellent way to begin sharing our history with the rest of Fairydom."

"Good point." She nearly jumped out of her wings at a bellow from behind her. Turning to see what was going on, she could hardly believe that so much sound had come out of the small woman standing at the head of the corridor.

"Listen up!" A Wrangler Major consulted the papers in her hand. Judging by her cold gear, she'd just come from the shipyard. "Boarding will start immediately, in this order. *Itxar. Sazko.*"

Cassidy didn't really hear anything after *Itxar*, the name of her windship. Others were already threading past her when Agnes gave her a gentle push forward.

"Hey, Doc." Skite grinned and held the line up a little for her. He'd seen enough green Wranglers going for their first windship flight to have an idea as to why she looked paler than usual. "Let's get your tunic on you, Doc." Snagging the article from her, he nudged her to one side of the corridor, allowing those that were ready to brush by them. Held it while she slipped her arms inside, then patted her shoulder. "That's better."

Cassidy kept up after that, letting the living stream of fairies flow around her, guiding her along… They all wore the same cold gear that she did, but there were subtle differences. The Wranglers all sported wide bands on both upper arms. The officers' bands bore simple symbols of rank and coordinated by background color with their units. Apprentice bands stood out from the rest with their large embroidered letter A's.

Judging by the way the streams of fairies were moving, the *Itxar* must've been the windship furthest from the entrance. All the new sights and sounds occupied her—right up until her line reached the edge of the outcropping.

The outcropping they'd been walking on had huge, irregular gaps, making it impossible for her to walk around the edge of the cavern to get closer to the windship before she had to…to…

Pressing a hand to her stomach, Cassidy moved back from the edge, bumping into fairies behind her.

"Hey." Isaac landed beside her, smiling as he pulled her aside. Looking out over the shipyard, he took a deep breath of the cold air. "Exhilarating, isn't it? We make the best windships in Fairydom in the Deep Woods. See?" He pointed at a massive, triple-thick oak leaf windship. "That's a Hawk-class windship we're building for the Sky Fairies. She'll have fifty guns and four masts when we're done with her."

"Oh?" Cassidy could barely force the word through stiff lips. "Why so m-many guns?"

"Are you shivering? Are you that cold?" Isaac began rubbing her arms. "Cass? What's wrong?" Peering into her white face, he racked his brain for a solution. "It's not for war, I promise. The mountains, they're dangerous. All sorts of birds live in them. Huge birds." She was still staring at him as if transfixed. "Birds big enough that you sometimes need the extra firepower to drive them off. And that's not what's bothering you, is it?"

She dropped her eyes and focused on the stitches on his leather tunic, counting them in her head to distract herself.

"Alright, then…what is it?" He felt her shudder violently in his arms when someone hollered.

"Keep it moving!" Roared an officer somewhere. "We want to leave an hour after dawn, not at dusk!"

"Let's get onboard the *Itxar*," Isaac suggested, suddenly recognizing that a crowded outcropping wasn't the ideal circumstance for the sharing of secrets. "You can tell me there." Her hands, which had settled on his arms, contracted like iron bands around his biceps. Her grip was so fierce that he felt each individual fingertip even through the layers he wore.

"Don't take me out there. Please. Please."

Cassidy screwed her eyes shut and strained to breathe.

"I won't." His promise came out a pained croak and he half-wished for a pry bar to wedge under her hands. "Cassidy, let go. Your hands. You're killing me here." Abruptly her death grip relaxed and blood again flowed through his veins. Exhaling in relief, he managed a faint chuckle. "You are *so* much stronger than I realized."

"Don't take me out there," she repeated. "I'll fall."

"Fall?" He stopped mid-flex to try to comprehend what she was saying. "You won't fall. You'll fly. Just like everyone else." He turned to point at the *Itxar*, to show her the line of Wranglers making their way to it, but the last of them had already landed on deck. The last of the crew except for himself and Cassidy.

In fact, the other windships were nearly all boarded as well. Any minute now, everyone was going to look to the *Itxar* to start the launching sequence. And here he stood, holding a badly shaking Cassidy. Because she wasn't shivering from the chill. She was shaking, from head to foot.

A glance around showed that things were moving smoothly without him—no surprise, really, everyone here was hand-picked—so he allowed himself to focus on Cassidy.

"Listen to my voice." Isaac pulled her as close as their cold gear would allow. "Can you hear me?" He waited until she nodded, eyes still closed tightly. "Who am I?" One eyelid opened just enough for her to peek at him. "Who am I?" he repeated sternly.

"Isaac, I don't want to play games." She eased his hold on her, afraid he was going to squeeze her breakfast out the rest of the way.

"Lady Cassidy Botere." He pressed one palm to her cheek. "Darling. Who am I?"

This time she opened both eyes. Studied his face. The ice in her veins thawed marginally. "I can't look down."

"You don't have to." Dropping a light kiss on her lips, he took a step back. "Just listen to my voice."

She had to try twice to get her voice to cooperate and then it came out hoarse. "I can do that."

"Good." Releasing her hands, he instructed, "Stand right there."

The dock was quieting down and Isaac could sense eyes on them as he carefully turned his back to Cassidy. Well, what of it? If he rushed her now, he would never get her on board the *Itxar*.

"Give me your hands." He waited as patiently as he could, his hands just above his shoulders, while she came closer, then hesitantly put one of her hands in each of his.

"Good. Now, hold still." He drew her arms forward as he moved back toward her, spreading his wings slowly.

"I want you to close your eyes," he told her, positioning her hands so that she could grip the front of the harness that was built into his cold weather gear. "And keep them closed until I tell you. Can you do that?" He felt her breath stir the hairs on the back of his neck in the agonizingly long second it took her to respond.

"I love you. My eyes are closed." Cassidy buried her face in the soft, thick fur of his tunic.

"I love you, too." At first, Isaac took them straight up a twig or two. Leaned forward until he was facing the ground. She shifted into a better position, her grip tightening convulsively on his harness. Taking that as his cue, he flew straight for the windship, arms stretched out behind him.

It felt good to stretch his wings, especially after the weeks of treatment and getting bruises from the cursed wingboard, but he was most thankful that there were no cross-breezes to navigate. The greatest danger to them both right then was Cassidy's fear.

That and his own weakened state. He'd been cleared for light flying and finally for regular flight. Luckily, Cassidy had forgotten that he hadn't flown double, or even while carrying a pack, since before his injuries.

Someone rose from the deck of the *Itxar* and flew toward them, reaching them before they hit the halfway mark. Skite nodded gravely to Isaac and assumed a safety position just above and behind them.

Isaac wiped drops of sweat from his face, but persevered. Only a handful of flaps more. Three…two… Close enough at last, he curved his wings, bringing their hind edges down, slowing his velocity so that he settled softly, softly on the deck.

Before he could catch his breath, Skite was beside him. "A duty-fit Wrangler can carry twice their own body weight on the wing, just in case they need to do a rescue carry," he announced to the gaping apprentices and civilians. "You never know how bad hurt you can get 'til it happens." Slapping Isaac lightly on the shoulder—and coincidentally shaking Cassidy to bring her around a bit—Skite continued, "It's showing off a might to do it just for the fun of it, but." He shrugged. "I reckon Prince Isaac's feelin' his oats after bein' grounded for so long."

Cassidy somehow pried her hands loose from Isaac's harness and managed to stand beside him, though she hoped nobody realized how heavily they were leaning on each other. He was in no shape to have carried her that far and she should never have allowed it.

Chapter 9

"Get that deck cleared!" Keddy, the vessel's captain, bellowed from his position forward.

Anyone who'd stopped to stare at Isaac and Cassidy suddenly resumed their scrambling to get below. In an instant, there wasn't a stray piece of gear or fairy to be seen except for Cassidy and Isaac.

Smiling tightly, Isaac looked from Cassidy to the nearest companionway. He wanted to see her safely below, but… "I have to stay on deck a while."

He didn't know what else to say. No matter how much he wanted to stay with her, to take her below decks and hold her during the launch, he couldn't. Sure, he could assign someone else to oversee things on deck; it wasn't as if the captain *needed* a landlubber underfoot. Except, as the leader of the expedition, courtesy and tradition dictated he remain on deck for the launch.

"I'm alright now." She was, she told herself, squaring her shoulders. The action created a gap between them and she missed his warmth instantly. "But!" She frowned. "I want you to report to me as soon as you can. I need to examine your wings."

"They feel fine," he assured her. Whistles

began sounding from the other windships and he abruptly turned her toward the companionway. "Skite! See her safely below. Now."

Cassidy got a glimpse of the world beyond the railing and lurched backward, slamming into something reassuringly solid. Her hands fisted around sweating palms. It wasn't Isaac. She didn't know how she knew, she just did.

"Steady on." Skite's voice was all business, something she'd only heard once, when Sugar was in mortal danger. His hands gripped her shoulders gently. "Close your eyes if you like, but ahead we must go."

Gulping, she closed her eyes and allowed him to walk her forward. He was a first-class idiot on the subject of practical jokes, but she knew him well enough to trust him not to throw her over the gunn'ls for a laugh.

"Safe to look, Doc." Skite put her hand on the solid wall ahead of her. "In fact, I recommend it. Otherwise, you'll probably hit your head."

She sneaked a peak and saw that she was boxed in on three sides. Skite stood behind her and stairs descended before her.

"Hurry, Doc!"

In response to the urgency in Skite's tone, she lifted one leaden leg. Then the other. Her feet become lighter, her movements quicker, as she descended into a comfortingly cramped hold.

By the light of a few hanging storm lanterns she could see stacks of gear, secured behind cargo nets where it would balance the windship during the flight. A small cast-iron stove sat on a sheet of metal at the far end of the hold. Beside it stood a large box that looked ready to burst with its load of firewood. Steam came from a large pot on the stovetop, which was being stirred by a wiry older Plant Fairy who grinned as he gabbed with the Wranglers.

"Here, Doc." That was all she had a chance to see before Skite all-but carried her to the nearest empty spot and seated her firmly on a bench. "You can secure yourself with these." Reaching around her waist, he pulled two pieces of rope away from the wall and handed them to her.

The apprentice Wrangler beside her on the bench snickered, but she tied the rope around her waist just the same. With a sturdy bulkhead behind her and a hold lit only by hanging storm lanterns, her frantic heart rate began to return to normal.

The windship rocked unexpectedly and she nearly choked on a suppressed squeak. Swallowing hard, she closed her eyes and tried to convince herself that she was in a Water Fairy vessel, tucked safely beneath the waves.

On deck, Isaac grimly clipped a safety line to his harness—as much to keep himself from going to check on Cassidy as from any concern that he might go overboard. "At your pleasure, Captain Keddy." A quick glance at the hourglass showed him it wasn't as late as he'd thought and he exhaled silently in relief. They needed every minute of sunlight for their flight that they could get.

"Hoods and goggles! Wing flaps down and locked!" Keddy barked and the ship's mate relayed the orders to the two crew members currently on deck. The captain needed two hands to smooth his wiry blue hair under his hood before fastening the front so that his whole head and neck were covered. Goggles on and secured, he gripped the wheel tightly in anticipation and shouted, "Loose the slings!"

Isaac chuckled to himself while he finished securing his protective gear. All the forms on deck looked remarkably like walking gloves, with arms and legs in place of fingers; faceless except for the goggles that would shield their eyes from the bitter cold outside.

Dock workers, crew, and even the crews on the other windships cheered as the *Itxar* slid free.

Gravity did the work at first as Keddy kept her pointed toward their exit, a smallish door built into the massive one that kept the ice and snow out, if not the cold. To the inexperienced, the smaller door probably looked like an impossible target. For Keddy and his elite crew, though, threading a target barely larger than their windship was as easy as telling up from down.

Isaac's feet were barely touching the deck by the time the stout little vessel nosed her way free of the shipyard and plunged into the sunlight. She shuddered a little as a playful breeze tickled her sails, then shook off her winter malaise and sprang forward, making Isaac tighten his grip on the rail as the brief sensation of weightlessness passed.

Covered from head to toe against the cold, the five on deck nevertheless turned to the sun. Her heat warmed their bones, chilled over a long winter living by firelight.

Keddy broke the spell with more orders and the *Itxar* came about sharply, pointing north toward Lauta.

Isaac watched the next two ships launch without trouble, then broke out his telescope for the last three. The mate and both windfairies stood at the waists, watching as well. A careful record was made in the logbook of when each of the other windships left visual range. It didn't take long, even with the branches still bare of leaves.

Stowing his glass, Isaac saluted Keddy. "Permission to go below, sir?"

Keddy grunted. "Aye, you'll be wanting to see that doctor of yours."

Isaac scowled, then remembered the captain couldn't see his face through the shield. Which might be for the best, at the moment. The shields were a necessary evil at these temperatures, especially while out in the open air on a rapidly moving windship, but at the same time they could severely hamper communication. The only solutions were for the mate to stick close to the captain and hand signals often supplanted verbal commands.

"Doctor Clark is the doctor of everyone on board this vessel, captain, as you well know."

Keddy shrugged, clearly unimpressed. "Happen someone should be injured on deck, what use do you s'ppose she'll be?"

Isaac gritted his teeth against a hasty response. "You think she's afraid of heights?"

"I do. And a stranger thing I've never seen." Keddy gestured at the world around them. "If the weather were fine, we'd be wavin' to traders on branches as we passed. What sort of fairy is she, that she's afraid of heights?"

Again, Isaac controlled a waspish retort. Seconds grew into minutes as he considered everything he knew about her.

"I don't think that's it." He met Keddy's piercing blue eyes, slightly obscured by the goggles, without blinking. "She's never hesitated to fly anywhere in Weetu, not the second or even the third levels. It's something else." Summoning his best diplomatic training, Isaac finished with, "You made a good point, though. We'll be flying most of the day and someone may be injured. Let's plan on summoning a senior Wrangler first for on-deck injuries. If it's beyond their capabilities, I am confident that Doctor Clark will find a way past her fear to help."

Keddy growled something unintelligible, which was probably just as well for both their sakes, and nodded sharply.

Accepting that as a dismissal, Isaac unclipped his safety line and descended the companionway. Passing the second crew of windfairies on his way to the wood-burning stove, he noticed one of them slip away to go on deck. They rotated crew members rapidly when it was this bitterly cold.

"It is *cold* out there!" Isaac shivered for effect and spread his hands over the stove. The heat bit into his chilled fingers like a squirrel into an acorn and he almost yelped in pain.

"Do tell?" Skite led the snickering from where he lounged. He met Isaac's eyes and tilted his head fractionally to his left, indicating Cassidy's seat.

Isaac swallowed hard and made a mental note to never again complain about Skite's stupid practical jokes. He was trying to estimate how long was long enough to stand at the stove before he went to check on Cassidy when a young voice asked an ancient question.

"How much longer afore we get there?"

Amidst the answering laughter, Isaac gave a

half-frozen windfairy his spot at the stove and made his way down the line of Wranglers to sit by a wan-looking Cassidy. He relaxed for the first time in an hour when her hand slipped into his. They couldn't discuss it privately, so he doubted they should discuss it at all. Then again, if he knew anything about spring expeditions, it was that privacy would be almost as scarce as gourmet meals.

Pressing his shoulder against hers, he murmured, "Walk with me?"

"Time to examine your wings?" With a shaky smile, she rose.

"That can wait." He headed for the aft companionway, but stopped the instant he felt her begin to tense. "This is far enough." Glancing back past her to where the others remained clustered in the hold, he loosely trapped her by placing his free hand on the wall by her shoulder. "I'd kiss you," he whispered, "if we didn't need to talk." Her answering blush was the first color he'd seen in her cheeks since he'd found her on the shipyard walk earlier.

"I'm sorry." She took a deep breath and let it out. "I am so, *so* sorry. I didn't know that would happen. I mean, I've only heard stories about places like the, um, the…" Her eyes narrowed and she shook her head, frustrated that she couldn't think of the word.

"Shipyard?" he supplied.

"Yes." Even standing there, more or less in Isaac's arms, her heart began to race at the memory of the gaping, yawning hole.

"Cassidy." Dropping her hand, he gripped her shoulder instead. Shook her lightly when she took too long to respond. "What is it? What about the shipyard scares you?"

She brought both hands up and put her palms flat against his chest. The contact steadied her. "Big. T-too big. Empty."

Confused, Isaac just stood there, trying to grasp what she had just said. The shipyard was big. No. It was 'too big.' And 'empty.'

Except it wasn't. She had to have seen the partially constructed windships; they were all over the place. Every tribe lost windships in the recent pirate offensive. They had orders for military windships that would keep them scrambling all year. There was even some talk of opening a second shipyard to accommodate civilian orders, the kind that didn't need cannons mounted or reinforced hulls.

"I'd like to tell you I understand." He eased her the rest of the way into his arms, not even caring whether or not anyone noticed. "But I don't. Too big? Empty?" He shrugged his shoulders, forgetting for a moment that her hands had moved to his arms. "I don't understand that." Feeling her start to stiffen, he slid his fingers into her hair and held her more tightly. "Fear, though. I know fear all too well."

Her heart resumed a near-normal beating in her chest at his soothing words. "Thank you," she whispered. She hugged him back, savoring the moment, all of her senses filled with Isaac.

"No need for thanks." He smoothed her hair as he released her. "We'll figure this out, alright?" *We have to.*

She nodded, wanting to believe him. The sound of metal striking metal snapped Cassidy out of her pensive state. "Isaac?" Disentangling herself, she squinted into the dim interior. "Something's wrong."

"What? Where?" Isaac dragged his thoughts away from some very vivid potential future catastrophes, all of them involving a petrified Cassidy, and tried to concentrate on the situation at hand.

"That man. He's not well. Excuse me." Cassidy slipped into doctor mode without even realizing it as she walked back into the hold in time to catch a cup of hot broth that was about to slip through stiff fingers.

Isaac leaned against the bulkhead and folded his arms across his chest. He knew basic first aid, enough to keep someone alive so the squad medic could get there and take over. Wrangler medicine was often a brusque business, however, composed of direct questions and equally direct answers.

Watching Cassidy, Isaac envied the subtle mix of authority and compassion she exuded as she assessed the windfairy. She drove straight to the truth and, under threat of a full examination, he admitted that he'd hit his head while on deck.

Leaving Cassidy to her work, Isaac went up to talk to the captain. For the next several hours, he kept himself busy with the details of the expedition, taking care to make eye contact with Cassidy every time he returned to the main hold. For each routine bit of business he did, his racing brain raked him through the coals of different ways Cassidy's fear could contribute to tragedy.

It only got worse when he finally sat to catch his breath, a mug of hot broth cupped in his chilled hands. He didn't even smell the savory odor as he slipped into his thoughts, trying to find a way to help her before something went horribly wrong.

"Sir?"

Isaac blinked and looked up from his seat on the bench into the slightly bewildered face of the short, swarthy windfairy addressing him. "Yes?"

"Captain's respects, sir." The windfairy touched two fingers to his sky blue forelock. "The hackberry grove is in sight and he'd like all officers on deck, scanning for a landing position."

Isaac waited a beat to see if there was more forthcoming, then nodded briskly. "We'll be up in a moment, thank you."

"What was that?" Skite spoke from beside Isaac as soon as the windfairy was out of earshot.

"You saw it, too?" Isaac scratched his ear and sighed inwardly, resigning himself to donning the hood once more. He'd have to remember to check with that windfairy later and ask what was bothering him.

"Uhh…?" Skite's eyebrows rose. "I saw you not answer the first two times he addressed you." Skite paused to polish a smudge off his goggle. "I thought you'd fallen asleep with your eyes open."

"Really?" Isaac flipped his hood up, tucked his hair firmly behind his ears and willed it not to tickle his ears. Skite's explanation told him he didn't have to worry about the windfairy; he just had to worry about himself. Wonderful. "Nope. I was just thinking."

Getting to his feet, Isaac relayed the captain's request. Cassidy offered him a tremulous smile from where she was talking with the cook, a burly Plant Fairy, and Isaac forced himself to start trudging toward the companionway.

"Let's get this right the first time, folks!" Bellowed the captain from where he stood at the windship's stem as the Wrangler officers clipped on their safety lines. "The sooner we land, the sooner we can batten down for the night!"

"Truer words," muttered Skite as he opened his field glass.

They stationed themselves around the gunn'ls, leaning on the waist-high barrier that ran around the deck as they peered into the hackberry grove, seeking the best landing position. They needed more than a spot big enough to accommodate a windship, much more. They needed protection from the elements. A clear line of sight for the sentries. Proximity to dead, dry wood was desirable. Above all, it had to be in full sun for as many daylight hours as possible.

The junior officers called out when they sighted a likely position and the captain, Isaac, or Skite reviewed them as quickly as they could. As yet the sun was keeping the frost off the deck, but they only had an hour or so until nightfall.

"We're running out of grove," grumbled the captain after ruling out yet another site. Patches of snow ran along some of the flatter, more desirable landing spots and he refused to chance slipping off a layer of ice that might be hidden underneath.

"That's it!" Isaac beat his arms against his body and stamped his feet against the cold. "Leave the grove and catch an updraft. We'll come back around and make an approach from east to west, not south to north."

"Staying on the south side of the grove, where the sun shines hottest the winter long.

That might work." The captain paused to wipe ash and grit off the compass as he passed it. Smoke, issuing from the stovepipe near the foremast, drifted across the deck and coating everything in its path. While this added a degree of traction to the relatively slippery deck, it also got on equipment and clothes.

At the call of, "Captain has the helm!" everyone braced themselves and the windship started a wide turn.

Isaac desperately wished he could wave his officers below, but they'd no sooner reach the hold and have their hoods off for a mug of hot broth than the call would come for them to be back on deck. So instead he gritted his teeth and focused on not letting his glass slip through numb fingers.

He lurched unsteadily as the windship found the updraft, his safety line catching him when his own reflexes failed.

"Eyes open!" Shouted Skite as the windship swung around for a second pass. "Sing out if you spot our new home!"

Isaac brought his glass up to his goggles. Frowned when he saw only white nothingness. Clumsily, he reversed the glass and wiped the frost off the far end with his mitten.

"Over here!" They were all on the same side of the windship now, looking north toward the south edge of the grove. "I've got a patchy white spot. Looks like borer holes!"

"Identify the tree!" Roared the captain, who had no intention of traversing half the deck to stand at the officer's elbow.

"Northwest, approaching fast. To our left of a tall tree with brooms in the upper branches," sang out another voice. "Branch a third of the way down."

Isaac finally spotted the tree and brought his glass to bear. The captain was already issuing landing orders by the time Isaac was getting a good look at the site. Trusting the captain's decision, Isaac expanded his visual examination.

"Tree looks healthy enough," observed Skite. "I only see a small section of holes. On this side, anyhow. I'll take a crew out in the morning to start reconnoitering the rest of the tree."

"Not before we draw lots for woodcutting duty," snorted Isaac. Collecting wood to burn in their never-ending fire was nobody's favorite task, but it had to be done. "I'm not seeing any old bird or wasp nests."

"Is that a good or a bad thing?" Skite wasn't kidding. Birds and wasps kept the spider population down.

"Don't know yet." Isaac closed his glass and put it away. A glance around the deck showed that he and Skite were the last Wranglers on deck. "Let's get below before we freeze clear through. And you can forget about the outside of the tree tomorrow. First order of business is to scout the borer holes. Once we're sure we have them to ourselves, we can start making permanent plans."

"Understood." Skite began moving stiffly toward the companionway. "One good thing. We're high enough up on this branch that we could relocate if we had to."

"Don't let Captain Keddy hear you say that. I don't know which is worse, an emergency landing or an emergency takeoff." Isaac eyed the stairs unhappily, but ventured to start down them despite not being able to feel his lower legs. "Let's hope it isn't necessary."

Chapter 10

"Take your seats!" Skite barked the order as they bolted into the hold. He grabbed a coil of rope that hung from the ceiling just in time to keep from tripping over a careless apprentice. "We're on approach."

Cassidy, a fast learner, clamped the lid shut on the mostly-empty pot of broth to keep it from spilling everywhere—the pot itself was already held down by an ingenious device—and hurried over to Isaac. Any concerns they might've had about his tribe taking exception to their relationship faded into the background as they found a spot on the bench where they could sit together.

"This is going to be a bumpy landing." Isaac held still while Cassidy took off his goggles and threw back his hood so he could breathe more easily. "But don't worry, Keddy knows exactly what," he almost bit his tongue when the *Itxar* started jolting along the branch, "he's doing."

"Good." Cassidy's reply came out sounding like an empty gourd being drug across a ribbed washboard, the result of the *Itxar's* persistent bouncing. Her fingers dug into the edge of the bench beneath her and she braced her booted feet on the planking.

It was over almost as suddenly as it had begun. Cassidy stayed right where she was, gritting her teeth against the next impact…while several others exploded into action.

"Move, move! Get those anchors in place!"

In the blink of an eye, Isaac, Skite, the deck crew, and Cassidy were almost the only ones left in the hold. The handful of apprentices crowded the portholes, watching eagerly as the Wranglers worked to tether the *Itxar* to the tree bark. Keddy had skillfully guided them into a furrow between raised ridges of bark—a sheltering valley for their relatively tiny craft.

"Welcome to Lauta." Isaac announced to nobody in particular.

With an effort, Cassidy released her grip on the bench and lurched to her feet. She'd gotten so used to the subtle motion of the craft over the last few hours that she had to stand still for a moment to reorient herself.

"You all," she took a deep breath, "are freezing. Stay there and I'll bring you some hot broth."

"I'll do the totin'," offered the cook kindly, his voice strangely high-pitched and breathy, like a squeaky tin whistle. "You'll do well to keep yer feet planted fer a bit, lass."

Cassidy smiled gratefully and began filling mugs for him to pass out. She was scraping the bottom of the pot when the others began filing back in, but the cook just shooed her off.

"Apprentices, to me!" ordered the cook. "We'll need more'n hot broth to see us through this night!"

Realizing that Isaac didn't have a mug, Cassidy ducked through the commotion to take him the last of the broth and was surprised when he pulled her onto the bench again.

"But I can help!" she protested, indicating the miniature kitchen springing to life at the far end of the hold.

"You will, trust me." Isaac winked and let a sip of the hot broth slide down his throat. It was a wonder none of them caught fatal chills on these voyages. It was hard to tell under the bite of the spices, but did he detect doctor's water in the aftertaste? As much as he usually hated the vile-tasting medicinal concoction, right now he didn't even care.

"We'll be out here for weeks," he reminded Cassidy. "Cutting wood and cooking food are the two constants of a spring expedition. Let the apprentices help tonight. Maybe they won't complain as much when they're detailed to cut wood tomorrow."

She shook her head a bit doubtfully, but bowed to his experience. "Speaking of tomorrow, I'll need a look at the flood plain."

"Tomorrow? No, not tomorrow. We'll be clearing the borer holes tomorrow and some of us," Isaac frowned as he finished his broth in a gulp, "may have need of our doctor."

She stopped fidgeting and stared directly at him. Every speck of fight in her screamed that she had to find a way to keep him from getting hurt. His betrothal ring, trapped under layers of cold gear, seemed to dig into her skin, reminding her of all she stood to lose.

"Cassidy. I didn't mean…well, whatever you're thinking. It won't be that bad." He put his hand, still cold from his time on deck, over hers. "We found exactly what we hoped to, which also means we have all the equipment and training we need. That being said, it's better to be ready in case of the unexpected." If there were adult flathead borers waiting for them, they would be at a severe disadvantage. Thankfully, nothing worse than pupae should be in the borer holes at this time of year.

Should be. He didn't voice that last.

Somehow Cassidy managed to draw a full breath, but she had to pull her hand away before she could think clearly. Professionally. Despite the ache in her heart.

"I better examine your wings first." She expertly repositioned him and stretched out his hindwings one at a time. "What kind of injuries are we expecting?"

Isaac smiled, relieved at her business-like tone. "If everything goes well, minor acid burns."

"If it doesn't," Skite inserted flatly, "broken bones. Sprains. Wrenched shoulders. Crushed wings." He returned Isaac's glare without an ounce of remorse. "You do us no favors by trying to shield her."

Cassidy caught a glimpse of herself in the underside of a pot lid, worn smooth by years of use. Its concave shape turned her face upside down and enlarged her features. She might've laughed if not for that momentary peek at the deep furrows in her brow, however exaggerated the reflection might be.

Had all her lessons with Rosie been for naught? She knew well and good that the odds of injury were high on these spring expeditions. Now was hardly the time to start acting like a dramatic first year medical student.

Smoothing her face, she said firmly, "Thank you, Skite. It's important for me to know so I can prepare." Patting Isaac's shoulder, she nodded that she was done. "No damage that I can see. You're all right to fly tomorrow." Her voice dropped to a whisper despite her best intentions.

"Thanks, Doc." He waited a beat, but she refused to meet his eyes. "I had no intention of deceiving you," he promised. Seeing no point in attempting to defend himself further, he moved on to the next point. "Let me show you where the medical supplies are stored and then I'll help you prepare them for tomorrow."

Somewhat mollified, she allowed him to lead her to a corner of the hold where the wooden chests were labeled plainly with the red maple leaf that marked medicinal materials. She watched quietly as he untied a knot and began deftly moving aside the cargo net that had kept the chests from hurling themselves every which way during their takeoff and landing. He didn't cast the net aside carelessly, she noticed, but pleated it like a child's paper fan, as if it needed to be ready for use at a moment's notice.

"What I meant by helping you," he murmured quietly as he secured the netting to its storage hook, "is that we need to talk about open spaces."

Cassidy nodded slowly. Behind her, someone was trying to start a song but no one could agree on *which* song. That and the noise of scraping and clinking being made by the kitchen crew would cover their conversation nicely.

"We'll do what we have to do to keep you safe," he promised, opening two chests before he realized she wasn't looking at anything in particular. "Cassidy." Taking her by the shoulder, he tried shaking her lightly.

"Yes? Um, *yes.*" She corrected herself hastily. "I'm here." And better 'here' than the shipyard, which was where her mind had tried to slip off to.

"Good, because you're the doctor." He watched her eyes closely to make sure she stayed with him. Satisfied that her thoughts were on the here and now, he added, "And I need to know how to help you."

"Yes." Irritated at her repetition of the word, she stopped and cleared her throat. "You're right." Steeling herself, she directed her thoughts back to her time as a medical student. "I believe most Water Fairies suffer from anxiety in large, open spaces."

"Anxiety." Isaac nodded to keep from blurting out the question of why she was just now telling him that! "And how," he chose his words carefully, "do they handle swimming? Like your dad did, I mean. You can see for a long way through your facemasks, can't you?"

"Diving? Oh, that's completely different." She spread her fingers in front of herself and raised her hands slowly, demonstrating as she explained, "You can always feel the water around you. It presses against you, makes you feel safe."

"I see." He made a mental note to never go diving. On a positive note, his instinctive desire to avoid doing anything like what she had just described gave him a better insight to how she felt about the surface world. "Tell me, Cass. What can we do?"

He began rearranging the contents of one of the chests, trying to keep busy to give her time to think. The group had finally chosen a song and while they'd most likely starve if forced to sing for their supper, he knew it gave them something to do besides watch the light streaming through the portholes fade to darkness.

At last, Cassidy blew out a breath. "It's not much of a problem for most of us," she admitted. "We're content to remain in the seven regions, snug in our tunnels and caverns. I know of no tonic or," she lifted a shoulder, "cream. No easy solution. The only thing I've ever heard of anyone trying, with any sort of success, is replacement thinking."

"What?" Isaac folded his arms across his chest and leaned against the hull, giving her his full attention. He'd finished organizing things for tomorrow a few minutes ago and saw no point in continuing to shuffle things around. "What's that?"

"Replacement thinking," she repeated. "For example…" She paused and scratched the back of her neck, wishing she'd had her hair cut short so it couldn't tickle and itch. "Imagine you've just walked into a room. You're alone and the only light is coming from a candle, which is throwing shadows."

Isaac made a short mental leap and guessed, "Candles flicker. If I'm at all tired or edgy, I might mistake a shadow for a threat."

"Exactly. Our minds can trick us." Cassidy winced at the sound of someone hitting a false note. She was relieved to hear the singing quickly reach full force again, deafening though it was. "With careful planning and effort, we can control that process."

"Great!" That was an understatement. It killed him to think of her shivering with fear at the thought of walking through a door or looking out a window. "How do we begin?"

"Begging yer pardons, sir. Doc." A young apprentice interrupted them apologetically, her cheeks still flushed from proximity to the stove. "Cook says to eat while it's hot. Reckons it'll ward off the night's cold."

"Don't mind him, Patience." Isaac accepted a mug with a sympathetic smile for the hint of nerves he detected in the apprentice's voice. "The old gloomy bucket has survived nearly three dozen expeditions just like this one and keeps volunteering for more."

"Then we won't freeze?" Patience asked hopefully.

"Not so long as we keep the fire burnin' bright." Skite, who'd also just come from the galley, answered the question mildly. He'd noticed the lass forgot the utensils, so he now handed Cassidy and Isaac each a spoon. Addressing Patience again he suggested, "Hurry on and get yourself some stew. I'm about to tell a story."

Cassidy raised one smooth, pink eyebrow as Skite wriggled both of his bushy ones. "A story about what?"

"I ain't quite decided yet." Skite hedged until

the lass had scurried off, spreading the word as she went. "S'long as it takes their minds off'n the cold," he continued more quietly, "I can't see as how what it's about really matters."

Isaac shook his head as he chewed a bite of the hearty stew. "The first night's always the worst," he told Cassidy, motioning for her to eat her stew. The cook wasn't kidding about eating while it was hot. Temperatures in the hold would continue to drop so that by morning they'd be able to see their breath when they spoke. Sunrise would warm things back up, but that was hours away. "Hard as we try to prepare them, this is all new to the apprentices."

"And to you." Cassidy was still eyeing the stew doubtfully. As an amused grin spread across Isaac's face, she sought to explain. "Have you ever been here before?" When he shook his head, she nodded hers. "So it's all new. Every bird call; every creak of the branch; every whistle of the wind. You don't know what to expect tonight, or when it will happen, any more than the rest of us do."

That said, she shifted uneasily and told herself to ignore the rapidly darkening porthole. It would be better when it was dark and she couldn't see out of it at all, wouldn't it? She'd been avoiding glancing out the portholes for hours and now she wouldn't have to worry.

"Smart girl." Isaac chuckled and risked planting a quick kiss on her cheek. "I'd appreciate it if you kept that between us, though. If the apprentices catch on, none of us'll get any sleep tonight."

Cassidy wanted to seal the promise with a proper kiss, but knew better.

Isaac must've sensed the direction of her thoughts anyway—or perhaps they matched his own—because he cast a longing look at her lips.

"I'll have to work out just where to start with my," she breathlessly changed the subject, "my, um, replacement thinking."

His lips twitched, but his eyes were serious. "So you'll have to think about what to think about?"

"Yes. Exactly." Worried about what she might say or do next, Cassidy spooned some stew into her mouth. Made a face as she started to chew.

Isaac chuckled a tad ruefully, then excused himself to go talk to Captain Keddy. They still had to set a watch and he wanted to personally make sure the companionway doors were battened down for the night. Small, metal grates built into the doors cost them precious heat but allowed the even more precious fresh air to circulate.

Soon enough blankets began to be handed around and Cassidy gladly traded her now-empty mug for one of them. Some of the veteran Wranglers started stretching out hammocks across the hold at different heights and she tossed her blanket over her shoulder so she could help.

"Ouch!" She shook the finger that she'd just snagged in the hammock webbing. "This is harder than it looks."

"Slow down," recommended her lanky partner with a friendly grin. "We got all night."

Chuckling, Cassidy took his advice. They traded names and Knewt helped her master the finer points of setting up hammocks correctly.

"I've never slept in one of these before," she confessed, tugging on the last hammock curiously. "Don't they hurt your back?"

"Nah." Knewt spread the hammock out side-to-side, turned around, and sat, rocking on his heels. "Unless you fall out, of course."

He said it with such a straight face that Cassidy had to consider his words twice to realize he was teasing her.

"Thanks for the tip," she muttered wryly.

"You betcha." Deftly, Knewt swung his feet up into the hammock and shifted into a comfortable position. Pointing toward where Skite stood, surrounded by a seated, enraptured audience, he grinned. "We're missing the story."

Selecting the hammock next to her new friend, Cassidy arranged her blanket in a loose ball at the end where she planned to put her head. Next, she spread the hammock, turned, and…it had collapsed. Frowning, she studied it a moment. What had she done wrong?

Mentally, she reviewed the actions she'd just seen Knewt demonstrate and finally settled on the fact that she'd let go of the far side when she turned. With a little more concentration, she was able to keep the hammock spread while she turned, then sat. Success!

Well, so far. The blasted thing wobbled the instant her feet left the floor, prompting her to hastily plant them on the planks again. Finding that Knewt was watching her expectantly, she offered a faint smile.

"It's not as easy as you made it look."

"You'll be alright," he assured her. "Takes getting used to, is all. First few times, you'll want to lay back as soon as your feet are in. And hold real still, so it don't dump you out."

"That's a cheerful thought," she grumbled.

One or two of the others decided to stretch out, too, and she watched carefully as they entered their hammocks. It was more or less as Knewt said, as far as the motions went. The others were so relaxed, though; sitting and twisting into position as casually as if the lively hammocks held as still as desk chairs. Or beds.

Oh, what a relief a real bed would've been! But there were no beds aboard a scouting windship. Here it was hammocks all around.

Grimacing on the inside, Cassidy forced her shoulders to relax. Took a deep breath and twisted as she raised her feet.

"Not bad," came Knewt's favorable comment.

She continued to lay there, staring up at the bottom of the deck, and trying to ignore the lumpy blanket, which had rolled down to lodge under her shoulders.

"Comfortable?" Isaac's voice asked.

She looked on either side, then tipped her head back and found him smiling down at her. "I…mostly."

"Hmm." Spotting the blanket, Isaac came around to stand beside her hammock. "Here, let me help." He held the hammock steady while she sat up long enough to snatch her blanket. Taking it from her, he shook it out and draped it over her, then showed her how to arrange the face shield inside her hood to make a softer pillow.

"What's he doing?" Cassidy nodded toward the cooking area, or galley, as she'd heard others call it.

"Hmm?" Isaac toyed with one of her curls as he followed the direction of her nod. "Cook's starting bread dough for tomorrow's breakfast."

"Oh." Reaching up, she caught his hand and laced her fingers through his. They stayed that way for several heartbeats, not saying anything, just enjoying each other's company.

Skite's story, a wild-eyed adventure about a spider, reached its high point, disrupting the moment and prompting Cassidy to squeeze Isaac's hand.

"Don't let him worry you." Isaac brought her hand to his lips and kissed it. "He only tells that story to apprentices, and it gets bigger every time."

"I'll try not to." Exhaling slowly, she dragged her thoughts away from Skite's dramatics. "I think I've figured out where, um, what to think about."

"That's wonderful." Isaac rewarded her with a smile. "Can I help?"

She hesitated. "I'm not sure yet."

"Alright." He nodded, reminding himself that she was the expert. "For now I'll see to it that you're assigned duties inside the hold."

"That *will* help." She couldn't believe he'd thought of that first. "I'll let you know what I've learned at lunch tomorrow."

"I may not be back by then." He watched the corners of her mouth start to turn down and hurried to explain. "The borers will take most of the morning. And there's wood to haul and stack. I'll need to coordinate with Skite and Keddy…"

"It's alright." She patted his hand, which still held hers. "I understand. Just be careful. Please?"

"I promise." He kissed her hand again, then reluctantly backed over to the nearest hammock, where he settled in for the night.

Chapter 11

Cassidy was below decks, sitting with her back against the wall and listening to the others joke about how cold it was.

Perhaps that was why she got to her feet. Because she was cold. Whatever prompted the action, it brought her to eye level with a glass porthole. She avoided looking at it as long as she could, but it drew her to it like a shrimp to green lights.

The inner surface of the porthole was covered with frost. Thick enough that when she reached up to touch it, she found she had to scrape it away with her thumbnail. The frost formed a pile ahead of her thumbnail and she watched it grow, temporarily mesmerized as she cleared a single line from right to left, barely enough to peek through.

As her cold hand neared the far side of the porthole, the remaining frost thinned, then vanished, leaving her with a petrifying view of an empty expanse. Pale blue, it seemed to stretch on and on and everywhere she looked: up and down; side to side. It was an ocean of nothingness.

It pulled at her, clawed at her, dragging her right through the windship's hull!

She screamed as everything fell away. But there was no sound.

Sometime between lights out and sunrise, Isaac was relentlessly dragged from his slumber by a sound he couldn't identify. Lying awake in the dark, he strained to hear it, but all was…

His head turned sharply toward Cassidy's hammock. The whisper of blanket sliding along blanket, followed by the faint grunt of a discomfited sleeper reached his ears.

He was on his feet in a flash, hand over her mouth to stifle her scream. Lips next to her ear, he alternated between soothing words and calling her name until she came awake.

"Isaac?" Confused, Cassidy tried to sit up, but the room started to rock. Clinging to him, she demanded, "What's going on? Why is Weetu moving?!"

"Listen to me, Cassidy Clark." He resorted to her full name to reach past the fog of sleep that still held her captive. "You're safe. Do you believe that?"

Eyes squeezed shut, cheek pressed against his shoulder, she nodded slowly. "I believe that."

"You had a bad dream. That's all." Scooping her out of the hammock, blanket and all, he carried her to the bench and sat down with her on his lap. "You're safe," he reiterated, smoothing her hair.

"A bad dream… Yes, I remember." In the blink of an eye, she relived it.

She curled into herself, drawing her knees to her chest and gripping the front of Isaac's tunic for security. She was awake. She was inside the *Itxar*. The porthole was dark.

Isaac tightened his hold and kept murmuring to her until she gradually dropped off to sleep again. Reluctantly, he carried her back to her hammock, depositing her gently and covering her with her blanket.

Sternly telling himself that he could do nothing to protect her from further bad dreams, he made himself climb into his own hammock. Where he lay, staring either at the ceiling or at Cassidy, neither of which he could actually see.

Despite his grave concerns, he'd hard a long, hard day, much of it in the brutal cold. His body warred with his mind and heart. But, in the end, he slept.

It was well that he did, for of a necessity he rose with the sun. There was work to do and, after checking on a still slumbering Cassidy, he forced down some breakfast, donned his leathers, and left with the others.

Not long after, Cassidy came awake all at once, and lay stiffly in place. As was often the case these last few months, her first complete thought was, *Where am I?*

She blinked rapidly, trying to sort out the strange sounds that had woken her—voices, perhaps? And…snoring? The back half of her body felt like she'd spent the night tied up in a closet, and the distinctly smoky taste in her mouth only added to her confusion.

"Morning." An apprentice approached Cassidy's hammock warily, not wanting to startle her into tumbling out. "Isaac asked me to keep an eye on ya." His breath as he spoke left puffs of white in the chill morning air.

Cassidy turned to look at the voice, which belonged to the same lanky young man who'd snickered at her for tying herself down during the windship launch yesterday. She paused to process what he'd said, then smiled.

"Morning." As her mind continued to clear, Cassidy rubbed a thumb along the rough hammock webbing. She'd spent nights curled up on a cave floor during her survival training and suffered less.

"Hungry?" He showed her the covered plate he was carrying.

"Yes." She tried to sit up and bit her lip when the hammock immediately began rocking. Why did that seem so familiar? "Is there a, um, secret to getting out of these safely?"

"Practice mostly." He stood there uncertainly, wanting to help but too shy to do so.

"I see." She couldn't help the little laugh that escaped. "What's your name?"

"Harry." He replied tersely, then watched in astonishment as she rolled right up and over the edge of the hammock, catching herself on her arms and toes when she hit the floor. A few of the sleepers, mostly windfairies who'd risen with the sun to check the anchors and whatnot, stirred, then lapsed back into their deep slumber. Those Wranglers who'd had the late watch, ending just at sunrise, didn't even flinch.

"That's one way to start the day," Cassidy muttered to herself. As long as she was down there, she stretched, arching her aching back until it popped. Her mind whirled, wondering why she could smell Isaac so clearly on her hands. Did it have something to do with the almost-memory that she couldn't quite shape into coherent thought?

"Er…" Harry rubbed the back of his neck. "After breakfast, maybe I oughta show you an easier way to do that. Get out of the hammock, I mean."

"I'd appreciate it." Cassidy smiled as she got to her feet and briskly dusted her knees. She'd wrestle with her maybe-dreams after her stomach stopped shouting for attention. 'Breakfast' was a hot grain mash with chunks of fruit and a sausage baked inside a biscuit.

While she ate, Harry occupied himself by scrubbing dishes and she pitched in as soon as she'd swallowed her last mouthful. She'd remembered where Isaac and the rest of the Wranglers were and it was either work or give in to the twitches of inactivity mixed with fear.

Harry gave her the easy part of the job, taking her plate from her and pointing at the tub full of hot rinse water and a towel. As cold

as she'd been when she woke, she was soon
surprised to find herself mopping sweat from
her forehead.

"I guess this is the only really warm spot on
the whole ship." She offered him another
smile, but all she got in reply was the discernible
clenching of his jaw. A dozen thoughts popped
into her mind like bubbles on the surface of the
pot boiling on the nearby stove. "Are you mad
at me?"

Harry shot her a startled glance. "You're a
direct sort, ain't ya?"

"Saves time." This time her smile was more
a wry twist of her lips. "Something *is* bothering
you."

He hunched his shoulders briefly. "Nah."

She waited a minute, then gently prodded,
"Where's Cook?" As she'd expected, Harry's
shoulders hiked toward his ears again.

"Collecting ice shavings."

Deciding to give him some space, Cassidy
scanned the interior of the hold. Noting that
hers was the only unfolded blanket, she dried
the last handful of utensils and hung the towel
where she'd found it.

"Here." Harry took the towel and dropped
it in the rinse water. "I'll be over in a bit to
help you with your hammock," he promised
and added soap to the clean water.

Cassidy left him to it, admiring his sense of
duty as he washed the cloths Cook and his

helpers had used so far. It didn't take her long to fold her blanket, so she practiced the initial maneuver for getting into the hammock. With Harry's help, she next worked on exiting the hammock gracefully. Harry's inexperience as a teacher produced some laughable miscommunications, but by the time Cook and two of the other apprentices returned, she'd more or less gotten the knack of it.

"Thanks." She grinned at Harry as she settled her feet firmly on the planking one last time. "That'll save me a lot of bruised knees."

"Hey, Doc." Cook, still in his full gear and identifiable only by his voice, leaned one fist on his worktable and sucked in a shallow breath. The older he got, the harder it was for him to breathe in this confounded ice cold air. "Best get yerself ready. We seen the Wranglers comin' back and some of 'em are bein' carried." His message delivered, he turned to oversee the apprentices as they scooped ice shavings from huge bags into the stove's built-in water tanks.

Cassidy stood where she was, her smile fixed on her face. *Isaac.*

"Doc?" Harry nudged her. "I'll help if you'll tell me what to do." He waited tensely. She owed him this. Why, it would make up for being left off the regular duty roster to babysit her if she'd just…

"I need a place to examine the wounded." She forced the words past stiff lips.

Figuratively speaking, she boxed fear's ears and stood it in a corner. However bad things were—no matter whom was injured—things would only get worse if she wasn't ready when they arrived.

"Usually they get laid out on a hammock," answered one of the Wranglers who'd stood the late watch. Roused by the rattle of ice shavings in the metal funnel, he'd heard enough to know what was going on. Scrubbing a beefy hand over unfocused eyes, he swung his legs out of the hammock. "I've got lots of experience with these kinds of injuries. Best if you let me handle it."

"No." Cassidy bit the word off at the end, then cursed herself for an ingrate when all eyes turned to her. Who did she think she was, turning down a seasoned Wrangler?

A fool, she silently answered the unspoken question.

"They'll be exhausted and half-frozen when they get here." She eyed his broad shoulders and hastily offered an alternative. "Will you please take charge of getting the patients into their hammocks? Bring the worst injuries over here." She pointed to the boxes Isaac had rearranged just last night.

The burly Wrangler set Harry to helping with the ice shavings so the companionway would be clear and rousted the rest of the sleepers. To those who protested he simply declared, "Ye'd have been woken soon enough." And moved them to different hammocks to keep sleeping if they could.

Cassidy used some of the hot water to prepare a treatment for the acid burns and quizzed Harry, as soon as he became available, on how to tend muscle sprains and strains.

"Good. Get your kit." She directed the speechless lad to stand on the other side of the hold and treat the minor injuries as they came in.

The sounds of booted feet on the deck, then in the companionway, contributed to a slight trembling of her fingers as she bound her curls back.

Organized chaos erupted in the hold and Cassidy busied herself with her patients. Her stomach churned as she realized that none of the burns had been washed yet. In some cases, fresh blisters were developing before her eyes.

"Here." Cook sloshed up to her with a smallish pot full of water. "We're meltin' the shavin's fast as we kin."

"Thanks." Cassidy accepted the pot, then handed it to Patience, one of the apprentices. Grabbing for a pair of scissors, she trimmed away the melted edges of the Wrangler's shirt. "Blast," she muttered, realizing that her own gloves would provide only minimal protection for her. Ripping them off so she wouldn't spread the acid, she ordered Patience to rinse the wound.

"Doc?" The burly Wrangler from before hailed her as he carried an unconscious patient over. "His leg. It's busted bad."

"Knewt!" Bile got as far as Cassidy's throat at the sight of her friend's mangled limb, but she forced it back down. "No, not a hammock. Set him on a bench, please." She couldn't hope to work on that kind of an injury on a swaying surface. "It would seem you were right, Corporal," she told her aide as she rolled up her sleeves. Someone veered toward her and dropped an apron over her head, which she promptly adjusted and tied in place. "I'd appreciate it if you would take over the acid burn cases."

"Yes'm." Without another word, he waded back into the chaos.

For an instant, she glimpsed Isaac across the room. He had an armful of gauze and was busy dispensing it to those working on the acid burns. She allowed herself a small sigh of relief that he looked well enough, then set her mind to the task at hand.

Skite was suddenly beside her, a med kit in one hand and a sturdy-looking box in another. "Best take a seat, Doc." There was no humor in his eyes as he set her up beside the bench. "Looks like we'll be here a while."

She wasn't sure at first, but in the end, she was grateful that Skite stayed by her. His hands, which she'd only seen employed in sleight of hand, proved to be nimble and knowing in medicinal matters as well, aiding her deftly in cleaning the wound and easing bone fragments back in place.

"Here, Doc." Skite opened a jar she didn't recognize and showed her its glue-like contents. "Daub it on any solid bit of bone," he demonstrated, "then assemble the pieces around it."

"That's astounding." The gluey stuff stiffened quickly and only after a few clumsy tries was she able to begin using it to effect. Willing as she was to accept it as standard Wrangler practice, she had a few questions. "How does it work?"

"The bone's broke, right?" His hands never stopped moving as he talked. "This'll hold it together until his body absorbs it. Won't have to splint the leg right away, either." Stripping off soiled gloves, he readied the silk and needle. "It's a regular hodgepodge of things that prevent infection, nourish the bone, reduce pain, and such."

"I see." Finished, Cassidy removed her own gloves and washed her hands thoroughly. Absent-mindedly she removed her apron and relinquished it to Harry, who was helping clean up. Picking up the rather plain-looking jar, she studied it. Aside from an instantly identifiable image of a broken bone, it had no markings. The odor was quite pungent, however, and she lowered it to get it away from her nose. "I thought you used potions for broken bones?"

"Sure do." Skite gripped the needle tightly, but made no move toward the open wound. "Break like this though," he wiped his mouth on the back of his sleeve, "needs all the advantages it can get."

"We probably shouldn't sew this right away." Cassidy offered him the open jar and held her hand out for the needle, which he placed carefully in her palm. "I'll watch for infection for a while first."

"Good." Skite gripped the jar with white-knuckled fingers. "I mean, good thinking."

"Thanks, Skite." She put the needle and silk away, whereupon Skite's breathing evened out. "I couldn't have done that alone." The worst of the injuries tended to, she automatically began examining the rest of her patient. In the end, she added three broken fingers, a head contusion, and more bruises scattered over his body than she wanted to count.

Skite looked from her to their patient, then gave the jar in his hand an odd look, as if he'd forgotten it was there. "You may have more such work, Doc." Lidding the jar, he put it away. "Wasn't just fat, sleepy borers in there. Spider got Knewt. We still have to get *it*."

"Here, you two." Isaac appeared, a plate in each hand. "You've worked right through lunch."

Surprised, Cassidy tried to turn her head to look around the hold and flinched as fire screamed down the side of her neck, driving all thoughts of the spider from her mind.

"Uh-oh." Isaac, having already given Skite his plate, caught her by the elbow and maneuvered her over to the now rather messy collection of medicine chests and supplies. "Why don't you eat while I try to do something about those sore muscles?"

"That's not going to work." She smiled wanly and motioned for him to sit beside her instead. "If you rub a knot the wrong way, I'll get a forkful of food in my lap."

"Good point." He surrendered the plate.

She cut into the ham, but left the piece sitting on her plate as she looked around the once-peaceful hold. "I didn't do very well, did I?"

Isaac had to lean forward to catch her words. "What are you saying? You did fine!"

"Did I?" She gestured at the hammocks in use. Some of them were filled with patients wearing slings or wraps or braces for their muscle injuries. The rest she guessed were recovering from acid burns. "A dozen patients came in today and I helped one."

"That's not fair." Isaac picked up her abandoned fork and speared the piece of ham on it. "Eat this and listen to me." He took it as a sign of her depressed feelings when she meekly obeyed. "Cass, you're one fairy. One doctor. Nobody expected you to…to split in two and tend two patients at once. That's ridiculous."

"No, of course I couldn't do *that*."

He ignored her attempted interruption. "Harry did fine. And it was smart to put Berns in charge of the acid burns, he has years of experience. Cook had plenty of hot food ready for us and…" He stopped to notice how she was looking at him. "And none of us could've taken care of that broken leg the way you did. Ah, I know. Skite showed you the sludge." He desperately wanted to kiss her on the nose that she wrinkled at him, but one kiss usually led to another and this wasn't the time or place.

"Sludge? Is that really what it's called?" Wearily, she cut another piece of ham and put it in her mouth to chew on.

"No." Reaching around her, he eased the band that held her hair captive. "It has a fancy scientific name that's much too long when you're in a hurry."

"Oh." She fidgeted with her fork. The ham was a bit tough. "Skite did more than show it to me. A lot more."

"Yes, I saw." He smiled, relieved to hear her rouse herself to defend Skite. "We've all got *some* experience with traumatic injuries. You were faster, Cass. As soon as he got you started with the sludge, he got out of your way."

The wave of Isaac's hand encompassed everyone in the hold. "You, you're the only doctor here. It's your level of training and skill that will make the difference between a man walking straight and a man hoping not to lose his leg to an injury that severe."

It was a grim way to look at it, but she gave him a tired smile. "I think I see what you mean." She was pleased to notice that someone had already begun mopping the floor under and around the hammocks.

"Excellent." Tapping the plate she'd balanced on her knees, he suggested, "You should finish that while it's warm. Then I'll take a crack at those shoulders."

"And then," she cut the rest of her ham and filled her spoon with beans, "I better work on my replacement thinking."

"How's that going?" He hadn't decided whether or not to talk to her about her nightmare. Exposing it to the bright light of day might chase it off permanently. However, he'd known a few whose dreams got worse after allowing them to invade their wakefulness, too.

She chewed slowly, trying to decide how to answer without wiping the too-bright smile off his face. "It's only the first day, Isaac. On top of that, I slept late and then all of *this* happened. Aside from a few minutes while I was rinsing dishes, I haven't had time to think at all."

"I understand." This time he did press a quick kiss to her hair as he took her dishes. He washed and rinsed them to give himself time to think. He should've known better than to hope for a quick solution.

He made a show of stretching his fingers as he returned to Cassidy, who laughed at him. Seating himself, he shifted her so that her back was to him. At least he'd made a decision about the nightmare. Unless she had it again or brought it up on her own, he wouldn't mention it.

She sighed without meaning to when his hands settled on her shoulders. "How can your hands be so warm, when it's so cold in here?"

"It's the wash water." He chuckled and scooted closer so he had a better angle. "Don't fret. You'll get another turn at the dishes." He was rewarded by a soft laugh and a discernible release of tension in her muscles.

"Isaac." She wanted to bask in the glorious relief of his ministrations, but she had to ask. "How was Knewt injured?" She sensed a hesitation in the movement of his fingers, then his breath stirred her hair. It must've been a very deep breath, by the feel of it.

"Well, Doc, we're not quite sure. Knewt went ahead of his group to check the location of the borer." He shifted his attention to her neck, tenderly loosening the last few knots without drawing so much as a flinch from her.

"We'll know more after he wakes up, but for now we're thinking he got distracted and the spider surprised him."

"Distracted?" She turned to face him, capturing his hands in her own. She didn't have to ask which team Knewt was on to know that Isaac held himself at least partly responsible for what happened. "By what?"

"By the task at hand. He was just supposed to check on the borer, report its condition and location. But…" His lips twisted bitterly. "Wranglers should know that the danger we expect is never the only danger. We're just about the smallest thing in these woods, Cass. Almost everything out here will either eat us or step on us and never notice. It's not safe to focus on any one thing."

Her gut clenched and her heart sank to hear him put it so bluntly, but she couldn't argue with the truth.

Chapter 12

Isaac was soon called away, and Cassidy arranged herself in a seated position near Knewt. Closing her eyes, she took a few deep, steadying breaths, then reached back in her mind to just before her first memory of the shipyard. She'd bid Agnes goodbye. Bumped into Skite, who'd taken her under his wing.

Ah, there it was. Stopping the memory as she left the hallway and entered the shipyard, she concentrated on her feelings. Finding no fear in that moment, she let things edge forward.

Something that stuck out plainly in her memory was the noise. Unlike the sober, nearly silent hallway, the shipyard rang with sound. Shouted orders. Thuds. Laughter from the Wranglers as they neared the beginning of the journey. Creaking noises from…what?

She must've wondered, must've looked, for it to stand out so vividly.

In her memory she saw a large, slender stick with a hinge in the middle and a huge cargo net dangling from one end. It began to move, rotating the cargo net away from the outcropping where they all walked. The harder she tried to watch the cargo net, the hazier things became.

Suddenly she realized that something else

~ 167 ~

was coming sharply into focus. A windship! Not the *Itxar*, but another one. Ignorant of design, she knew only that it had masts and wings; a slender nose and a boxy tail. It hung loosely, almost casually in what looked like a string cradle. No, not string. The lines around the windship were much too thick to be string. Belts? Or at least, thick straps of leather?

Her curiosity compelled her to look up. The masts were tall, so very tall! What could the straps be attached to and still be out of the way of the masts?

Cassidy abandoned her memory with a jerk and stared, wide-eyed, around the hold. Sturdy, solid bulkheads met her gaze in all directions. Rising, she lifted off and touched the ceiling, just to be sure.

Settling back down, she sagged onto the bench by Knewt.

The windship she'd seen hung from the shipyard ceiling. *So far* above her.

"You alright?"

She blinked, trying to throw off the vivid memory of her fear so she could answer coherently. Except, when she looked around, no one was there.

"Over here." The voice spoke again. It sounded tired. Painfully tired.

"Knewt!" The memory fled from her as she met his eyes. "You're awake!" Rising, she held a tin cup under the tap of a water keg, then added a splash of treated doctor's water. "How are you feeling?"

He licked chapped lips, eyeing the cup greedily. "Like I got rolled on by a bull ant."

"Just about." She laughed, relieved to hear him joking, and held the cup to his lips. Best of all, he seemed to be breathing easily, which eliminated broken ribs from her worries. She'd been pretty sure, but it was nice to have him awake to confirm it. "Not so fast," she warned as he drank. "Your stomach's empty. Think you could handle some food?"

"If the food ain't still," he winced at an unnamed pain when he tried to shift on the bench, "kickin' I can."

"Good." She refilled the cup, half and half with the doctor's water this time, hoping that would slow him down. After making sure he could handle the cup with the hand that only had one broken finger, she hurried over to the cook stove.

"Sure we got food." Cook harrumphed and grabbed a plate. "Say what they will, an' I've heard it all, ever'body knows cookin's the most important job on an expedition!" He started ladling beans and what looked like chunked-up pieces of that afternoon's lunch ham onto the plate. When he had a small mountain, he handed it over to Cassidy with a small sniff. "Knewt usually eats enough for an army. Tell him there's plenty more iff'n he can get that down and keep it down." He stressed the second half of the condition.

"I will." Somehow she kept a straight face while she reached for a spoon, then let her smile out on her way back to Knewt—who was surrounded by Isaac, Skite, and Captain Keddy? They parted to let her approach, but their grim expressions made it hard to maintain her smile, even for Knewt's sake.

"There it is! Oh, will you look at that." Knewt fairly drooled as he reached for the plate.

"Steady lad." Keddy stopped him with a hand on his chest. "You'll never keep that plate right side up with those hands."

Isaac and Skite were already in motion, one fetching blankets while the other positioned himself to raise Knewt's shoulders.

Cassidy bit her lips to keep from protesting that they should've asked first and admitted to herself that they did a good job of keeping the rest of Knewt still as they propped up his torso to make feeding him easier.

"Isaac." Catching his arm when they'd finished, she tugged him over to her side. "What's going on?"

"Remember how I said I'd know more about what happened once I'd talked with him?"

"What, now?" She frowned, not liking the idea at all. "You know better than I do what he's just been through. He needs to rest."

"He will, I promise." Taking her by the shoulders, Isaac looked her squarely in the eyes. "But we have to know what he knows. We're going out again tomorrow and he may be able to tell us something we can use."

"Going out to-tomorrow?!" She stuttered, she was so boggled. Only a finely developed sense of propriety kept her voice low as she flared, "I have enough patients to keep me busy as it is. What is so deucedly important about getting that spider tomorrow instead of the next day or the one after that?"

"Isaac." Keddy's raised eyebrow spoke volumes. Knewt was awake, but for how long? His body badly used, he'd eat and fall fast asleep again, and then where would they be?

"Coming." Giving his full attention to Cassidy, Isaac offered his best compromise. "You're asking excellent questions. I'll answer them as soon as I can."

She glared at their backs as they surrounded Knewt. Mayhap it was well that she did. It didn't take long to see that Keddy was 'an old hand at shovelin' food into someone else's mouth,' to quote Knewt. Though Skite and Isaac questioned Knewt intently, they also proceeded kindly, taking time to ease blankets underneath him when he complained the bench was too hard.

And then there was the little matter of what

she heard. She knew about spiders from her time with the younger apprentices at Weetu. However, knowing and seeing were two entirely different things.

"All yours, Doc." Isaac was glad to see something like understanding in Cassidy's eyes after they finished. Nodding toward Skite and Keddy, who were moving off to the corner of the hold they'd claimed for private meetings, he continued, "There's planning to do. Can we talk, um…?"

"Later is fine." Troubled by what she'd overheard, Cassidy now more fully grasped the urgency of their mission. A hungry spider, aware that there was food in the area—even food as small as fairies—would start hunting. "Go on." She made shooing motions with her hands. "I've got a patient to tend."

As they faded away, she prepared a needle and silk. "This won't hurt," she promised Knewt, showing him the numbing salve she'd brought. "You can close your eyes, if you'd like." Deftly, she sewed together the edges of the cut, telling him as she worked that his bone was healing nicely.

Cassidy spent several minutes fussing over Knewt after she'd finished, staying until he fell asleep, a tired smile on his drawn face. Once she'd checked on the worst of the acid burns and other injuries, she paused to assess her new situation. With her suge in hand, there was little enough that frightened her. Not that she was stupid enough to underestimate a barely-known predator. No, it was simply that she trusted her weapon and what she could do with it.

Which brought her to her fear, and its consequences. She could hardly be a full-fledged member of the expedition if she wasn't capable of going outside the *Itxar*. There was wood to cut, ice shavings to fetch, the small matter of helping to prevent a flood of all southern Fairydom, and showing that she was a capable partner for Isaac and an acceptable future queen...

She stopped and shook her head. A certain degree of authority was inherent in being a zaldun of the seven regions, especially one from the Botere tribe. Even as a youth she'd been called upon to settle squabbles, set rules, and generally take the lead. Would all of that be adequate preparation for ruling a tribe of hundreds of thousands, perhaps *millions*, of fairies? The harsh surface world contained dangers she'd never dealt with, hardships that never troubled those of the seven regions. Especially remote villages site like Lauta would be.

"Cass?" Concerned by the way she was glaring at the stack of medicine chests, Isaac placed himself between her and the rest of the hold. "What's wrong?"

Lifting her eyes to the face of the man she loved, Cassidy sighed and walked into his arms. Burying her face in his chest, she held him tightly as she willed away the doubts. It was silly of her to worry about being queen while there still was one. Why, Queen Fiona and King Walter were young yet. They might live to see their great-great-great grand-children! Plenty of time for Cassidy to learn the surface ways.

Isaac, who knew from his younger sister that 'sometimes a girl just wants to be held!', matched the strength of his hug to Cassidy's. Meanwhile, his mind whirled with possibilities. Knewt might be in worse shape than they'd thought. Isaac might've interrupted her in her replacement thinking exercises. Or, though he hated even to acknowledge the possibility, Cassidy might be having second thoughts about marrying him.

So, as he rested his cheek against her soft curls, he closed his eyes and focused on everything wonderful about holding her.

"I love you."

The whispered words made his eyes pop open. He could breathe again. She loved him!

"I love you, too." Watching her eyes for permission, he stole a kiss that made him want another.

Laughing, she pushed him away after the second kiss. "You know everyone's watching."

He made a wry face, but didn't argue the point. "Are you alright now?"

"Better." She nodded. "But I need to look out a porthole. Will you come with me?" Her sense of dread eased significantly at his prompt response.

"Of course." He kept an arm loosely around her shoulders as they approached, worry building inside him. "Cass, are you sure? I mean, earlier you said you hadn't had time to work on this and now you want to look outside?"

She rubbed her arms, cold despite the heat being constantly pumped out by the galley stove. "What will I see?" While looking out a porthole was a small flit forward, it *was* a flit.

"What will…oh." He raked his fingers through his hair.

"Don't try to protect me," she warned. "Just tell me what I'll see."

"Not very much." He answered honestly. "Even on the wind, there's always a wing in the way. You'll see out, straight out, as far as the wall of the bark canyon. And maybe up." He checked their position between the bow and the stern. "Yes, this one will have a good view of the sky."

"Alright." Bracing herself, she marched the last few steps to the porthole and thrust her face up to it.

It was exactly as Isaac described. A tall, light

brown ridge lay beyond the wingtip. Enormous ice crystals, their once-smooth surfaces and angles now gray and pitted with soot from the stovepipe, were clearly visible. And the sky, so bright that it was only barely blue, stretched up and away forever.

Exhaling sharply, she retreated to Isaac's arms.

"I've got you," he murmured into her hair. She nodded and burrowed closer, shaking, though not as violently as she had in the shipyard. He was helpless to do more than hold her. Or was he? Remembering the analogy she'd used to help him understand replacement thinking, he asked himself if he'd ever flinched at a shadow while in good company.

Taking a deep breath, he started to sing. "Jaunty Jack, brave village lad, sat by the fi-ire, a sorrowin'!" Other voices soon took up the song, the tale of a restless boy who left home for a grand adventure.

At first, Cassidy gritted her teeth, irritated that he'd so casually hijacked her replacement thinking exercise. As the song progressed, however, a wondrous change came over her. Even with her thoughts fixed on the never-ending sky outside, the song—and Isaac's warmth—soothed her.

Halfway through the second verse, a positively ridiculous bit about 'Jack' stealing an entire honeycomb from wild bees, Cassidy turned and approached the porthole again.

Fists clenched at his sides, the song forgotten, Isaac watched her. This time, when the sunlight hit her face, her eyes half closed and she smiled. Then, her eyes opened. Several seconds passed before he realized that she had been looking out for *several* seconds. That was good—right?

Relaxing marginally, he moved closer.

"Ask me what I see." She prompted without turning from the window.

"Tell me." Curious, he peeked out as well, the action bringing his chin to rest on her shoulder. The view was no more than he'd expected. Slowly melting ice crystals and a blank canyon wall.

"I see hope." Cassidy leaned back, inviting him to put his arms around her again, and sighed with happiness when he did. "I hope to go outside tomorrow."

Isaac tightened his hold on her waist, careful not to move her from her chosen vantage point.

"Can you be ready at dawn?" He chose that question out of dozens swarming him. Questions like, 'Are you sure?' and 'Didn't you just tell me you needed more time?' If she was willing to face the outside, he had no desire to discourage her.

"So early?" She squirmed briefly, then sighed.

"I can if you'll wake me."

"I can try." Turning her so she faced him again he asked, "Anything I should know about that?"

Large hazel-green eyes blinked up at him, clearly puzzled. "About what?"

"About waking you." He tugged gently on a tempting curl. "I've woken many a fairy to stand their watch and they're all different. Some come awake all at once. Some *say* they're up, then go back to sleep. A few smile and most are grumpy." He'd learned to duck when waking certain fairies, come to think of it.

"Just give my arm a shake," she told him with an amused smile.

"It's a plan, then." *Plan...* Remembering why he'd initially come over, Isaac released her shoulders and folded his arms across his chest. "Speaking of tomorrow, Doc. I need to know who's fit for duty."

She blew out a breath, chilled by the sudden shift. "What kind of duty?"

He hesitated, sensitive to the trepidation in her voice. "Ice shaving collection is probably the easiest outside duty. And both the wood cutting and the ice parties will need lookouts." Deliberately, he avoided mentioning the spider hunt.

"You'll be short-handed, I'm afraid. Many of today's muscle injuries will be well enough for the ice parties by morning." Pointing out the remaining fairies, those with the most serious injuries, she added, "These should remain onboard, at least until I can look them over."

"Morrison." Isaac frowned, recognizing one of the women she'd pointed to. He'd never seen her hesitate to put herself between danger and her comrades. "Figures she'd get banged up the first day."

Unsure what to make of Isaac's remark—his impressed tone didn't seem to match his words—Cassidy moved on to discussing the acid burn patients.

"Most of them were lucky. The heavy cold gear protected them from all but superficial burns." Still, she named three that she needed to keep an eye on.

"Alright." Isaac nodded. That gave him just enough for two fighting squads—*if* he pulled every uninjured Wrangler from the ice and wood cutting parties. He didn't dare take less than two squads on a spider hunt, but he couldn't leave the chore parties unprotected, either. Spiders had a nasty habit of turning up where they weren't expected. "I have to ask, Ca...um, Doc." For an instant, he'd forgotten this wasn't a routine conversation for her. "What's your assessment of their fighting capability?"

She had to cough to clear her throat before she could force the answer out. "They're all drinking doctor's water. Stiverson and Wilks, well." She shook her head, as much to clear it as to indicate a negative. "I'll apply a liniment tonight and rewrap them."

Isaac opened his mouth to thank her, but a patient called out and she almost ran to check on them. Or more accurately, she *did* run away; from him and what he'd had to ask her to do. Closing his mouth on the urge to call her back, Isaac marched himself over to Skite and Keddy to report what he'd learned.

There were more songs as the sunlight faded. Supper was the same as lunch, though there were hot rolls this time. Cassidy volunteered to help wash the dishes, earning a nod or two of approval from the others, and the hold grew quiet as everyone retired to their hammocks.

"That's enough, lass." Cook patted Cassidy's shoulder and nudged her aside. "Go on to bed now."

Exhausted, she relinquished the last of the pots to Patience and yawned her way over to her hammock. Tired as she was, would she be able to sleep? Or would she have nightmares about twenty-some tiny fairies trying to surround a monster that blurred when it moved and had a dozen eyes?

"Hi." Isaac waited by her hammock. He'd tried to go to sleep right after supper, but found he couldn't. Not until he'd talked with Cassidy.

"Allow me." Opening her hammock, he held it for her.

"Thank you." Seating herself, Cassidy swung her feet up and lay down, letting the hammock curl up and around her. Blast. She'd forgotten her blanket.

Isaac picked up her blanket and shook it out, then tucked her in. He touched her cheek softly, unsure whether he needed to apologize or bluntly tell her he had no choice. Wood had to be cut. Ice shavings had to be fetched. The spider had to be hunted.

She caught his hand and squeezed it. "I understand. I've never carried the weight you are right now, but." Turning his hand, she cupped it to her cheek. "I thought about it while I was washing dishes and I do recognize the burden of command."

"Dishes are wonderful for thinking." Bending close, he touched his lips to forehead. Would she have a nightmare tonight?

"I think I have a lot to learn." She shifted to brush her lips against his. "I'll try not to make your job harder than it is."

"Let's learn together." Smiling, he kissed her goodnight and retired to his hammock where sleep came reluctantly, but at last it did come.

Chapter 13

The next morning, after an uninterrupted sleep, Isaac and Cassidy took turns changing behind a hanging blanket. Clad in fresh woolen layers and leathers, they crept through their still-sleeping comrades to the forward companionway.

Isaac eyed her suge skeptically. "You really want to bring that?" It hung from her belt in a protective pouch made of a material he didn't recognize.

"Yes." She cocked her head at him. "Why do you ask?" Wiggling her fingers inside the insulated mitten, she tried to imagine herself doing a suge taithí while fully suited up. It wasn't a pretty picture. Once she'd conquered her fear, she'd have to start practicing.

"Because it's cold out there." He suited action to word, pulling his hood up. "I've seen ordinary blades chip in these temperatures."

"A suge is not an ordinary blade," was all the answer she would give him. Buttoning her face shield down, she slipped her goggles into position. Her stomach did a back flip when Isaac nodded for the guard to open the first door, but she said nothing.

Together they climbed onto the stairs, the door closing instantly behind them. In good weather, only one companionway door would be closed. Now, with overnight temperatures cold enough to bite and leave a mark, doors at the top and bottom were both closed for added protection. Fresh air circulated through a brace of hand-sized metal grates in each door.

"Keep your wings tucked," Isaac warned when they reached the top. Under the gruff reminder ran a streak of concern for her that, like a throbbing toothache, refused to give him any peace. Hand on the doorknob, he stopped to look at her. Or try to. The lighting was bad and the goggles only made it worse.

"I'm trusting you to tell me if you can't do this." So much for not discouraging her!

She tried to laugh, but it stuck in her throat, coming out as a muffled croak. "Open it, please."

Cold blasted in as the second door opened, knocking Cassidy back on her heels. The weak light of dawn filtered in more cautiously, allowing her to catch her first real glimpse of outside.

"Come on!" Isaac grabbed her arm. "If we're not going back, we have to move forward!"

The simple truth rang within her, calling on her to act. Cassidy boldly pushed herself through the door and stood, blinking, on the deck.

"Welcome to Lauta." Isaac, suffering similarly, turned slowly as he scanned the area for danger.

"Well." Cassidy tried to wipe her eyes and was frustrated by the layers separating them from her fingers. "This is awful."

Isaac barked a laugh. "Is that an improvement?"

Cassidy surprised herself by laughing, too. "Sadly, yes."

"Great! Now what?" He shot her a look, then resumed scanning the area.

"Now," she started to take a deep breath and grimaced. "Is there a way to wash these nose vents? They stink after the first day."

"It's not hard. I'll show you once we're done up here."

Accepting the nudge, she skipped straight to her explanation. "Now I start collecting new thoughts to facilitate the replacement thinking process."

While Isaac stood guard, Cassidy looked to the edge of her sight. There was no 'ceiling,' but for as far as she could see there was a floor of sorts. That, and her constant awareness of Isaac, kept her mind from spiraling out of control.

"Hey." Isaac took her face in his hands. The temperature was rising with the sun, but it was a rookie move to stay out any longer just because safety was a few steps away. "You're freezing. Come on." Turning her toward the companionway, he coaxed her down the stairs.

"Th-thank you." The warmth from the hold made her shiver as they entered it. "D-d-didn't realize how c-c-cold…"

"Here, give 'er here." Cook's wiry hands gripped her shoulders. "Plenty of hot broth waitin'."

"Um." Isaac looked at Cassidy over the plate of hot food an apprentice shoved into his hand. "I'm kind of late for…"

"The spider hunt." Cassidy nodded. Everyone not elbow deep in dish water or wearing bandages was already outfitted and waiting. For Isaac. "Go. I'll be fine."

"Happy thoughts." Isaac took a big bite of his breakfast and allowed Skite to shepherd him away.

"Have a seat, Doc." Cook planted Cassidy on the bench near Knewt, who was wide awake. Taking a plate from Harry, he placed it in her hands. "Let's get that face shield off."

"Thank you." She lowered the plate into her lap, letting it warm her hands while Cook worked.

"Doc?" Knewt watched her curiously. His crew was getting ready to leave and here he was, still stuck on the bench. "What's got you up and out so early?"

And so Cassidy found herself telling Knewt everything about her fear and how Isaac was helping her overcome it. As she ate, her brain thawed and caught up with the conversation, leaving her twisting her fingers once someone came and took her plate away.

"Does it really work?" Knewt waved vaguely, not seeming to notice his splinted fingers. "This replacement thinking stuff?"

Surprised, Cassidy nodded. "Yes, it… That is, I'm my own first patient." Embarrassed, she tucked a curl behind her ear. "So far, though. So far it seems to be working."

"Good." Knewt gestured at the hold in general, it seemed. "You'll have to let us know how we can help."

Startled, Cassidy turned to find that they'd acquired an audience. Cook. Most of the apprentices. *All* the windfairies.

"Have ye had this affliction long, lass?" Cook asked, his weathered old face a picture of concern.

It wasn't that much different from the expressions the others wore, though Cassidy thought she detected a faint, lingering horror in the way the windfairies watched her while they waited for her response.

She coughed, trying to clear the embarrassment out of her throat so she could answer. "I believe it comes from being raised in the seven regions. We live in our tunnels and caves all year, not just during the winter."

Some of their reactions were a bit gruff, but they all expressed genuine concern. One Sky Fairy, who probably thought he was whispering, announced, "What a turrible way to live!"

Cassidy wasn't sure whether she should hide her smile or laugh outright.

"Will ya tell us about 'em?" One of the apprentices she hadn't met yet blurted. "Them regions, I mean."

"The seven regions?" She blinked in surprise. "Why, yes. Yes, of course."

"Hold on." A large hand settled on the apprentice's shoulder. "Tolden, you know we work while the sun's high."

"Yessir!" Tolden, who'd had his back to the Wrangler, answered at parade ground volume, making everyone else wince.

The small group broke up with a laugh and a few of them pounded a beet-red Tolden on the back as they formed up for chores. In a wink, as it were, they had gone.

"Don'tcha worry none." Cook grinned at Cassidy, revealing a gap in his teeth. "Berns is a hard task master, but a fair one. They'll be back soon enough and wantin' that story."

"Not to mention one of your hot, nourishing meals." Cassidy returned the compliment easily. "How can I help?"

"Well, now." Cookie rubbed his hands together. "Have a look round at yer patients, then come t'the stove. I'm bound to have a job fer ye."

She took her marching orders with a grin and a playful salute. Helping Cook mix up a batch of 'meat' pies took her mind off of Isaac and the spider hunt. After that, she fed lunch to her patients that couldn't manage their own utensils, did dishes, and helped sew patches over the holes in their leathers.

Whenever she had the chance, she channeled her thoughts through exercises she hoped would eventually allay her fears. She'd learned a lot during her time on deck. For one thing, not being surprised made a remarkable difference in how manageable the fear was. For another, 'outside' wasn't as empty as she'd expected. Branches and even taller trees spread across the sky, creating a clear boundary for her to cling to.

She wasn't ready to walk to the edge of a cliff, to look both down *and* up at the same time. No, it would be a while before she reached that point. However, that didn't stop her from congratulating herself on making progress.

The sound of boots on the deck sent her hurrying to the aft companionway, where she joined the line passing baskets of ice shavings to Cook, who poured them into the reservoir. A short creak preceded a tremendous rattle from over by the wood box and she was startled to see wood dropping in through the ceiling.

"Clever, ain't it?" Cook shook out the last of the shavings and set the empty basket aside.

"Wish they'd make a deck hatch fer the shavin's, too!"

Cassidy filed the new meaning of the word 'hatch' away for later and shivered at the icy blast of fresh air.

"Any news from the huntin' party?" Cook called over the rumble of wood.

"Nothin' yet," came the reply. "Don't reckon they had any luck, though."

"That ain't good," Cook muttered as the hatch closed with a thud and the creak of a latch.

Both parties were inside in short order and everyone wanted to know about the hunt.

Berns let them clamor a moment while he warmed his hands at the stove, then shrugged. "Caught a glimpse of them as we was comin' back. They wasn't comin' here with wounded and I didn't see survey gear. Looked to me like they was trackin'."

The answering silence was so profound that Cassidy could hear forks shoving the meat pies around on plates. Her own hunger gone, she wished she could scrape her untouched food back into the pot. Unfortunately, she needed the nourishment to survive, even in the relative protection of the hold.

Tracking. All she knew of it came from the pitifully few hours she'd spent in the Wrangler apprentices classes. The average Wood Fairy could follow a large land animal, meaning anything from a mouse on up, at a flat out zip. A semi-skilled Wrangler knew which kind of bird left what marks in the dirt or on bark. The *best* trackers, often but not necessarily Wranglers, could trail insects across wood or even hard-packed earth.

This business of tracking a predator, though. There weren't many tasks more dangerous than that.

Cassidy rubbed her arm, trying to make the prickles go away. She might well go mad waiting for the hunting parties to return!

"Doc?" Berns pushed his food together in a large pile at the center of his plate, as if preparing to scoop some into his mouth. "D'you think you could tell us one of your stories after supper?"

She recognized his distraction tactic. Her thoughts straying to Daphne's unfinished manuscript, she couldn't help smiling. Not that Berns was making the request for her sake alone. The mood in the hold had fallen flatter than a whipray.

"I think I can manage that." Aware of the responsibility resting on her, Cassidy made a valiant effort to eat her food so that the others would eat theirs while they were waiting. When she couldn't manage another bite, she took a big drink of water and cleared her throat.

The apprentices jumped up and began clearing away plates with such alacrity that she half expected them to gather on the floor around her feet. Ah, but they were too old to be quite so undignified.

Once everyone was seated comfortably, Cassidy began by telling them about the large domes of volcanic glass that sheltered much of the seven regions from the briny waters of the Margua. They were deep in a discussion about whether or not the lava tubes that connected the domes to each other and to several medium-sized caverns might be enlarged to permit casual flying, when noises on the deck told them the hunters had returned.

"What luck?" Berns was the first to speak after the companionway door closed behind them.

"None." Skite accepted a mug of a hot saffron steep and drank some with a grimace. "Found plenty of tracks, but never caught sight of the beast itself."

Isaac bypassed the others to come sit beside Cassidy, smiling wearily. "Cold out there." He flexed stiff fingers and wiggled half-frozen toes in his boots.

"You must be starving." She started to rise, intending to bring him a plate, but the apprentices were already attending to the hunters.

Isaac accepted the meat pie gratefully and with a side wink at Cassidy. He loved her always, but especially for thinking to take care of him.

"I'm sorry you didn't catch the spider." She cocked her head to one side. "I think."

"We all are." He leaned back against the bulkhead. "The only thing worse than tackling a spider when it's your idea is being taken unawares by one."

Several voices murmured agreement, then settled into the low conversing of tired folk.

Cassidy held her peace, unwilling to disturb Isaac while he ate. Thinking back to Skite's stories of the first night left her wondering how many patients she would have when they found the spider, even if everything went as planned.

After scraping his plate clean, Isaac surrendered it and his utensils to Harry with a satisfied sigh. "You know, I never trust myself to assign expedition cooks. I always have to put the names in a hat and draw them out to make sure it's fair." He grinned at Cassidy, feeling alive for the first time in hours. "We certainly got lucky this time."

"Hmm." She disciplined a smile when he moved to put his arm around her again. "Would you mind turning around?"

"Huh?" He blinked, thinking he'd misheard.

"Turn." She nudged him in the direction she wanted him to go. "I need to look at your wings."

She sensed impatience rippling through him as she spread his hindwings, carefully checking for weak spots in the recently reconstructed areas. Mindful of the months he'd gone without flying, she still took the time to poke and prod the muscles in his lower back, trying to decide whether or not he'd need a liniment treatment.

"Doc." The half title came out as a sigh. "I'm fine."

"Yes. I agree." She released him and went to the medicine chests. "You should still have a dose of doctor's water." She gasped when Isaac, who'd followed her, spun her to face him. Guessing his intent, she remarked breathlessly, "I thought we were going to be discreet about our engagement."

"About the engagement, sure. Not about our feelings." He smiled and caressed her cheek. "Though we will probably have to tell them eventually."

"Oh?" She eased closer. "Eventually?"

He ignored the implicit question in favor of a soft kiss. "Soon," he whispered against her lips. "We'll tell them soon."

"Don't think this gets you out of drinking the doctor's water," she countered, making him laugh.

Skite's voice, a smooth baritone that hardly seemed to match his often impish behavior, rose over the quiet group. Others joined in, singing soothing harmony as they related the tale of Master Donny Gibbons and the beautiful apple tree where he lived.

"And sure in spring," lilted a lovely soprano, "the blossoms were the fair-est in the wood. From groves around, came they all for to see."

Cassidy closed her eyes and rested her head on Isaac's chest, trying to imagine the stark branches she'd seen that morning—had it really been only a few hours ago? not a few days?—covered with freshly-sprouted green leaves and the dainty blossoms from the song.

"Someone's tired." Isaac chuckled when he noticed her yawning. Bending his head, he kissed her temple. "Looks like an early night all around, in fact."

A good thing, too. They'd all worked hard today and had a lot more to do. If they could only find and dispatch that spider, they could get on with their intended business of surveying the area and scouting for resources.

"I better see to Knewt." Cassidy let Isaac steal one more kiss; then, cheeks warming as she noticed others smiling at them, went to settle Knewt for the night.

"I sure miss doin' my own walking," he grumbled as she sent Harry for a mug of doctor's water and Patience for another blanket.

"Good." Cassidy looked up from where she was studying his leg. It was absolutely incredible how quickly it was healing! "Because I think we're all getting a little tired of doing things for you that you ought to be doing yourself."

"How's that?" Knewt stared at her, shocked.

"You heard me." Finished rewrapping his leg, Cassidy shook a finger at him. "Just you wait. I'll get you up come morning and Cook'll run you ragged."

"You mean it?" Knewt's grin dwarfed the lanterns in its brightness. "I can walk tomorrow?"

"Hobble, more likely." She patted his good knee. "But it's doing so well that, with a crutch, you should at least be able to get your own meals. Maybe take a turn around the hold."

He was about to shower praise on her when Harry arrived with the doctor's water.

Cassidy somehow managed to keep a straight face while she lingered, as if to make sure Knewt didn't cheat. She'd had doctor's water and knew it tasted ghastly, which only added to the fun of watching the moment play out.

Knewt coughed into his hand. Accepted the mug and tipped it enough to see inside, raising one eyebrow as though surprised at how full it was. Gave Harry a friendly thump on the chest when the lad leaned too close.

"Down the hatch!" Taking a deep breath, Knewt held his breath while he guzzled the stuff. "Oh, that's bad." He shook his head.

"I should think you'd be used to it by now," Cassidy observed dryly as she started to inspect his fingers. The much thinner bones healed almost overnight thanks to the doses of Wood Fairy potion, which meant that Knewt could join them in sewing tomorrow.

A chorus of laughs at her quip reminded her that there was no such thing as privacy in the hold, as did the friendly shoulder slaps and well wishes for her own 'recuperation' as they all headed for their hammocks.

"Cass. What do they mean?" Isaac asked when she went to her own hammock at last. "Your 'recuperation'?"

She fussed with her blanket for a moment, then met his eyes shyly. "I told them about my fear today." She'd told them a lot, come to think of it.

"Oh. And is everything alright?" Isaac searched her face, worried that she might feel anxious now that her secret was known to the entire expedition. Instead, he found only peace in her eyes as she smiled at him.

"Better than alright," she promised, sensing what he was thinking. "You heard them. They all think I can overcome it." She slipped into the hammock with minimal effort and shook the blanket down over her feet. "That makes me think I can, too."

With a final, shared smile, they whispered their goodnights and settled in to rest.

Chapter 14

It snowed overnight, turning the world outside the *Itxar* into a blinding nightmare of ice crystals. Majestic arches. Wicked-looking spikes. Columns as thick around as two fairies—not counting Sugar, of course. And each of them as big as a summer market, bewildering in their deadly beauty.

"Ice goggles!" Isaac called to the Wranglers still waiting in the companionway. From a small pocket in his left sleeve, he withdrew red-tinted goggle rounds and fastened them into place. "We'll need axes and saws!"

"Yep." Skite passed him a heavy ax and kept the saw for later.

"Thanks." Isaac wrapped his mittens around the ax handle and stifled a groan. He hated fighting for a grip while he worked. "Have the wood and ice crews clear the other companionway and the wood hatch."

"Already on it." Skite pointed behind him as the sound of an ax biting into ice rang through the frigid air. "Shall we?"

"We shall." Bracing himself, Isaac took a swing at the column of ice blocking his way. It was as thick as two ordinary fairies, possibly three, and took him several minutes to pare down enough for him to slide through the gap.

Trading Skite the ax for one end of the saw,

Isaac settled into a rhythm.

Pull. Push. Pull. Push.

By the time he and Skite had completed two cuts in top and bottom of the column so it could be removed, they were both sweating dangerously.

"C'mon." Skite waved for Isaac to follow. "We'll have to change."

"Blast." Isaac muttered under his breath as he descended the companionway, stripping off his top layer as he went. "It'll take us all morning to free that up properly."

"Mayhap it's for the best." Skite stepped behind a hanging blanket to put on dry inner layers. "We should be focusing on getting into those borer holes. Lauta's going to be a village in name only at this rate."

That brought Isaac up short. "With a spider around? Particularly one who thinks of those holes as a feeding ground?" He kept his voice down, not wanting to worry the others.

"All the more reason to get the engineers busy clearing out those carcasses." Skite emerged, clothed in clean woolen layers. "The sooner we lay claim to those holes, the better."

"I'll think about it." Isaac took his turn behind the blanket, then stepped into fresh leathers. He stank—everyone did by now—but the important thing was that his clothes were dry.

Topside again, they worked more carefully,

trading off with the others so that none of them worked up a sweat. As Isaac predicted, it was lunchtime before both companionways had a safe exit, but at least he'd made up his mind.

Over lunch he relayed the change in plans. He made sure to assign himself to one of the carcass crews so that no one could complain he didn't do his fair share, then worked with Skite and Captain Keddy to divvy up the rest of the work.

"Can't say as I like sendin' my crew out with a spider around." Keddy folded his arms across his chest. He and the other Sky Fairies were assigned to Weetu as windfairies, crewing the windships. It was one thing to agree to assist with the rest of the expeditionary goals and quite another to expose themselves to unnecessary danger.

"None of us likes it," Isaac assured him. "But it's the best we can do right now. We'll post double guards while we work. Berns will set spider snares, and we'll get the holes cleared as soon as we can. We'll all be much safer once we're inside the tree with proper gates in place." He deliberately avoided pointing out that it would happen much faster with the Sky Fairies' help.

"Alright." Keddy agreed at last. "Let's get started."

Relieved, Isaac got to his feet and turned to look for Cassidy, intending to wave to her before he left. He never expected to find her standing by Cook, intently listening while she adjusted her scale armor.

"Go." Skite nudged Isaac's arm, having also spotted Doc. "We'll get started checking the holes so the engineers can get in there."

"Right. And, thanks." Isaac made his way over to Cassidy and arched an eyebrow at her. "Looks like you're planning to go somewhere."

"Yes." She nodded. "With everyone working on the holes, I thought I could help with the ice shavings today."

"I see." He dropped his eyes to her gauntleted hands for a moment, then returned his gaze to her face. "I'd feel better if you stayed inside until we take care of the spider."

Her mouth drooped, but a spark flashed in her hazel-green eyes. "I won't be a liability, Isaac."

"I know you believe that. And I want to believe it, too." Isaac hesitated. How far could he trust her self-diagnosis? He had to ask that question. He *had* to. There were too many others at stake.

"We'll take good care of her," blurted Harry. Arms full of unwieldy baskets for the shavings, he nevertheless squared his shoulders.

"It's true, sir." Patience, likewise burdened, spoke quietly from beside Harry. "We know about her fear. We discussed it over breakfast and have a plan and everything."

Isaac stared as all of the apprentices began nodding. A small part of him whooped for joy at their whole-hearted acceptance of his beloved. The rest of him threw up its hands disgustedly and admitted defeat. Nothing short of a direct order would prevent this from happening. And the slightly defiant look on Cook's face confirmed that he did not want to go there.

"Alright." Isaac caught Cassidy's gaze and held it. "But stay as close as you can to the *Itxar*. Eyes open. And I don't care which lookout yells or how far away you think the trouble is, at the first sign of trouble you all drop what you're doing and run." He waited until Cassidy nodded before turning to the apprentices.

"Yes, sir!" They chorused obediently.

He stood there, hands curled into fists at his side, and watched them leave. Cook led the way and the others formed up around Cassidy, talking and laughing and generally working to distract her as they ascended the companionway to the deck.

"Isaac!" Someone hailed him from the forward companionway. "The engineers are moving into the first hole."

Groaning within himself, Isaac set off to do his job. It was a cold, foul job, hauling the carcasses along a row of uneven twigs, rolling it along the bottom of the tunnel to dump it onto the ground far below.

Over the course of the next several hours, the Wranglers swept each tunnel for the spider, then stood guard while the engineers prepared the next carcass for removal.

"Return!" The guards cried from their perches. "The sun will set soon!"

"Time to go." Isaac stretched to one side, then the other, his back popping gloriously. "Pack it up!"

"But we're almost done." One of the younger Wranglers protested. "Another half an hour. Please. Then tomorrow we can start straight into…"

"No." Isaac grabbed him by the shoulder and propelled him toward the mouth of the tunnel. "We go now. Look." The lad stumbled into the waning light, blinking rapidly. "We could survive a night here. Probably. But my stomach is scrunched so tightly together that I'm in danger of developing a permanent cramp in my digestive system if I don't eat soon."

A round of laughter saluted his jest and they all flew through the rapidly cooling evening air to the *Itxar* and their waiting supper.

Isaac, despite his joke, bypassed the line to the food and sought out Cassidy instead.

"Isaac!" Her face lit up when she saw him. She started to reach for him, but stopped herself when she saw her hands. They were covered in yet another marvelous Wood Fairy medicine. "Let me…um." Laughing, she pointed at Knewt. "I'm almost done."

"You don't have to sound so happy about it." Knewt tried to keep a straight face, but it really was too perfect an opportunity to tease them both.

Isaac enjoyed waiting while they bantered back and forth, talking about how they'd spent their day. Still, he was glad when Cassidy turned to him with a smile and clean hands.

"You're still here?" Seizing his arm, she pushed him toward the galley. "When was the last time you ate?"

"Hmm, let me think." He slipped his free arm around her waist. "This is supper, right? So I guess I must've last eaten at lunch."

She laughed at his terrible humor, then leaned into his half embrace, creating a bubble of space just for them. "I'm fine," she whispered.

"Really?" Not wanting to release her just yet, he lifted her off her feet enough to move them along with the line. Unfortunately, that brought them to the stacks of plates and utensils, where he let go with a sigh.

"Yes. I'll tell you about it while we eat." Accepting a plate from him, she smiled at Cook, who gave her a generous scoop of the salt pork hash she'd helped him make.

Finally, they were settled on a couple of medicine chests and able to talk.

"I take it today went well?" Isaac prompted, eager to hear more.

"So well!" She sat back and looked at him. "Did you know it's not actually empty out there?"

With a little prompting, she told him all that she'd seen. "Fields of ice crystals! They seemed to go on forever. I couldn't…it was just…amazing! I can't believe how huge they are! And *so* beautiful." Trees, everywhere she'd looked. Oh, and branches! The branches gave her something to hold onto when she looked up at the sky.

She blushed a little as she remembered her scale armor getting caught or 'hung up,' as one of the apprentices called it, on a prong of ice. Since they'd freed her at once, she left that out, not wanting to worry him.

He interrupted occasionally to laughingly remind her to eat. While she chewed, he filled the time with small insights. That the sky changed color with the sun, or when a storm was coming. How green the forest would be soon.

"As it gets warmer and warmer, we'll start seeing the first shoots of new growth," he promised as she polished off her food. Much to his surprise, her smile disappeared.

"I have to see the forest floor tomorrow," she said quietly. "If I am to help prevent the surface from flooding, I must see the land."

"We have detailed topographical maps," he started to offer, but stopped when she shook her head.

"My father and I studied those thoroughly. Now I must see what kind of ground is there." Reaching out, she stacked their plates. "It isn't just about where the slopes are or how big. I have to find the water path, determine how to redistribute or impede it." That was all she knew how to put into words, so she stopped speaking and looked at him, hoping he would understand what she couldn't express.

"I'd better tell Keddy and Skite." He yielded without further argument because he sensed the simple truth in what she'd already said. He had no concept of what it would take to stop the flooding from an early spring. Yet both Cassidy and her father Volt believed that a single Water Fairy could do exactly that.

Relieved, Cassidy took care of their dishes and allowed herself to be persuaded to tell another story about the seven regions.

"You mean it?" Tolden asked at the end. "No predators? At all?" At her nod he pressed, "What do you need warriors for, then?"

"That's a story for another night." Isaac, arms folded, spoke up from where he'd been listening at the back of the group. "We start working the tunnels tomorrow, so we all need to get some sleep." He'd arranged to have the windfairies assigned to the daily chore details, which freed all of the Wranglers for tunnel work, guard duty, and escort duty.

Cassidy smiled at the token protests and went to thank Isaac for interceding.

"What will I tell them?" she asked in a low voice. "That, of all the tribes, we're the only one still living as if the war had never ended?"

"Were," he corrected mildly. He'd never thought of it in those terms before, yet she wasn't wrong. Except that it was all changing, and her presence on the surface had a lot to do with it. "The Water Fairies *were* living as though the war raged on."

The creak of hammocks as the others settled in filled the silence while Cassidy thought.

"Maybe I can think of another way to say it," she sighed at last. "Perhaps if I tell them about the dangers in the sea?"

"Come on." He squeezed her shoulders and walked her over to her hammock. "Sleep on it. We want to present your tribe in the best light possible."

"And the only way to do that is to tell the truth." She agreed without waiting for him to state the obvious. "I just." She blew out a breath. "It would really help if I knew how to share it in such a way that all sides saw why an ancient decision made sense."

"A feeling I know well," Isaac agreed.

Smiling ruefully at each other, they retired to their hammocks, where neither slept well. They were more amused than surprised to find each other in the galley at dawn, working first to prepare breakfast with Cook, then to pack a hearty lunch for their trip.

"Good luck, Doc!" Knewt mumbled around the handful of pins he held between his lips in preparation for the mending in his lap.

"You, too!" She waved back, her scale armor jingling with the motion, and followed Isaac up the companionway. Stopped when he stopped, a few steps onto the deck. "Isaac? What is it?"

She was perplexed when he didn't answer beyond moving further away from the doors, which allowed the others to come on deck and close things behind them. In another moment, she noticed that all the Wranglers that made up their party were eerily still. All of them gazed off into the grove, their bodies facing different directions.

A trickle of condensation tickled its way down her face and she groaned without meaning to. She might live to go on a thousand spring expeditions, but she would never grow accustomed to the leathers.

"The forest." Isaac broke the silence, his voice hushed and awed. "It's waking up."

Cassidy watched, stupefied, as the Wranglers

removed their mittens and unbuttoned their face shields. Her own instincts kicked in belatedly and she actually looked at the deck. Small, hard lumps of ice glistened in the morning sun where the grand ice sculptures had stood.

"The ice." Her voice was grim as she hurried across the deck to look over the side. "It's melting."

Isaac joined her at the gunn'ls and frowned at the rising water level. "We have to get into those tunnels soon."

"Today would be best," Cassidy agreed. "As the day warms, the ice will continue to melt and the water level around the windship will rise, but when temperatures drop tonight…"

"The water will freeze all over again. It might crush the *Itxar*'s hull or just overflow across the deck." Isaac drummed his fingers on the gunn'ls, sorting through what could be done and what had to be done. "Either way we'll be lucky to survive."

"I have to warn you." Cassidy put her gauntleted hand on his arm when he turned to fly away. "This makes my visit to the forest floor all the more important."

"We'll leave as soon as I return." Isaac zipped across the deck and disappeared below.

Exhaling shakily, Cassidy copied the others, freeing her hands and face. She couldn't figure out how to comfortably tuck her leather hood under her scale armor while still wearing the armored coif, so in the end she left them both to dangle between her shoulders. Turning to face the faint breeze, she extended her tongue to test the water it carried.

"Alright, let's go." Isaac spotted Cassidy as he resurfaced; started to check on the others, then jerked his gaze back to her. *What* was she doing? "Um. As soon as you're ready."

"That breeze worries me," she announced as she turned to join the group. "We need to hurry."

"You can close your eyes if you need to. I promise I won't fly you into any branches or anything." He winked, trying to embed a visually full scene in her mind.

"I'll be alright," she promised, gripping his hand. "Just don't let go."

"Here we go!" Isaac extended his wings and led the way off the *Itxar*.

Luckily, the branch extended in the direction they wanted to go, and he kept them flying above it for as long as he could. It slowly narrowed down to nothing, forcing them to fly between trees, but Cassidy didn't hesitate to plunge into the gap with him at her side.

"There!" He pointed with his free hand when their destination came into sight. "That's where the water enters the grove."

"I need to see where it comes from!" Water Fairies kept meticulous maps of all the waterways in Fairydom, including those that ran along under the surface, carrying water to and from Margua. Unfortunately, she'd spent very little time with those maps in the last hundred years or so, preferring her laboratory and the operating room.

"You're sure?" Isaac reassessed the situation rapidly. At her nod, he drew up to consider the available tree limbs. "Going up!" Aiming for the likeliest limb, he landed, then cupped his hands around his eyes and squinted. Satisfied, he motioned to the Wrangler carrying the telescope. "Packs off, eyes open. We'll take a rest here."

"It's half a day's flight from the *Itxar* to the stream," Isaac explained to a bewildered-looking Cassidy. "We'd never make it back in time and we have nowhere safe to spend the night except the tunnels." He deliberately omitted the list of fairy predators that frequented tall grass and stream areas.

"Alright." She bit her lip, frustrated yet aware of her own ignorance of the woods. "I can at least examine the…" She was about to indicate the northern edge of the grove when Isaac interrupted.

"Here." Isaac beckoned her over to where the telescope waited. "We can't go as far as the stream, but we can bring it to you."

She approached the metal tube curiously. As long as her arm and standing on a three-legged stand, it had one large round end and one smaller round end. In a way, it reminded her of her microscope.

Putting her eye up to the smaller glass lens, she gasped in wonder as the distant horizon leapt forward to meet her.

After studying the stream through the telescope, as they called it, Cassidy was glad to settle on to the forest floor. There was only so much one could learn by studying something through a glass.

"We'll eat lunch here," Isaac ordered as he shucked his pack, one eye on Cassidy, who looked remarkably like she was going to wander off on her own. "Keep a sharp watch, now."

"What do we do with these?" The men hadn't complained about carrying Cassidy's peculiar equipment, but by now they were ready to hear that the heavy metal stakes and rolls of wire had a specific purpose.

"Guard them well." Isaac grinned cheekily and hurried off to join Cassidy.

"Here." Cassidy touched the front of the pitted stone cliff that ran along the northern edge of the clearing. Tapped it and listened. "When the water rises over the stream bed, it seeps across the grass to the edge of the forest. The trees and slopes force it through a narrower and narrower channel until it's comes through here. By then, it's going fast enough to erode the soil; and, over time, even stone."

"From here it travels the length of the Deep Woods." Isaac looked over his shoulder, in the direction the water would run. "Ordinarily, it dissipates along the way. A shallow pool here and there; and of course, watering the forest for its spring growth."

"But this year will be different." Cassidy flew back a ways, far enough to give her a better view of the water's course. If her armor hadn't jingled with her motion, she would've forgotten she was wearing it. "This year, the foothills and lower mountain peaks will melt too soon, while your tribal land is still sodden with the last of its own snow."

"Yes." Isaac's heart sank at the thought. He'd only heard stories of the lives and property lost to the last early spring, yet it still sickened him. "Can we do anything to prevent the runoff from reaching the Plant Fairies?"

"We'll do our best," she promised. Flying straight up, she spun in a slow circle. Then dropped down again, landing on a hillock bare of ought but hardy moss.

"Cass!" Isaac landed beside her and grabbed her hand. "You have to stay near me! We're not the only ones enjoying the warmer weather today."

"Oh. Sorry. I'm not used to thinking about that." She tapped her suge pouch and eyed the bushes, suddenly wishing for a bit *more* open space where predators couldn't hide. "I'll be sort of all over the place for the next hour or more, following the water."

"I understand, but you can't go off by yourself, alright?" He was genuinely worried. How could he watch for predators while keeping an eye on her? Inspiration struck. "Keep talking to me. That will help me keep track of you."

"You make me sound like an errant child." She wrinkled her nose at him, determined not to let the threat of predators keep her from her task.

Whatever Isaac might've said—or done—in response to her teasing was preempted by the call to eat.

"Is it lunchtime already? I didn't realize we'd been out so long," Cassidy admitted in surprise.

"We don't always eat on the clock on expedition." Retaining a firm hold on her hand, Isaac lifted off. "We mostly eat when we're hungry."

"Very wise," she laughed.

After they finished eating, Isaac sent the others to scout and set snares for prey, then allowed Cassidy to resume her work. He didn't understand much of what she told him, but he never lost track of her again either, and that was the important thing.

Finally, she landed on the tip of a broken stalk and looked back over the area she'd been studying.

"We can do it." In answer to his quirked eyebrow, she gestured at the rocky waterway. "We'll have to work quickly, but I believe we can divert a significant amount of the runoff. And possibly dam up quite a bit more here."

"Enough?" he asked eagerly.

"I don't know." She frowned. "There's a lot of ground between here and the Plant Fairy boundary. Not to mention any number of things that could've changed over the winter. Fallen branches or even fallen trees between here and the boundary. I'll do the best I can with what we have here."

He took a moment to digest her answer, then smiled. "That's all we can ask."

A distant shout brought his head up and he looked around to where the hunting party hovered.

"Good grief." Glancing about, he suddenly realized how deep the shadows were. "Your equipment. Do we need to bring it back? Is there anything in there that might freeze or be damaged if we leave it out overnight?"

"What? Oh." She blinked. "No, it's just wire and metals stakes." More or less.

"Safer than we would be, then." He waved at the party, starting them back to Lauta. "Come on. It's getting dark."

"Well." She frowned. "Let's at least put them over here." She scooped up a pack and hauled it over to a shallow overhang.

"Alright, but let's hurry." His hands were full of pack straps when movement caught his eye. "Cass! Look out!"

The urgency in his voice brought her about sharply, in time to narrowly avoid a glistening white rope. *Rope?* Adrenaline shot through her as though filling an otherwise empty space. Hand already moving toward her suge pouch, she leapt to one side.

"Get out of there!" Isaac yelled at her even as he flew forward, remembering belatedly to drop the packs. He couldn't hear them hit the ground over the roaring of blood in his ears. He'd never reach her in time.

Another white projectile shot toward her and Cassidy flipped her suge out to meet it, sliding to her right in the classic crab defense while her eyes scanned the landscape. Where was it coming from? It should've been so easy to just follow the white line back to its origin...

The severed end of the second damp projectile landed limply on the ground, tempting her to stop and find something to poke it with. There was no question in her mind of the unfriendly intent behind what she could only think of as attacks, yet her curiosity was peaked.

Isaac jerked to a stop just in time to keep from getting her shoulder in his chest.

"Isaac, wait!" His arms closed around her shoulders, blocking her right hand from using the suge to any effect. They were just starting to lift off when time slowed to a crawl as she saw more rope-stuff coming at them with all the speed of an arrow loosed from a bow.

Only this time, how could it miss? Isaac's wings were fully extended, tripling the target area. A real rope would've bounced right off, but this stuff—it was damp. Damp? And sticky?

"No!" Tossing her suge hilt to her left hand, Cassidy executed a wild figure eight. There was no time for finesse.

Isaac stared in shock as pieces of the freshly spun spider silk struck the ground at random, looking lost and perhaps a little forlorn at her sloppy treatment of them. Any pity they might've provoked fled in the next instant when an enormous, eight-legged beast scuttled out from behind a withered leaf. Its mottled brown and black coloring had hidden it perfectly.

"Blast." He tried to shift his grip on Cassidy, to put her in a better position to use her suge, but the rough edges of her scale armor gouged him so badly he began to bleed.

"Drop me!" Cassidy struggled against his hold. "We can't get away like this!"

"Never!" He tightened his grip.

"Isaac! Drop me!" She was a heartbeat away from forcing him to release her when at last his arms opened. As she fell toward what she recognized as a spider, she heard him shouting after her.

"Come on!" He started to rise away from the spider, only to realize *Cassidy was going the wrong way.*

"Get clear!" Transferring the suge hilt to her right hand again, she hoped fervently that Isaac would do as she'd asked. Everything she'd ever learned about spiders said that they didn't attack fairies in ones and twos, which made this spider either exceptionally hungry or insane. Whichever it was, the rules also said *she* was insane for charging it.

Tucking her knees, she somersaulted in midair over a strand of the rope-stuff. It had a better name, but she'd worry about that later. A powerful flap of her wings, which she immediately re-tucked, lifted her above the next strand.

As she tumbled and braked and rose and plummeted, she came ever nearer the spider's six beady eyes. Soon it was impossible to evade the rope-stuff, so her suge darted ahead of her, frantically chopping the strands into pieces.

A cold calm enveloped Cassidy when she saw a strand forming and knew she didn't stand a chance of escaping it. Ignoring the danger, she tucked her wings and executed a final series of forward strikes.

Isaac, who'd been watching the deadly air ballet in numb, horrified fascination, snapped out of his trance. "No. No! NO!" The spider silk ignored his anguished plea and struck Cassidy squarely.

He dove forward, then jerked to a stop, confused. The spider lurched violently. It reared up on its back legs. Then crumpled onto its side, shuddering.

"Cassidy!" He nearly screamed her name as he streaked toward her, a faint smudge lying in the shadow of the spider's legs. "Be alive. Be alive!" His training and experience told him that her leathers would protect her from most of the venom, with only her hands and face exposed.

Hands. His hands. Bare. Bleeding. Bad.

Jerking on his mittens, he wove his way through spider legs to her side, where he hacked uselessly at the envenomed spider silk until his belt knife was trapped in the vile, sticky mess. A failed attempt at retrieving it left one mitten permanently behind.

Suddenly remembering her suge, he yanked it loose from the spider's carcass and began cutting the spider silk away from her face, taking care not to cut her or himself.

"This is impossible," he muttered as the strand parted under the suge's blade. "*Nothing* cuts fresh spider silk."

Except here he was, doing it. And he had nearly finished removing the silk from her cheek! Regrettably, he'd had to sacrifice some of her curls in the process—which would grow back, he reassured himself.

More importantly, now he needed to find a way to remove her from the *rest* of the spider silk without exposing himself to the venom. He was no good to her dead.

Setting the suge aside, he stood up to study the situation.

"Isaac! Get outta there!" The Wrangler hunting party, alerted by the commotion, had spent the length of the fight trying to return in time to help. Spurred to greater lengths by his agonized cry, they surrounded him and dragged him away from her body.

"Ya can't save her!" A second voice shouted.

"Let me go!" Isaac slammed one of them into a spider leg. His elbow connected solidly with the midsection of another, and something gave under the blow. Reversing the arm motion, he twisted at the waist and threw a punch that snapped his next foe's head back.

In the confusion, nobody noticed when the suge was kicked hilt first into a mound of spider silk.

"Sorry, Yer Highness."

Too late, Isaac realized one of them was behind him. Something struck the back of his head and he pitched forward into darkness.

"Poor lad." A Wrangler, nursing his cracked ribs, shook his head sadly at the unconscious prince. "They was turrible in love."

"Didja see that?" Asked someone else. "She took this monster on single handed. And won!"

"That's one way of lookin' at it," remarked their leader dryly. "I'd ruther live to tell the tale, myself."

"She's still breathin'!"

Shocked, they gathered as close as the legs and silk would let them.

"Are you sure?" barked the leader, a weathered fellow by the name of Saltz.

"Sure as I am of me own name," retorted the speaker.

"Grab the med kit." Saltz jerked the nearest Wrangler to him, then shoved him toward the packs. "Get the antivenin. Everyone else, mittens on!"

Their prince forgotten, the Wranglers threw all their efforts into extricating their crazy new heroine and saving her life. Thanks to Isaac's careful work, her skin was free of the envenomed silk, but her leathers and scale armor were a total loss.

After administering the first shot of antivenin, they rolled her onto her stomach, where they encountered the back of her armored shirt.

"Remind me," grunted one of the Wranglers as he fought to pry apart the links, "ta tell Sven I don't want nothing like this."

"Agreed," huffed his partner. "'Tis one thing

to live in our armor. Another to be buried in it!"

"Or because of it!"

"There it goes!" Saltz took their places as the armored shirt finally yielded and used his razor sharp knife to slit Cassidy's leathers up the back, freeing her from the rest of the silk. He'd already done the same for Isaac, who was beginning to shiver. Well, the flight back to the tree would warm the lad up.

By then the others had dumped out the packs and fashioned them into a crude sling that they gently rolled Cassidy into.

Grimly, they lifted off into the rapidly descending darkness. They hadn't gone far when lights winked into view; not in the sky above them where they ought to have been, but directly ahead of them. Or so it appeared.

"All right, you knuckleheads!" Skite's irritation-laced voice pierced the night. The only thing worse than being second-in-command was having the boss go missing. "What in the name of good sense is keeping you out after sunset?"

"Spider," snapped Saltz, surly from the worry thrust upon him. "Stow your gab and fill your hands!" They'd been taking turns carrying the sling, but Lauta was a long way off yet.

Skite and the others in the small group of volunteers came at once to relieve their weary comrades. Someone whistled when light from the dancing torch flames revealed who the invalid was.

"Lively, now!" Skite's voice flicked like a lash, prodding them on. "To the tree!"

He sent the weariest of them on ahead—except for Isaac, who refused to leave Cassidy—and pushed sternly on in the cooling temperatures.

Cook and the apprentices met them at the tunnel gate with plates of hot food and another dose of antivenin for Cassidy, who hadn't roused more than to moan a bit when they shifted sling bearers.

"How much venom did she get?" Berns was the next to greet them, if it could be called that. "How much antivenin?"

"You can see on her cheek." Isaac indicated a large patch of space on his own, anyway. "Fresh silk from a spitting spider. I don't know how long it was on there. Five minutes? More?" He looked dazedly at the galley stove and briefly wondered where he was. His gaze wandered up and along the stovepipe, which ran across the ceiling to outside. Um, outside the tunnel. Ah, there. He had it now.

"Five minutes?" Berns squinted at him. "You got it off?" He wanted to ask how Isaac had managed to do it, but that could wait.

"Yes. Yes." Isaac started toward Cassidy and nearly fell. "I...um..."

"Get some food into him," Berns ordered. "And bandage those hands." Lowering Isaac onto the nearest flat surface higher than the floor, Berns tilted Isaac's head back and looked in his eyes. When they started to close, Berns used his fingers to open them wider. "Got some venom yourself, I fancy."

"Will he need the antivenin, too?" Patience asked. She would've wrung her hands except that they were full of food for Isaac.

"Hard to say." Berns gave Isaac a cursory examination; at least, the bit of him that wasn't covered by his woolens. "Feed him for now. Mind how he swallows. Fetch me if you notice he's havin' trouble either breathin' or swallowin'."

"Yes, sir!" Patience pushed the swaying Isaac back against the wall and offered him a bite of rabbit stew. "It's good, sir," she promised, touching the spoon lightly to his lips. "Happens we found a frozen rabbit carcass. Fox got most of it but left parts entirely untouched." Having succeeded in getting him to take the first bite, she tried another, still talking. "Course it doesn't take much to feed fairies, or even a whole group of fairies like us."

She didn't know if her talking was doing him any actual good, but it steadied her own nerves, so she kept going, updating him on the progress made on the tunnels while they were gone.

"We'll have to go back to the *Itxar* tomorrow for the rest of our hammocks," she finished as he ate the last spoonful. "And a few other odds and ends. Lauta's finally taking shape, though." Not knowing what else to do, she fashioned a bedroll from some blankets and coaxed him to lie down. "All in all," she cast a glance toward where Cassidy already lay, still as death, "I guess the day was well used."

Chapter 16

Isaac, still woozy the next morning, nevertheless insisted on moving closer to Cassidy's pallet. He felt so ill that he barely noted when Skite selected the chore details and got the day going.

"Isaac." Captain Keddy sat on the floor beside him, ankles tucked under his knees. He waited until the prince's eyes slowly focused on his face before proceeding. "I was talking with the lads from your detail. They tell me there's danger of a bad flood." The whole truth was that Skite had tasked him with finding out everything he could on the subject. Particularly how to keep it from happening, if at all possible.

"Flood." Isaac put his hands up to his head to stop it from spinning. Bandages? Why were his hands bandaged? He'd cut them. "Oh. Yes. Cassidy…"

"She's fine." Keddy spoke abruptly, worried that Isaac's attention might wander. "Tell me about the flood."

"Cassidy," Isaac repeated. "Said could stop." Getting the words from his brain out through his mouth was like pulling taffy. They stretched and stretched and didn't want to leave, so that he had to force them out.

"I see." Keddy scratched his stubble. "None

of your lads knew ought of that.”

“No,” Isaac agreed. “Did not tell.” His stomach contracted unexpectedly and his breakfast nearly gained its freedom. Wiping sweat from his face with trembling fingers, Isaac concentrated on breathing evenly.

“Right.” Keddy patted Isaac’s shoulder, more than a little concerned about the prince. “That’s enough for now.” Rising, he went straight to Berns, the closest they had to a doctor at the moment.

The next thing Isaac knew, he was submitting to another, more thorough examination from Berns. He didn’t resist as his pulse was taken, gums prodded, and eyes checked, but a groan escaped him when Berns poked two fingers into his abdomen.

Tight-lipped, Berns fetched a dose of antivenin and injected it in Isaac’s arm. His *prince*’s arm. It was all too easy to forget that under Isaac’s Wrangler uniform beat the heart of the tribe’s crown prince. A good man, one Berns wouldn’t hesitate to accept as king when the time came.

Coughing to clear his throat of the emotions crowding it, Berns remarked cynically, “Hope that’s the last spider we tangle with a’fore the reliefs get here.”

“Don’t tell me we’re running low on that.” Keddy grimaced and indicated the empty vial.

“More or less.” Looking over at Cassidy,

Berns was surprised to find she was starting unblinkingly at him. "Doc knows what I mean, don'tcha? The more of it we have to use, the less there is left."

Cassidy managed a weak nod. Ran a swollen tongue across dry lips.

"Here." Berns fetched a mug of doctor's water and the straw he'd whittled last night while trying to stay awake to keep an eye on his patients. He helped her take a few sips, steadied the mug when she tried to push it away. "Now, don't be s'hasty. You've sweated out more than that in the last hour. I know you know how much you need this, like it or not."

Weakly, she complied, drinking until he nodded.

"There's a good lass." Passing the mug off to Patience, he mopped the sweat off Cassidy's face. "Sleep, if you can. You're goin' ta be real tired for a week or more."

"Isaac?" she croaked.

"He's fine, lass. We fed him and tucked him in bed, just like you." Berns smiled reassuringly.

"F-f-flood," she whispered, the doctor's water starting to ease her words. "Stop."

Keddy's head came up. "What's that? Can you tell us how to stop the flood?"

Berns stepped between them. "She can only whisper and barely that. We've to let her rest and heal. Then she can tell…"

"Now."   Cassidy's eyes, bright with determination, met Berns'. "No time."

Frustrated, Berns scrubbed his hand across his face. He didn't want anything to happen to the Plant Fairy Tribe any more than they did.

"Talk fast," he ordered.

"Equi…equip…" She stumbled over the word.

"Equipment?" guessed Keddy, coming closer so he could hear her. At her nod he explained, "They left it all there last night."

"Yes." She shuddered at a stomach cramp. "Need branch. From tree."

"Makin' a dam, eh?" Berns glared at Keddy. "There. You have what you need." He would've said more except that Cassidy's cold fingers settled on his wrist.

Keddy, not noticing Berns' abrupt halt, muttered under his breath about the impossibility of a group as small as theirs moving anything as massive as a tree branch.

"Equip-ment help drop branch." Cassidy tried to swallow, but the sides of her throat stuck together, making her cough instead.

"That's it." Berns added plain water to the mug and helped her take another drink. "She's resting now."

Cassidy ached too much to complain, especially her jaw. *How* could she communicate her idea to them? Quickly. She might not know surface weather, but she knew water.

And the water in the air told her they were running out of time.

She lay quietly the rest of the morning, trying to come up with a way to teach them what they needed to know. At some point, her head cleared enough that she remembered Water Fairy law governing the use of lightning. That was when she knew it was impossible. They couldn't create the dam fast enough without lightning and she couldn't even tell them it existed.

She would have to do it herself. The important parts, at least.

Catching Patience's eye, she beckoned the young woman over and asked for paper and quill by acting out the motion of writing. She wasn't the least bit surprised when Berns was the one who brought them to her.

"You must be mighty tough." He tapped the blank pages he was holding, reluctant to hand them over. "Most folk'd likely be unconscious after the dose of spider venom you got." Her lack of verbal response added to his discomfort and he gave her the supplies with a sigh. "Try not to kill yourself off, hmm?"

She accepted the papers with a weak smile, then held up a finger, asking him to wait. Again, she mimed what she wanted, dragging the dry tip of the quill across the top page in a wobbly line, then pretending to mark a spot on it.

"Map?" he guessed. "You want a map? Of where?" As quickly as he asked the question, he decided it was a pretty silly one and added, "Of here?" Her smile was all the answer he required. "Hold on."

This time it was Keddy who brought what she'd asked for. After checking to make sure she had the chart she wanted, he settled nearby so he could keep an eye on her.

Patience stayed even closer, helping where she could by removing the ink bottle stopper, then holding things steady each time Cassidy dipped her quill. When she saw Cassidy was struggling to read the map, Patience showed her where they were and where the spider attack had occurred.

By the time Cassidy had learned enough to write a coherent line of instructions, she was too tired to even hold the quill, but she made Keddy read it back to her before sending him to share it with Skite.

"There, now." Patience gave her a drink of doctor's water. "You better hold still a while."

"Isaac?" Cassidy whispered.

"Doing well," Patience assured her. "Sure and he'll be up and about long before you are."

She slept briefly after that, but the antivenin was working and soon she became restless enough to start looking around for Keddy. Or Skite. Or even Berns.

"Hey." Isaac coughed into a handkerchief

and sniffled. "You look like you're feeling better."

"You sound like," she paused to take a sip of the doctor's water Berns had left in reach, "you have a cold."

"I got off lucky." He stayed where he was, not wanting to give her his cold. He didn't know how to say what he wanted to about…what had happened, so for a moment he just stood there awkwardly. At last he ventured, "Keddy tells me you've found a way for them to stop the flood."

"Us," she corrected. "If we work together, it can be done in a day or two."

"Cass, you can't even stand up. It'll be two days, maybe three, before you can even carry yourself as far as the clearing." He paused for a sip of doctor's water. "I promise we'll do exactly as you say. Alright?"

She shook her head firmly. "I may have to be carried there, but I must go." She gripped her blanket, fuming inwardly at Water Fairy law. Would it always come between them? "Some things only a Water Fairy may do."

"I see." He frowned, remembering the communicating machine and how closely guarded it had been. He doubted she planned to talk the branch into falling, yet whatever she had planned, it was clearly something she couldn't share. "We'll start tomorrow, then."

He raised a hand when her mouth started to open, presumably in protest. "The day's half gone, Cass. Skite didn't get your instructions in time to do anything about them."

She rubbed her forehead, semi-relieved to notice it was her worst pain point. The stomach cramping was over, she hoped.

"You're right." Sighing, she lifted both shoulders. "I look forward to tomorrow, then."

With that in mind, Isaac made a point of buttonholing Skite, Keddy, and Berns for a meeting as soon as they'd finished their supper. Thankfully, Keddy agreed to oversee the wood and ice details the next day, leaving Skite to command a hunt for fresh meat while Isaac and Cassidy took ten men to the clearing.

Despite the warmer weather the next day, Isaac bundled up in full leathers and a warm woolen hat.

"Oh no." Cassidy groaned from where she hung in a borrowed hammock. "My beautiful scale armor!" What little she could see of it was draped around the edges of a hardened silk strand. The rest, she supposed, was embedded inside the strand, lost forever. Her suge had vanished, though she couldn't imagine how. Certain knowledge of her loss sent a tear trailing down her cheek, which she wiped away quickly.

"Here we are again." Isaac was more concerned with the spider's carcass. Soon the ants would find it, and while it was possible to domesticate ants, that wasn't their mission.

Clearly agreeing with his unspoken assessment, the others made short work of repacking and transporting Cassidy's equipment to the branch she designated.

Once they were all safely in the tree, Cassidy perched on a bark outcropping and asked, "Is there a best place to cut this branch?"

"A weak spot?" Isaac squinted at the object in question. The thought of cutting the thick branch staggered his mind, but he didn't dare question her. The men would be curious enough when they were made to retreat while Cassidy used her Water Fairy machine. "Maybe."

With practiced ease, he overrode the other Wranglers' muttering and set them to examining the branch for cracks, soft spots, or anything else that would make the job easier.

The reports all added up to the same thing—the branch was solid.

"Pity." Cassidy's disappointment, if so she was, didn't change what had to be done. Wiping her forehead with a handkerchief Patience had pressed upon her when they left, Cassidy motioned toward the piles of metal stakes. "Please hammer those in into the branch in a straight line from one side to the other. Starting in the center of the branch."

Isaac picked up one of the stakes, twirled it,

then asked, "How deep do you want them?"

"I need to be able to access the rings on the sides." She nodded when Isaac poked his finger through the ring on the stake he held. "And they shouldn't be more than an arm's length apart. Please." She took a sip of doctor's water to cover her discomfort at giving orders she couldn't hope to help carry out.

"Will do." He dropped a wink that only she could see, then turned to face his team, leaning on the stake like a too-tall cane. "Hands out, everyone." Luckily, the cuts on his palms had been shallow and healed quickly.

Cassidy watched in some amusement as they extended their dominant hands, made a fist, then on the count of three, raised and lowered them with fingers poking out.

"Right." Isaac gave the circle of hands a cursory glance. "Odds hold the stakes. Evens swing the hammers." He'd held out four fingers himself, so nobody could complain he was playing favorites.

Anyway, it didn't stay like that for long. They all knew how important this was, if it worked, so as soon as a stake was set and would stand on its own, the stake holders moved down the row. Hammerers traded places with holders and in short order, all twenty stakes were set.

Isaac caught Cassidy's eye before dismissing the men to rest, then stayed as long as she would allow, helping her string the wire through the rings of the stakes.

Eventually, Cassidy had to ask him to leave, too. The miniature lightning machine she'd brought from Weetu only took a few moments to assemble, and much longer to charge.

Setting the delay switch, she wobbled her way to the bark outcropping where she'd rested while the men prepared the stakes, and ducked behind it, plugging her ears.

Three, two… The branch swayed violently with the result of the lightning discharge and Cassidy flattened herself still further when a head-sized chunk of smoldering wood landed nearby.

Alarmed shouts and cries warned her that the men were returning and she raced back to disconnect the machine and shove it in a discarded leather bag before anyone saw it.

Predictably, Isaac arrived first and stared, open-mouthed, at the fresh gash in the branch's surface. At a guess, he would estimate the trench at sixty twigs long and ten wide. Not quite waist deep. How… He shot Cassidy a look, but she was pretending to be wholly occupied with re-rolling the ball of wire as she pulled it free of the stake rings.

"What happened?!" The same question was asked a dozen or more different ways by the ten men as they surrounded the gaping trench in the branch.

"Yowch!" One of them jerked his hand back from the stake he'd reached for. "That's hot!"

"They all are." Cassidy's composure cracked when the breeze picked up and the branch swayed again, with a creak that was definitely new.

Isaac looked from the trench to her, then wiped damp palms on his trousers. "What's next?" he asked hoarsely.

"Let the stakes cool. Then hammer them in as far as they'll go again." Acutely aware that her legs had begun trembling from the exertion, Cassidy put the ball of wire down and reseated herself on the raised bark patch.

"Right, fellas." Isaac jerked his head toward the food bags. "Have a snack, then we'll get back at it."

Cassidy didn't move a muscle as the men filed past her, but was honestly afraid to look Isaac in the eye.

"Why didn't you tell me?" He looked down at the top of her head, wishing she'd look up at him. Dropping to one knee, he took her cold hands in his. Waited for her to lift her hazel eyes to his. "Cass, I'm...I'm not asking you to divulge any grand secrets. Not even a tiny one. But a wee bit of warning that whatever you did would sound like thunder on a clear day." He sucked in the breath his lungs were screaming for after so many words. "That we'd come back to a gash big enough to hide a hundred Wranglers in."

She cupped his cheek in her hands. "You're right. I should have."

"And?" He waited a beat. "Why didn't you?"

"Because I've never done this before. Not *this* exact thing." She looked over his head to where the stakes stood like uneven sentinels and shivered. "I knew it would work. I just wasn't sure of what that would entail."

"You've never…" He kissed both her palms, then clasped her hands between his. "Cass, my darling, my love. Whatever possessed you to take a chance like that?!"

"Why, to stop the flooding, of course." Seeing that she'd left him speechless, she ventured to add, "I wouldn't call it taking a chance, though. It was more of a calculated risk."

"You're mad." He drew her in for a kiss. "Quite, quite mad."

She giggled, then yawned. "Oh, for pity's sake. How long," she yawned again, "am I going to be tired for?"

"Probably until your body recovers from the venom." Chuckling, he steadied her. "Now, what're we going to tell the men?"

She grimaced, but let him lift her to her feet. It was the stew, heating over a small, hot fire, that inspired her simplified explanation.

"You boiled the liquid in the branch?" summarized one of the men.

"Basically."

"And that made the rippin' big hole?" Another leaned forward.

She nodded, concerned that more words would only make things worse.

"Do we, um, want ta know how?" asked someone else.

"Lady Clark," Isaac intervened firmly, "is not at liberty to disclose how it was done. Finish your stew, lads."

That finished the question and answer session, but Cassidy was glad to note they resumed their hammering with gusto. Here and there she caught a snatch of an idea, all of it about how grand it was that they were helping to prevent the flooding. Rather than being afraid of her, they seemed wholly focused on completing the task before them.

In fact, they cheered when Cassidy's second go brought the branch down.

They were still celebrating upon their return to Lauta, where they regaled the unfortunates who'd spent their day at menial tasks such as wood and ice cutting with the details of the day's great adventure. Such details as they knew, anyway.

Isaac was called on to verify the truth of the story, which he did with such flamboyance that Cassidy elbowed him in the ribs to stop him.

"Next you'll tell them that I chewed on the branch until it fell." As she'd hoped, her flippant accusation drew a round of friendly laughter.

"I'd never do that." Isaac pressed a hand to his heart, as though wounded. "I will, however, say this." He looked into her eyes soulfully. "If that was how you'd decided to do it, I have every confidence you would've succeeded."

Exasperated, and yes exhilarated by their success that day, Cassidy took his face in her hands, and kissed him right in front of everyone.

Chapter 17

Life fell into a pleasant routine after that. Over the next few weeks the Wranglers hunted and surveyed, the apprentices rotated chores, and the engineers worked on expanding the tunnels to accommodate the anticipated villagers. Lauta began to look and feel like a home.

Cassidy, her lethargy a thing of the past and her 'special' Water Fairy knowledge no longer needed, cheerfully pitched in wherever she could. Given her otherwise limited skills, that usually meant fetching and carrying—thankfully, they'd had no more medical emergencies—but she didn't mind.

"Doesn't this damage the tree?" Cassidy asked Harry one day as she helped haul wood chips away from where the engineers were enlarging the tunnels.

"Nah, she'll never even notice. In fact, she'll live a lot longer with us around to keep an eye on her." Harry, who had impossibly grown even lankier since their departure, winked. "Wranglers do more than sing and eat, y'know." He stopped a few steps shy of the tunnel mouth and lifted an eyebrow when she hesitated as well.

"I know, I know." Sighing, she hooked on the safety line they'd rigged especially for her, and walked the rest of the way by herself. How could such a short distance seem so long? "This was my idea."

It would be too easy to get comfortable in the tunnels and forget there was a much, much larger world outside. Determined to prevent that, each day she set herself a task that involved at least poking her head out. Oddly, the days where she actually went outside with the others were easier to abide. On those days there were plenty of things to occupy her mind. She'd even begun to learn to navigate the massive grove.

Today, however, she merely had to dump the wood chips out onto the forest floor. Which was so, *so* far away. She jerked her gaze away from the prettily falling bits of wood and forced herself to look out at eye level instead. Though nights were still cold, the trees were busily sprouting new, green growth, filling her sight everywhere she looked. Except down, that is.

"Hey, Doc." Harry started to speak from beside her.

She squeaked and jumped, nearly falling out of the tunnel.

He dropped his basket to reach for her. It hit the floor with a thud, spilling chips everywhere. The basket wobbled from side to side, then tipped itself right out of the tunnel.

"Good grief," Harry muttered, remembering

where they were. "You've got me doing it!" Releasing her arm, which he'd grabbed to keep her from falling, he gave the safety line a good yank to demonstrate that it was firmly attached to the wall. "See? You're not going anywhere." Still grumbling, he took the twig broom from where it leaned against the wall and sent the rest of the chips tumbling out with a few practiced strokes.

"Sorry." She guiltily peeked over the side, but the basket was long gone.

"Forget about the basket." He folded his arms and looked sternly at her. "We're going flying."

"What?" She pointed in disbelief. "Out there?"

"Just as soon as I tell someone where we're… Oh, shucks." He unbent enough to run his fingers through his hair, which was starting to get in his eyes these days. "I was coming to tell you the engineers have called lunch." His stomach growled and his young cheeks pinked.

"That's alright," she hurried to say. His restless gesture reminded her of the gap in her own hair, where Isaac had cut it to save her from the envenomed silk. She made a mental note to ask if someone could trim her hair so it was all one length again. Returning to her conversation with Harry, she added, "I don't mind waiting."

"I'll say you don't." A smile tugged at his mouth and he threw up his hands. "You gotta decide for yourself, Doc, but take it from me. Life'll be a lot easier once flying isn't your second or even your first thought, but your natural reflex." Shaking his head, his longish hair fluffing with the motion, he steered her through the hole that now existed between two of the tunnels and toward lunch. The hunting party had salvaged untouched fish from an otter's breakfast and the smell of it cooking was making his mouth water.

"Special for you, Doc," joked Cook when he handed her a heaping plate with a flourish. "I'll be wantin' your opinion, naturally."

"Mmm, it smells delicious." Since they were at the tail-end of the line, she made a point of scooping up a small bite right there. "I've never had freshwater fish before. Oh, it's delicious!"

Everyone was surprised to hear that she'd never eaten trout or bass or any such fish before, which led to a conversation about saltwater fish, crustaceans, and shrimp.

As soon as she'd finished eating, Cassidy excused herself to help with the dishes. The look on Harry's face when he dropped off his lunch things told her he knew exactly what she was doing, but he didn't say anything and she mentally patted herself on the back for succeeding in thwarting his plan.

"Here, let me in there." Isaac grinned and winked at the windfairy who was helping to dry the dishes. "I'm a few days behind in helping with this chore." The windfairy looked from Isaac to Cassidy and surrendered the dish towel without a word.

Cassidy had a sneaking suspicion that she was in for a lecture. Trapped behind a pot of hot, soapy water and a stack of dishes as tall as her shoulders, she wasn't going anywhere for a while, either.

"Want to trade?" Isaac offered generously. There weren't that many plates left, not really, before they reached the pots and pans. Granted, this cook wasn't prone to burning things like some others Isaac could name. Still, the larger pots were heavy enough to be quite a wrestle.

"No, thanks." She smiled and transferred a few plates to the wash water. "What brings you to this neck of the woods?" she asked, experimenting with her surface jargon.

Chuckling, Isaac rinsed a handful of plates and arranged them so they could drain and dry on the warm stovetop. "A lovely lady." He answered in Margua, hoping he'd chosen the right words from his small vocabulary.

She blushed and rewashed the plate she'd just finished. "Your pronunciation is improving."

"Thank you." He bowed slightly. "We should

practice more often. I'd like to be able to speak to the Water Fairy ambassadors and ministers in their own language."

"That is very considerate of you." She agreed after a thoughtful pause. "We have so much to learn, to get used to. I'm sure they will appreciate not having to rely on an interpreter; or, on their own limited knowledge of the surface tongue."

"That's all quite true." He looked at her solemnly as he shook water off a new bunch of plates and set them on the stove. "And what will my wife think about it?" His heart seemed to pound louder with each beat he waited for her response.

"I'm sure she'll think you're wonderful." Suddenly shy, Cassidy flicked a glance around the room to check if anyone was listening. Sometimes at night she slept with his ring on her finger, though she was always careful to put it back on the chain before anyone saw it.

"Cass." He reached for her.

"Alright you two, break it up." Cook barged into the area, arms full of a withered-looking berry. "We're havin' fresh pie with supper and I can't bake with you makin' eyes at each other."

"Fresh pie!" Isaac swapped spots with Cassidy before she realized what he had in mind. "Let me at those pots. We'll be out of your way in a jiff, Cook."

Suspicious of Isaac's slightly over-eager behavior, Cassidy nevertheless did her part to rinse and dry and tidy while Isaac whistled his way through the heavier dishes.

"There you go!" Bending, Isaac opened the tap that allowed the wash water to drain outside through a hose. Catching Cassidy's hand, he backed away from the galley. "I can taste that pie already!"

Once they were at a safe distance, Cassidy murmured, "What *are* you doing?" She paused when he did and wondered why he would need the crossbow and quiver he picked up.

"You'll see." Slipping an arm around her, he flew her outside in a twinkling. "I found a beautiful spot the other day while we were surveying. I've wanted to show it to you ever since."

"Oh!" She gulped and closed her eyes. Then, gritting her teeth, she opened her eyes little by little until she could see all around.

"Ready?" he asked.

"For...for what?"

He slowed to a hover. "To fly." He winced as her grip tightened. "Cass. You *know* you can do this."

"Harry told you what happened," she accused.

"Of course he did." He met her gaze steadily. "He knows you can do this, too."

She had no defense against that. And yet...

"You should have asked me."

"You're right." He grimaced. "I wanted to surprise you; but in retrospect, the way I did it was selfish. I'm sorry."

"Thank you." She looked around, biting her lip. As long as they were already outside… Extending her wings, she focused on his presence beside her while she began flying on her own.

"That's it. Stretch them out. Yes. Let the air flow around them." Isaac carefully drew back to arm's length once he thought she was ready. "Now, there's something I wanted to show you. It's not far from here. But, we're also not far from Lauta. Where would *you* like to go?"

Warmed by the consideration he was showing her, she yielded to the temptation to see what he was so eager to share with her. "With you."

He hesitated, not sure what that meant.

"I mean," she laughed, suddenly realizing what she'd said, "I want to go with you to this new place."

Relieved, he showed her how to turn so that they were flying side-by-side, inner wings overlapping. "Like that, yes. Now, we flap at the same time and it's easier for both of us."

"We," she gulped when a faint breeze rocked them, "um, we forgot to tell anyone we were leaving."

"What?" Isaac spread his wings as they approached a safe-looking branch. His shoulders rose and his feet dropped, toes down a bit, and he landed softly. "I would never take off without telling someone. It's a rule."

She leaned on him for support as she landed and was glad to feel a solid surface beneath her feet again. He didn't release her waist, though, which made her smile despite her exasperation at his high-handed tactic in getting her out there.

"I suppose you think I'm going to kiss you now." Cassidy arched an eyebrow. It wouldn't hurt to reinforce the boundary she'd just laid down regarding her flying 'lessons.'

Hearing her tone, Isaac changed his answer from 'of course' to, "Well, if you insist." Despite his teasing words, he stopped short of touching his lips to hers. Watched her eyes.

Though she resisted briefly, it was just for show. And she'd never enjoyed surrendering so much.

After some moments had passed, he whispered, "I love you."

"I love you, too." Pushing away, she turned to look at their new surroundings.

A smile grew on Isaac's face as he watched the wonder on her face. This was all new for her. Hundreds of white flowers surrounded them, dangling from whip-slender branches. Their soft scent filled the air, making each breath a delight. Here and there, closed green pods hung, still waiting to bloom.

"What is this tree?" Awed, Cassidy reached out to touch a silken petal.

"This is a silverbell." Taking her hand, Isaac lifted off and took her on a tour, both eyes open for predators. "It's really more of a bush," he explained as they went.

When he showed her the first indications of the plant's fruit, she shook her head in wonder. "I never knew the surface had such a variety of foods."

"Ah, we're flush with food in the spring." Isaac slipped his hands in his pockets as he looked over his forest with pride. "That's why we want the galdu to come now. The more hands collecting food to store for winter, the better." He could only hope that the galdu were choosing their tribes wisely. It wasn't enough to merely have brown hair or brown eyes. Wood Fairies had a special knack with the animals and the forest.

Cassidy turned from the petal she'd been stroking and frowned. "We just had winter. Are you already planning for the next one?"

"We must." He offered her an arm and kissed her forehead when she came to stand close by him. "It's hard work, nobody can deny that. But with a plentiful crop like this year promises to have, it shouldn't be a problem to harvest enough for a bountiful winter."

She considered the idea, and how it would impact her life. "Isaac? Why is it that your tribe doesn't live closer together? In a single tree or one grove of trees?"

"I think we used to." He scratched his chin with his free hand, trying to remember how long ago that would've been. Details eluded him, so he shrugged that question off. "A long time ago."

"Water Fairies travel to all of the seven regions year round. I think I'll miss that." Cassidy didn't realize she was frowning. Tilting her head back on his shoulder, eyes still on the delicate-looking flowers, she asked, "Why did you stop living near each other?"

"What? Oh. We, um… That is." He did his best, but it was no use. Her lips were entirely too close to his to ignore. "First things first."

She laughed, then kissed him back. Snuggling in so that her cheek was pressed against his chest, she coaxed, "Now will you answer my question?"

He chuckled and scanned the area for danger. "If I recall my history lessons correctly, we began to spread out because we lost a lot of folk to a windstorm. Part of a tree blew down and there weren't many survivors."

"I'm so sorry." She hugged his waist.

"Yes, that was a tragedy. Hoping to prevent it from happening again, we searched out new trees and made them our homes. One thing led to another and now we have major settlements in each of the most important groves in the Deep Woods."

They walked as they talked a bit more about what made each of the settlements special: berries; nuts; choice lumber; and so on.

"I see," Cassidy nodded. "Your tribe depends on the efforts of everyone in those settlements to provide the materials you export as well as what you'll need to survive each winter."

"Exactly." He smiled, pleased at how succinctly she'd stated it. "You are going to make a wonderful queen."

She ducked her head, not really comfortable with the subject.

"Isaac, look!" Pulling away, she hurried over to kneel beside a curly green nub. "What is this?" She stroked it with one fingertip, the action producing a slight squeaking sound.

"That?" He joined her, perturbed at her hasty change of subject. What was wrong? "It's a brand new leaf."

"A leaf?" She considered the dozens of flat, banner-like leaves surrounding them, then sent him a skeptical frown.

"No, it's true." It took a moment, but he spotted the leaf he wanted and pointed at it. "See? That one's not much older than this one." The second leaf wasn't exactly flat or curly; it was somewhere in-between.

Lowering his hand to his thigh, he asked gently, "What made you want to talk about leaves all of the sudden?" His heart constricted when she persisted in staring at the leaf rather than answering. Well. His father always counseled patience and an open heart. He'd even mentioned it to Gallica and Stuart in the final family council before the wedding. So, Isaac could wait.

Cassidy listened to the sound of her heart beating. It seemed painfully loud in the growing silence. Oh, the leaves chuckled as a breeze tickled them. A bird sang in the distance. And Isaac sat quietly.

"It takes a lot," she raised her eyes to his, "to make a queen."

He opened his mouth to agree, and perhaps to even begin listing the attributes of a good queen. He'd been schooled on them often enough over the years. The way that Cassidy's shoulders rose—as though she was taking a deep breath in anticipation of being lectured—prompted him to close his mouth and reconsider.

His self-reflection was well rewarded. He already knew what *he* knew; and reiterating it would do nothing to advance his understanding of Cassidy's discomfiture.

"What does it take?" When he saw her brow knit in confusion, he clarified, "You said it takes a lot to make a queen. Can you give me an example?" Leaning against the leaf, he shifted so that his legs were outstretched in a relaxed fashion, crossbow on the ground, but easy to reach; as though he had all day to listen. Truthfully, they were running out of daylight, for the days were still fairly short.

Some of the tension eased out of her as she searched his face. Sensing only genuine interest, she exhaled the breath she'd taken when she thought he was going to tell her there was nothing to worry about. Dropping her eyes, she took his hand in hers and spread his fingers, then pressed her palm to his. Her developing callouses were nothing compared to his, yet she liked that it was something they had in common.

"A wedding, for one thing." She peeked at him from under her lashes and had to bite her lip to keep from laughing at his comical expression. His features didn't seem to know which emotion to portray. His eyes remained wide with shock even as a slow grin spread across his face.

Then his hands were on her shoulders and hers pushing against his chest.

"Isaac, wait!" She nearly succumbed to the longing in his eyes, which only matched her own, but held firm. "A wedding, *our* wedding, won't be about us. Every eye in the five tribes will turn to it, every minute detail will be scrutinized past bearing."

He hated that she was right, but that changed nothing. "Let the wedding please them," he said at last. "So long as the marriage pleases us." Her lips compressed slightly and he asked, "What? Did I say something wrong?"

"No." She shook her head, pink curls bouncing. "No man in love could've said it better. And," she brushed her lips against his, "I love that you did say it."

"And…?" Still confused, he prodded her for more.

"And I'm ready to start making plans."

<h1 style="text-align:center">Chapter 18</h1>

They got back to Lauta shortly before the gates closed for the night. After checking with Skite and Captain Keddy to make sure everyone was safely in, Isaac led Cassidy to the medical area.

"Wood Fairies!" He called over the conversation. "Sky Fairies! If I may have your attention, please."

Both groups quieted and turned to him expectantly.

"Cassidy Clark, Lady of the Water Fairy Tribe and Doctor to our expedition, and I wish to share our good news with you." Isaac did his best to appear calm while he waited.

Cassidy reached up to her collar and lifted out the chain she always wore. Someone gasped as the ring at the end came into view and the women began whispering. Her fingers trembled, making it next to impossible for her to unhook the clasp. Finally she succeeded in removing it from her neck and offered it to Isaac.

"As some of you have no doubt already guessed." He tenderly took the ring from the chain, unwrapped the protective fabric cover and held the ring up for everyone to see. The stones flickered blue, red, and white in the lantern light. "Cassidy and I are engaged."

Cassidy did her best not to flinch when the tunnel erupted in cheers. In fact, she even managed a laugh, for the reaction was so typically Wrangler. And so completely opposite of the polite applause such an announcement would've garnered at a Water Fairy gathering.

Isaac surrendered good-naturedly to enthusiastic back-slapping while Cassidy was swarmed by Wrangler and Windfairy women alike, eager to see the ring.

For the next four days, their engagement was the only thing that was discussed more than the soon-to-arrive galdu villagers. Now that the weather had steadied out, lookouts were assigned to watch for the galdu windships every day.

When she and Isaac finally stole another afternoon for themselves at the silverbell bush, she wasn't sure whether to laugh or cry as she told him, "I think everyone in the entire expedition has asked me what a Water Fairy wedding is like."

Isaac studied the new spoon he was carving for Cook, evaluating the depth of the bowl with a practiced eye. "And then they each came to tell me whether or not they thought we should have a traditional Wood Fairy wedding."

Groaning, Cassidy buried her face in her hands. "I never realized it was possible to have too many friends."

Chuckling, he set the spoon aside and went to hug her. "I wonder if this is how Hugh and Rebecca felt."

"Who?" She rested her cheek against his. The names sounded vaguely familiar, but she couldn't quite place them.

"Hugh Lawson." He supplied the last name this time. "King Hugh of the Silver Fairy Tribe, now. And Queen Rebecca. I don't think you've met them."

"I've only met a fraction of the surface folk, silly." Laughing, she pushed him away. But not too far away. While she'd grown accustomed to actively checking the area for danger, she still trusted his instincts over her own. "Why do you think of them, though? Surely two Silver Fairies had no such troubles planning their wedding."

"Ah, but they are not both Silver Fairies. Not exactly." That even sounded confusing to him, so he explained, "Hugh is the son of a Plant Fairy princess and a Silver Fairy guardsman."

"Really?" Cassidy couldn't help being surprised. "I thought surface royalty married tribal nobles. For example, Gallica and Stuart."

"That's most often the case," Isaac agreed, brow furrowing as he tried to remember details. His eyes roved the foliage, wary of predators. "In this case, Princess Alicia was actually betrothed to Prince Nathaniel when she fell in love with a member of her Silver Fairy Guard and they were secretly married.”

“So,” Cassidy clarified the salient point, “there *are* occasionally marriages between the royal houses.”

“Yes.” He rubbed his chin thoughtfully. *Hmm.* He turned abruptly to face her. “Did you always want a Water Fairy wedding?”

“Did I…?” She shot him an exasperated look. Before coming to Weetu her marriage prospects consisted exclusively of the galdu and Water Fairies.

“Right, of course you did.” Isaac held up both hands, forestalling the rest of her answer. “What I meant to ask was, would you mind *not* having a Water Fairy wedding?” He waited eagerly, excited to share the solution that had just occurred to him. It would make everyone happy!

The question made her pause. She wasn’t sure he’d like the answer.

“I think it is little enough to ask.” Cassidy struggled not to look away from his intense brown eyes. This was the sort of thing they needed to discuss—that they needed to be honest about—if they were to keep resentment from growing up between them. That didn’t make it easy, though.

“Oh.” He frowned, annoyed with himself. She’d already agreed to live in Weetu. How much more could he ask her to sacrifice?

"Wow. That, um, that makes sense. We'll make it work, darling. I promise."

Cassidy's head slowly tipped to one side as she tried to sort out what had just changed. Clearly he was disappointed with her answer, but there was a subtle…something else in his reaction. Curiosity got the better of her.

"Why did you ask me that?"

"Hmm?" He folded his arms across his chest and shook his head. "Oh. It doesn't matter. What matters is figuring out how I'm going to memorize an entire love poem in time."

"First you have to write it," she reminded gently. Then, moving closer, she put her hands on his folded arms. "Please tell me why you asked me if I wanted a Water Fairy wedding."

"I just had a thought." He looked down at her hands and back into her hazel eyes. "Everyone's opinions so far are based on us having either a Wood Fairy or a Water Fairy ceremony."

"And?" she prodded when he lapsed into silence.

"And I had the crazy idea that we could do something entirely different." His lips twisted in a pained smile. "Plant Fairy ceremony. Silver Fairy ceremony. Might've been a nice touch with the galdu joining us after so long."

Her gaze drifted down and to the side. Stepping away from him, she cupped her right elbow in her left hand and brought her right hand up to pinch her lower lip. Agnes would've called it her 'thinking pose.'

"Bad idea, I know." Worry mounted in his chest, tightening it as she distanced herself from him. "But let's talk about our Water Fairy wedding. Especially this poem I have to write. I'll do it, naturally, but is it alright if I have a little help from a friend?" He knew just the man, too. Prince Cambrian Bijou of the Sky Fairy Tribe was an accomplished poet and a friend.

"I like it. This idea of yours." She turned to face him again. "I think we should at least discuss it."

He froze. "You like it. Truly?"

"I do." Closing the gap again, she kissed him lightly on the lips. "It *would* be difficult to have a full Water Fairy ceremony on the surface. Also, I'm not confident that the royal families of the surface tribes would be comfortable joining us in the seven regions."

They shared a grimace at the idea of spending every spare moment leading up to the ceremony in assuring their royal guests that there was no danger of them being kept as political prisoners.

"So this is a chance to find neutral ground, then." Isaac tucked her arm under his and began to pace. "Which means it can't be in the Deep Woods, either. Logically, we should ask the Silver Fairies to host. They are the diplomats of Fairydom."

"The logical choice is the predictable choice, and not always the *best* choice." She winked as she quoted something he'd said recently.

"That's true." He laughed and shook his head. "But we're not sparring with the Silver Fairies."

"No. We're sparring with Fairydom." She wished they didn't have to worry about what all of the other tribes thought, but there was really no choice.

Some might sneer that Isaac was being sacrificed to guarantee the safety of his tribe from the formidable Water Fairies. Others could make the argument that this was a dangerous alliance—dangerous to the rest of the tribes, who would now have to scramble to make their own alliances to maintain the balance of power.

Confident he had taken her meaning, Cassidy moved on. "Besides, while the Silver Fairies would no doubt be the most gracious of hosts, would they be excited to do it?"

"Excited? Do we need them to be excited?" He had a funny feeling he'd veered into someone else's conversation. If they were willing to host, wasn't that enough?

"Excitement is contagious. If the hosting tribe is excited, not merely polite, then the guests will be more likely to be excited, too. Or, at the very least, to view our marriage less as a political decision."

"Yes, I see." Isaac sighed. "And yet, I suppose anyone with any political experience will suspect ulterior motives." He frowned. "But what about a host with no political experience? Someone who will be flattered and excited and probably think it's terribly romantic, all at the same time?"

"How young is this fairy?" Cassidy joked.

"Abigail? Fifteen hundred? Two thousand? I honestly have no idea." The more he thought about his crazy idea, the better he liked it. King Hugh's adoptive mother had spent centuries traveling Fairydom with a troop of performing fairies. "From everything I've heard she's a delightful woman. Astute, charming, and well-versed in the traditions of all the tribes."

"But *not* politically experienced?" Cassidy interrupted with a raised eyebrow.

"Trust me. She knows the tribes, loves her plants, and if it can be arranged, will the best hostess we could possibly hope for. She was staying with the Plant Fairies last I heard." He snapped his fingers. "And we can send our petition to her as soon as we get back to Weetu! We'll be able to head back as soon as we've got the galdu villagers settled."

At the sound of a trump, Isaac's head snapped toward Lauta. Then, without any explanation, he caught Cassidy close and kissed her thoroughly.

"That, my love, is probably the last kiss we'll have time for until we return to Weetu." He rested his forehead against hers, waiting for his heart to stop pounding.

Her lip turned down in a pretty pout. "Why is that?"

"The first windship from the coast is here."

"Windship?" Still reeling from his kiss, it took her a moment to grasp his meaning. "The galdu. We have to go! I have to be there when they arrive!"

"Let's fly!" He let her lead the way, thrilling at how easily she navigated the route back to Lauta. As they landed, he caught her hand. "I have something for you."

"It's a good thing we finished the windship cradles last week," she told him, looking around in confusion when he pulled her into the tunnel where they all slept at night. "Isaac, what are you doing?"

"Close your eyes," was his only answer as they reached his hammock.

She wanted to roll them instead—this was hardly the time to play games!—but she indulged him.

Isaac lifted his blanket carefully aside. "You can look now."

When she did, she couldn't believe what she saw! Her scale armor and suge lay on his hammock, glistening even in the faint light.

"What? How?" Lifting her suge free, she checked around her, then uncoiled it for a short figure eight. Satisfied that it was in perfect condition, she fingered the armor. "Did you repair this yourself?"

"Yeah, once I got it out of the spider silk." He held up both hands when she frowned at him. "I was *very* careful. But the armor links just needed recrimped, so I spent some time on it each day until it was done."

"It's beautiful, Isaac, thank you." She kissed his cheek, mindful of their perpetual audience.

"Now you can wear them when we greet the galdu." He grinned, proud of himself.

"Mmm. No, I don't think that's a good idea. I'm the expedition's doctor and that's all." Taking up her weapons, she returned them to her hammock where she placed the suge in its protective cover and hung the armor from a peg on the wall. Finding Isaac at her side, she explained quietly, "The galdu were forbidden to own weapons or learn to fight. If I show up at the docking in armor and carrying a suge, that's how they'll always see me."

"I hadn't thought of that." He rubbed her arm, frowning sympathetically. A bad first impression could last a fairy lifetime, and would do nothing to make the Wood Fairy galdu comfortable with her as their next queen.

"Right. Well, I'll give the order that we're going weaponless."

"No, please don't." She gripped her hands tightly in front of her. "*You* should wear your weapons. All of you. And your uniforms. The more formal the greeting, the better. They're home now. *This* is their home and the Wranglers are their new authority." The smile growing on his face made her stop and give him a funny look.

"Sorry, I just." He shrugged. "I love how enthusiastic you are about it. And, I think you're right. The surface is a dangerous place in spring. We'll come prepared."

"Um, now would be a good time!" Berns, who'd caught the tail end of their conversation, beckoned to them. "That windship will cradle in less than an hour!"

"Just the one?" Isaac called as he headed back to his area to find a set of clean leathers.

"So far," Berns confirmed. "We'll have the second cradle ready, though."

And so the scramble commenced. There were no dress uniforms on expedition, but they all did their best to spruce up and look official.

Cassidy washed her face and put on a clean woolen shirt; brushed her hair and tied it back. Hoping to look as doctorly as possible, she slipped the strap of a medical kit over her shoulder, then hurried out to line up on the branch with the others.

"Oh my," she whispered when she got her first good look at the windship. *Atska* was painted in bold letters on her nose and she could have held two or even three of the *Itxar*. As the *Atska* swung around to make her cradle approach, Cassidy could see faces pressed against the portholes that lined her side.

A tall windfairy positioned herself near the cradle and guided the windship in, whereupon the other windfairies zipped out to secure the straps around its keel. The baggage gangplanks were thrown out before Isaac could even salute the ship's flag and ask for permission to board.

"Permission granted, Your Highness." The Sky Fairy captain made a point of saluting the crown prince as he came aboard, for diplomacy's sake. Then, with some relief, participated in a firm handshake.

"Welcome to Lauta. I hope you had a smooth flight, Captain." Isaac grinned, eager to get past the formalities.

"All in one piece still, even your new settlers." The captain was likewise ready to move things along. He didn't mind the occasional question from his passengers, but this lot never let up! "The second windship can't be more than a day behind us. They had some trouble with a wing." He shrugged. "Easily repaired."

"Glad to hear it." Isaac turned to greet the ranking Wrangler officer aboard.

"Lieutenant Lekue, sir." She saluted crisply.

"Lieutenant." He returned her salute. "Welcome to your new post."

Paperwork on our new tribesfairies, sir." She handed him a packet. "Names. Occupations. The lot."

"We'll go over this later," he promised as he accepted it. He looked over her shoulder at the Wranglers assembled behind her. Then over his own shoulder. More than two hundred passengers aboard and no sign of them. Surely they weren't still below?

"Ah, yes. Something does seem to be missing, doesn't it?" Pivoting, the captain shouted for the companionways to be opened. Then he stepped closer, almost shoulder to shoulder with Isaac, and observed in an undertone, "They're an odd bunch. Three days aboard and I could hardly get them to leave their quarters."

Isaac twitched involuntarily. *Could it be? Did the galdu suffer from the same affliction as Cassidy?* A glance at the lieutenant's carefully blank face told him nothing.

"I'm sure we'll be fine," was all he said aloud. Bowing slightly he extended the traditional invitation to the captain. "Will you join us for supper tonight? I'm sure Captain Keddy will be glad for any news you bring." After nearly two months away from everyone, they were *all* looking forward to news.

"Delighted." A salute and another bow later, they went their separate ways.

A stirring to Isaac's left caught his attention and he turned to find a group of five fairies approaching him. It was startling to see green and blue hair with brown eyes, and even brown hair with green eyes, but he hoped he kept his surprise from showing. Two of them were women that he would guess were his mother's age; of the three men, one had hair so pale and yet so unquestionably brown that he must be in his eighth or even ninth thousand years. He and two others carried carved, off-white staffs that reached to just above their shoulders. Though they were all warmly dressed, the older man was the only one wearing leathers.

Lieutenant Lekue came to attention. "Your Highness, may I present Zaggi, akoa of the *Mirotza* clan?"

Isaac reached back into memories of lessons with Cassidy and dredged up the fact that 'akoa' was the galdu word for the family elder. Accordingly, he bowed to the pale-haired man in the center of the group.

"Zaggi Deitu," the lieutenant continued the introductions, "may I present Isaac Bristlecone, Wood Fairy Crown Prince?"

Isaac hurried to prevent Zaggi from kneeling to him. "No, sir, no. Please, everyone." He indicated the others, who were following Zaggi's example. "Stand."

"We must kneel to our prince," Zaggi insisted. "It is customary."

"An old custom, good father." Isaac held out his right arm. "Welcome home."

Zaggi stared at Isaac's proffered hand, then slowly extended his own. His eyes filled with tears as they stood there, clasping forearms.

"Come." He released Isaac's hand and beckoned to those with him. "Come and meet our prince."

Isaac felt a tear slip down his own cheek, but didn't bother wiping it away. If Zaggi could cry, so could he. And so did the others as he greeted each of them.

"Now." Isaac cleared his throat. "You must be ready to see where you're going to live. I'm afraid Lauta's a little rough as yet; we've only been here a few weeks. But I'm sure by winter it will be very comfortable."

"Lauta." Zaggi spoke the word slowly, as if savoring it. "We are eager to see it. All of us." He spread his arms, as if to include a much larger group. His weathered brow wrinkled further, yet he lapsed into silence.

After waiting as long as he dared for Zaggi to continue, Isaac inquired, "Zaggi, I wonder if you would permit me to introduce Doctor Clark? You'll meet all of my officers soon enough, but I think she might be able to help us bring your folk safely to the tree from this windship."

Zaggi's eyes lit up and he nodded. "Yes, please. I would like to meet this doctor." Behind him, his small council exchanged relieved looks.

"I'll fetch her," volunteered Lieutenant Lekue.

"No need." Turning, Isaac spotted Cassidy amongst the others waiting in formation on the tree branch and beckoned to her. He did his best to ignore the startled gasp from the galdu when she spread her wings and started forward.

"A Water Fairy?" sputtered one of the women, tightening her grip on her staff. "Your doctor is a *Water* Fairy?"

"Hmm? Why, yes, she is." Smiling brightly, he looked over his shoulder at Cassidy, who was already touching down on deck. "Doctor, surgeon, friend. A fair hand at singing. We're really very fortunate to have her along." He spoke as nonchalantly as he could manage.

And, by the time Cassidy touched down nearby, the galdu had relaxed considerably.

"Hello." Cassidy shifted the strap on the medical kit she carried and smiled. "How may I be of assistance?"

Chapter 19

Zaggi hesitated, baffled by this apparently affable Water Fairy. After five thousand years in the seven regions, he was accustomed to being ordered about or sternly reminded of curfews. This was an entirely new experience for him.

"Is someone ill?" Cassidy ventured to ask. Surely if Zaggi—or any of them—could say one word to her, whether it be 'yes' or 'no,' that was a beginning.

"Not ill, exactly." Hard green eyes stared at Cassidy out of a pale oval face. The woman who spoke hesitated when the others looked at her, then plunged ahead. "They're just not used to this…" She waved at the air around her.

"To seeing this much?" Cassidy supplied. Drawing on the strength of her years as a doctor, she persevered despite their lack of response. "I had much the same reaction myself."

"We don't need Water Fairy help," ground out one of the men in a deep base.

"You may recall," Isaac's voice was deceptively mild, "that this is *Doctor* Clark. Our doctor and yours, for the time being."

"I was actually going to recommend a course of action that would require all the Wranglers to help." Cassidy tried to sound somewhere between professional and amused. In the end, she worried that she just sounded emotionless. "I'm sure that your folk could cross safely with a Wrangler to guide them."

"Excellent notion." Isaac looked steadily into the eyes of the man who'd objected. "Don't you agree?" All he got was a grudging nod, but it was enough.

Lieutenant Lekue didn't wait for Isaac to give the order. "Zaggi, if you and the others will explain what's going to happen to your folk and send them on deck when they're ready, please?"

"We really should get inside," Isaac encouraged the galdu. "There's a hot meal waiting for you and sleeping arrangements to make." That seemed to shake them out of their daze and they hurried below, leaving Isaac and Cassidy 'alone' amidst the bustle.

"How do you think that went?" Cassidy asked, daring a step nearer.

"I think they just need time and," he took a deep breath as he looked pointedly around the spacious grove, "a little space." He chuckled as the lieutenant marshalled the Wranglers to stand in lines by each companionway.

"Spider!"

Cassidy and Isaac jerked toward the shout. A huge, hairy black spider perched on the tree trunk not far above them.

"Get them in the tree." Isaac grabbed Cassidy and shoved her toward a companionway. "In the tree and safe. This windship won't hold against a spider."

"Windfairies, to me!" Cassidy stepped in as both groups of Wranglers flew to intercept the spider. "Windfairies, to me!"

Captain Keddy reached her an instant before the captain of the *Atska*. "What d'ye need, Doc?" He ignored the sharp look the new captain gave him.

"These galdu, they're like me when I first arrived. I don't know how many of them can cross the gap on their own and we don't have time to find out," she explained tersely.

"Too right." Keddy shouted an order to his men. "Take them gentle, but get these fledglings into the tree!" It wasn't his windship, but he glared at the other captain until he passed the same order on to his crew.

Cassidy turned to find herself face to face with the same grim galdu man who'd spoken against her.

"Change of plans." Reaching past him, she picked up the first little girl she could reach. "The Wranglers will handle the spider." *They would!* her mind insisted. "But we have to get everyone off this windship now and worry about who likes it later."

Her message delivered, she stepped back and handed the girl over to a windfairy. "He'll keep you safe," she promised.

"Come out one at a time," the galdu man

called into the companionway. "No dillydallying!"

As fast as the windfairies went, there were still gaps that left Cassidy with far too much time to observe the battle going on above. Someone screamed and fell.

"Harry! You're in charge!" She flung the words at the startled apprentice as she zipped to the far side of the deck and dove overboard, wings extended.

Sighting her patient, she tucked her wings and dove. Tears streamed from her eyes, but she clung relentlessly to her flightpath until the last moment.

Seizing the injured Wrangler by her harness, Cassidy extended her wings all at once. Her muscles screamed in protest at the rough treatment and she nearly dropped her prize, whom she now recognized as Morrison.

"Come on," she urged, fighting the instinct to save herself. Her wings couldn't take much more, but if…she could just…

They struck the ground before she could bring them to a safe speed. Cassidy clung to Morrison with both hands, twisting and turning and using every trick she'd ever learned to keep herself between Morrison and the ground as they bounced, rolled, and crashed along.

Finally, she was able to turn to take the contact on her bent legs and…collapsed.

They'd stopped moving, but Cassidy's head spun.

Adrenaline still coursing through her veins, Cassidy got her hands underneath her and pushed herself onto her knees. She tasted blood and spat. A quick survey revealed no broken bones, so she shook her head to clear it, staggered to her feet, and stumbled over to Morrison.

The Wrangler lay unmoving, arms and legs akimbo. One forewing was crushed under her torso; the other draped over her, a jagged tear in it. If she was bleeding, it wasn't obvious—even the wing injury had missed the veins—so Cassidy started with the basics.

Seating herself clumsily, she addressed her patient. "Alright, Morrison. Let's take a look at you." Cassidy shifted the medical kit so it wasn't digging into her side and reached to feel for the other woman's pulse. As she fumbled with the uniform collar, her fingers encountered a cord. Something made her tug on it and she pulled a silver whistle free. Of course! She'd seen the hunting parties wearing these when they returned. "Brilliant."

Cassidy used her belt knife to cut the cord, knotted the loose ends, then slipped it over her own head. After determining that Morrison's pulse and breathing were steady, Cassidy started to check her pupils.

"Oh, no!" Discovering a discolored patch

on Morrison's left cheek, which had lain hidden until then, Cassidy resettled her head gently and wrestled the medical kit into an accessible position. She picked through the supplies until she had a gauze pad and some doctor's water.

Wetting the pad, she wiped Morrison's cheek, taking pains not to get any of the venom on her own skin. Tossing the pad a safe distance away from them both, she dug out the antivenin and administered it.

"Hope they're doing alright upstairs." Cassidy closed the kit so she couldn't spill it and moved down to Morrison's legs. She'd just checked and straightened the second one when a horrible *crunching* thud reached her. "Did you hear that?" she asked Morrison, peering toward the noise.

At their present level on the forest floor, she couldn't even see over the grass blades to be sure which direction the hackberry tree was in, so after a moment Cassidy shook her head and got back to work.

"I'm sure that wasn't the *Atska* falling. I'm sure everyone got inside and that things are just fine." Cassidy smiled tightly at Morrison as she worked her way past cracked ribs to find a severely sprained shoulder under the torn wing. "We'll have to immobilize that arm." Opening the kit again, she retrieved a sling. How many other patients were waiting for her in the tree by now? "I'm glad you're unconscious, but I sort of wish you were awake. You could tell me what you thought that racket was and then I'd feel better."

She sat up straight at the sound of a whistle. Lifting Morrison's whistle to her lips, she blew for all she was worth. Two whistles responded, then three.

"They're getting closer!" Cassidy blew again as she gently fitted the sling over Morrison's elbow. "We've got to get you ready to travel!"

"Over here!" someone shouted.

Cassidy kept at the whistle until she saw someone.

Lieutenant Lekue dropped from the sky as it were, though with considerably more grace than Cassidy and Morrison had. Two windfairies were hot on her wingtips.

"Doc, you're needed at the tree." Lekue shot Morrison a worried look. "Can she travel?"

"Cracked ribs, torn wing, strained muscles. She's had one dose of the antivenin, but may need more." Cassidy somehow got her feet under her. "Brace her neck and she can be moved."

"On it." One of the windfairies began rifling through the kit.

"You can barely stand." Lekue's lips compressed to a thin line. "Think you can hold onto me?"

Cassidy almost laughed. "Think you can carry me?" Cassidy wasn't tall but she had a finger or more of height on the tough-looking Wrangler.

"I've got her." Isaac landed beside Cassidy, his face white with concern. Cassidy was sporting a rapidly blackening eye, a bloody nose, and favoring her left knee. "Lekue, get these fairies back to the tree safely."

"Yes, sir." Lekue didn't waste energy saluting.

Scooping Cassidy up, Isaac cradled her close as he lifted off. "You," he murmured, lips against her temple, "scared me out of a thousand years. We haven't even set up regular patrols in this area. Do you know what might've been waiting down here?"

Cassidy closed her eyes and let him scold a little longer. He meant well. When he finally stopped for a breath, she asked, "What kinds of injuries are we dealing with?"

Isaac spent a moment grappling with himself, then refocused. "They were still bringing in wounded when I learned you were missing, so I'm really not sure." He landed in the tunnel where they kept the supplies and hesitated. "Can you walk?"

"If you'd carry me to the worst patient," her knee had begun to throb during the flight, "I'd appreciate it."

"Clear the way!" someone shouted. "Let the

doc through!”

The sea of galdu fairies parted and Cassidy would’ve cheerfully melted into the floor than face their open-mouthed stares. This wasn’t the first impression she’d wanted them to have.

Isaac didn’t seem the least bit aware of them as he ran-stalked to the center of the action.

“Wow, Doc.” Harry whistled as he approached, med kit in hand. “You look a bit worse for wear.”

This time she did roll her eyes. It hurt. “Left knee,” she told him. “Wrap it tightly, please, but…”

“Not so tight it cuts off the blood flow. Got it.” He was already opening his kit, so he missed seeing her smile.

“Doc.” Berns and Skite converged on her location. “Are you alright?”

“Close enough.” She shook off someone who tried dabbing at her mouth with a wet washcloth. “Never mind that. Tell me what’s going on.”

“We’ve got mostly broken bones and some venom patients,” Berns began.

“Treating those as we speak.” interrupted Skite. “Nothing too serious. The real problem is…”

“Traumatic wing injuries. We’ve got half a dozen, at least,” finished Berns. A passing fairy muttered something derogatory about spiders.

"There's one more coming. Let me know when Morrison gets here." Cassidy flexed her fingers. She hadn't noticed their friction burns earlier. She could go on ignoring them now. "I need a windfairy from the *Atska*. Preferably the captain." Harry had finished, so she rose carefully.

Berns disappeared into the crowd, shouting at the top of his lungs.

"How is it?" Skite asked as she put weight on her leg. Both of his arms were bent at the elbows, as if he expected to have to catch her.

"Won't be cutting it off anytime soon." *Oh, it hurt!* She signaled to Patience, who hurried over to help her with an apron.

"Here he is!" Berns returned, a windfairy officer in tow.

"How can I help?" Captain Norbai couldn't tell who was in charge, so he addressed the question to everyone in the small group.

"You were to bring supplies from the coast. Water Fairy medical supplies." Cassidy changed her mind and took the wet washcloth. The dried blood on her chin was starting to itch. She must've had a nosebleed at some point. "Did you bring starfish sheets?"

"I have no idea." The captain was bluntly honest. There was no time for anything else. "I can get the bills of lading for you."

"She'll be busy." Isaac intervened. "I'll go with you and some of your crew. If we find the sheets, we'll bring them straight back." With that, they were gone.

"What do we do in the meantime?" Berns wasn't the hand-wringing type, but traumatic wing injuries didn't keep well.

Cassidy hissed in pain as she ruthlessly scrubbed her hands in a pan of hot, soapy water. "Show me the patients."

By the time Isaac returned with supply crates from the *Atska*, Cassidy had her patients arranged in order of severity.

"Let me see." Cassidy stepped in as they pried the lids off. "Yes. Yes, this. And this." She lifted a bottle from one crate and a flat box from another. "Patience?" She handed the things to the apprentice, then showed her and Berns how to prepare what they needed.

Isaac, realizing the area was filled with folk just looking on, began gently encouraging them to move along. The Wranglers with minor wounds he sent to the galley, assuring them that Cook would have something for them. He thanked the galdu who'd pitched in, then recommended that they clean up and seek out their family.

"Bit more excitement than we expected on the first day," one of them remarked, wiping his hands on a rag.

Isaac chuckled in agreement and slapped him on the shoulder. As he turned to the next bunch, he hid a grimace of guilt. He'd never know for sure that this was the spider that got Knewt. Or that it wasn't.

Cassidy knew nothing besides her work until she'd finished the final surgery. Skite practically had to force her to sit on a stack of boxes during the third procedure, for she'd even forgotten her wrenched knee.

"Alright." Isaac intercepted her when she finished. "You've done your part. They can take it from here." He nodded at the apprentices who'd hovered for most of it, fetching, carrying, and watching Cassidy worriedly.

"You're worn out!" Patience untied Cassidy's apron and removed it. "Please go lie down."

"We'll clean up," promised Harry, passing Isaac a bottle of doctor's water.

"Drink this," Isaac ordered her, pressing the bottle into her hands.

Cassidy yawned, but complied. "Ugh." She made a face. "I really have to talk to Rosie about the way this tastes."

"Later. With your permission?" He eased her off the boxes and into his arms.

"Hmm." Relaxing against his broad chest, she took another sip. It didn't taste any better, but she minded less. "Where are we going?"

"Just keep drinking that." The crowd parted on its own as he carried her to her hammock. Settling her tenderly, he unwrapped her knee. Tried rolling up her pant leg, then used his belt knife to cut it when the swelling prevented him from going further. "Fire blight, Cassidy."

"What?" She stared at him, eyes wide. She recognized the frustrated tone, but not the words.

"Sorry." He scrubbed a hand over his face, then began rummaging in the med kit he'd brought. "It's just…look at this! It's black and blue and…what *is* that color?" Gingerly, he smeared a salve over the swollen muscle. "This will relieve some of the pain."

"I can already feel a difference." She took another gulp of the doctor's water. Held still while he daubed the salve on her nose and one of her eyes.

"This is for you." A gruff voice said.

Isaac and Cassidy both looked around. The man from the windship, the one who'd declared they didn't need a Water Fairy's help, stood next to Cassidy's hammock. He cleared his throat and shifted his weight from one foot to the other while carefully balancing a bowl of stew.

"Cook said it was just what you needed."

"Thank you." Smiling, Cassidy corked the water bottle and accepted the stew. She'd discovered some loose teeth, but if she chewed carefully, she should be alright. "I'm sorry, I didn't catch your name."

"Tiko." He frowned, clearly not yet happy about finding her at Lauta.

"Tiko, I'm Cassidy." She stirred her stew, trying to think what to ask him.

"How are you at chopping wood?" Isaac finished repacking the med kit and reached for Cassidy's blanket.

"I don't know." Tiko looked down, embarrassed. "I've never tried."

Isaac fought to keep his face neutral despite the shock. "Tomorrow's a big day for you, then."

"Really?" Tiko squared his shoulders. "You'll teach me?"

Oops. Isaac had intended to spend tomorrow with Zaggi and Lieutenant Lekue, going over the list of galdu names. He particularly needed to know how they'd scored on the Wood Fairy aptitude tests. That would help guide him when it came to assigning chore details and more permanent tasks.

"Of course he will," Cassidy inserted. "It's a pity Queen Fiona isn't here, though. She's the one who taught me."

Tiko gaped at her. "*Queen Fiona* taught *you* to..." He couldn't finish the sentence.

"That's right." Cassidy calmly took another bite of stew. The salt burned a spot on one cheek, which she must've bitten at some point during her fall with Morrison.

"Everyone contributes." Isaac lifted Cassidy's

injured leg and slipped the folded blanket under it. "Even stubborn doctors." She had a point, though. Once the novelty of chopping wood and hauling water wore off, they could remember that Prince Isaac did it without complaint.

"Who're you calling stubborn?" Cassidy wanted to know. She wanted to know anything that would take her mind off her knee right then.

"Rosie, of course." Grinning, Isaac leaned in for a soft kiss.

"I'll, uh." Tiko cleared his throat again, but there was more thoughtfulness and less animosity in his eyes as he looked at Cassidy this time. "I'll just go and, um…"

"We'll need more volunteers to cut wood if you can find them," Isaac suggested. "Five at least. They don't have to be any particular size, so long as you'd trust them with something sharp."

Tiko practically saluted him. "No problem."

Cassidy smiled as she watched Tiko hurry away, a man with a purpose.

"As for you, young lady." Isaac slung the med kit over his shoulder and tried for a stern expression. "I expect you to rest that leg."

"I will. *If.*" She qualified her pledge, "If you'll come sit with me a while. And tell me more about this Abigail fairy and why you think she should host our wedding."

"I'll even bring paper and quill," he promised huskily. "So we can start drafting a letter to her."

Skite, who'd been about to hail Isaac, stopped abruptly. Spotting Berns and Captain Keddy heading in the same general direction, he quickly moved to divert them.

"Hey!" Berns growled at Skite. "What's the big idea?"

"Oh, nothing much." Skite looked over his shoulder at where the engaged couple were sharing a moment. "I just thought we could talk about…"

"Um, something. Over there." Berns was quick to suggest.

"I suppose that would be alright." Keddy agreed when he saw what they'd been about to interrupt. "It looks like they're busy right now, anyway."

Thank you for reading <u>Fusion</u>, I hope you enjoyed it!

I'm not sure how many of you have had the pleasure of reading a review of your own work. Personally, I check for new reviews often and love reading them!

More Titles by Lea Carter:

Contemporary Romance
Gifts of the Heart series:
Four single Latter-day Saint women find love in the small, fictional town of Cadmia.
A Country Mile
In Due Season
Food For Thought
Home Free

Fantasy
Silver Sagas series:
The ongoing adventures of the royal fairy families.
Silver Princess
Silver Majesty
Silver Verity
Troubled Skies
Dress Blues
The Seeker's Storm
Heartwood
Wedgewood
Fission

Coddiwomple series: Three high-flying adventures in the fictional world of Jattori.
Dragon Sparks
Dragon Fugue
Dragon Thunder

www.ingramcontent.com/pod-product-compliance
Lightning Source LLC
Chambersburg PA
CBHW071234190726
48292CB00007B/2288